I0535313

Broken Notes

A HEAVY INFLUENCE NOVEL

Ann Marie Frohoff

AMF Publishing
Ann Marie Frohoff
heavyinfluencetrilogy@gmail.com

First Print Edition: December 2014
This book is a work of fiction. Names, characters, places, and incidents are
the product of the author's imagination or are used fictitiously. Any resem-
blance to actual events, locales, or persons, living or dead, is coincidental.

Frohoff, Ann Marie, 1971—
Broken Notes: a novel / by Ann Marie Frohoff.— 1st edition

Summary: When Jake and Alyssa begin to build a life together in New
York City, a death and an unfortunate set of events rattle Jake's very existence. Alyssa clings to her own dreams. Jake's blurred take on life may end
what they've fought so hard to keep.

ISBN-10: 0991657225
ISBN-13: 9780991657223

"They've promised that dreams can come true – but fail to mention that nightmares are dreams, too."
~ *Oscar Wilde*

Chapter 1

JAKE

Arriving at JFK airport at the hour of five-thirty a.m. wasn't something I dug. I was tired. My bedtime on any given day was about three a.m., so going to sleep wasn't an option. Aly was finally graduating from high school, and I was going to surprise her. The only person who knew I was coming was her brother, Kyle. Four months had gone by since I'd last seen her, and I couldn't wait to feel her again. Daydreaming of our time in London made my blood rush. I squirmed in my seat, tugging at my pants, adjusting myself. Before that, I hadn't seen her for nearly three years. What was the point? I'd been thrown in jail for not staying away from her, amongst other humiliating reasons.

The band and I moved to New York, and it was the best thing for us. Aly and I were both a mess. We were both so caught up – her grades and sport paid a high price, as did my band and my relationship with my mother and surrogate father and manager, Notting. Our relationship had become volatile, with me slipping back into using drugs and booze to mask the pain of all the bullshit. The last straw was the meltdown with Mike drugging Aly and the epic battle that followed, landing my ass in jail for the *second* time. It took her months to get over the fact that I chose to leave. She felt abandoned and lied to. Everything had gone up in smoke, and she hated me. I was heartbroken, but something had to change. Everything was slipping away, from the both of us.

I'd kept tabs on Aly through her brother, Kyle, and found out it took months for her grades return to normal. I hadn't realized the impact our breakup had on her. After six months of not talking, we began again and maintained a virtual love affair for three years, until London. She'd come to London for her eighteenth birthday. I was what she wanted, and she'd gotten what she came for.

I'd stayed in Europe touring for another two months after our rendezvous. With Dump being sick, finding a fill-in drummer had been a challenge. Dealing with my mother and her overextended visit to London was less than ideal. She'd smothered me with love and attention and I still didn't get it. Thank God for Notting, my constant buffer. I seriously had no idea how he put up with her. Coming back to the States meant another round of touring and recording. Aly being three thousand miles away and with her volleyball schedule and school made it impossible for us to see each other. I wanted her more than ever, now that I knew I could have her.

Sitting in my first class seat, I took my sunglasses out of my jacket and put them on. I closed my eyes, recalling our last encounter that cold February day.

Seeing her standing curbside at Heathrow was hard for me to believe. She was bundled up in a snug-fitting black wool coat. Her head was down, and she didn't notice me pulling up. She looked different, taller and more beautiful than I'd imagined. She wasn't the tear-streaked girl I left standing in the driveway. Her face had thinned out a bit and her hair was lighter and longer. She'd grown into herself, and the picture and video chatting images only told half the story. She was radiant. I sat there staring at her for several seconds. I had to admit I was nervous. This was her idea. I knew the inevitable was near, and it had me locked in. Knowing nothing could keep us apart had my mind spinning out of control with the possibilities of our future and the little box sitting in my nightstand drawer.

"Hey Alycat." I got out of the car. She didn't hear me at first. "Yo, Alycat!" I said louder.

"Oh my God, Jake," she said, breathless. She beamed and my knees went weak. I was shaking from the excitement.

As if no time had passed, she threw herself onto me, hugging me tight. I took her face into my hands. The sound of her sigh made me want to take her right then and there. We stood, making out, until the airport cop pulled us from our love-drunk haze.

She'd never been to London, and she was wide-eyed with excitement as we made our way through the tight cobble-stoned streets of my temporary neighborhood. She marveled at how small the cars were. —

"They look like oversized roller-skates," She mused. She would be with me for only a week, and rambled on about how she wanted to squeeze in every possible thing before she left.

I couldn't take my eyes off of her.

———

We stood waiting for the elevator to take us up to my pad. She'd moved behind me, sliding her cold, soft hands under my coat and rubbed lightly against my skin, sending that intense, familiar current through me. She was the only one to ever have that effect on me.

"I've thought about you every day, a million times," she said, resting her head on my shoulder. "I've missed the way you smell, your body."

I'll never forget the look on her face when we walked through the front door. Her eyes went as bright as the sun when she saw the pictures we'd taken of her all those years ago, installed on my wall. I loved seeing her happy; it fueled me. Thinking back to that moment I presented Aly with the ring I designed just for her made my palms sweat like it was yesterday.

Damn, I really did ask her to marry me. She didn't say no, but she didn't say yes either – I had to ask her dad if I was serious. I didn't realize girls still wanted it to go down that way. Maybe I wasn't ready to marry her if I was too chicken to ask her dad for her hand. I still wanted to marry her. Maybe she'd say yes now, now that we'd be living together. I seriously contemplated having a talk with her father when I got there. As the plane filled with people, my thoughts drifted to her black lace bra and panties, and her flawless, soft skin. A ripple of chills ran over me. I closed my eyes, enjoying the sensation, and continued my daydream:

"So this is it, this is what you want?" I said, kissing and sucking the inside of her thigh. "You sure about this?"

"You're not gonna tell me no again, are you?" she asked playfully, and moaned with pleasure as I fondled her smooth wetness. She grabbed me and pulled up to her, holding me firm. "I've waited for you, and just traveled half way around the world. I could cry, I want this so bad."

Her soft mouth pressed against mine and she gently licked my lips. Her firm body and soft skin beneath my hands, pressed against my body, had me permanently altered. Being inside of her was more than I could handle. She was wet, hot and tight…I could barely hold on. I'd waited three years for that moment, and it was as insane as I'd dreamt it would be. We didn't leave my flat for over a day, and just like before, I didn't go to rehearsal.

—

A pretty blond flight attendant roused me from my recollection. "Mr. Masters, did you choose your meal?"

"Ah, can you come back?" I gave her a weak smile, grabbing the menu. I lifted my glasses, blurry-eyed, and I tried to focus on my choices.

Gnawing on a bagel and cream cheese while I stared at the eggs Florentine that she placed in front of me, I contemplated my next steps. It was hard for me to maintain my current relationship, one I shouldn't have been having. Life with the girl I'd been seeing, Sophia, was now meaningless. All I could think about was Aly. I knew I had to break it off with Sophia, and I should have done it months ago. I thought of Aly and how she told me she'd broken up with her boyfriend before coming to see me in London.

It wasn't that easy for me. I *hated* confrontation. We never really talked about our other relationships in depth, only that I'd promised I'd break it off with Sophia before she got to New York. Aly was booked to fly back with me to New York in a week, and I'd yet to tell Sophia anything. *Fucking kill me*, I thought as I wiped the cream cheese from the side of my mouth. Sophia had no idea that'd I'd gotten a new pad to live in, too, all newly furnished and ready for me to move into when Aly arrived. My only saving grace was that at least Sophia didn't live with me.

I was beyond stoked to begin a new life with Aly, but dread spread over me. I thought about pulling a dick move and telling her what was up via text, but that would be lame. I'd waited all this time and pushed it off since London. What was really fucked? I would be flying back with Aly and having her move in with me. I was being a complete douchebag, and I knew it. I had to tell Sophia face to face, as soon as I returned. Why did I have to do everything at the last minute? I was a loser for waiting so long, but I struggled with how to let her go. The guilt I felt was overwhelming.

Sophia took me for what I was worth, and accepted my demons. To her, Aly was one of them. She'd always known about Aly, and knew I was stuck on her. Our split wouldn't come as a surprise, but nonetheless, I knew it would hurt her and I felt terrible. But I had no choice now. I was standing at the cliff.

I eventually had to come clean with Sophia that Aly had come to visit me in London. She had heard the lyrics to a new song I'd written, and to her it was apparent. She called me out on it.

"When was she there?" Sophia's voice cracked. "Do you think I'm an idiot, Jake? Did you think I wouldn't read between the lines?"

My stomach sank. I knew this day would come sooner or later. I stood there, staring down at my black Chucks, listening to my voice and music flood the room. The song ended and we stood there silent. I searched for the right words to make her feel better, but there were none. I loved her, but I wasn't in love with her.

"I never lied to you."

"What's that supposed to mean, Jake?" She moved closer to me, lifting my chin.

She made me look at her. Her green eyes were watering, and her face was flushed.

"Sophia, when we met and started hanging out, I confided in you about Aly," I reminded her. "You know what she is to me. This doesn't change the way I feel about you." Those words were the truth when

I spoke them. I didn't want to hurt her. I should have broken it off right then – what an idiot.

Thank God I never let Sophia stay with me. That was my rule. The only girl I would let stay the night in my bed would be Aly, and she'd be moving in with me to attend NYU for college. I feared she didn't want to move to New York, because she kept asking me to return to Los Angeles.

If it was only me, I would move back in a heartbeat. I had the band to consider. I'd dragged their asses to the East Coast, and it turned out to be the best thing that could have happened for us. The songs we'd cranked out after our move were the ones that really put us on the map. Creativity in the time of pain made for a true connection with people. The fact was, misery did love company.

———

Arriving at LAX, I was exhausted. I hadn't seen my mother since she'd surprised Aly and me in London, and I hadn't been back home since I'd moved to New York over three years prior.

Kyle was waiting for me at baggage claim.

"Fucking A, bro!" I said, hugging Kyle and adding a back slap. "Look at you! Where'd the scholar go?" I joked. He looked like someone I would hang out with. He wore a black faded t-shirt and holed-up denim jeans. He even had a tattoo on his forearm. "When did you get the tat?"

"Aw, man, I can ask the same about you!" he laughed, pointing at the beginnings of the emblazoned sleeve I had growing on my left arm. "Shit, it's good to see you, man!" Kyle said, giving my shoulder a squeeze. "Where're your bags?"

"You're lookin' at'em," I said, holding up my backpack and a small duffle. "I'm only gonna be here a week. Where's your sister?"

Kyle breathed in deeply, pausing. He grabbed the top of his head with both hands. He blinked, concerned. "Dude, you shoulda told her you were coming."

"Why? What the fuck man, spit it out."

"She's been hangin' out with that guy, Nathan, again. She's with him right now."

I laughed. "Dude, you had me scared. I don't care about that guy. Let's go find her."

Kyle's face lit up with a crooked grin. "You guys have the most insane relationship. I don't get it." He shook his head. "My parents are gonna die when they see you."

My stomach turned when his words hit my ears. "Dude, don't remind me. Do your parents know Aly's coming to New York with me?"

"Yep, they sure do," he sniggered. "They're just concerned you're gonna ruin your lives together. That my sister's gonna quit school, get pregnant, and you'll fail and not be able to take care of her."

"Don't mince words. Wow. I'm glad they have so much faith," I said dryly. I was pissed. They obviously had no idea of where I was in my career. I guess I couldn't blame them, though. We were a train wreck when I left. "Well, I'm gonna go over there to break the tension, then I'll meet your dad for coffee, you know, explain how things'll go down."

A stunned look flashed on Kyle's face. "Dude, you're not gonna ask her to marry you, are you?"

I choked. "Fuck, are you crazy?" I said flatly, trying not to look like I was lying. Aly obviously hadn't said anything to him about my *already proposal,* and if she was gonna tell someone, it would have been him.

"Well, shit man. Sitting down with my dad? Alone? Who does that unless they're gonna pop the question?"

I chuckled, a bit jumpy, and caught myself grabbing the back of my neck – my anxious reflex. Shit. I wondered if Kyle noticed the same habits as Aly did. "Naw, man," I laughed it off. "I just wanna make sure he knows where I'm comin' from. Dude, I want her to move to New York permanently and go to school out there."

———

It was just after nine in the morning, and the summer weather was here. It was seventy-three degrees and warming up; the sun was already shining brightly. Gone was the usual cloudy marine layer. I missed it. It was hot and humid back in New York, and I hated it. You couldn't walk outside without becoming instantly moist and sweaty. Thinking about the upcoming week, I looked forward to chilling with Notting and not having any band shit to deal with. This was the first vacation ever.

Driving down the familiar streets out of the airport, I wondered where Aly was at again. "Aly's with Nathan, huh? So she stayed the night with him?"

"Dude, I don't…" he paused.

My insides turned at the thought of her sleeping with someone else. "Don't be a pussy, Kyle. I wanna hear it."

"I don't know," he stammered, shrugging his shoulders. "I went to the house on the way to get you, to see what Aly was up to and she wasn't home. Mom didn't know where she was at or if she'd come home. Only that she was with him."

9

"Does she stay with him all the time?"

"Not that I'm aware of. They've been on and off since you've been back in the picture."

Huh? It sounded like she didn't tell him anything about her trip to visit me, or that she'd supposedly broken up with Nathan. *Fuck, maybe she lied to me.*

This news made me feel better about my Sophia situation. Seemed like we were both playing games. Not that it really mattered, but hearing she was with someone else right now made my blood boil. I wanted to find her. Whoever this Nathan fuck was, I didn't give a shit about hurt feelings. This was it. We agreed to be together. I laughed inside at the hypocrisy of my thoughts, seeing I'd just been with Sophia a few days before and had yet to break up with her.

I didn't have to wait long. Kyle sent a text to Aly, asking her whereabouts. She was having breakfast at our local beach joint, The Kettle.

We arrived in no time. My heart raced as we pulled into the metered parking space right out front. My mouth went dry. As if I was still in high school, I wondered whom this dude was, and if he'd be a dick and wanna fight me.

Come on, it's all good, I told myself.

I spotted her right away. She was sitting in a booth, facing the front door. Her hair was rumpled, like she'd just woken up. She wore a white tank top that clung tightly to her boobs, making them look especially great. I simmered at the thought of Nathan staring at them, too. Standing there, I waited for her to see me, wondering what her reaction would be.

Her eyes lit up as soon as she saw me. She quickly got up, making her way towards me. A look of surprise painted her face and her smile was genuine. Relief flooded over me. She wrapped her arms around me. I stared at Nathan, who was looking over his shoulder, peeved. I couldn't help but smirk. Fuck him with his pretty boy blond hair; another fucking sporto, of course.

Sometimes I wondered why she chose me. Usually girls stuck with the same type of guy. Other than Mike, she'd never dated another musician. This just made me love her more. She wasn't some band whore like all the others, including Sophia, who'd gone out with her share of famous frontmen.

Aly barraged me with questions, searching my face and squeezing my waist. "What are you doing here? When did you arrive?"

"Just flew in. I wanted to surprise you," I answered, looking at her lovingly. Her excited state had me zinging inside.

"Come on, let's go," I said, staring down at her flawless face.

"Jake, I can't just leave him." She laughed under her breath, glancing in Nathan's direction.

"Did you eat already?"

"Yeah."

"Then you can. Go say good-bye. Tell him the truth and let's go." I held her tight to my chest, kissing her again.

She paused, pushing away from me, and sighed. Her lips pressed together and her head bobbled from side to side. "Okay. I feel bad though."

I looked at her with raised eyebrows as she backed away, wearing a helpless expression. She turned and slowly walked back to Nathan. Kyle stood behind me, silently timid and not wanting to get involved in any way, which took me back to our childhood for a split second. I watched Aly intently as she pulled nervously at the caramel tips of her hair, making up some sort of an excuse. Aly grabbed her bag and gave him a hug. To my gut-wrenching surprise, Nathan got up and followed her. I could only imagine what was going through his head.

Fuck – confrontation.

Nathan approached us and Aly took my hand. He stared me up and down, and I stood taller, meeting him face to face. My heart thumped in my throat then he spoke.

"You don't deserve her," he growled under his breath, then walked away before I could form a comeback. Aly clutched at my arm, stopping the torrent of anger coursing through me.

Fuck him.

"Sporto didn't take this well," I said smugly.

"Get over yourself." She nudged, trying not to smile. "Of course he's not gonna take it well. But I told him when I got back from London what was going on, and he chose to keep hanging out with me."

You clearly liked hanging out with him too, I thought hypocritically.

Draping my arm around her shoulder, I pulled her close to me as we walked to Kyle's car. I decided to tell her about Sophia when we got to my house.

Chapter 2

JAKE

Aly hung over the back passenger's seat, her arms wrapped around me. I kissed her hands and fingers tenderly, over and over again. I wished I'd gotten a room somewhere instead of thinking I'd stay with my mom at the house. All I could think about was being alone with her in a king-sized bed. One of her hands slipped down into the neck of my shirt, and her fingers lightly brushed my skin, giving me the chills. I could have jumped into the backseat then and there.

Soon enough, we were pulling into Aly's driveway. I stared at my childhood home, where it all began: *everything*. I tensed up, knowing I'd be face-to-face with my mother. Strange, I thought. We'd actually been getting along really well since her trip to London – we'd still yet to talk about anything *life-changing*. Not sure what my mood was all about. My mom had only joined me on the road twice in Europe, and Notting made sure to take charge, keeping her at arms' length. There wasn't really anything that she could control now that I was grown and on my own.

I sighed loudly, gripping the door handle. "Okay, here we go," I announced. I opened the door, swinging my legs out and walking to Aly's side of the car.

"What's wrong?" she said, shutting the car door. "Aren't you excited to be home?"

"Of course I am, come here." I reached out for her, pulling her tight to my body. "It's just weird. The last time we were here together, it was…crazy."

Aly nodded her head, stepping back away from me. She held my hand, swinging it back and forth, staring at it. "I don't wanna talk about it."

A jolt went through me. Was she trying being cute?

A smile peaked at the corners of her mouth. "Wow, no pun intended, but now that it's out there, nice song," she said dryly.

We never did talk about the song I'd written and recorded after we officially broke up. *The* song that got mass airplay all over the country, the song – *Talk About It.* I guessed now, maybe, we'd talk about it.

I smiled weakly at her. "I'm sorry how that all went down."

"Yeah, a pretty sucky time. When I heard it for the first time on the radio, it made me hate you more."

What was I gonna say to that? We stood staring at each other for a long moment. The song said it all. "That's all behind us now. Let's go say hello to Kate."

I began walking away, but Aly didn't follow. "Um, I think maybe you should go alone, text me in a bit, and I'll come over."

I totally understood where she was coming from. I didn't look forward to my face to face with her father, either.

14

I shook my head, walking back to her. "Okay. It's prob-ably better, seeing she has no idea I'm here." I chuckled. "I'll text when the excitement fades. Then you and I are gonna do cartwheels." I winked at her, leaned down, and kissed her goodbye.

———

I stood staring at my front door. Nothing about its off-white surface had changed. The same potted, neatly trimmed suc-culents lined the steps. I bent down, picking up two tree-trim-ming leaflets someone left in hopes of new business. I took a deep breath and rang the doorbell. I counted all the way to ten before I heard commotion come from behind the door, and then it swung open.

I smiled sheepishly. "I'm home!" I said, raising my arms. My mother beamed and gave me a radiant smile. I felt a tinge of burn in my nose and my eyes tingled. When I went in to hug her, I got misty-eyed.

She held me firmly, all the while whispering, *"Oh my God, oh my God, oh my God, my baby's home."* She'd never used the words *my baby* before. I held her snugly in return.

I pulled away and noticed that her hair was different. A lot about her appearance had changed since I'd seen her last. Her hair now grazed the tops of her shoulders. Gone were long the golden blonde waves. She was still blonde, but more grey peeked out from behind the blonde strands.

"What are you doing here? Does Notting know? Oh, geez, Jake Masters. How could you do this? I'm not ready for you." She kept chitchatting in excited bursts.

"Mom, relax. Take a breath," I laughed.

We slowly walked through the foyer and I glanced at the wall. I noticed all the black and white photos that I'd left behind were now gone. Lined side by side were black and whites of me and the band, performing at various venues and stadiums. "Wow, when did you get those?" I asked, pointing.

"Oh, Notting and I…" She paused. "He came home with one as a gift on my birthday one time, and then it just grew from there."

I got the feeling she didn't want to admit that Notting and her had taken things to another level. "Is Notting living here?" I saw her gulp and surprise flashed in her eyes. *Whoops.* She certainly didn't expect me to ask that so quickly. "Come on, Mom. It's no big deal."

Her chest rose as she took in a breath and held it. Her eyes searched mine and she let out a big sigh. "Jake, Notting does stay here from time to time."

I smiled at her impishly. "Mom, I'm not thirteen anymore. It's okay to have a boyfriend. I already know you guys have had a thing going on for years."

She grew rigid, standing taller, then turned, sitting down on the sofa. "Notting and I are very good friends, Jake, and…"

"Mom, it's okay. Don't you get it?" I said, interrupting her. I still couldn't believe after all the time that went by, and how long I'd been gone, that she still couldn't admit anything about Notting. "Did you hear what I said? I know about Notting."

The skin on her cheeks flushed pink and I immediately felt bad. I totally put her on the spot, but it needed to happen. She should be happy to have everything out in the open. "What's the problem?" I probed.

She fidgeted with the rings on her fingers. "I want to hear about you." She blinked. "Who met you at the airport?"

I laughed, shaking my head. "Okay. Let's see something." I turned around and walked toward her bedroom. She didn't say anything until I was all the way into her room.

I heard her voice faintly. "Jake, what are you doing?"

I stood facing the neatly made bed with its white comforter pulled and tucked tightly against its mattress. I glanced around the room. I spotted Notting's camel-colored travel satchel. I knew it was his. It had the familiar scars of travel, and Dump's branded cigarette-burned happy face stared back at me.

"What are you looking for?" she said, coming up behind me. "Notting's not here." I didn't answer her and walked toward the closet. "Jake?" she said, her voice strained.

Just as I thought, Notting's razor sat on the side of the sink, across from the wall of closet mirrors. I pulled open the doors, and men's clothing hung there.

I shot my mother an ironic look over my shoulder. "I guess I'm doing what you would do; just seeing for myself." I stared at her, smiling, waiting for her to admit it. "Can't we all just move on?"

Her forehead knitted together. "Jake this is not how I wanted you to find out."

"Mom, you're acting like you got caught cheating or…" I stalled as the words darted from my mouth, thinking of my father. "I mean, come on. It's okay. I'm a big boy." There was something that flashed in her eyes. What was her problem? "Look. I know I caught you off guard and I'm sorry. I think I'll just stay at a hotel until you work whatever it is you need to work out," I said, swinging my arms around.

"No, no, no. I want you to stay here." She reached over, grabbing a little black elastic band from the bathroom counter, then tied her hair back. Instantly, she looked ten years younger. She exhaled loudly. "Come." She turned, walking toward the bedroom door, and I followed. "Notting won't be home for a while. I want to hear about what's been going on with you. Notting, of course tells me everything, but I want to hear your version. Are you still dating Sophia? Or is this thing with Aly still happening?"

Kill me before the pink elephant swallows me whole, I thought.

I didn't want to talk about Sophia with her. I decided not to lean on my mom anymore about Notting; instead, I'd just ask him directly. I was shocked he never said anything to me in the first place. I felt strange about the whole thing. Why wouldn't he tell me, especially after all the intimate talks we'd had in the past?

I sat at the kitchen counter as my mother did her usual frittering around, making food I wasn't hungry for.

"Are you still seeing Sophia? I really liked her. She seems like a good one."

Not as good as Aly. "Um, about that…" I paused.

She shut the stove carefully. "What happened?" she asked, sadly. "Did you break it off because you and Aly are getting serious again? I had a feeling since London…but with her school and all, are you sure you want to have a long distance relationship? It wouldn't…"

I sucked in a deep breath and stood up. "Look, Mom," I interrupted her babbling, "actually there's something I want to tell you."

"Okay." She kept shredding cheese, without looking up at me.

"Aly is coming back with me to New York." I held my breath. My heart thumped hard in anticipation of her reply. She smiled softly and kept shredding for a moment longer.

18

She looked at me, wondering if I was kidding. "This *is* news. I'm not sure what to say."

Really? She didn't have *one* thing to say about it? I waited. She most definitely had to have something to say about it.

Gulp – nothing. Lick my lips – nothing.

She looked away from me and began placing the cheese in a bowl.

I wasn't about to go after this. Or was I? Reverse psychology at its best.

"No other questions?" She shook her head. I nodded. "Okay. So. Um, I guess I'll go get checked into a hotel and come back in a bit. I wanna spend some time with Aly, too." I stood blinking, dumbfounded.

"I'm making enchiladas. Will you please come for dinner?" Her voice sounded funny. It pitched higher, and the mood that filled the room was nothing I was used to. She sounded small, insubstantial, unlike herself. This yanked at me.

"Yeah, of course. I just don't want you to feel weird about Notting, Mom."

"Don't be silly." Her lips turned up at the corners, but I knew she didn't mean her tiny gesture. She was faking it, like me. A faker knows a faker, a con. "Notting and I are working through some things. Trying something new." She paused and sighed. "I don't want this to affect you, Jake."

I huffed, disturbed by her ridiculous concern. "Stop it already. You can't be serious." She had to be kidding. Was she trying to milk me for attention? "I'm really not sure what the problem is. I want you and Notting to finally be together, and it's obvious that you've had a problem with me knowing about it for years."

She leaned against the counter as her eyes diverted from mine and snatched a nearby dishtowel up, holding it to her face. Fuck, was she crying? "I can't do this, Jake." Her muffled voice squeezed through the rag. "We can discuss this later."

I gulped. Holy shit, she *was* crying. I hadn't seen her cry in a long, long time. Like a time warp, I felt six-years old. "Mom, what's wrong?"

She removed the towel from her eyes, which continued to pool, and she sniffled. "I wanted to tell you, not have you find out like this. I'm sorry," she said, holding back more tears. "It's just very emotional for me, moving on." Then she laughed ironically, tossing her head back. "I'm supposed to be the parent, and here I am crying to you. It shouldn't be this way."

She shook her head and her forehead creased with sadness. She shouldn't be sad; she should be happy to be moving on with her life.

"But it is his way," I remarked. I wanted to go to her, but I stood paralyzed. I wanted so badly to tell her not to be sad, that she deserved better than my father and his going with another women behind her back.

She smiled and put on a brave face, tucking the stray hair behind her ear. "I want you to be happy, Jake, and successful. That's all I've ever wanted for you. It seems you're about to have everything you've ever wanted. That's all I could ask for."

I laughed to myself. She was the master at diversion.

"I just wanted to love you and provide for you the best I could, in memory of…" she paused, sucking in her tears, "your father and to not have anything in my personal life affect you in any way, and it could have many, many times. So I made you my number one priority, and I still do. I'll do it until the day I die." Oh geez, *why* was she always so melodramatic?

I sighed. "I know, Mom, I know you did." Now it was getting really heavy, and I couldn't take it. This was her issue; she was right. I needed to go. I wanted Aly. I scooted to her side and gave her a gentle hug. "What time do you want me back?"

"Seven." She turned, going to the fridge. "Jake. Please stay here. There's no reason to spend money on a hotel."

I laughed. "Mom, there are other reasons I want to stay in a hotel." I hoped she'd get the hint as I turned and walked out of the kitchen. "I'll be back."

Chapter 3

ALYSSA

The warm afternoon air pressed against my face as I walked into the Shade Hotel, our towns local boutique hotel. I prayed that the person at the front desk wasn't someone we knew. I was relieved that I didn't recognize the lady with short brown hair and sparkly gold earrings, punching away at a hidden keyboard. I glanced around for any familiar faces. Just what I needed was for my mom and dad to hear they saw me with a boy, checking into the hotel down the street. My heart raced like I was gonna get in trouble or something.

I wondered if this paranoia would ever go away. I mean, I was eighteen after all. I'd traveled all the way across the globe and back and my parents knew about it. What was my problem? This lady obviously didn't recognize either of us. I breathed a soft sigh of relief as I waited quietly behind Jake, keeping my head bent down, as if that would thwart anyone noticing me.

My fingers traced the sweeping dark blue and black lines permanently etched onto Jake's left bicep – he'd gotten more ink work done. I tried to make out what he was going for; the only markings I could make out were the little musical notes.

He told me it was a surprise, so I stood there wondering, waiting for the elevator door to open. Walking through the hallway, I could barely feel my feet hitting carpet. I was tingling all over, and could hardly contain myself as he swept me up into his arms and walked through the hotel room door.

"Honey, we're home." He smiled seductively.

I took his face in my hands, feeling the slight roughness of his unshaven cheeks, and kissed him deeply. I wanted him so badly, I couldn't feel any other part of my body except my lips, tongue, and the intense ache that radiated through my hips and down my thighs. It was as if he was my life's breath, and I would die if I didn't inhale every bit of him. He laid me gently on the bed and lingered above, pressing into me. Sliding my hands up underneath his shirt, his skin felt like silk. I pulled the shirt over his head, and he stared down at me with his blue, dreamy eyes. He was now firm against me, and it made me wet with desire. *Wow.* I wrapped my legs around him, wanting us to melt together for eternity.

We feverishly yanked at each other's clothing and tossed them across the room, giggling and laughing like I don't know what. Was it nervous laughter? Mischievous laughter? Maybe it was both. It'd been so long since I'd been with him, and my insecurities were looming over me. Would I be able to satisfy him again?

"You're the end-all, Aly," he whispered, looking at me intensely. My breathing was erratic, and I was ready to explode. His words continued, caressing my ears. "I love you. I wanna show you how much I love you. I'll move mountains to be with you; nothing's gonna keep us apart now."

His hand caressed my thigh and he kissed me softly, licking my lips. He moved down my neck, sending chills over

every inch of my body. Tender, warm, wet kisses covered me
all the way down to my stomach, then to my thighs. He took
me into his mouth. Toe-curling doesn't even begin to describe
how he made me feel. I was in a complete pleasure blackout,
and it ended way too soon. I'm sure the whole universe heard
me scream, but I didn't care at that moment; all I wanted was
more of him.

"Oh my God," I said, breathless, covering my face.
"Mmmm." I closed my eyes, reveling in the sensations that
were still flowing through me.

"I love drinking you up. You're so fuckin' hot." His voice
was husky with desire.

"I still ache for you," I whispered, sitting up. I took him
into my hand, and he was as hard as a rock. I stroked him. "I
need more of you."

He smiled softly. "You want more, huh?" His eyebrows
rose in amusement.

"I wanna make your eyes roll into the back of your head,"
I purred, giggling, and poked him in the chest.

I wanted to be as close to him as I could. I wanted to be
a part of him. I prayed that it wouldn't hurt like it did the first
time. I wanted to get off with him inside me; that hadn't happened my entire time in London.

"You drive me crazy, you feel so good," he moaned
in my ear, moving my hips as close as they could be. He
filled me completely. I wanted to wince through the first
several thrusts, but the pain ebbed and didn't return. Only
warm, pulsing goodness ebbed through me. Watching the
pleasure-filled pain wash over Jake's face made me feel
something I'd never felt before; for the first time, I felt like
a woman.

Our blur of lust was finally satisfied, leaving us spent and curled up in each other's arms. "Do we really have to go to dinner at your house?" I whined.

I wanted to stay in bed with him for the rest of the night before I had to face my father. He'd been acting like Jake didn't exist, talking like I would be around all summer. He conveniently forgot that I would be in New York during our annual family vacation.

Jake propped his too-handsome head up in his hand and stared at me with his devastating blue eyes, making me melt into him. I kissed his chin and neck over and over again. He sighed. "We don't have to. But I don't wanna be a dick. I left my mom crying and all emo." He collapsed onto his back and rubbed his face, staring at the ceiling. His muscular arms made his new tattoos beyond hot. "Notting moved in."

"What?!" The news propelled me to sit up, pulling at the sheets to cover my boobs.

Jake smiled. "You know, you don't have to cover them. I think they like being naked, having me admire their perfectly round perkiness….and being played with." He reached out, squeezing one.

"Stop it," I giggled, hitting his hand away. I crossed my legs, thinking more of Notting and his mom. "You know I never thought anything of him being around with out you there. But now that you say it, his truck was *always* parked at your house."

"Yep. My mom didn't tell me. I found out because I asked and she got all tongue-tied." He half laughed, getting out of the bed. His butt was perfectly round, like an athlete's. His legs were strong, and I admired them as he disappeared into the bathroom.

"You need to get some sun. I don't recall you ever being this white," I shouted, smiling. I heard the shower turn on. "What? Doesn't the sun shine in the city?"

I heard him laugh. "Not like it does here!"

———

I sat staring at Jake. *Are you kidding me?* He *still* had a girlfriend and she had no idea that he was essentially leaving her to move in with me, into a brand new apartment.

"I seriously can't believe you," I said, flabbergasted. I couldn't think of anything else to say at that moment, and paced back and forth. I should have been angry, but instead, I felt overwhelming sympathy for what was to come for Sophia. "Are you fucking kidding me?" I shouted.

He breathed in deeply. "You're not mad?"

"I don't know what I am! I guess, yeah, I'm mad! I'm also sad for Sophia! What the fuck are you thinking?"

He shook his head and looked at the ceiling in frustration. "I didn't want to deal with it. I'd been blowing her off and not seeing her as often, and I guess I hoped it would just go away."

"It? You mean *she*. You sound like you're ten years old, Jake," I jeered. Now I was getting truly angry, and I huffed, pointing at him. "You need to call her. I don't wanna show up somewhere and have her there, not knowing what's going on."

"I can't do this over the phone. I told you that. I promise I'll take care of it as soon as we get there. I promise you won't have to deal with any of this."

"I sure hope not," I squeaked out, already convinced that this was not going to go over easily. Scenes from the Rachel episodes flashed in my head. "This is gonna be a repeat of Rachel, you just watch."

"No, no it's not. Sophia already *knows* about you. She knew we were together in London." He rubbed his hand over his face. "I'm sorry for dragging it out."

This made me feel worse for her, and I stared at Jake wondering, what else he was going to spring on me. I sulked into the bathroom to take a shower without another word. I wanted so badly to ask if he'd still been sleeping with her, but I was too afraid of what the answer would be. I didn't want to hear a *yes*. He was fully mine now. Sophia was just a formality

Chapter 4

JAKE

Aly had her damp hair pulled into a tight bun. Her face was luminous against the setting sunlight streaming through the car windows. She was the most precious thing in my life, and I'd never been happier. Everything I'd ever dreamt of was happening. I was alive and healthy, my band was whole, and everybody in my life was right where they wanted to be. Dump seemed on the mend from his sickness and he had given up smoking. He and Sienna were happily set up in Midtown. Devon, our fill-in guitarist, still toured with us even after Bobby returned, and Bobby and Marshall were still together.

Even with all of it ostensibly falling into place, uneasiness churned in my stomach. Aly didn't seem as excited about coming to New York as I thought she'd be, even before I sprung the whole Sophia debacle on her. I squeezed her hand. She smiled, leaning her head back against the headrest and looking out the window. I turned the corner into our neighborhood, my nerves itching at me.

"How you doin'?" I rattled her hand.

She sighed quickly, and then an even bigger sigh followed. "I'm just nervous about everything. I don't think I'll be able to eat."

"Don't be nervous." I said reassuringly. I also worried how it'd go over. Aly and my mother hadn't seen each other since before I'd informed her that Aly was moving with me to New York.

The evening moved along, with my mother lost in the kitchen as Aly and I watched TV. I wondered when and if Notting would come home, or if my mom had asked him to stay away. I'd bet any amount of money that she asked him to stay out; that's just how she operated.

As all these thoughts ran through my head, I glanced at Aly, who looked petrified. She didn't return my affection, begging me under her breath to leave her alone. I playfully taunted her until she punched me hard in the arm, leaving a charlie-horse as a reminder for me to behave.

"Kids, dinner's ready!" my mom shouted. Aly glanced at me, rolling her eyes. She whispered her under her breath, "*here we go.*"

———

I pushed the rice around my plate. It was palpable that Aly was on edge. I could feel *it* as she quietly carved away at her enchiladas, unable to look up from her plate, even though my mother kept an upbeat demeanor. My mother cleared her throat, glanced at me, and then looked at Aly. Aly held her stare. All I could do was chew my food, wondering what the fuck would happen next. My mother opened her mouth to speak, and to my surprise, it was Aly's voice I heard.

"Kate," Aly said. She placed her fork and knife on her plate, never taking her eyes off of her. *Oh shit.* "I know a lot has happened." She shook her head, looking between the both of us, smiling ironically. "And I'm sure it's as hard for you to sit there as it is for me to sit here, pretending that we don't have a past, but I just want you to know that I love Jake more than you could ever know. No matter what happens, I'll always have his best interest at heart."

I could see my mother gulp as she blinked, surprised at Aly's bold, mature attitude. I was more astonished.

"Alyssa, dear." She smiled, then pressed her fingers between her eyebrows before she spoke. "After the time we spent in London, I've come to believe that you do care deeply for Jake. I know you understand what he's been through in his life and how hard he's worked. You're both grown now, so there's not much else to say." She shrugged. "I've chatted with your brother over the last few years, and it seems you've really got it together. You have your pick of colleges. I'm sure your father is proud." She chuckled, shaking her head. "I can only image what he must think about you going off with Jake to New York, after all that's happened."

Aly chuckled softly, and her eyes grew wide, brightening the energy in the room. "Yeah, he's pretending it's not gonna happen, or I don't know what. Maybe he really did forget."

"I doubt it," I guffawed, almost spitting the food out of my mouth.

"I'll be reminding him soon enough," Aly said a bit loudly. Her hand slipped under the table, clasping my thigh, sending a warm sensation pulsing through my veins. Crazy, I thought, how one simple move could have such an affect on me.

"Speaking of, I, um," I stammered, "Mom, I was hoping that you'd do me a huge favor."

"What?" Her eyes narrowed and her lips pressed together.

"Um, I was hoping that you'd go over and talk to Aly's dad, you know, and tell him that you're aware of what's going on and stuff like that."

"Stuff like that?" She crossed her arms to her chest. "No, I will do no such thing. You're twenty-one, and I have nothing to say to that man." She looked at Aly, smiling sadly. "I'm sure you understand. He'd have to come over here and be accountable for all the insults. I don't care how much time has gone by; I'm not having it."

"I'm really sorry about all that, about everything, Kate." Aly rung her hands, "I don't know what we were thinking back then, any of us."

I totally regretted saying anything to my mom in front of Aly. I was simply hoping that Aly and I would be able to leave as one big modern family, all made up and happy – as if.

I cleared my throat, wanting to change the subject. "That was a long time ago, it's time to drop it. Sorry I brought it up." I stood, pushing my chair away. I gave my mother a hard stare, silently telling her to move along to a different subject, and grabbed my plate.

"You're right. The past is the past. Just know that sometimes the past can come back to bite you."

"What? A past that you're just letting go of, finally?" I lightly huffed, shaking my head. "I really don't think we need to talk about pasts, especially with you."

"Jake, stop it!" Aly scolded me.

"No, Aly, he's right," my mom remarked calmly, looking at me, then back to Aly. "On another note, he's so quick to judge, yet has no idea what he's judging."

I threw my free hand up. "And that's my fault? I practically begged you this morning to tell me…"

"Jake!" Aly chimed with an edge I'd not heard before. "Like you said, I think we need to move on."

Her courage took me aback and perked me up. Twice in a row, I wasn't used to her speaking up. Especially since it was against me, though I couldn't keep the smile from peeking out at the sides of my mouth. I was intrigued by her new personality trait. It was hot. I drank her in with my eyes for a long moment, and the aching pressure of yearning ran through me. Her slender arms hung motionless at her sides as she stared me down, daring me to keep giving my mom shit. I forced myself to stop fantasizing about what I would do to her if my mother hadn't been sitting right in front of us.

I stepped over and grabbed the plate that sat in front of her, then gave her a peck on the forehead. Her hand lightly wrapped around my calf as I stood next to her, making me go weak. It spurred me to clear my throat self-consciously. "So, when's Notting gonna be back? Been missin' that guy." I didn't look at my mom or Aly as I walked to the sink. I focused on rinsing the plate in my hand.

"Well, he actually should be back here any time now."

"Why didn't he have dinner with us?" I turned the water off and looked around for a towel.

"I wanted to be alone with you for a little bit." *Control freak,* I thought. This irritated me. It was never-ending; poor Notting, being kept away from where he lived. I ran my wet hands through my hair.

33

"You didn't have to do that." I glared at my mom.

"Jake," Aly broke in, rising from her seat. "I think I'm gonna get going."

My eyes darted to Aly. "No, no. It's cool." I motioned with my hands for her calm down. "I'll stop. I just don't get it." I said, looking at my mother and shaking my head.

My mom ignored my remark and began clearing a few things off the table. "Are you excited to be graduating tomorrow, Aly? Ready to embark on your new adventures?"

Aly looked at me, smiling. "I'm ready to move on with my life. Yes, I'm very excited."

"I'm sure tomorrow will be quite a stir at the ceremony, having Jake there." Her tone was a bit condescending.

What? What was that supposed to mean? I glanced at Aly, and she looked perplexed too.

"What? Mom, she had no idea I was coming."

She sighed loudly. "I hope it doesn't turn into a scene, that's all."

———

Aly had such a knack for sneaking away unheard. It was her graduation day and our D-Day. My stomach flipped, thinking about seeing her mom and dad at the ceremony and conversing with them about our future. I rolled over into a ball, staring out across my hotel room, wishing I could just avoid it and be on the plane back to New York. I glanced at the clock. It was still early, 8:30 am. I decided to make my way to the gym, wondering if my membership was still valid.

Arriving at the gym, I was stoked the parking lot wasn't at full capacity, which meant no waiting for machines. Walking through the familiar foyer brought me back to when my mom would force the band to work out as part of *the deal*. I chuckled to myself. Maybe her demands made an impression on me, because it was now always important for me to stay in shape and clean. Even during my relapses into using, I still made sure to work out, telling myself it would clean out my system faster. Maybe it did.

A pretty blonde with big brown eyes stood behind the counter, ready to greet me. "Hello, your name?" she said, smiling brightly as I approached closer.

"Jake Masters." I smiled in return. "I'm not sure if my membership is still valid."

She batted her eyes at me, then looked back at her screen and back up at me, blinking twice. "Yes, you're still active. Your account is on auto-pay."

"Really? Hmm. My mom must have forgotten about it." I shrugged, feeling a bit embarrassed to have mentioned my mother. "I think it's about time that I switch over the account. Can you put it on my credit card now?"

"Sure."

I tossed my credit card onto the counter. She took care of business while I checked out the scene. It was, as I'd thought, nearly empty.

As I made my way into the locker room, I kept having a pretend conversation with Aly's parents in my head. As if it would go that way, but hey it was making me feel better to be somewhat prepared. Rounding a corner, I was surprised to spot Notting. He was stuffing his things into a locker. Did he pass right by me in the lobby? He must not have noticed me. I wondered if my mom was there too.

"Not, hey man!" I said excitedly.

He looked over his shoulder with a huge smile on his face. "Saw you at the front."

"Why didn't you say anything?"

He shrugged. "You were taking care of your business."

I embraced him in a tight bear hug, patting him on the back as I released him. "Missed you last night, man. Sorry Kate's still being weird about stuff." I wanted him to know I was aware of what was going on.

He sighed deeply and shook his head. "Son, I'm not sure about things," he said sadly.

My stomach sank. Shit, maybe my mom's time had run out. She was finally out of rope with him. I gulped and felt hot under my collar. I just stared at him blankly. I had no idea what to ask or to say, and before I'd realized it, a few words sprung out. "But you just moved in, right?"

"Jake, I'm sorry. I shouldn't have said anything. I don't think I should be discussing our issues with you."

"Not, man, I think you know it's all good with me. I *know* mom has issues, big ones."

He looked at the ground somberly. "Yeah. I'll be on the treadmill," he said. He squeezed my shoulder on his way by.

I stood with my backpack dangling in my hand for I don't know how long, just staring at the space where Notting once stood. Mixed emotions thundered through me. What the fuck was going on? I had to find out. I hastily stuffed my shit into a locker and took off after him. I found him walking at a brisk pace on one of the treadmills. There wasn't anyone else around. Notting stared at the soundless TV screen in front of him, perhaps reading the closed-captioning.

"Hey," I said unhappily. "Tell me what's going on." *I had to be blunt, right?*

Notting took in a deep breath. "I'm not sure, really." He reached out, pushing at some buttons on the machine, slowing his stride just as I pushed at mine to get started. "Things were great when I first moved in. And then one day, about four weeks into it, she was distracted, almost distraught, and very emotional. She wouldn't tell me why, making up something about her friend, Cassidy. Something just didn't sit right with me. It's gotten better, but something's still off."

I walked, staring down at the black tread gliding underneath my feet, and my mind tried to grasp what it might be. Fear ran through me. "Do you think she's sick? Like cancer sick or somethin'?" I grabbed the rails of the treadmill. "I mean, she says that's not it, but that unexpected trip to London has me really wondering. She was all weird then, too."

"No, no, no." He shook his head. "She swore to me that it wasn't anything health-related. Then told me she was working whatever it is out with Cassidy. She asked me not to bring it up anymore."

"What the hell is that supposed to mean?" I guffawed uneasily. "I mean, oh, okay. She just get's to make all the calls, still? She acts lame, treats you differently, and can't tell you the truth?"

"Jake." Notting's tone warned me to cool it.

I hit stop on the machine and stared at him. "I seriously don't know what to say about the entire thing. It's like one big long drama. You have no idea how long this drama has been going on. It's one thing or another, starting with my dad, and then her…*issues* and now you're officially dragged into it because you're living with her."

He stared at me pensively, running his fingers through his wavy hair in frustration as his other hand gripped the handle of the treadmill. I jumped when he practically punched the emergency stop button and then glared at me angrily. "I have been a part of this drama since before it was drama, Jake. Don't tell me I have no idea," he growled. He shook his head as his shoulders slumped. "I don't think we should be discussing family matters anymore."

Notting stepped off the treadmill without another word. I hadn't meant to upset him. I thought I was the only one upset about our history. I went after him. "Notting, man, I'm sorry," I said, tripping over my own feet as I followed him back toward the locker room. "Don't stop your workout because of me. I'll leave."

"I'm no longer in the mood to be here. I'll see you later." He didn't even look at me.

I stood there feeling stupid and glanced around to see if anyone was staring at me. A few people were. I was embarrassed. I looked in the direction of the café, only to see someone taking a picture of me with an iPhone. I instantly saw red and almost went off yelling something I'd regret before I noticed a gym attendant walk up in front of the woman, thwarting her motives. I didn't stay to watch how that panned out and took off toward the free weights, thinking about leaving.

My heart was thumping wildly. I looked around and spotted a few instructors gawking at me, which only made my mood worse. Before I knew it, I was standing right in front of them. "Do you have a question? You need somethin'?" I hissed, my arms out to the side, daring them to say something stupid. "Don't people mind their own fucking business around here?"

A girl standing by, wearing pink tie-dyed workout gear, choked out her words. "Uh, no. I'm sorry if we've offended you." Her eyes bounced around behind me, never making contact with mine, only with her bearded and muscled-up coworker's. "Um, Mark, I'll talk to you later," she said and finally looked at me. "My name is Trisha. I'm the nutritionist here. If you have any questions, don't be afraid to ask…I hope your day gets better."

Trisha walked away. Now I felt like a dick as *Mark* looked me up and down. "Jake? Masters? Right?"

"Yeah," I grumbled, not looking at him

"I thought that was you. I know you. Trisha…" he said, pointing in her direction. "Actually knew you from a few years ago, before you hit the big time. Great music, man."

Faux enthusiasm sprung to my face, dipping into a tight smile that ticked at the corners of my mouth. I thanked him, looking around, trying to decide which bench I would land on. I wanted to be alone, and not have *Mark* carry on about my shit. Thankfully he got the hint and didn't mention anything about *me* again, saying goodbye. As cordially as I could, I returned his gesture.

Chapter 5

JAKE

So typical of me; I didn't let myself down. I was officially the number one procrastinator in the entire world. I'd waited until the last possible moment to talk to Aly's parents about her move to New York. Aly was graduating in a few hours and we were leaving tomorrow. I stood in the driveway, leaning against my mother's black Escalade, my heart thundering in my chest, waiting for her parents to come over. I couldn't take my mother telling me to sit down and relax anymore, so I moved outside to greet them.

Mr. Montgomery was the first to come out of the gate, crisp as usual in his light blue checked button-down and black slacks, looking like the lawyer that he was. My hands began to sweat. *Fuck.* I pulled at the collar of my t-shirt and wished I'd dressed nicer. It was bad enough that he already thought I was a piece of shit. I could have at least looked like I wasn't one, in my faded jeans with holes in the knees and a black t-shirt with a bleach stain. I gulped and stood straight. I had to stop myself from shoving my hands deep down into my pockets like I was twelve.

I stepped away from the truck as Aly's parents moved closer, and tried to smile as sincerely as I could. "Hello, thanks for coming over," I said, extending my hand to Aly's father, Frank. I smiled sincerely at Mrs. Montgomery, who looked like she'd been crying. Great. She gave me a tight smile, as if she were holding back tears. "Um, you wanna come inside?" I offered as my voice pitched higher.

"Jake, maybe we should talk over at our place." Frank scratched the top of his head and ran his hand over his face. "I don't think Kate would really appreciate us coming into her home after all that's happened."

"Look, Mr. Montgomery. All that was a long time ago..."

"Jake, first we need to apologize to Kate," Aly's mom interrupted, shooting Frank a look of contempt. "And then we can talk."

I was shocked that Frank just stood there, silent, looking off in the distance. He was probably cursing her in his head for embarrassing him. It was obvious Mr. Montgomery was being forced to play nice.

"Okay, um, look I know you and I…" I said, looking sheepishly at Mrs. Montgomery. "We never talked about what happened like Frank and I did before I moved away. I should also be apologizing to you. I was out of control. I was on drugs, and I should have known better. Even before I was high on those pills, I should have paid attention and cared more about what was going on with Aly. I was selfish. I admit it. It took me a long time to figure that out and let go." I paused, reliving that moment when I'd told Aly I was moving to New York and going on tour with Eva James. I felt a pain in my stomach as if I'd just admitted, all over, that I'd also been seeing Eva. I shook my head. "Leaving was the only way I knew to make it all better."

Mrs. Montgomery covered her mouth with her hand, trying to bottle up the tears that welled in her eyes. Her red nail polish caught my attention. It was an appealing accent to her otherwise natural beauty. She had the same long brown hair as Aly, with the exception of the light dusting of grey that framed her face. For the first time, I saw my future. Aly was going to be beautiful forever.

Silently we walked toward the house and I opened the front door and ushered them in.

Mr. Montgomery stood unnerved at the entrance to our kitchen. My mother was rigid behind the counter, staring down at her hands. I couldn't really say there was tension in the room, but some weird vibe was pulsing. I wondered who would be the first to speak. Then I decided to go for it first, clearing my throat. "Mom, you know I thought it would be a good idea for all of us to get together since Aly and I will be leaving in the morning."

She stared at me blankly, nodding and looked directly at Frank, waiting for him to apologize for all his harsh words aimed at her three years earlier. She crossed her arms to her chest drumming her fingers against her bicep.

"Look, Kate. I'm sorry. I can't say I remember what I said back then. I just know it was heated. We were in shock that Aly and Jake had been running around behind our backs, with the lying and ditching school…and I just don't run my life like…other people."

He hung his head and stammered, searching for words that wouldn't offend my mother more than he already had. I saw a glint of amusement in her eyes as Frank continued, struggling to apologize. "I'm really sorry for the insensitive things I said. I was out of line. I know you didn't know what was going on either."

I glanced over at Mrs. Montgomery. She was crying, wiping away the tears from her cheeks with trembling hands. It was as if a heavy wool blanket had been lifted from my face and I could breathe fresh clean air. Over three years of bitterness was gone in a matter of minutes. My mother was misty-eyed too as she came from around the counter with her arms outstretched to hug Mrs. Montgomery.

"Thank you, Frank," she said as she held Aly's mom tightly. "Carolyn, thank you, thank you both for coming over here."

Carolyn stepped back from my mom. "Kate. This has been the most agonizing and longest three years of our lives," she admitted, shaking her head. "Frank here likes to ignore the situation and move about like nothing's going on."

"Now Carolyn, that's not true. I just know there's nothing I can do about any of it anymore, so I carry on with my life. Just like the kids did."

For the next hour, I explained to Aly's parents my plan for having her in New York with me. I even invited them to come for a stay, which they politely declined. Then I was shocked out of my tree when he told me that Aly hadn't yet decided on what college she was going to attend. How she'd been grappling between NYU and Pepperdine. She'd gotten offered a full ride scholarship to play volleyball at Pepperdine University in Malibu. My heart sunk into my gut. *What the fuck? Academically to NYU – she never said anything to me.*

"Didn't she already have to make that choice if she's supposed to start school in the fall?" my voice cracked. Fuck,

I didn't want to come off as desperate. *What the hell was she thinking?*

Mr. Montgomery hemmed and hawed, finally offering something I could use. "She mentioned she would make her choice over the summer and start in the spring. She has to make a choice fast; they won't hold her spot for long."

Great, I thought. My stomach cinched in knots. Did I really have to convince Aly that NYU and New York were going to be her new home? I couldn't say goodbye to her parents fast enough. My mind was scrambling, wondering why after all that we'd spoken of, she'd be wavering about moving. What did that mean for us? Looking at the clock, I was relieved it was almost time for Aly's graduation ceremony. Notting came home, looking a bit confused when he saw Aly's parents, but engaged them kindly. I hadn't been keeping him apprised of much in my life since their visit to London. I politely said goodbye. Five PM was rolling around pretty fast.

———

I sat in my truck with a nervous anticipation I hadn't felt in a long time. I watched the students and families walk through the parking lot of our local community college; all shiny, pressed and fluffed, ready to graduate. Students milled, some with excitement painted on their faces and some staring blankly off in the distance, perhaps afraid of embarking on a new life, fearful of being an adult. I wondered what Aly was feeling.

Anxiety was churning. I thought of Amy, my sponsor, and her words echoed in my head. I didn't need anything to take the edge off. No booze, no pills, nothing. I was going to be fine. All of these gnawing, uneasy feelings would pass; that

I wasn't good enough for Aly or that I would be a failure, a has-been, and not able to provide for her. My eyes bounced around from face to face as I fought my restless thoughts. Was I truly a coward because I was too afraid to face Sophia? To show her the respect that she deserved? *Yes.* I had to man up, I told myself. That thought spurred me to think of my father, too, wondering if that's how he'd felt about his situation with my mother all those years ago, afraid of conflict.

With a deep breath, I closed my eyes as I took a reluctant first step through the gate, toward the football field and up into the stands. I turned to see white chairs precisely lined one by one next to each other, row after row. I never did get to sit in one of them. I scanned the area, not really making eye contact, not wanting to invite people in, not wanting anyone to recognize me. But it didn't take long for the buzz of the crowd and the stares to reach me. This was one of those times when I wished I could just fade into the background. Even though our town had its fair share of celebrity sightings and professional athletes milling around our local joints, it was nothing like being born and raised there, where everyone knew you before you did anything special, which made them feel entitled to come up and be nosey with backslapping familiarity.

I just wanted to be left alone as I sat next to Aly's bother and sister, Kyle and Allison, waiting for the ceremony to begin. I didn't get what I wanted, though. One by one, I shook hands and repeated myself over and over again about what I was doing and why I was there – *"I'm here for Alyssa Montgomery."* Or *"Yeah, we're back together."* Or *"No, things are great between us, don't believe everything you read or hear."* I wanted to punch half of these nosey motherfuckers in the face.

Chapter 6

ALYSSA

The last few days before graduation blew by like a hurricane. I could barely remember anything except Jake's body, firm against mine, and his lips roaming every inch of my body. It was all I wanted and it's all I thought about. I hardly cared that I'd graduated high school. The party my family threw me was all just a blur of festivity and happiness from everyone around, with lots of tears on my mom's part.

Jake made his best effort to hang out, speaking with everyone, finally coercing Kyle into going to Guitar Center with him. I didn't blame Jake for wanting to leave; people kept asking him way too many questions *and* asking to take their picture with him, even those we've known our whole lives – *so fucking annoying*. It was irritating to watch. It was also strange having him in my house, with my mom and dad.

No one spoke about me going to New York *with* Jake; that subject was off limits. My father's last words about it were – *"I don't want you talking about going to New York with Jake. I know NYU is one of your schools, but people are already talking about how we're letting you run off with some rock star."* Some rock star? *Really,*

Dad? But I didn't blame my dad for wanting to stay away from subjects involving Jake. I actually preferred it.

All I wanted was to be on the plane to New York and to experience a new life for a while before the reality of college slapped me in the face. The looming loneliness of Jake being away on the road again taunted me. I tugged at my bed covers, tightening them and smoothing them out. It would be a long time before I'd sleep there again. I glanced around at every surface and met the gaze of my own eyes in the mirror. I inhaled deeply, feeling as if I could cry. *Wow.* I sucked in another breath and exhaled out heavily, shaking my head.

"You wanted this, Alyssa," I said out loud, staring at my reflection. "You got what you wanted, completely." I nodded, checking myself out one last time. I wanted Jake to be proud to have me at his side. I had no idea what to expect, really. If being home and having all these people tripping over themselves to get to him was intense, I wondered what it would be like outside of our hometown.

I was so engrossed in obsessing over my outfit and the way I looked that the knock at my door startled me. "Yeah," I said, grabbing my chest. The door cracked open, and it was Nadine. My heart ached. I was going to miss her so much.

"Look at you, hotass!" She rushed in, swinging the door shut behind her. "With your little tie-dyed cut offs and booties. Legs much?" she teased, coming in for a hug.

"Oh my God, Nadine. I'm going to miss you so much! I'm gonna cry just thinking about it." My tears welled up as I squeezed her tightly. "I don't know what I'm going to do without you. You have to come to visit as soon as possible."

"I'm so there, are you kidding? I just have to save some more money. I have enough for air fare, but I need some for shopping, duh!"

I stood back from her, wiping away the trickle of tears from under my eyes before they had a chance to ruin my mascara. "You have to come right away. I won't know a soul there, and who knows, I'll probably be battling Jake's ex."

"What?" Nadine squealed. "What the hell is going on? Jake's ex? Who? That girl Sophia? He always let on he wasn't serious with her. You know that! Bobby said he never even let her stay at his apartment. Calm down."

A torrent of emotions ran through me. I was happy to hear her words, but she had no idea what he'd told me.

"Nadine. He'd been seeing her, period. For a long time, he's been in a relationship with her...regardless of what you or he wants to call it. It's no different than what I was in with Nathan. He told me he'd still been seeing her, and she has no idea that I'm coming with him to New York. I'm almost certain he's still been fucking her up to this point." *Ugh* – hearing myself say it out loud made me want to vomit.

Nadine just stared at me with her mouth hanging open.

I agreed with her silent sentiment. "Yeah, right?" I said, and turned, grabbing my luggage from off the bed. "I can't be mad. I mean, what? I'd be a fraud myself. It makes me sick to think about."

Nadine followed me silently down the stairs as I struggled with my bags, dragging them down the stairs – *thump, thump, thump*. I was waiting for my dad to shout out at me. I wasn't used to Nadine not having some witty comeback. I looked at my phone, and it lit up – 11:30 AM. Jake would be arriving any moment to go to the airport. I could hear Kyle in the kitchen, talking to my parents. An overwhelming feeling of sadness flooded through me. I was going to miss them all so much. I'd never been away from home for more than a week at a time, and now I was going to be away for nearly three months, maybe longer.

In our foyer, Nadine and I sat on the tiled floor at the bottom of the stairs, sprawled out with our legs in front of us, facing each other. The bottoms of our feet pressed together as we waited for Jake. We'd always sat like that when something important had to be discussed. I leaned against my luggage as Nadine leaned against the wall. Her hair had grown out long, past her boobs. She had it tapered around her face now. Her features had thinned out; gone were her full cheeks. She'd gotten prettier, only because she'd lost the need for all the makeup. She still had a million differ-ent boyfriends. She majored in marketing and worked a paid internship at some clothing company in Huntington Beach. I was proud of her accomplishments, and looked forward to my own.

"Aly I'm excited and terrified for you. You're brave, braver that I'd be," she whispered. "I coulda gone anywhere for school, and I chickened out and stayed here."

I leaned my head back against my bag and glanced in the direction of the voices, listening, making sure they weren't paying attention to us. I hung my head. "I'm so in love with him, Nadine. I never ever in my wildest dreams thought that we'd work out, but here we are. Here I am about to move to New York, maybe permanently. I'm afraid to disappoint him."

"Wait, what?" she leaned in closer to me. "What do you mean *maybe* permanently? I thought it was a done deal. NYU, baby."

I gulped. "I pushed off making a choice until spring. I mean, I have to choose soon. But I won't begin until the spring; I have the whole summer and fall off." Finally admitting that to someone other than my family felt good – the bag of bricks lifted from my chest. "I haven't had the heart to mention it to Jake. I'm totally committed to him, just not sure about college. I guess I'm chicken too." I tapped at her feet with mine, pressing into hers, rocking her gently.

Nadine wore a serious expression. "He has no clue?" Skepticism laid across her forehead.

"I don't know." I shrugged. "I get the vibe he knows I'm nervous about this move, but I don't think he thinks anything else of it." Kyle's laugh carried through the house and I could hear my mom and Allison giggling right after. I was happy they were preoccupied. I continued quietly, "You know how you dream and dream about what you want? Or you get excited about something that's coming up but don't believe it when it's time? That's me right now. I'm in shock. Ever since Jake arrived. I'm in a cloud."

———

I stared at our boarding passes. I'd never sat in first class before – 5A was my seat. Jake's was 5B. I was dreaming. I had to be. As we strolled through the airport, I was very aware of the subtle stares and nudges people gave to each other when they recognized Jake. He acted as if he didn't even notice. Maybe he was used to it by now because of all the rag write-ups. I'd stayed clear of that sort of celebrity tabloid news during Jake's rise, only hearing of his appearances on one of those Teen Nick TV shows, David Letterman, and Ellen. I never watched them, though. It was too painful. I kept all of that far away, concentrating on my real life. I couldn't stand seeing pictures of him with other girls. He'd kept seeing that pop princess, Eva, for a long, long time and I couldn't take it. Jake and his band were always being written up *everywhere* – "They're Just Like Us!" – *yeah, whatever.* Perez Hilton's blog loved Bobby, who had officially come out last year and was a fave of Perez's since they'd met at the MTV Video Music Awards. "Rita's Revolt" had won for Best Alternative Video.

We made our way to the American Airlines Admirals Club, hand in hand. I'd never been in there either and always wondered what it would be like. Jake kept kissing the inside of my wrist, his silky lips teasing at my skin. Each time he did, it sent a warm, fuzzy vibe through me.

"I think you need to stop that," I whispered into his ear before I sat down. "I'm gonna have to take you into the bathroom when we get on the plane."

He smiled broadly at me and placed my carry-on bag he'd carried for me onto a chair. He looked around and bent down, nuzzling my ear. "Don't say things you don't mean, Alycat. I'm not a member of the mile-high club yet, but I'd def join it with you," he provoked, his blue eyes sparkling. "I'll be right back."

I watched him as he walked towards the bar, wearing his staple black slim-fit denim jeans – his ass filled them out perfectly. There weren't very many people around. I was a ball of nerves. I could see Jake ordering me a glass of champagne. The bearded bartender glanced over at me when Jake pointed in my direction. Would he ID me? *Shit. Add that to my nerve rating.*

I looked away, trying to be inconspicuous, casually glancing around like I didn't have a care – but every fiber in my body was having a raging party. There weren't any other types like us in the lounge, only business people with their heads down, staring at their computer screens or having serious conversations on their cellphones.

Jake strolled up nonchalantly, smiling at me like he'd gotten away with something, handing me the slender flute filled with golden bubbling liquid. I stared at him, wide-eyed, with a tight grin, and glanced at the bartender, who paid us no attention. *Phew.*

Jake chuckled and sat down next to me, throwing his arm around my shoulders. "What's that look?"

"I don't know," I laughed quietly. "I thought maybe he'd ID me."

"Nahhh. Not today, Alycat." He leaned in, kissing me on the cheek. "Cheers, baby; here's to our new adventure."

I was bursting inside. "Cheers." Our glasses clinked together, and we sipped in unison. I sighed happily, leaning back into the crook of Jake's arm, and he squeezed me.

"I love you," I whispered into Jake's neck.

"I love you more." He smiled down on me, kissing the tip of my nose. I couldn't get enough of his lips touching me – anywhere.

I sipped on my champagne while Jake's attention was on his phone. I watched as people entered and exited the lounge. I spotted an attendant, tucked neatly into her blue American Airlines blazer. She looked like she was walking toward us. I glanced at Jake; he was still engrossed in his phone, tapping away at an email. She smiled at me as she approached, and I nudged Jake's knee with mine.

"Hello, Mr. Masters?" she questioned, making sure, smiling as she greeted us. She was older, like my mom's age, with shoulder length hair and perfect makeup. The kind of makeup you'd see on a beauty queen.

"Yep, that'd be me," Jake confirmed and moved to get up. He knocked back the rest of his champagne, and I did the same. Jake held out his hand to help me rise. "This is Alyssa."

"Hello, Alyssa, nice to meet you. I'm Margaret."

I smiled at her. "Nice to meet you, Margaret."

"Thanks for helping us out." Jake smiled at Margaret and rubbed my back, taking my hand into his.

She nodded happily at us. "I made sure your bags made it onto the plane, and boarding is nearly complete." I was a little confused as to what was going on, and looked at Jake. He just winked at me.

"Alright, let's do this." He rubbed his hands happily and grabbed my carry-on bag from the chair next to him. I hooked my arm through my purse handle, and we followed Margaret out into the very busy terminal. We arrived at a nearly empty gate. The line was almost gone. Everyone was already on the plane. We followed Margaret to the front of the line, and I could hear whispers of wonder – *"Do you know who they are?"* and *"Who is that?"* – I guess not everyone knew who Jake was. After all, maybe people just stared because of our special escort.

I pressed my fingers to my mouth, smiling. "What?" Jake said softly, nudging my shoulder."

"Nothing, shhh." I didn't look at him. I felt like the entire world was staring at us.

"Better get used to this, Alycat," he warned quietly, tugging at my fingers.

Chapter 7

ALYSSA

I never wanted to fly coach ever again. The champagne flowed, the food was hot, the utensils weren't flimsy plastic and the best part was that Jake and I were practically alone. There were only two other people in First, and they were on the other side of the plane. It made for easier fondling without feeling like people could see us – our faces were stuck together practically the entire time.

The flight went by in a blink of an eye. I could barely believe we'd arrived in New York. Even walking through the terminal to the exit and seeing the *Welcome to New York* sign didn't seem real.

The whole experience was unlike my last trip, where I was packed in coach and schlepping my bags all by myself. Nope; everywhere we went, someone was tending to us, taking my bag and leading us to where we needed to go. Jake tempered his annoyance with me as he stood there next to our driver and a luggage cart, practically tapping his foot. I ended up taking two large pieces of luggage that needed to be checked. He'd asked me to ship my things, but I just couldn't get my shit together, and still didn't know what I wanted to bring until I just threw whatever into them.

I watched the baggage belt go round and round eagerly, looking for my bags. I glanced back at Jake, and he threw me a tight smile. I gave him a – *What?* kind of look, and he stepped over to me.

"I fucking told you," he growled playfully in my ear. Jake wrapped his arms around me, pressing his body against my backside. "We need to be home, in bed."

His words made me ache. All that fondling on the plan left me damp between the legs. "Mmm. I can't wait!" I spun around and kissed him hard, sighing happily.

Jake pointed. "Watch for your bags."

I finally spotted them and pointed them out to James. Yes, *James* (I had to laugh at how ironic it was), our driver, wrestled my two forty-five pounds bags onto the luggage cart, and we were finally on our way.

"What the fuck do you have in those things?" Jake shook his head in puzzled amazement. "I mean, really, Aly?" He laughed in spite of himself.

"What? I needed my shoes. I didn't know what to bring, so I brought all of them."

"Oh geez. That's the type of shit you shoulda shipped here."

I pursed my lips. He was right. "I'm sorry." Jake just shook his head and smiled at me.

As soon as we walked outside, the humidity poured itself all over me. *Holy shit is it hot!* – I thought. I pulled my hair up into a bun, watching James and Jake lift my luggage into the back of the black SUV. I moved to open the backseat door and slid inside. The cool air swirled around me. I fanned at my face as if it would help. Jake crawled in next to me, and I reached up, gently wiping the perspiration from his forehead. He took my wrist, kissing it, and his warm tongue swirled against my skin. I felt like a kid going to Disneyland for the first time. I had no idea what to expect. I'd seen a million movies with New York as the backdrop, but I knew nothing would compare to actually living in it.

The traffic was insane, but it wasn't anything I wasn't used to with our 405 Freeway gridlock. I was in awe of all the buildings towering over us. There were people filling the streets, everywhere and from all walks of life. The higher the street numbers went, the more it was clear we were headed to a nicer part of town.

It took us over an hour to get to West 71st and Central Park West. We'd chosen a two-bedroom apartment across from Central Park, near the famous John Lennon Memorial – Strawberry Fields. He'd only sent me options in that area of town to choose from. Jake was a fan of John Lennon's drawings, and had sent me pictures of Lennon Lithograph artwork he'd wanted for our apartment – limited edition prints of John Lennon's black and white family sketchings. They'd fit well with Jake's black and white photographs.

We pulled up in front of a green canopied-thirteen story building, not the tallest on the block. We were on the 8th floor. My heart was racing with excitement. Jake said he wanted to surprise me. He'd become of fan of decorating, always texting me pictures of home furnishings – go figure. I supposed it was because he was a creative type and it was just another creative outlet. I had no idea what to expect when I walked in, but as soon as we walked through the door, the only thing I saw were the pictures of me hanging on the far wall.

I looked up at Jake, dumbfounded. "Where's the furniture?"

"I bought a bed." He nodded, smiling.

"A bed? That's it? You don't have anything from your other place that you wanna bring?" I said as I walked into the expansive empty space. I didn't expect the unit to be as big as it was, a blank slate with white walls and dark hardwood floors.

"All we need is a bed, Alycat." He gestured at me, holding his hands up and trying to sound convincing.

"Indeed." I hummed as I walked past what would be the dining area – there was a double beveled glass door that lead into a full kitchen. Jake followed me quietly. I looped around back into the foyer and headed toward a short hallway that had a half bathroom at the end. Perpendicular to the bathroom were the two sets of bedroom doors. I stuck my head into what was to be the guest bedroom, and that's where the boxes I did ship sat waiting for me. I turned and entered the large master suite. This was the only room that was furnished. It looked like a hotel room, with plush white bedding and fluffy pillows. The furniture was an eclectic mix of mid-century modern with a bohemian flare. Jake had been trolling through antique and thrift shops for furniture.

I took in a breath when I saw the picture I took of him while we were in London, sitting atop a bedside table – my side of the bed. "Oh Jake!" I twirled around and hugged him. "That's why you asked for that picture… you…" I sung out as I poked at his chest, smiling up at him. He picked me up, cradling me in his arms and kissed me.

"Welcome to your new home," he said as he let go of me onto the bed. Our clothes came off in a fury. Feeling his hot body on top of me gave me the chills. I ran my hands through his hair, clutching it in my fists. He dipped into me, sending pleasure pumping through every inch of me.

I watched Jake sleep for I don't know how long, listening to his soft and easy breathing. He was so perfect in so many ways...and maybe even more flawed as I thought of what he'd yet to take care of – *Sophia*. I turned lying flat on my back, staring up at the ceiling and watching the light from the TV bounce around. I tried to believe that I was there and a resident, at least for the foreseeable future. I looked out the window; it was dark, and I realized I was hungry.

I slid out of bed and padded to the window. The park was across the street, and it was black with the night, but the perimeter of the park was alive with street lights. Pedestrians walked their dogs, carried shopping bags and just moved about their business – at 10:30 at night.

I walked into the hallway and flipped the light switch, peeking around the corner and looking for another light switch in the other room. It felt strange walking through the unfamiliar, empty dark space. I flipped on more light switches and dimmed them down, then stood there, glancing around at the nothingness of the rooms. Me and the Lennon sketches stared back at each other.

My stomach grumbled, and I hoped there was some sort of food in the kitchen. Maybe Jake had an *Emily* here, too, to prepare our meals and clean up after us. Nope, no such luck. *Good*, I thought. I wanted to be Emily. I'd planned on investing in some cookbooks and giving my skills a run. I'd already looked into taking cooking classes. I was happy the fridge was bare. I sighed and got a bit nervous when I thought to go to the market alone. Certainly, there had to be one around the corner, and the doorman could point me in the right direction.

———

Miguel, our broad-shouldered, goatee sportin' Argentinian doorman, chatted me up for a bit, welcoming me to the city. He walked me outside into the warm night air. It felt lovely; the humid stickiness was gone. Wearing only my black strappy knee-length sundress and flip-flops, I strolled toward what would be Columbus Avenue. *Turn right*, Miguel had said, and sure enough, there was the market; D'Agostino's.

I pushed through the door. The cool air wrapped itself around me, giving me the chills, I rubbed at my arms and looked around for a basket. This store reminded me of the local market in London, small and stuffed from floor to ceiling. The carts were tiny. I quickly wheeled around, tossing things into my cart; chips for snaking, strawberries, grapes, cheese, and crackers. I was craving a tuna melt (of all things) and threw those ingredients in the basket. *Breakfast* – I'd make French toast in the morning. I searched for what I needed. I went to reach for a bottle of wine near the checkout stand as I waited, only to realize that I couldn't buy it. I wasn't old enough here. I missed London and their reasonable drinking age. The US really needed to get with it. I mean, we allow citizens to risk their lives by being in the military and going to war at eighteen, but we weren't allowed to drink – legally. *What a crock of shit*, I thought, shaking my head the ridiculousness of it.

I struggled with the two stuffed bags I held in each hand. I'd forgotten I had to walk home. No wonder all the people carried shopping bags around. I was too embarrassed to put anything back. People here probably had to stop at the market everyday. Miguel was standing outside, talking with neighboring building's doorman, and rushed up to me, helping me with my bags.

"Miss Aly," he chuckled. "Next time you need more than a few things, I have a cart for you."

I laughed, embarrassed. "Thanks, Miguel. Where I come from, we have cars and large carts. I wasn't thinking when I got to the checkout, and didn't want to put anything back."

He helped me to my door, and I thanked him. Jake was still sleeping when I peeked in on him. Now my stomach was growling louder than ever – *tuna melt!* it roared. Thankfully, the kitchen had all the pots, pans and dishes that anyone would ever need. I thought about how we would have been fine in a studio apartment, simple and cozy. It was nice, though, not to worry about waking Jake as I banged around the kitchen.

As I waited for my sandwich to brown in the pan, gooey, yummy cheese melting out of it, I began to open the drawers. Most of them were empty. Then I came to one filled with some papers. My curiosity got the best of me – there was an envelope with Jake's name written on it in neat girlish script. It was torn open – and I assumed he'd already read it. I picked it up and inched it open, getting a look at what was a letter. My heart raced. I left it there, flipped my sandwich, and went back to stare at it.

I turned off the stove; my sandwich was ready. I went to check on Jake one more time – thinking of only the letter. I gulped as I walked back, making a beeline for it. I took it out and set it down next to the plate, where my sandwich sat. There was nowhere for me to sit, so I hopped up on the counter and took a bite, staring at the letter. I took a few more bites and wiped my hands on my dress. I took the letter out and went straight for the last page – *Love Always, Sophia.*

Chapter 8

JAKE

I found Aly sitting on the counter in the kitchen, eating. She'd looked adorable sitting there, with her legs dangling, looking windblown and reading something. As I approached her, she looked up, and her hand dropped suddenly to her side. She looked pained and shocked to see me. I noticed immediately the letter and looked at the opened drawer I'd put it in. I'd forgotten to throw it away – *fuckin' great*.

She waved the letter at me. "You *were* living with her." Aly threw the letter at me and picked up her sandwich, chomping into it angrily.

"No I wasn't," I said, and picked up the scattered pages from the floor, crumpling them into a ball.

"It says for you to come pick up your things," she said through a mouthful.

"That's because, yes, I have some stuff over there."

She swallowed and shook her head, hopping off the counter. "I don't believe you." She stuffed the last bit of her sandwich in her mouth and walked past me without another word. I just stood there, staring at the ball of paper in my hand, kicking myself for not throwing it out right after I read it.

Aly sat in the chair in the corner of the bedroom with her phone in her hand, staring blankly at it. "Aly, I swear I wasn't living with her. I mean, of course we stayed together. We lived in the same building." She finally looked up at me upon hearing those words.

"I don't believe you." Her chin dropped back down to her chest. "I feel terrible for her. How could you let this go on? She says she knows this has to do with me...how?" She paused, totally confused. "I mean, is that my future? Jake?"

"No! No it's not!" My heart raced as I tried to convince her. "Look, I told you everything that I thought you needed to know. I know I should have taken care of her months ago. I'm sorry. But it's not like we haven't talked about this. You knew she was still around, just like I knew you were still hanging out with what's-his-fuck."

She glared at me. "His name is Nathan...and I wasn't still fucking him."

Ouch – I'd never admitted that, but I wasn't gonna deny it.

"Jake, I just want this to go away. I'm here. I've uprooted myself for you...for us, for the promise of us. You're being a complete sorry-ass..."

I stood there, feeling like a total skid mark. "You're right. Aly, I'm really sorry. I told you how I felt about this in London. It's just a tough one, you know, because I don't want to hurt her. I didn't want to hurt her. I don't want to hurt you either." I sulked over to the bed, deciding to lay it all out there. "When I moved into the same building as her, we became quick friends. I didn't know anyone here except the guys. We were friends for over a year before we hooked up. She's a good-time, light-hearted, a bit of a party girl, but nothing over the top. She's in the band scene, a promoter for clubs. She was a great wing-man during those dark days of getting over you."

Aly stared at me with empathy in her eyes – probably for Sophia. "How does she know this whole thing has to do with me?"

I sighed heavily. Aly didn't know about the song I'd recorded after her visit – it was ramping up for release as a single to our next record. "I recorded a new song, and she heard it and called me out on it. She knew, she just knew." I shrugged, shaking my head, thinking about how intuitive it was. Girls always *knew* when shit was fucked up.

I spent the rest of the night holding Aly and reassuring her that there was no intent to outright lie to her. She impressed me with her resilient attitude. I'm not sure I would have been as forgiving or accepting under the circumstances. I felt like I didn't deserve her; maybe I didn't.

Our conversation drifted to the apartment. I curiously watched as Aly scoured the Internet for local home stores and she plotted our pursuit of furnishing. For a moment, I thought of bringing up what her parents revealed to me during our apology session – her choice of colleges and the possibility of her *not* staying in New York. I didn't think she would be so into stuffing the apartment full of things she loved if she wasn't planning on staying, so I didn't bring it up.

———

I'd tossed and turned all night, watching Aly sleep, tempted to brush the hair from her face, to kiss her supple pink lips. I had to stop myself on a number of occasions. I'd told Aly I'd take care of Sophia first thing, and I did by waking up at seven AM and showing up at her usual pilates appointment – at least, I'd hoped it was still *usual*. My heart beat erratically in anticipation of seeing her. I paced the lobby, waiting. Watching the minutes change on my phone.

Sophia came through the door, and my heart stopped. She had her blonde hair pulled back into a tight ponytail, and wore black body-hugging workout gear. She looked great. I felt like such an asshole. She saw me right away, and I thought immediately that I should have let her know – alarm covered her face. She glanced around at the other women making their way into the lobby, undoubtedly hoping no one would notice me. I walked to meet her with damp palms.

"Hey." I stuffed my nearly dripping hands into my pockets, and she just looked at me with gloomy eyes.

She looked over her shoulder and back at me, tucking her arms tight to her chest. "What are you doing here?" she said bitterly.

"I just want to say I'm sorry."

"Okay," she said, and blinked, nodding her head twice. She turned to walk away from me and I grabbed her elbow.

"Hey, don't do this," I begged.

She swiftly turned, yanking away from me. "Don't fucking touch me!" Her voice echoed loudly around the grey marbled lobby, taking me aback. I held my arms up in surrender. I looked around, and for a millisecond everyone stopped breathing, looking at us. "Have a nice life, Jake Masters. Come and get your shit out of my house," she barked without turning around.

"I'm sorry, Sophia," I shouted out at her, not caring who was staring at me. I looked at the ladies who remained in the lobby. "I'm sorry," I said to them, and walked out the door.

At least I tried, I told myself, but I deserved her hatred. *I have to do better,* I repeated in my head over and over again during my cab ride home. As we approached my pad at 71st Street, I decided to walk from there.

"You can pull over here," I instructed the cabbie and paid my fare. It was just after 9 AM, and my phone chimed out a text message from Aly, who was wondering where I was.

I replied with – *I'M AROUND THE CORNER, BE UP IN A SEC.* I was heavy-hearted and hoped that Sophia would forgive me someday. I wiped my damp forehead. It had warmed up fast and the air grew thick with humidity. As I approached the corner, I spotted a couple paparazzi – *Great, what the fuck do they want?* Then I realized one of them was Marty – my usual stalker. I stuffed my hands into my pant pockets and pretended that my sunglasses were an invisible cloak – it didn't work.

"Hey Jake," Marty greeted, overly excited, pacing me. Marty Jones was a tall, studious-looking guy who wore blue-rimmed glasses and neatly pressed button-ups. He wasn't the usual t-shirt sportin', bark-in-your-face pap. "Who's the girl?" he asked as he shuffled next to me up the street. "Is it your high school sweetheart? I think I recognize her." – "Is this your new address?" – "What happened with Sophia?"

I abruptly stopped, grabbed his shoulder, and noticed a younger version of Marty following behind us, snapping pictures. "Who the fuck is that?" I pointed to the exclamation point of a boy, his hair sticking straight up.

"That's my little brother, Michael." Marty pushed his glasses up higher on his nose and gulped. His hand shook.

I sighed, looking between the both of them, not sure what to think, and began walking again. "I'd like to make sure I have my information correct, but I'm pretty sure that's Alyssa. Your muse."

Hearing the word *muse* made me stop. "Marty, you need to get a real job." I encouraged.

"This is my real job. I'm a music journalist." He stood tall. He was proud of the label he gave himself.

"What publication do you work for?" I'd never asked him that; actually, I'd never spent anytime conversing with the guy, always smiling, but waving him off. No wonder he was shaking like a leaf in a windstorm.

Marty cleared his throat. "I work for myself. I have a music blog."

"How old are you?"

"Nineteen."

Even though we were nearly the same age, I felt so much older. "You in college?"

"No."

I wanted to lecture him that if he wanted to be a serious journalist, he needed to go to college, like I was some fucking expert or something, but I refrained. I decided to throw the guy a bone. Hell, I had a dream once. I knew what it was like. "Yes. It's Alyssa. Yes, this is where we live, but if you print that anywhere, I'll have to kick your ass. I don't need people showing up here."

"I promise." He swallowed, looking at his little brother. "You better not say anything either. This is important stuff." He pointed at Michael, who watched, in awe of his big brother. Marty's face was flush. I felt for the guy.

"I tell you what," I said, smiling at Marty. "Alyssa and I are going for a walk soon. Hang out, and I'll let you take a shot of us without breaking your camera." His eyes lit up like he'd just hit the lottery. "Ask something intelligent, and maybe I'll give you an answer."

Chapter 9

JAKE

"Where'd you go?" Aly inquired as she pulled eggs and bread out of the fridge.

My stomach churned with unease. "I took care of Sophia."

Aly stopped moving and stared at me as the fridge door swung itself shut. "Really," she said dryly, her eyes locking in on mine. "And?"

"It's done." I shrugged. Her chest heaved with a heavy sigh, but no words followed. She placed the food on the counter and went back to the fridge, removing more items. I wasn't used to her being tight-lipped. "Not much else to say. Just relieved it's over."

"Me too." She smiled softly, a hint of sadness in her eyes. I assumed she felt for Sophia; I did. I waited for Aly to unload the customary cache of questions, but she never did. So unlike her. It made me wanna ask *her* questions, but I let it ride, and instead she changed the subject to our search for furnishings.

Aly cooked a delicious breakfast of thick, crunchy French toast sprinkled with powdered sugar and bacon – reminding me of home. The whole notion brought me peace and an overwhelming feeling of contentment, something I'd not

71

recalled having ever since my father died. My hope for my future with Aly was at an all-time-high.

Without haste, we left and made our way through the lobby. The excitement of spending the day doing normal couple things had us giddy, and seeing Marty standing outside waiting for us made me stoked to officially unveil Alyssa to the world. Just like Marty said, she was my muse, and I wanted everyone to know. I picked up her hand and kissed the ring that I'd bought for her. I hoped that one day, maybe soon, that it would be moved to the other hand.

Miguel held the door open for us, and we walked out into the damp warm air. Marty immediately bounced over to us, snapping pictures. "Hey Jake. Who's this beauty?"

I stopped and smiled down at Aly. "This is Alyssa."

Flash – the sound of the camera's shutter moved at a rapid pace. "Ahh, the infamous Alyssa. How does it feel to finally have your muse at your side?"

Aly looked at me, surprised, not sure if she should smile or frown. I looked back to Marty. "It's awesome to finally have her with me. It's been a long time coming."

"When will you be releasing new music? There's been a lot of chatter that you'll be releasing a slew of singles instead of an album. Is this true?"

"Partially true," I nodded. "New tunes are comin' soon." I took Aly's hand in mine and decided that I'd do Marty Jones the biggest solid of his life. "Marty, give your info to Miguel inside." I pointed. "I'll give you an exclusive."

Marty's mouth hung open, and he slowly dropped the camera to his side. He went white, and I worried he'd pass out. I looked at his little brother, and he too was slack-jawed.

Marty gulped, regaining his composure. "When?"

"I'll be in touch."

I tugged at Aly's arm. She was stunned. "That poor kid. I think he wet himself." She giggled, covering her mouth as we walked away. "Wow, I think you just made his entire life. Did you see his face?"

It made me feel good to do something like this for someone like Marty. My label and my agent were going to have a fucking aneurysm, but I had a feeling about that guy, like he wasn't the usual scum pap. He was always respectful of my space when Sophia and I would show up at events. I wanted to know *his* story.

I kept glancing at Aly as we walked up 72nd to the Amsterdam Avenue subway station. She looked ethereal, wearing a flowing teal and white spaghetti-strap sundress – natural, beautiful and completely unaffected by the stares or what had gone down with Marty. She was fully enthralled by her surroundings, and I got kick out of watching the wonderment in her eyes. I loved experiencing life with her.

"Get ready."

"For what?"

"For the world to really know who you are." I wrapped my hand around the back of her neck, bringing her face to mine. "You are what made me. I'm nothing without you."

As we strolled closer to the subway entrance, steam rose through the sidewalk subway grates, and Aly pointed. "You know that famous picture of Marilyn Monroe? Isn't that, like, where she stood, when her dress flew in the air?"

"Yep, pretty much," I replied. She nodded, and her lips puckered, tempting me to kiss them, so I did.

She giggled as I tripped over my own feet. "Maybe you shouldn't sneak up on me like that while we're walking down a city street." She pulled me back to her by the hand.

"Noted," I chuckled, a little embarrassed by my clumsiness. "I'm just head over heals for you," I whispered into her ear. She squeezed my arm, sighing happily.

"Pinch me," she beamed.

I guided her around the corner, down into the doldrums of New York City's veins, with the tight masses of humanity. People jockeyed for position to purchase their Metro Cards at the automated stand, I had my prepaid card at the ready. I swiped it at the turnstile, pushed Aly through, swiped it again for myself. I grew a bit anxious knowing that before we embarked on our treasure hunt, I'd be taking her to my original apartment. I wanted to prove to her that I never lied to her.

———

"So this is The Village? Greenwich?" Her eyes glimmered, taking in the neighborhood as we ascended the stairs from the subway station.

"Yep. We're almost to our first stop." We cruised a couple of blocks, and the closer we got to my old place, I grew tense. It'd been over a year since I'd seen my apartment. My renter was out of the country. I pulled at her hand, stopping right before we reached our destination. "I wanted to do one last thing to prove to you that I wasn't lying about living with Sophia. I want to show you my old place."

Aly's shoulders slumped. "Jake you don't have to do this. It's over. You said you took care of it." She glanced around, nervous. "I don't want to run into *her*."

"I know. We won't. She's across town…I need to prove this to you." I sighed, holding her hand and swaying her arm back and forth. "I guess I need to do this more for me than for you. I have to communicate better."

We walked up to a single door of a nondescript, eight-story brownstone building, and I pushed the small red button at the intercom. A moment later, a buzz came, unlocking the door. I sighed as I pulled it open, hoping and praying that Sophia remained the creature of habit that she was, and was still across town sitting and reading at the coffee joint she went to after her pilates class.

This will be a quick one, I thought.

"No doorman?" Aly gave me a tight smile, nudging me.

"Just no elevator," I chuckled. "Sebastian is the doorman here, but it's on the down-low." Just as I mentioned his name, he came to greet us from around the corner.

"Mr. Jake." He smiled broadly with open arms, taking me into a firm, back-slapping bear hug. "It's been far too long."

He backed away, and looked at Aly and back at me. I saw a bit of confusion register in his bloodshot blue eyes, wondering who she was. I wrapped my arm around Aly's waist. "This is Alyssa." I smiled, a bit uncomfortable, as the last time he saw me, I was with Sophia. "My girlfriend from California. She just moved here."

Sebastian didn't miss a beat. He knew my story. He'd been by my side during many of my late night fights to not relapse, counseling me about love, loss and addiction in the very lobby we stood in. He had his own family stories. I was lucky to have met him too. His eyes crinkled at the sides like an accordion, smiling. "Ahh, Miss Alyssa, it's a pleasure to meet you."

Chapter 10
ALYSSA

My first morning in New York City was everything I'd imagined it to be, with the exception of the Sophia issue. I refused to let her dominate my mind or my future. I'd trust in Jake, and that would be it. What did it matter if he lived with her, anyway? I was just jealous. I mean, what other choice did I have but to let it go? I'd either make our lives miserable browbeating him, or I could enjoy my summer and be concerned with making important decisions in the fall.

The one firm choice I did make was that this would be my home, with Jake, no matter where I chose to go to school. I reasoned with myself throughout our breakfast, and I grew more excited about our planned day. I found out Jake didn't have an Emily in New York, yet. He'd said, *"We'll choose an assistant together."* The whole idea of having someone picking up after me regularly nagged at me, and I worried about the cost of everything.

I thought about getting a job. I had a few thousand dollars saved, and the money I'd gotten as graduation gifts, but it wouldn't last long if I wasn't careful. I grew uneasy at the thought of milking Jake for money. That's the last thing I wanted. I wanted to be my own person. I definitely would start looking for something to do with myself.

I wondered about Jake's schedule. The band was on a short break, from what I understood. The new music was set to be released soon, and details of touring and such were being finalized.

Our conversation drifted to Jake's concern about Dump. He was apparently on the mend from whatever was wrong with him. I guess the doctors said he was anemic or something like that. Jake didn't know what to think, because he was hearing conflicting things from Bobby vs. Dump. Bobby seemed to think Dump was sicker than he was letting on. Hearing Bobby's name made me think of Marshall. Marshall and Bobby had an on-and-off relationship, but they seemed be going strong, regardless of their status. Marshall was hell bent on going to FIDM, the Fashion Design Institute of Los Angeles, so I knew better than anyone that it would be tough keeping something going when the other person was never around.

Jake changed our meandering conversation to focused action when he realized how late in the morning it was getting. He swatted my butt to go get ready and took over doing the dishes. "Alright Alycat, get going." His eyes sparkled, making my love and lust for him surge.

I suddenly didn't want to go anywhere. I wanted him in bed. I tilted my head and reached out for his arm, running my hands over his bare skin. "I think you need to come get ready *with* me."

He threw me a mischievous glance, grinning, and turned off the water. "Don't tempt me, Alycat." He looked at the clock on the oven. "It's already 10:30, and I have something to show you, but we don't have much time."

I pouted and turned on my heels, walking out of the kitchen. "Fine. I won't be naked for long." I threw out one last lure – he didn't bite. I heard the water turn back on, and I wondered what it was that he had to show me.

What I didn't expect was to be dragged to Jake's old apartment. Standing on the street corner, I focused on the hot dog vendor and tried to stave off tunnel vision. The last thing I wanted was to be anywhere near the life he had in New York before me, but there I was, meeting a grey-haired Russian man named Sebastian, Jake's old doorman. Who apparently knew our entire life story.

After our introduction, Jake and I began to climb five flights of stairs. I found it hard to believe that people lived in buildings with no elevators. I couldn't imagine moving furniture in and out of these narrow hallways and stairwells. The floors had that old black-and-white checkered vinyl covering. The fixtures were old and baroque, and each floor landing had a beautiful two-tiered chandelier that lit up the windowless hall. The walls were clean, and painted grey with white trim. We ran into a sixty-something woman as she came down the stairs, wearing a dated eighties sweat outfit. She greeted Jake, happy to see him, and asked where he'd been. He politely answered that'd he'd been on tour and pushed me up the stairs, saying his goodbyes in as many ways as he could not to offend her.

"That's Margo. She's been here for forty-five years." He stepped up the stairs, taking a mouthful of air. "She's too fucking nosey."

Winded, we finally reached the intended floor, where there were four doors. Jake took a set of keys from his pocket and unlocked the door at the farthest end of the hallway. He stood holding it open for me. I didn't know what to expect, but I immediately saw the black and white photos of myself when I came through the door. The place didn't look like anyone lived in it. It was clean and modern, with a single red L-shaped sofa sitting in the middle of the living room, a contrast to the rest of the building. The floors were sealed concrete, and the kitchen was much like the kitchen in London, with black granite countertops and stainless steel appliances. It was smaller than our apartment, but since this was a top floor, it had skylights. The walls were white, and the only things on them were the framed black and white pictures of me and a TV mounted over the fireplace.

I rubbed at my arms. "Jake we didn't have to come here," I said, turning to face him as he shut the door.

"I know, but I wanted you to see. Come…" He walked over to me and grabbed my hand, towing me to a door down a short hallway. He took the keys back out of his pocked and unlocked the door, pushing it open. There sat a bare mattress and frame, boxes, keyboards, and an entire drum kit. "I moved my shit in here when I sublet the place. The master bedroom is on the other side." He walked over, sliding the closet door open, and there hung only men's clothing.

I felt ashamed for reading Sophia's letter. "Jake I'm sorry. I should have never read that letter. It was private, and I feel like such a jerk." I wanted to cry and hang my head. I gulped back the tears as I let my hair fall down to cover my face. I was relieved that all this existed, but felt so wrong. I sat on the bed. "I won't look or open your things anymore."

I stared at my feet, unable to look at him. "Hey," I heard him say in a comforting tone. I still couldn't look at him. Then I heard a faint knock, and that made me look up at him. He had his head turned, facing out the bedroom door.

"Huh," he questioned. "Probably Sebastian. I still get mail n' shit here." He walked out the door and I stood, following him.

I sat on the red sofa, staring at the images of myself. Then I heard Jake's surprised voice. "Sophia."

A rush of words poured out of a woman's mouth. "I just ran into Margo. She said you were here, and I just want to say I'm sorry. I know…" Jake shot me a glance. Sophia stepped into the apartment, and stopped talking when our eyes met.

Awkward, I thought as my heart raced up into my throat. She was way prettier than the one grainy image I had of her. I closed my eyes and looked away.

"Oh my God," she gasped.

I heard Jake shout out her name. "Wait, Sophia!" he said again. I could hear their voices strangle together in the hall and down the stairwell. Then I heard a door slam, then silence. Finally I heard footsteps. Jake came back in through the door. His hair was messy from running his hand through it, and I stood to face him. He looked overcome with regret. I trembled inside from disbelief.

"Let's go." I approached Jake without touching him and whispered, "I'm sorry."

I walked out the door, and he followed me. Hearing the door slam shut, I went to step down the stairs, but Jake pulled me back up to him by my elbow. He took me into his arms, hugging me tightly. "No, I'm sorry."

I didn't know how to respond. We were both sorry for our own reasons, but we wouldn't have been there if it weren't for my nosey, prying eyes reading that letter and accusing him of lying to me. I was wretched inside, and held tightly to Jake's hand as we took each step down the stairs. I looked at the doors that lined the floor as we passed down the next flight of stairs. Sophia was behind one of them, probably burning Jake's things.

We said goodbye to Sebastian, and Jake promised to stay in touch. We both breathed a sigh of relief when we were a block away. I reached up, correcting Jake's hair, and kissed him on the jaw. I felt his hands grab my waist. His arms wrapped around me, sending a warm, comforting feeling down into my gut, battling the apprehension that stirred. My paranoid imagination was in full swing. I looked over his shoulder, fearful that Sophia would be behind us, watching our every move.

"I'm exhausted," I whispered into his collarbone.

Jake chuckled, uneasy. "Me too." He spun me around when the light turned green for us to cross. "I don't know about you, but I need a drink."

"I know, right?" I quipped.

"Let's catch a cab."

Jake went to hail a cab, and I watched him closely. He stepped out into the street, watching the cars and cabs fly by. He threw his arm into the air, but a cab passed him.

"Why didn't he stop?"

"Probably already going to pick someone up."

"Why aren't the other empty ones stopping?"

"Out of service."

Hmm, okay. I watched as the empty cabs went by and realized that the light at the top was the indicator. *Smart.* I laughed at my ignorance – *a million movies I've watched with cab scenes, and I never knew there was a system.*

Our short drive into SoHo had my butterflies fluttering, and I clutched Jake's thigh as I took in the sights. The streets got a little tighter, and the storefronts more picturesque, with narrow one-door stoops, reminding me of London. I looked above the storefronts, and noticed that they were quite likely residential units. I smiled.

"Don't you think it would be cool to live in this part of town?"

"Why? You don't like where we're at?"

"I wouldn't know yet." I shrugged. "I just dig how everything is right here. You have all your stores and then live above."

"Yeah, this is my second favorite part of town." He nodded. "But I like being near the park. I like seeing the green, open space. But this, this area is def on the radar. One of my favorite restaurants is here. That's where we're going. They have the best steak and fries *and* the best French onion soup I've ever had." He pointed, announcing to the cabbie, "you can stop here."

We stood in front of a red-canopied restaurant named Balthazar and Jake moved around the smokers to open the door for me. It was packed with well-dressed patrons. My eyes roamed the room, meeting many other eyes, as heads perked up to see who was coming in. *Typical.* Two tall model-type women greeted us, and one knew Jake immediately.

"Hey!" the one with long dark wavy hair and green eyes chirped. "It's been a along time!"

"Hey Ingrid." *Ingrid?* Okay, he knew her name. I sucked in some air, pushing down my immature feelings, and smiled at her beautiful face. I felt so small, even though I stood eye-to-eye with her. "This is Alyssa, my girlfriend. She just moved here from California."

Her eyes registered with surprise, but happily creased as she smiled. "Nice to meet you, Alyssa. I'm Ingrid and this is Macy."

"Nice to meet you both." Why were my hands sweating? Thank God she didn't try to shake my hand. *What. The. Fuck. Calm down, Aly.*

"We're just gonna grab a seat at the bar." Jake threw a gesture over his shoulder and winked at the girls, thanking them. I clenched my wet palms as Jake steered me by the small of my back.

I eased onto the barstool and placed my purse on the counter as Jake scooted closer to me. "What say you, Jake!" I startled, hearing Jake's name, looking to the bird-nosed man behind the bar.

"What's up, man? Good to see you!" They shook hands firmly. Bird-Man looked like he was shining from the inside out; he was delighted to see Jake. "Just rolled back into town. Been in Europe, then back home to Cali to get this little beauty over here with me." Jake's eyes roamed my face adoringly and looked back to Bird-Man. "This is Alyssa."

"Welcome to New York. I'm Chuck." He smiled and threw cocktail napkins out in front of us. "What can I get you two?"

"I'll have a glass of champagne." I looked to Jake, then to Chuck and smiled, trying to exude twenty-one-ness. *Own it, Aly*, I told myself.

"I'll have a vodka soda."

Chuck eyeballed me a moment longer, and then eyeballed Jake, and pressed his lips together as if he was deciding to serve us or not. Thank God he did. As soon as the bubbles hit my stomach, I relaxed. Clearly a placebo effect, but the idea of them calmed me, and I took another sip. Before I knew it, my glass was empty and I was really feeling the buzz. I asked Jake for another one.

Chapter 11

JAKE

I threw back that first vodka in nearly one gulp, and I watched Aly as she emptied her glass just as quickly. The threads of anxiety tightened as I battled to break them. What a cluster fuck that was with Sophia. No doubt she truly hated me now for bringing Aly over there. I pacified myself by reaching out to Aly and scooting her stool closer to mine. We didn't really say much to each other while we sat there, ordering another drink. Aly dug in her purse, taking out a few sheets of paper and unfolded them. She pointed to a picture of a white sofa with black and white patterned pillows.

"You like that?" I looked at the picture thoughtfully. "White?"

"No, silly, this is the place that I want to go to. They have new and used furniture."

"Ahh." Chuck placed another drink in front of me with a wary eye. "Thanks. This is the last one."

"You bet it is," he replied, throwing me a cautionary nod.

"What was that?" Aly whispered under her breath when Chuck turned away.

I began to explain Chuck was a friend of Amy's, my LA Narcotics Anonymous sponsor. Chuck's vice was heroin, just like Amy's. He was my crutch when I first moved to New York. He had never served me a drink, nor did I ever ask, until one day Bobby demanded it after a particularly bad day – *"Serve him a fucking drink. He popped pills, he didn't drink himself to death's door!"*

Then my phone rang out – speak of the devil, it was Bobby. I took the call outside. When I returned, Aly had paid the bill and stood to leave. She immediately noticed the worry etched on my face.

"What, what is it?" She clutched my forearm with concern in her eyes.

"It's Dump. He's in the hospital. He passed out."

"Oh my God," she gasped, hand covering her mouth. "Is he okay?"

"I don't know." I was worried. His sickness had been going on too long.

Aly and I rushed to the hospital and found Bobby hunched over in the packed, no-frills lobby.

"Bobby," I said, startling him. "What's up?"

He shook his head. "Not sure. Sienna hasn't come out yet." He turned to Aly. "Hey Aly, not a very nice welcome being here, is it?" He stood and they hugged.

We sat down in the waiting room and stared at each other in silence. Nearly every seat was taken. I held my breath, hearing the gurgling cough of the older man sitting next to me as he leaned over onto his walker. Aly wrung her hands, and Bobby searched my face, leaning his elbows down on his thighs. He hung his head.

"Dude, Dump's gotta be really sick." He shook his head, staring at the floor. "I just know it. He's lost too much weight."

"What?" I asked, surprised. "I just saw him two weeks ago. He seemed like he was getting better."

"Yeah, so did I. I guess he's had no appetite, though."

"Do you live with them?" Aly chimed in.

"Yeah, just moved in a month ago, temporarily. Until I find something." Bobby looked at me. "Sienna asked me to stay as long as I want. She's got shoots booked, and doesn't want Dump alone."

"Why didn't you guys tell me? Why isn't Sienna calling me? Or Dump? I mean, fuck. Why am I just hearing all this from you?" I got up, pacing, and Aly grabbed my hand. I snatched it away, sitting back down. I was pissed that no one thought I should know anything. When I glanced up, I spotted Sienna walking towards us. She was red-eyed, holding back tears. I hugged her.

"Hey…hey," I said, rubbing her back, trying to comfort her. "It's gonna be okay. What's going on?" I wanted to shake her for not calling me directly. My heart raced.

"No it's not," she wailed, shaking her head violently. Saliva bubbled at her lips as she sobbed, trying to catch her breath.

I glanced at Bobby, and he looked horrified. "Is he dead?" Bobby gasped, clutching his chest.

I wanted to throw up. "Is he okay?" I nearly shouted. I grabbed Sienna by the shoulders.

"He has cancer…lymphoma something…" She leaned into my chest, sobbing harder. I couldn't believe what I was hearing. I went numb. I looked at Aly. She had tears streaming down her face. Bobby stood there with his mouth hanging open, as shocked as I was.

Holy fuck.

The hospital admitted Dump, and two hours later, we were sitting in his hospital room, staring at each other. He was as pale as I'd ever seen him, making his tattoos look that much more vibrant and dark. He wore a black beanie that had *Live or Die* embroidered on it. How ironic, I thought.

I pointed at it. "Did you plan that?" I chuckled at my morbid humor, trying to make light of his serious situation.

He took the beanie off his head and stared at it. A smile peeked at the sides of his mouth. "You know it, motherfucker," he said, and tugged it back over his bald head, squeezing his eyes shut. He pinched the bridge of his nose. My heart thudded a million miles per hour, watching his emotions bubbled at the surface. His eyes were red, and his face twisted, holding back tears. "Those fucking cancer sticks," he choked, sucking in a breath. Sienna rubbed at his forearm.

Seeing Dump break down pulled at my heart. I'd never seen him scared or upset. "Man you're gonna beat this."

Dump shook his head. "I dunno, man."

"Yes you are!" Sienna piped. "People beat this shit all the time."

"What's going on, man? Did you know?" Bobby said in an accusatory voice.

"I knew I wasn't well." He stared off in thought. "The fuckin' docs over at that quack office kept misdiagnosing me...and then I just...I just didn't wanna know, you know. I was hoping I'd feel better. I stopped smoking, started eating better...it was too late."

"I'm so sorry," Aly said softly as she rubbed my shoulders. "You *are* gonna beat this."

"Yes, he is," Sienna agreed, smiling at Aly's positive comment.

The doctor came in wearing a grim expression, needing to speak to Dump and Sienna. Aly and I didn't stay too much longer. We were later informed that Dump was Stage-4 non-Hodgkin's lymphoma, and he'd begin immediate chemotherapy treatment. Dump was in a fight for his life, and I was in complete shock.

He was too young to die.

We spent the later part of the afternoon floating around the city, from SoHo to Midtown to the Upper East Side, in our disconnected mental state, looking for furniture. We didn't know what to do with ourselves. I knew I should have called Notting and my mother right away, but I didn't have it in me to explain what was going on. They'd be on the next plane out when I did. I'd wait until morning.

Dump's life was now a waiting game, and I didn't want to think about the possibility of the band without him. I kept thinking back to Sienna and her devastation, how she desperately clung to me for comfort. Her whole life was Dump, just like mine was Aly. All I knew was, I didn't want to let go of Aly. The warm feeling of her skin beneath my fingers consoled me as we weaved up Park Avenue. I wanted to dash the mayhem of the city streets and made a left at 76th Street toward 5th Avenue and Central Park.

The moist heat of the day was tempering down, and the warm breeze was soothing. A walk across the park toward our home would provide a welcomed distraction. "Hey." I squeezed Aly's lithe hand. "Everything's gonna be okay, Dump's a fighter."

Aly shook her head; trouble lined her forehead. "I hope so. Did you see Sienna? I'm so sick about this." She leaned her head against my shoulder as we waited to cross the street into the park. "I can't imagine my life without you. I mean really *without* you. Just knowing that I could never see you or hear your voice again…" She choked back tears, covering her mouth with the palm of her hand. She squeezed her eyes shut, and tears spilled onto her cheeks.

"Hey, stop it." I pulled her into my chest, hugging her tightly. "I'm not goin' anywhere." Aly's words stabbed at my heart, and I found myself swallowing back my own tears. I cupped her cheeks in my hands and kissed away her salty tears. "You wanna go through the park? Or take a cab home?"

"I'd love to go to the park." She turned and stepped off the curb, pulling me along. "Some first day. I can't believe it." I was surprised when a burst of laughter came out of her. "Actually I can. I'm not surprised…I don't know what I am."

The feeling was mutual, I thought, as we stepped up onto the sidewalk in front of the park. I spun her to face me. "I'm sorry, Aly. I'm sorry for dragging out…that shit with Sophia…" I stammered, looking down at the uneven cobblestones beneath my feet. "I need to be better about facing shit."

Her hazel eyes shimmered at me, blinking. "You have no idea how it felt to lock eyes with her. I really hope that was the end." She turned away from me. "I don't wanna talk about it anymore."

I went to speak again, but shut my mouth. I knew I'd probably dig myself more of a hole. It was the end, as far as I was concerned. I'd ruined a friendship, and I didn't deserve Sophia's forgiveness, let alone Aly's understanding. I didn't need the hovering drama in my life trying to make things right with Sophia. My main concern was now Dump *and* finding a drummer for the upcoming radio & TV station gigs. My

stomach churned with unease. I didn't want to do this without
Dump.

I held Aly's hand snugly as I steered her through the narrow and winding asphalt paths of Central Park. Its lush green-
ery was at a pinnacle, and the birds and squirrels were darting
and scurrying through the bushes and trees. Making our way
to the Upper West Side and our home, I savored the calm,
silent moment. Shit was gonna be miserable. My head spun
just thinking about the band's immediate future.

The late afternoon sunlight beamed through the trees,
and the peaceful faint rustling of the tree leaves made me pull
Aly off the trail to climb the nearby boulders. I wanted to
appreciate the calmness before I was thrown into my own survival mode. As I took a deep stride up the rocks, I turned to
help Aly up, but she was stepping her way around a less steep
area, holding her dress up over her knees.

Oops.

"Sorry about that!" I called out. She smiled, waving me off.
I observed her movement; the way she held her slender arms
out, balancing her way towards me, the way her hair swayed over
her face and bare shoulders, and her smile. I loved her smile. I
didn't deserve her or her smiles, I thought. I needed to prove
that I was worthy of them and her. I crouched down, sitting on
the hard, warm surface, and held out my hand to Aly. She took
my hand, standing next to me and looked up at the skyline.

"Wow. This is amazing." She dropped her bag on the
rock. "Such a juxtaposition, it's crazy."

"This is why I love being near the park." I tugged at her
arm. "Sit down."

Aly sat as close as she could that our thighs and hips
pressed together. I wrapped my arm around her shoulder

and we sat in silence. The warmth of her face pressed into my neck. I nuzzled her hair, taking in her clean, fresh scent. How could someone be so content and wretched at the same moment? But I was. I felt guilty about my happiness with Aly, while Sienna and Dump hung out with the Grim Reaper.

Aly cleared her throat. "I'm sorry about Dump."

I glanced at her, and she was looking up at me with misty eyes. "Me too. I hope he's gonna be okay. He's gotta be." I thought of Sienna and what it would do to her if she lost Dump. My sentiments went to Aly. I would die without her.

Chapter 12

JAKE

At 4:00 PM a month later, I found myself staring up at a five-story brick and mortar building way up town on East 96th Street. As I passed each black door with engraved silver plaques, it appeared to be all offices. Finally coming to number 402, it read *The Jones Show. Really?* I was trippin' that the wannabe journalist, Marty Jones, had a pretty legitimate looking set-up. I checked the doorknob. It was unlocked, so I tapped on the door as I cracked it open. There sat Michael, Marty's little brother and pseudo assistant, behind a simple black desk, working (probably playing) on a computer.

"Hey Michael," I greeted as I stuck my head in and slid my sunglasses on top of my head.

Michael's hazel-blue eyes lit up wide, and he slapped his forehead. "I didn't think you'd really come!" he said excitedly. "I didn't believe you! Marty always gets lip service and empty promises! Um, um, come in, come in." He waved eagerly. "Oh man, my dad's gonna shit when he hears you really showed up."

I couldn't help but smile at the kid as he took off into another room. I could see a green screen through another open door down the short hallway. Wow, those were at least eight grand, and the computer Michael was working on was a Mac desktop, the kind with the largest monitor you could own – not cheap. I wondered who Marty's father was, that he'd *shit* that I'd actually showed up for his son. Voices blended together, and soon enough, Marty, wearing another gingham checked button-up, was standing in front of me with a mile-wide smile.

He pushed his blue-rimmed glasses up on his nose. "Welcome." He tipped his head, pleased, and gratitude filled his eyes. He chuckled. "Man, thanks."

"No problem." I extended my hand to him, and he shook it and slapped my back. "You got a nice set up here."

"Thanks. I do graphic design work to pay the bills and interview bands for my blog."

"I see that." I nodded as I stared at all the pictures of him with famous bands, musicians and singers – Kings of Leon, Imagine Dragons, Gwen Stefani, Beyonce –*Fuckin'-A*, I thought, and pointed. "I had no idea, Marty."

He smiled proudly. "Most of those were before they got really famous, except for Beyonce. I kinda got her like I did you, following her around and being respectful." He smiled sheepishly. "Been doin' this since I was fourteen."

And here I thought I was doin' him the biggest favor of his life, Marty wasn't really a wannabe at all, he was doin' somethin' right…

"But I never had anyone like you, a Grammy winner…*after* they've hit the big time. I'm too little-time for their labels and managers now. They want Rolling Stone, MTV, n'shit. " He chuckled. "But it's all good."

We locked eyes and I searched his face. This guy was totally legit. I was about to do something that was gonna cause the biggest uproar with my label and Notting (not to mention my mother. I'd yet to tell anyone about Dump), and Marty was gonna be the messenger. "So where do you wanna start?"

Marty cleared his throat. "You gotta get outta here by a certain time?"

I shook my head. "Nope. I'm all yours."

A burst of breath escaped him, and he smiled, unbelieving. "I can't thank you enough for coming."

"Hey man. I got nothin' to lose if you're what I think you are, and by the looks of it, you are. Where do you sell your pictures? You know, those shots you've been takin' of me over the years? Of these guys?" I pointed to the wall, finally finding one of me performing at Madison Square Gardens.

"I don't sell my pictures." He sat up straight, looking serious. "I use them only on my website and for future publication. I plan publishing a book someday. A book of interviews and moments of music through my eyes."

I was impressed. "That's a lofty goal, Marty. I dig it." Now, more than ever, I wanted to help him, and I wanted to help myself. Sure, we as a band had media interviews, our displays for the world; how we wanted to be seen. There was *my* story, which Marty was ultimately interested in, but with Dump's illness and uncertain future, I felt the need to really document what was going on with us. *I think our fans would want that.*

That morning, before meeting with Marty, I'd met with Dump. He was four weeks into his cancer treatment, and the chemo and whatever else they had him on seemed to be working. He was up and around, weak, but pretty much back to his leathery persona. He'd taken up smoking marijuana to increase his appetite. I was optimistic about his recovery. I'd informed Dump about my plans, and he'd given me his blessing.

"Fuck those guys. We're free agents, and they're lucky we stayed with 'em. There's nothing in that new contract about media proxy," he'd said about our label. I'd originally wanted Marty to debut our next single, but seeing what a class act he was, I decided that not only could he debut our single, he would be the one to help me deliver the news about Dump to the world.

We'd moved into another office with black painted walls, more pictures of musicians I recognized, and a glass top desk. Another equally large Mac monitor sat upon it – graphic design must be paying him well. The building had clearly been converted into office space, and this unit used to be a two-bedroom. Marty rolled out his desk chair and ran his hand through his mussed black hair.

I sat down on a worn tan leather sofa watching Marty as he fidgeted nervously with his glasses. "Marty, take a deep breath." I chuckled. "I'm not gonna bite."

He closed his eyes, taking in a deep breath, and placed his glasses back on his face. "Out of everyone I've ever followed, you're the one that's made the biggest impact on me." He sighed. "My father is a pharmacist and was addicted to pills most of his life. When we nearly lost everything because of it, it was your band and you that got me through those days. Then you went downhill for the same reasons and came back, and it gave me hope that he would too."

"Did he?"

"Yeah. I actually used you as an example of perseverance during our family therapy sessions. My mother was gonna leave him…" He trailed off, revisiting the distant memory, and I wondered what he was staring at in his mind. I was glad Aly was never able to witness my fall from grace. I felt for

Marty's mother; it must have been awful. "And I played him your music. He was always a big fan of rock n' roll. And I told him your story, and let's just say he's doing okay now. He's a fan, too."

Wow. I was beyond humbled.

"That's heavy shit, Marty. I'm glad to know he's doing okay." I glanced around as the silence mounted. Marty was deep in thought. "Hey, we're lucky that we have people who have our backs. I'm fortunate this shit happened before the real fame. I'm happy I got a grip on it before I really fucked some shit up."

"Yeah. I read into all your lyrics and dissected them, sharing them with my dad. I don't know if what I interpreted was what you meant, but I think they saved my father's life, at least, I like to think they did." Marty wiped his forehead. "It's getting hot in here." He laughed ironically and got up, walking over to the window and firing up the air-conditioning unit.

Marty and I talked for over an hour. I was the one doing the interviewing. Whether he was telling me what I wanted to hear or not, our meeting solidified what I wanted to do. I wanted to invite him on the road with us, the next round. He showed me a bit of his footage, footage of famous bands in their beginning days, *and* footage of Beyonce sitting in the very spot that I filled.

"You never aired any of this?" I watched a silent, younger Beyonce on Marty's computer screen.

"Not at length. I wrote an article for my blog and just posted a thirty-second snippet."

I nodded, thinking, and then offered, "Marty, what would you say if I invited you to travel with us this next tour?"

Marty went speechless and pushed his glasses up his nose, blinking, dazed at my offer. "I would say yes." He gulped. I could see his wheels turning. "When?"

"Next week."

———

I opened my apartment door, and Marty stood there wearing a light-colored striped button-up. "Dude, it's fucking a hundred degrees and a million percent humidity. What are you wearing?"

Marty rolled in a single piece of luggage, carrying a backpack and what appeared to be two camera bags. He was barely perspiring. I would have been sweating my balls off, with pit stains to boot. He laughed. "It's nothin'. It's my thing." He shrugged, looking around, and abruptly stopped when he saw Aly sitting on the edge of our one piece of furniture that just arrived that morning – an L-shaped chocolate sofa with black leather piping.

"Hello," he said, waving awkwardly.

Aly stood, wearing little black denim cut-offs. She flipped her long hair over her shoulders. "Hi." Her slender tanned legs carried her over to us, and she extended her hand to Marty. "It's nice to see you again, Marty." She smiled favorably at him. "I'll leave you two to do your thang," she sang out, bouncing on her tiptoes, and leaned over, kissing my cheek. "Yoga calls. Be back in a couple."

I watched her taut ass dance out of the room, and a pang went through me. I was gonna miss her. I still couldn't believe she'd chosen to stay home. I shook my head at the thought and glanced at Marty, who was staring down the hallway where Aly vanished.

His mouth clamped shut and gulped. "I can see why you're in love with her. She's more beautiful in person than in pictures." He turned and gently put down his camera bags. "She's so…so….clean looking."

I laughed at his portrayal. "That's because she's California-grown, man." I slapped his shoulder. "Just like Van Halen said, I wish they could all be California girls."

Me and the band, including Dump and Marty, were set to leave that afternoon on a ten-city radio station tour, with a stop in California for an appearance on The Ellen DeGeneres Show, and finishing up back in New York with an appearance on Saturday Night Live. We were flying to each destination. I hadn't told Marty about Dump, and my stomach churned, knowing I was about to deliver the unsettling news.

I sighed and squeezed at the tension building in my neck. "You want something to drink? Beer? Wine? Water?"

He nodded. "I usually don't drink, but I think a beer sounds good." He grinned.

"Great." I went and grabbed a beer and a bottle of water.

"You said you wanted to record something now?" he asked when I returned, handing him the bottle of amber ale.

"Yeah, might as well start," I said as my nerves pricked at me. "I got something for you." I walked over to my satchel and pulled out some papers and an envelope. "I know I said I'd take care of your boarding and food. But I wanted to put you on the payroll." The look on Marty's face was priceless. He quickly twisted the cap off the beer bottle, taking a swig as he stared at the envelope in his other hand. "And I need you to sign this." I tossed one of those tax forms and an agreement in front of him. I kinda felt bad for putting him on the spot, but I had to protect myself.

"I usually don't sign anything that my attorney hasn't seen."

"Sorry man, you can't go with us if you don't fill that stuff out and sign that." I shrugged. "You're a smart guy, Marty, read it. You'll get it. All it says is the amount of money I'll be paying you on the first of every month for your services, and that you can't sell any footage, images of the band, or anything like that to a third party while under my employment, unless approved by me, to anyone else. But it does say that anything you capture you can use for your blog or any books you publish, things like that. It's a little convoluted, but you'll understand, I'm sure."

Marty's head swayed, and my heart thumped like I'd run around the block. I knew I should have done this earlier, like every other important thing, but fuck, I was busy. I tried to make myself feel better as I watched Marty's eyes dash over the words on the pages. He rubbed his head, took his glasses off his face, looked at me, and then back down at the last page.

"Do you have a pen?"

I felt the pressure in my chest release. "Yep." I dug in my bag and handed him a pen.

"Are you married to Alyssa?"

"No," I stated firmly. "Why? I would have told you that already."

"Well it just says in here that if anything happens to you, like if you die, Alyssa has to approve any material that I want to be released."

I shut my mouth and thought about the clause that I'd asked my attorney to add in. "I'm going to be making her my Power of Attorney. Alyssa is the only person I trust that would always do right by me."

For the next hour, we recorded the sad details of Dump's illness. I talked directly to the camera. I was beyond anxious, and my tongue was so dry and thick it felt like I'd smoked pot, but I sensed I had to do it this way. It felt right to all of us, Me, Bobby and Dump. As I looked into the camera, I wanted our fans to know I was speaking directly to each of them and didn't have our label or our handlers in mind. I didn't care that Notting or my mother would be blind-sided. I only cared that Dump and Sienna were okay with it, and that our fans would appreciate the intimate way we delivered the troubling news.

Dump finally arrived and joined me. We didn't hold back. It would be the first time anyone would see Dump's tears. It was hard for me to watch, and I strangled my own tears. That's when Marty took charge.

"If there was one thing you could ask of your fans right now, what would it be?"

Dump cocked his head, wiping his eyes. "If you're not feeling good, go to the doctor, man, and don't smoke those fuckin' cancer sticks. Since the beginning of our band, Jake told me not to smoke 'em. I waited too long on both accounts."

"It's not lung cancer, though?" Marty probed.

"Nah, blood cancer, Lymphoma, and it's now spread, but I go in for surgery after we get back. We'll just see how it goes," he said matter-of-factly, pursing his lips. I slapped his back.

"How are you feeling now? You look good," Marty complimented.

"I'm great. I'm about fifty percent. My first round of chemo just ended, and when I get back, I go into surgery and radiation. Shit like that."

"You're well enough to travel and play?"

Dump took a moment to answer. "It's all I know, man. I want to live a normal life for as long as I can."

"What else would you like to do?"

I watched Dump as he considered his next words with a trembling lip. I rubbed his shoulder, trying to comfort him, swallowing over and over again, trying not to cry myself. "You're gonna beat this, man."

Dump gave me a tight-lipped smile, nodding, and looked at Marty's pensive face. He leaned back and clasped his once-meaty hand around his mouth, looking up at the ceiling. Tears spilled out of his eyes. "I wanna grow old with my wife." He sniveled and bit his bottom lip. A long, silent moment later, he looked over at me. "I wanna grow old with this guy!" he said loudly, smiling and laughed through his blubbering. He wrestled my head into his inked-up arm, giving me a noogie. The painful sensation made me yelp, but I didn't fight Dump like I normally would have. I didn't want him to expend any more energy then he had to.

He finally released me. "I wanna keep playing and traveling and making music with my buds. This was a dream come true, and all of you fans…" He looked directly into the camera lens. "I wanna keep playing for you."

Chapter 13

ALYSSA

Finally, six weeks, and everything seemed to be in its place. I looked around, staring happily at our newly furnished apartment, but feeling equally melancholy about Dump and Sienna. They were all I could think about. I shoved them from my thoughts for the millionth time as I clutched the gift I'd just bought for Jake – well, really it was for our home, but I knew he'd love it – an *Annie Leibovitz: American Music* coffee table book. It had the stories and pictures of American musicians from the beginning of time. I walked over, setting it on the large glass coffee table, tracing the red letters on its cover.

I looked around, proud of what our apartment interior had become. I'd moved Jake away from his favored simplicity and modern lines by mixing in plants, comfy patterned pillows and earth-toned throws; nothing frilly, but homey and welcoming.

I sighed, wondering what next. I didn't have anything else to keep me busy other than my twice-a-week yoga class. I couldn't keep shopping. I'd gotten too accustomed to spending Jake's money, and every day it ate at me as I sat alone, thinking about what to do with myself. The only friends I'd made were with the forty-something-year-old ladies at the bookstore, Julia and Ashley. I had stacks of coffee table books lying around, and no friends to invite over to look at them. I sighed, bored, rubbing my stomach. The gnawing feeling of guilt for not contacting the coach at NYU crept in. I needed to keep up my conditioning and at least train with the team.

I laughed to myself – how pathetic was I? I knew what I needed to do; I just needed to get off my ass and do it. I attempted to befriend Sienna, but she was either tending to Dump or traveling around the world, modeling. The only thing I had to look forward to was Nadine's visit. She was finally coming, and would arrive in a week. I was giddy with anticipation and couldn't wait to show her the city. Jake had been away on a two-week, major-city-only tour for the release of the band's next single and upcoming EP release. He would be home in three days. He'd asked me to come along, and I thought I'd eventually join him for at least a few days, but getting the apartment together was more of a task than I had thought. I wanted our place to be finished for Nadine's visit and for his return.

I decided to go for my customary daily walk in the park. I was startled when I heard my name being called out at the corner of 72nd Street. "Aly!" A female voice shouted a second time. I looked behind me, and it was Sienna.

"Hey," she said, winded from walking fast. "I'm sorry. I should have called you. Jake told me to call you."

"It's okay," I said, rubbing her arm. "Is everything okay?"

She gulped, shaking her head, and began to tear up. "I'm sorry." She clasped her mouth. "He shouldn't have gone."

I knew immediately something happened with Dump. *Fuck – why hadn't Jake let me know?* "What happened?" I gasped.

"Let's go sit. Here, come on." I guided her by the elbow as we crossed the street and sat on a bench at the perimeter of the park. "Tell me."

She shook her head, picking anxiously at her red nail polish with trembling hands. "Jake just called a couple hours ago, and Dump is in the hospital in Philly." She sniveled. "Jake's been calling me every day, giving me updates, you know. He's been amazing through all of this."

My stomach tumbled. *Jake called her and not me? I haven't heard his voice in three days.* This wasn't about me. This was serious shit. Her husband was dying, I told myself.

"I'm so sorry, Sienna." Her eyes were bloodshot and puffy from too many tears. I was lost in her delicate, broken beauty. She looked way different than when she was in high school. Gone were the shoulder-length jet-black hair and heavy black eyeliner, replaced by true loveliness, flowing light brown hair, and long eyelashes. "What can I do?"

"I'm supposed to fly to Miami in a few hours. It's a big job for Ralph Lauren." Her lips trembled. "He told me to go… Dump did…but I feel so torn."

She wanted me to tell her what to do. My mind raced to give some sort of advice. *Go or stay?* "Is he stable? I mean what's wrong with him? I thought he was getting better."

"He's just so weak and tired. He has a weakened immune system…"

"What did the doctor say?" I said urgently.

"He needs to come home. Jake said they're coming home tomorrow, I guess a few days early. I can't keep track."

What?

"They must be really busy with details. I didn't know any of this," I offered. "I hadn't heard from him today yet." *Or yesterday, or the day before, with the exception of a few texts.* "Sienna, I don't know. I mean if he's gonna be okay. If he *says* he's gonna be okay. I'd probably go." I sighed. "I don't know. How many days will you be gone?"

"Just two."

"That doesn't seem too bad." Sienna stared off into the distance, lost in her tidal wave of despair. I didn't want to be the one to talk her into going and God forbid Dump die or something. "You know, if it was me, I wouldn't go," I said firmly. *And I wouldn't, no matter what. I'd be by Jake's side indefinitely if he was sick,* I thought.

She looked at me and gaped. "But you just said…"

"Sienna, if you're looking for someone to tell you what to do, I'm telling you to stay here and meet them at the airport." I reached out, caressing her hair down her back, trying to comfort her. I felt so awful, and all I wanted was to hear Jake's voice. I couldn't believe he hadn't called me after learning of Dump's situation.

———

I turned over, barely conscious, pushing the fluffy pillow just right under my head. I could hear a dog barking. *Ugh, shut the hell up.* I knew exactly which dog it was, too. I could picture the lady in my building with her platinum blonde hair and dark sunglasses, wearing a classic Calvin Klein ensemble. Her little Pomeranian barked at everything, every person, and *every* sound. She must be in the hallway, waiting for the elevator. I rolled onto my back and hit the mattress with clenched fists, squinting at the bright light that filled my room.

I rubbed my eyes and wondered what time it was. I'd tossed and turned all night, thinking about Dump, Sienna and Jake. Jake wasn't in the mood to talk. I didn't blame him under the circumstances, but it still bummed me out. I missed him, and had a pit in my stomach thinking about it. *He's coming home today*, I thought, and my excitement ignited. I threw the covers off and was startled when I saw Jake standing there, leaning against the wall, staring at me.

"Shit!" I gasped, clutching my chest. "Jake, what are you doing? How long have you been standing there?" I took in his disheveled appearance and instantly saw the sorrow in his dimmed blue eyes. I reached out to him with welcoming arms.

His lips curled up ever so slightly, a strained act. He kicked off his black sneakers and crawled across the bed, wrapping his arms around my waist. He laid his head on my chest. "Sorry for scaring you." His voice cracked and he sighed. "I'm so fucking happy to be right here, with you."

I embraced him tighter and curled my arm around his head, kissing his hair. The warmth of him swathed over me. "I'm so happy you're home," I whispered. "I'm sorry about Dump."

Jake wept into my chest. "He has to pull through." I clung to Jake as he choked the words out. He pushed away from me, rolling onto his back, wiping the tears from cheeks. He looked exhausted. "I have to find another drummer." He grabbed at his hair with both hands and squeezed his eyes closed, then looked at the ceiling. "We have SNL in a few days. Fuck. I can't do this without him, Aly. He has to be okay, he just has to be."

Jake told me every sorry detail. The trip started out fine, but as the days ticked by, Dump got more and more tired and began throwing up, having to stay back at the hotel, bludgeoned by high fevers and sickness, missing even the Ellen DeGeneres taping in Los Angeles.

Poor Dump.

I couldn't comprehend Jake's burden, but I felt for him. We laid there in silence loosely holding hands. I wanted to fix the problem. "What can I do?"

He turned his head to face me. His eyes roamed and studied my face, searching for an answer. "Come here," he said in a low, raspy voice. He wrapped his hand around my neck, bringing my face to his.

The heat of Jake's mouth filled mine, and my want for him pulsed. I ran my hand up under his shirt, caressing his chest as his thumb lightly played with my nipple. "Mmm, damn I missed you," he moaned as his sultry kisses traced my neck and jawline. His eyes brightened, diminishing the weight of his worries. "I need to hose off…" He smirked and his eyes glimmered. "And I wanna feel your wet skin against mine. Get up." He winked and dragged me out of bed.

For the first time, Jake wasn't slow moving or seductive at all. There was urgency and a roughness in his actions, and while I was dazed for a second by it, I liked it. I kissed him hard. He spun me around, pulling at my hair so my head would tip back under the water. As the water cascaded over my head, he sucked at my neck, biting into it tenderly.

"Ahh." I gasped, surprised that I liked it so much. "Mmm. What are you, hungry or somethin'?" I moaned teasingly.

"I'm hungry *and* thirsty for you. I wanna drink you up." His eyes had an intensity firing through them, and he was as hard as a rock. I took him into my hand, and he pulsed in my grip. Suddenly, he lifted me. I wrapped my legs around him as he slammed my back into the black tiled shower wall. He filled me, and I panted with pleasure, weaving my fingers through his hair, gripping it tightly.

"I love you, Aly."

"I love you more," I whispered into his mouth, kissing him harder and deeper. He twirled me around, kissing and gnawing at my shoulder and neck. His fingers slipped between my legs, fondling and pleasing me, making my knees go weak. His other hand pushed at the nap of my neck, bending me forward. He took me from behind.

Whatever had sparked Jake's sexual aggression, I was totally into it.

Chapter 14

JAKE

I woke up lying in dampness, naked. It took me a second to realize I was home and in *my* bed, and the reason *why* it was wet – Aly and I had stumbled, entwined, right out of the shower to finish what we'd started. It was dark. Fuck, I'd slept all day. Aly wasn't next to me and I wished she was, thinking about what went down – her wet and throbbing in my mouth. The thought of it gave me an instant semi. The room was dimly lit from the streetlights that filtered through the window, and my thoughts urged me to get up to find her.

What time is it?

I squinted, looking at the clock on Aly's bedside table – 10:30 PM. I laughed to myself and covered my face with my hands. *Wow.* My heart skipped and I wondered how Aly was feeling. I'd never let her have it like that. I'd asked her over and over again if she was okay, and she acted like she wanted more. I jumped up grabbing a pair of sweats from the closet and went after her, and as soon as I reached the door I heard voices.

Motherfucker – my mother and Notting.

I gulped and my stomach cinched into a ball. I wanted to punch the wall. I needed a break, a lifeline, anything to pull me from the black hole of drama. I stood with the door cracked open, trying to hear what was being said. Their voices mingled with the TV volume. Why was I surprised that they were there, anyway? I'd been ignoring both of their calls – all due to our exclusive interview released by some "no-name", telling the world about Dump's illness and streaming our next single before any major pub had the chance. I sighed, resigned to the fact that I knew this was gonna happen.

I purposely told Marty to wait on airing the interview until after we left California, so things would be as normal as we could play off. I'd told them *and Ellen*, Dump had the flu…and now here I was, feeling like I was sixteen again. I scratched my head and opened the door, walking into the lion's den.

As soon as they laid eyes on me, time stalled. My mother's eyes shot wide open and she covered her mouth, and so did Aly.

"What? What's wrong?" Aly looked horrified.

"Um…" An agonized look spread over Aly's face. "I think you need to go put a shirt on…and…oh my God." Aly covered her face, talking into her hands. "Oh my God, I'm so embarrassed."

My mother was flushed pink. She avoided my stare and looked down at the floor. Notting just shook his head at me and turned around, walking into the kitchen. I turned and rushed into the bathroom, flipping on the light…*shit!* I was covered in hickies! All over my chest and neck. There was even one on my jaw. I wanted to burst out laughing.

Perfect.

I was gonna look like a leper for our SNL appearance.

———

Sniffle – I heard Aly rush past me while I was in the guest bathroom, assessing my vampire wounds. I had to ask Notting and my mother to leave after I looked in on Aly to grab a shirt. She was pacing back and forth in our bedroom, talking to herself, trying to keep her hysterics at bay. My mother didn't say one word to me, only looking at me with pained frustration. Notting slapped my back on the way out – *"Well, son, we'll take up first thing."* Dismay etched across his face, deepening his wrinkles. My heart sank, realizing his disappointment. Why hadn't I at least confided in him?

"We had to track this place down. Bobby gave us the address after we visited Dump in the infirmary…" He carried on a few minutes longer, pinching his eyes closed, holding back his emotion. I wanted to ask about Dump, but didn't. I couldn't take it anymore, not right then.

I shut the door behind Notting and went to find Aly. She was curled up with her knees to her chest at the center of our bed. She shook her head at me in embarrassment.

"Are you kidding me?" She dropped her head to her knees.

I chuckled. I really did think it was funny, a silver lining in the portable shitter that was my current situation. "Hey…"

"Don't *hey* me!" she barked, and more words rushed out. "Look at you…oh my God! I'm so sorry. I had no idea…I really didn't…"

I hopped on the bed, scooting next to her, and put my fingers over her mouth, shutting her up. "Quiet," I sniggered again. "They'll go away."

She sighed and crossed her legs in front of her. "Some of them are so dark! Look at your neck and right here," she said, touching the one on my jaw.

I grabbed her wrist and stuck her index finger in my mouth, sucking on it. "You were totally fucking hot. It felt good, you tearing me up like that."

She yanked her hand away from me, trying not to smile. "Shut up," she huffed. "What did your mom say? Shit, I'm never gonna be able to look her in the face again."

I smiled. "She didn't say anything. But they'll be back first thing in the morning." I paused, rubbing her bare thigh. She wore a little black slip dress trimmed in lace, and she wasn't wearing any underwear. "Mmm," I teased as I ran my hand over her stomach.

She laughed and squirmed, pulling my hand out from under her dress. "Stop it."

"I'm hungry." I rolled over, pulling her closer to me.

"Jake!"

"No, really. I'm really hungry." I held up my hand in submission. "Food. Feed me."

Aly and I rustled to get ready. I switched out my sweats for some jeans and Aly plucked out a red lacy pair of panties, slipping them on, along with her black ballerina flats, and tied her hair up in a knot. She kept shaking her head, trying not to laugh when she stared at me. I didn't look that bad with a shirt on. Aly took out her make-up concealer and dabbed it on the exposed red suction marks. She sighed heavily and shrugged. "It'll have to do."

At 11:00 PM, the August night was at a perfect temperature. We strolled along the nearly deserted Central Park West – a long walk would do us good. I chose to take her to *Robert* at the top of *The Museum of Arts and Design* over at Columbus Circle. They always had some jazzy musician playing, and served a full menu late into the night. We took a table over-looking the park and ordered a bottle of wine. We hadn't had a chance to really talk. She'd mentioned how bummed she was that I'd been communicating with Sienna and not her, and it made my stomach sink.

"For the record, she called me first and asked me to call her as often as I could about Dump," I explained, still shocked that Sienna had come to talk to Aly in the first place. "Apparently he didn't want her to worry, so he took to limited contact because he didn't want to lie to her."

Aly sighed, looking out the floor-to-ceiling window. "I feel so bad for everyone. I feel guilty for wanting to live nor-mally with you."

I understood where she was coming from. I wanted it all to go away, too. "You're telling me. Don't feel bad." I paused, thinking about Dump and Sienna. "I'm surprised Sienna made the trek to come talk to you." Aly frowned at me. "What?"

"Why are you surprised she came over?"

"I dunno." I shrugged. "She's just busy with her shit, but thinking about it, I guess it doesn't surprise me."

"Whad'ya mean?" Aly tilted her head, confused.

"Even though she's had a successful career modeling, she's super clingy." Aly's eyes bounced around my face, but she wore a blank expression. I swallowed, thinking that I did kinda sound dickish. "I didn't say it like that to be mean."

"Define clingy." She tapped her fork on her knife.

"Okay, wrong choice of words." I caught myself raising my voice to counter her snippiness. Was this turning into a fight? "Okay, this is about *before* Dump got sick. She doesn't have any friends here. When she wasn't traveling for work, she was attached to us."

"So. Hasn't it always been that way?"

Why did she have to be so smart? "Aly, we're older now. We're not fucking teenagers. I just worry about her. Other than shopping and going to modeling gigs, she doesn't do anything for herself. Dump does it all. I don't even think she knows how to pay bills. He asked me to take care of her if anything happens to him." My stomach balled up, thinking about that possibility. "I don't wanna think about what she'll do if Dump…" I couldn't say it aloud, and looked away from her. I didn't want to ruin our night by dwelling on what-ifs.

Aly reached over the table, resting her hands palms-up in front of me. Her hair had come out of the bun, and splayed around her face and over her shoulders. She looked divine as the lights from Columbus Circle draped over her. I took her hands in mine and played with the ring I'd given her in London, when I first asked her to marry me. The ring that was meant for her left finger, but she wore it on her right. Would she say yes now? I smiled at her thoughtfully, feeling warm relief as she lovingly grasped my fingers. Just as I was about to speak, our waiter arrived with our wine.

I was never into wine until I'd first tried it when I dated Sasha, the blonde British heiress, while touring Europe. Then Aly surprised me when she asked for it during her trip to London. I was happy to know she was a fan of it, too. The first sip of the dark red liquid went down without a bite; that's what I loved about Pinot Noir. I liked the feeling a little too much, and the way it made me feel after a few more glasses, even better.

"Let's change the subject. How you feelin'?" I smirked, hoping she'd get my drift.

She laughed under her breath and looked around as if people would know exactly what I meant. "I'm a little sore." She smiled, tilting her head, and leaned in closer. "But you know how it goes. Even after a tough workout, you always go back for more."

Oh, the innuendo. "I'll have to give you a good rub down then when we get home, massage those sore muscles of yours." I winked at her. I leaned in over the table, holding her hands tight. "Marry me."

Aly's eyes sparked open in surprise, and she bit her lip. "Jake. You know I want to spend the rest of my life with you."

"Then marry me."

She squeezed my hands, and then pulled away, pouting a little. *What?* She played with the napkin in her lap, then looked at me. "You haven't asked my dad."

I sighed. "If I ask your dad tomorrow, would you marry me?" I wanted her to be mine for real, like Dump and Sienna, 'til death do us part.

"I'll marry you if you talk to my dad *and* after I finish college." Her eyes pleaded with me for understanding. "There are just certain things that I have to have…in order."

I took a gulp of my wine, wondering why it was so important for her to finish college *before* we got married. Thinking about it more…I was full-on chicken to ask Frank Montgomery for his permission. Why did she have to be so old school? "Understood. I know you already told me this in London. I guess I was just testing the waters." I tried not to sulk, but what a jab to my ego. "So you're saying yes?"

117

"I'm saying yes under those stipulations." She grinned softly at me, and spoke softer. "I want it all, Jake. I want you. I want this." She gestured with her hands and looked out over the half-filled room. "I want to figure out what it is I wanna do, you know. I wanna travel the world."

I scoffed. "Aly, you can travel the world with me."

"I wanna play volleyball, Jake. Just like you wanna play your music." Dismay filled her eyes. "The fact that I haven't trained in almost two months isn't good. Tossing around a ball in the apartment and running in the park doesn't count. I'm going to NYU tomorrow to see what my options are."

My stomach sank. I understood passion. I couldn't blame her for wanting those things. "A little bird told me you might not stay here for school." As soon as the words registered, her fire dimmed and she looked down at the table.

"I'm not even gonna ask who told you that…because it doesn't matter," she said bitterly, shaking her head. "I want to stay here. I wouldn't be here trying to make a life with you if I didn't want it. That's why I'm going to NYU tomorrow."

"Do you really want to stay here? Don't bullshit me, Aly." My mouth went dry, and I reached for the bottle, refilling my wine glass.

She sighed deeply. "Yes, but there's more to think about. I can't ask you to pay for my school."

"Marry me. That's what husbands do; they take care of their wives. You wanna go to school? I'll take care of it. What else do I have to spend my money on?"

"Please, stop. You know I'm not feeding you a bunch of crap. You know what my dreams are. I have real opportunities that aren't just about the money for school, Jake. My parents have invested so much in me. I want to do this for them, too."

I had to bite my tongue. I didn't want to argue with her. I knew how important it was for her to follow through with her school commitments. "I get it. I do. We've just fought so fucking long for this moment, Aly."

Our unassuming waiter, with his vintage bowl haircut (was that a thing now?), finally came to ask for our order – I was wondering where he went. My stomach was eating itself…or maybe it was the acids of uncertainty chewing holes in me. Aly ordered the salmon, and I ordered a filet mignon and another bottle of wine.

She leaned in over the table with hopeful eyes. "Move back to California."

Chapter 15

ALYSSA

Overwhelmed and awestruck, I watched the throngs of people line the sidewalk outside the Saturday Night Live studio as we slowly drove by, bogged down by a sea of yellow cabs. *Tents? Really? Fans camped out to see them?* Hidden by the tinted windows of our hired black SUV, we passed the NBC Studios marquee. Many of the fans held signs – *We Love You Dump!* – *Get Well Soon!* – *Bobby Let's Dance* – *Fuck The Big C!* – *Jake Marry Me* – *I Love You Jake Masters!* My heart thundered in my chest, and palms went damp – they couldn't *all* be for Jake and the band.

I swallowed down my simmering insecurities, looking down at my outfit: a black bustier, shredded-up dark denim jeans, and my very first pair of designer shoes – a pair of black stiletto Valentinos with red soles and silver studs on the heel. They literally made the outfit.

"You need to be the part of a rock star's girlfriend, Alyssa. Every girl in that audience wishes she was you," Sienna had said. I glanced at Jake as I played with the fake eyelashes I had expertly put on. I wasn't used to wearing make-up, and Sienna suggested I get them. *"They'll last two to three weeks, and you won't have to do shit*

but wear lipstick. I live in them," Sienna shared. One by one, a lash extension was glued on each of my own lashes. It took two hours. They certainly looked great, but bugged the hell out of me. I hoped I'd get used to them, and quick.

Jake appeared to be calm as he sat sunken down into his seat next to me, *always* working on his phone. He looked perfectly cast with his hair waxed back, wavy and precise. It was darker with the product, making his blue eyes pop even more. His black shirt with tiny white pinstripes fit him perfectly, showing the broadness of his shoulders. It was pressed crisp, and he had his sleeves rolled up past his elbows. With his shirt unbuttoned, his bare chest teased me. Those girls were gonna eat him up – I knew I wanted to. I was relived that I'd managed to cover all the hickies pretty well with my makeup, and I was certain the real SNL makeup artists would make them invisible.

I kept my eyes on the crowd sprawled on the sidewalk. I wasn't sure if it was a pang of jealousy or pride that ran through me, I concluded it was both. Was he totally unaffected by all the fans feathering the streets just to get a glimpse of him? This was the first time I fully realized what Jake had become, and it made my head swim. The paparazzi's and fans in London had nothing on this scene. I'd stayed away from almost everything pop culture, the TV news, the internet; anything to keep my sanity while I was plotting and planning my life for the last three years. All the while knowing Jake and I would make a go at it, but not knowing exactly how it would affect me.

Holy shit.

"Mr. Masters. I'm going to round the block once more. Are you ready?" our black suited driver announced.

Jake sat up, straightening his position and looking out the window. "Yeah. I just called Sarge, and he's already waiting out front. Thanks, Carl." He looked at me, clasping my thigh, and leaned over to kiss my cheek. "You ready, Alycat?"

"I think so." I glanced out the window too. "Better question is, are you ready?"

"I think so." He smirked, still staring out the window. "I'm actually shocked there're so many people out there for us. Those signs for Dump…I wish he was here." He shifted in his seat, leaning forward, and sighed, taking my hand in his. "So I have to tell you something, and it's not a big deal. Unless you make it a big deal."

"What?" *What the fuck now?* My heart raced even faster, waiting for him to tell me whatever *wasn't* a big deal.

"I'm pretty sure most of these fans are here for Eva James. She's the host of tonight's show."

I seriously thought I'd had an aneurysm, because I couldn't talk for a second. I flashed back to the moment in 9th grade when I found out he was seeing the Disney star turned pop-princess Eva fucking James, after we'd officially broken up. Though we were still involved secretly behind even *her* back, it still burned. I pictured myself screaming at him and bopping him upside the head. Then I snapped out of it. "What is wrong with you?" I said calmly, folding my arms around my waist. "Why is it you wait until the last minute to tell me things. Like seriously. What. Is. Wrong. With. You?"

He fussed like a grade-schooler. "Aly I didn't want you to back out. I thought maybe you wouldn't wanna come if I told you. I want you here with me."

"I'm not fifteen anymore, Jake. I can handle being around people you used to…screw."

His face fell. "Now come on."

"No, you come on…"

Carl loudly cleared his throat. "Mr. Masters, we're here." He spoke loudly, stopping our bickering.

I narrowed my eyes at Jake, disheartened. Next thing I knew, Jake was holding my hand tightly, waving and smiling at his fans, I followed, smiling as sweetly as I could at the screaming and crying fans, who had their arms outstretched, trying to get a feel of him as camera flashes blinded me. I caught a glimpse of Marty at the front of the barricade by the studio doors and waved.

We were swept along by two linebacker-sized bodyguards, and I looked back behind me, seeing Bobby and Devon slapping the hands of fans along the short distance into the studio. I was surprised to see Devon, the band's fill-in guitarist, I hadn't seen him since high school. I hadn't known he was still around. I was inundated by a million thoughts at once, and closed my eyes to get a grip, feeling my heartbeat thumping behind my eyes.

Finally, just inside the studio walls, the noise level cut in half as the doors swung shut. We waited for Bobby and Devon, and I tried to calm my rapid heart rate as my arms and legs shook from the adrenaline. Jake faced me, rubbing my bare arms, and his fingers clasped around my biceps.

"You're shaking." His blue eyes roamed my face, and his eyebrows furrowed with concern. He pulled me to his chest, hugging me tightly, kissing my forehead and hair, over and over again. "I'm sorry, I had no idea it would be nuts. There's never been a crowd like this, ever."

I took in a deep breath. "It's okay," I laughed, playing off my nerves. On top of the rabid fans, I was totally preoccupied and obsessing about seeing Eva. I looked around to see if she was standing anywhere nearby. "I just didn't expect all that. Being in the middle of it, it's crazy."

"It just started getting like this. LA was kinda nuts too, but not like this."

As he held me, I peered over his shoulder and spotted a gorgeous girl with cropped blonde hair, leaning against a door jam off in the distance. I immediately recognized her as Eva.

———

Jake and I sat alone in the band's assigned dressing room and I tried to get over the Eva encounter. I played her syrupy hello to Jake over and over again in my head – "*Oh my Gawwwwd! It's been forever!*" she'd said as she threw herself at him. *Vomit.*

I smiled as sincerely as I could, watching her as she clung to him like white dog hair on black fabric. She smirked at me as Jake stepped way from her, the kind of smirk that challenges you. I knew that look – she wanted to play. Jake introduced her, and she held out her hand to me, giving me the limpest shake I think I'd ever had. She felt icky and clammy. Even though she was beautiful, I wondered how he could even touch her after feeling her hand. Then I reminded myself he was high on drugs and alcohol at the time, trying to make myself feel better. I laughed internally. I knew I was being catty, but fuck her and the look she gave me. I bit my tongue and played stupid.

"That wasn't so bad, was it?" He looked at me uncomfortably, and I felt bad, telling myself it was circumstances.

"How did this happen again?" I asked, as if he'd shared that tidbit of information already.

He slumped down into a square, stiff chair. "We're with the same label and have the same agent, and it's just something that happened." He sighed and leaned forward, looking at me guiltily. Something always *just happens* with him.

"What?" I whispered sternly at him when he looked like he had more to say.

"They wanna send us out on another tour with her."

All I could do was blink at him as the fire and fear rose inside me. Life just kept throwing tomatoes at us. I was pissed that he would be essentially hanging out with her again, in such close quarters. I feared that maybe, just maybe, he'd end up hooking up with her. Irrational fear began to consume me – there was no reason to believe it would happen. But Eva clearly still had a thing for him and it made me sick to think she'd take any opportunity to tempt him. I attempted to bury my insecurities, stuffing them down as deep as I could. I didn't want to ruin the evening with immature intolerance, but it was tough.

"Well there's nothing I can do about that, is there?" I brushed past Jake, sitting down on the burgundy-colored sofa, trying not to sulk, and changed the subject. "Are you nervous?"

Jake blinked twice at me, and his eyes danced around my face. "I don't know what I am," he said despairingly, and looked around the room. Bobby and Devon busted through the door. "Hey Bobby, will you hand me a beer?" Jake pointed to a clear bucket filled with ice and selection of beer – Bud Light, Corona, Sierra Nevada.

"Hey Aly." Devon smiled shyly.

"Aly!" Bobby piped as he reached into the bucket, grabbing a Corona and tossing it to Jake.

"Hey guys," I smiled, happy to see someone was stoked to be there. Maybe their moods would lighten ours.

"I need an opener," Jake announced, waiving the bottle around in front of him. I watched in agitated silence, and Bobby looked around for an opener for the beer.

Bobby cleared his throat and grabbed a beer for himself. "Ran into Eva. She looks different with that short hair. I barely recognized her." His eyes nervously darted to me and then back to Jake.

"I like her better with long hair," Devon chimed, and dug around in his backpack, taking out drumsticks.

I knew who she was right away, short hair or not, I thought as watched Devon moving about. It dawned on me that he was holding drumsticks.

"You're gonna play the drums for Dump?" I asked curiously. I mean, who else would, now that I thought about it.

Devon nodded. "Yeah, drums are actually my thing." He shrugged. "I mean, I play everything, but I started out playing the drums."

"That's awesome, Devon. I had no idea." He threw me a lop-sided grin and went about his business of turning on the Bose system. Music filled the room.

I took in a solemn breath, thinking about Dump, and looked at Jake as he stared of into nothing, swigging his beer. He leaned his head back, resting it against the chair, and closed his eyes. My emotions shifted immediately. The last thing Jake needed was to worry about me. I got up and stood in front of him, nudging his knees with mine.

"Hey." My lips twitched upward.

He reached out, grabbing the back of my thigh with his free hand, pulling me to sit down in his lap. My insides swirled with longing to be close to him and for things to be normal – no sickness, no ex-girlfriends, no mom drama.

He parted his legs a bit more, and I sunk down in between his thighs. My lips brushed against his jaw. "I'm sorry," I whispered. "I don't mean to be a pain. I don't want you to worry about me. I'm a big girl. Worry about Dump…the more important things."

His fingers swept across my cheek, cupping it, and his lips hovered over mine. "I'm gonna worry about you for the rest of my life, Alycat." His warm breath danced over my face, and his lips met mine softly.

"You two get a room!" Bobby observed, throwing ice at us. "This'll cool you off!"

I could hear Devon and Bobby chuckle as I focused back on Jake. "Hey hey," a female voice sang out, jolting me to look toward the door. "They'd have their own room if you two would leave." Eva smiled slyly at us, locking in on Jake. Her little red booty shorts and barely-there top showed everything.

Jake squeezed my hip, and his lips lingered at my forehead. "Great idea," Jake piped. "Maybe you should all leave." Jake's lips curled up, and he half-laughed. A ripple of relief coursed through me knowing he was displaying unity with me, in front of Eva.

"Let's do just that, boys." She turned on her heel and threw Jake and me a cold shoulder. "I've got red velvet cupcakes in my room, and Bobby, I know you're such a sucker for them."

She vanished – *ugh*. Why did every pop star feel they had to practically be naked to be appealing? Eva actually had a killer voice. She didn't need to display herself like that. I laughed to myself, like I was one to talk. I ran around in little booty shorts *and* bikinis too – but that was different; they were the required volleyball uniform. Bobby shrugged his shoulders at us. "Duty calls." He disappeared in a sugar hunt frenzy.

"I don't like her," Devon said flatly as the door clicked shut. To know this made me happy, and I tried to keep myself from smiling, pressing my lips tightly together.

"Oh you like hearing that?" Jake tipped his head at me, amused.

I nodded. "Yes. I do." I jutted my chin out, defiant. "Sorry I'm not sorry."

"That's okay, I don't like Nathan either."

My heart thudded to my stomach, hearing Nathan's name. Not really sure what it was about, I just shook my head and pushed myself off of Jake, standing.

Jake looked at Devon. "Why don't you like Eva? She's been nothing but cool to us," he said, finishing off his last bit of beer.

He shrugged, not looking at Jake, fiddling with something in his backpack. "I dunno. There's just something off about her. She's weird."

The devil on my shoulder was pumping its fist. I was pleased to know that Devon would potentially become my ally while they were on the road without me.

A knock came at the door, and Devon hopped up, answering it. A curly-haired PA stuck his head in. "You guys are on in ten."

I moved away from Jake and sat back down on the sofa. He grinned at me. "You wanna stay in here while we rehearse? It's just a quick run through, but you might be able to meet the cast if you come."

I was excited to meet the cast. I'd looked forward to it. "I'll come and watch."

As I stepped into the hallway, I saw Marty leaning against the wall right in front of me, his camera was slung across his chest. "Hey Marty." I smiled, happy to see him. Marty and I stood side stage against the wall, watching the SNL staff of PAs and the prop and stage crew run around, switching and changing stuff out. It was organized chaos. I didn't fangirl as much as I thought I would when I saw Vanessa Bayer, Taran Killam, and Kenan Thompson. For a moment, I'd wished my visit could have been during the days of Kristen Wiig, Will Farrell, and Tina Fey.

To be *that* funny... geez – I watched as Eva ran through her skits and thought anyone could be funny with the material the SNL writers pumped out. Then, as soon as Jake took the stage, Marty moved and had his camera at the ready, shuttering away. They sound checked and played through a song, and just like that, it was over. The stage cleared and Marty met back up with me.

"Let's go back to the dressing room. They're gonna bring in the audience now."

I looked over Marty's shoulder for Jake. He was standing with the Director and Eva. My stomach simmered in aggravation, and there was nothing I could do about it.

This was Jake's life. I was just in it.

Chapter 16

JAKE

Aly didn't say much after the SNL gig, and I knew it was because of Eva. We didn't have time to talk due to dinner with the band and our agent after our SNL taping. Having people back to our apartment didn't help, either. She appeared to be having a good time, but I saw the discontent in her eyes. I just hoped she'd snap out of it sooner than later. I had to do what was best for the band, and Eva was still hot shit, only this time, we'd be the headliners.

Aly brought up moving back to Cali again while we were dozing to off to sleep. I actually seriously considered moving back. Dump should be near his mom anyway while he was battling the big C. He'd yet to tell her of his illness. He'd said he didn't think she'd care. I refused to believe that. Fuck, it was his mom, after all. I told Aly I'd consider it, but explained to her that there was too much going on overseas with the band in the near future. It'd be some time until I'd be able to make that a reality – it was just too convenient living on the East Coast. Not to mention I really did love New York, but I loved Aly more and I'd just have to see.

Morning light burned my eyes. I was over squinting at the bright light that always greeted me before I wanted it to. We needed window coverings, stat. I rolled over, and of course Aly was already out of bed. It was 8:30 AM. A rush of adrenaline flowed when I remembered Notting's text – *WE'LL BE THERE AT 9.*

"Aly!" I shouted. I propped myself up on my elbows and saw that the door was shut. I dragged myself out of bed and caught a glimpse of my bare chest in the mirror hanging above the dresser. I'd forgotten about the hickies since they'd been covered so well – my late night shower melted that away. I reached down for my shirt on the floor, slipping it on.

Walking into the short hallway, I felt the rug beneath my feet, plush and soft. It was black in the middle, with a cream and tan outline. There was a little table with an orchid plant sitting on top of it. *Huh* – I'd not seen all of Aly's little homey accents, and it made me smile. I slowly took in all the new details of our apartment that I'd failed to notice as I walked out into the living room, like the zebra-print skin rug that was placed in the foyer under a round dark wood pedestal table – I'd noticed the table before, but not the rug.

I watched Aly thoughtfully for a moment – she didn't notice me. She sat with her leg bent up. Her elbow rested on her knee as she pointed the remote at the TV, wearing sheer white pajama bottoms. I could see her perky nipples through her equally sheer white tank top that dipped down, exposing her cleavage. Her hair was tied up on the top of her head in a messy bun – she looked beautifully bedraggled and delicious.

"Good morning," I said and practically skipped over to her, diving onto the sofa, laying my head in her lap. She squealed with laughter as I tickled and squeezed her waist.

"Stop it!" she pleaded over and over through outbursts of giggles. She took me by surprise by punching me in the stomach, knocking the wind out of me. I gasped, and then she gasped.

"I'm so sorry. I didn't mean to punch you that hard," she said remorsefully, rubbing my belly. "You know I hate being tickled…I'm sorry."

"I know, I know…but damn." I smiled, still lying there with my head in her lap, looking up at her. Her amber eyes smiled at me, making me warm inside. I took her hand in mine, kissing her palm. "I love you, and I love what you did with the place."

"I love you more." She ran her other hand through my hair, combing it and then looked out over the room. "I really hope you do like it." She nodded happily. "What are you doing up so early?"

I placed the palm of her hand flat on my chest. "Notting is supposed to be here at nine, and that's twenty minutes from now."

She moaned, and her face drooped. "I can't look him in the face. Is your mom coming too?"

"I assume she is."

Aly's head tipped back and thudded against the wall behind the sofa. "Great." She sighed. "Thank God I'm leaving for yoga…get up." She nudged me. "I wanna get out of here before they get here."

"Aly…"

"No, please. I just can't look at them yet."

She pushed at my back, helping me to sit up. "We're gonna go visit Dump. He's finally back home."

She paused at the edge of her seat. "When?"

"I dunno, probably around noon, maybe." I scratched my head. "After I get the lecture on how unprofessional I am." I shook my head. "Maybe I need to hear it."

"What's going on?" Concern laced her voice.

"I just hadn't been answering calls from my attorney or the label. That thing I did with Dump, letting our fans know what's up…it's not gone over well with the Powers that Be. Apparently we had some agreement with MTV."

She gave me sympathetic eyes; then a wry smile sprung to her lips. "You can't run from this, Jake." She shook her head.

I threw her an ironic glare. "Coming from someone who's running out the door because she can't be accountable for the injury she's inflicted up on me?" I teased, playfully looking wounded.

Her head tilted. With puckered lips, she leered at me. "Okay. You got me." She tapped her foot. "But really…I was really going to yoga, and I'll be back in an hour or so."

Aly pecked me on the forehead and dashed out of view before I could thread any more words together. She disappeared out of the service door in the kitchen just as the front door buzzer called out Notting and Kate's arrival – *smart girl*, I thought. As soon as I opened the door, there was something in Notting's eyes that looked different. My mother looked like she'd been crying.

Dump.

"What's up? Is Dump okay?" My eyes bounced back and forth between Notting and my mom.

Notting held up his hand and then clasped my shoulder. "Dump is fine, for now." He pushed at my shoulder for me to turn around, and we all walked into the living room. "What's with the somber looks then?"

"These are somber times, Jake," my mother replied, and quickly looked away. Like she still couldn't stand the sight of the hickies or something. "But everything will be okay. It always is. Time heals."

I looked at Notting, and the odd look remained in his eyes. "Look guys. I'm sorry about the hickies. It's embarrassing. Aly's really embarrassed, and so am I." I laughed. "We're just trying to enjoy our time, and things got a little…"

Notting held up his hand. "It's okay, son. It's none of our business."

My mother laughed tensely. "I hope you covered those things enough that they didn't show on your SNL appearance." She grabbed my chin with her cool fingertips, moving my head from side to side to get a better look. "Jake, really. They may just have a field day with this. You'll probably get your own skit by next week."

Notting burst out in a hearty laugh. "Oh Katie!" he moved next to her and placed his arm around her shoulder, kissing her cheek. Watching him made me smile, but when his eyes met mine, they looked at me differently. Something was going on; I felt it.

Heavy-footed, I walked to the sofa and they followed me. "Spit it out. Let me have it. What are all the fucking suits sayin'?" I leaned back and sunk down into my seat.

My mother sat quietly, looking down at her hands. That's when I knew something was up, and it wasn't about the band. Maybe they were just as upset about Dump as I was, and they knew something I didn't?

"First things first," Notting began. "This is all very upsetting and shocking about Dump. I'm not sure what the both of you were thinking…" A long dramatic silence pulsed. I kept holding my breath, and finally he continued. "But none of what I was going to say matters, because what's done is done, and your legions are what matter in the end, I suppose. They're the ones who fill your pockets."

"Exactly." I threw my hands out, sitting up. "That's exactly why we went about it the way we did, and Marty was just the guy to do it."

My mother huffed. "What's upsetting is that you didn't care to let *us* know! Dump is family, Jake," she choked. Fuck, she was about to cry.

"Katie…" Notting reached for her leg, giving it a consoling rub.

"Mom, I'm sorry. Dump didn't want anyone to know for as long as he could hold on."

She continued to tear up, shaking her head. "Jake, it's just such a surprise, a horrible, dreadful thing. There are too many surprises these days." She sucked in a breath and suddenly got up and left the room. I assumed she was going to the bathroom, since that's what girls did when they got upset.

"Wow." I slumped deeper into the sofa, wanting to sink into the fibers. "This is heavy shit."

Notting cleared his throat. "Yes. Indeed." He paused, clearing his throat again, rubbing and stretching his neck from side to side. His tattoos moved animatedly on his skin as he tried to rub out the tension. "One of the issues is that Universal is *not* happy. They had an Agreement with MTV, and it's caused a problem and…"

"And what? So?" I raised my voice. I gave zero fucks about what the label wanted anymore. We'd given them too much already. Sure they gave us a break, but they took full advantage for the first two records. "I read that contract with our attorney and Dump, and there's no clauses in there that we'd be in breach."

"It was a booking, Jake, an interview, and live exclusive performance of the new music. But you'd know that if you'd answer your phone. Hell, I haven't even heard the final masters." He raised his voice. "I had to hear it on YouTube. The fuck?" He shook his head and gestured at me with open arms.

Shit, a swear word – now I knew he was upset.

"All of sudden, things are goin' all wonky again. Where's the communication between you and I?"

Wonky again? His comment made me think of Aly. "Look, I'm sorry. I hope you're not insinuating that me not communicating has anything to do with Aly." My tone was measured, but I was about to erupt. "I just got back in town, and Aly didn't travel with me. She was here."

"She wasn't with you at all?" His forehead rose.

"Nope."

He nodded, surprised. "I'm impressed."

"Impressed?"

"That Aly is independent of you."

I didn't want to discuss Aly with him. Notting sighed and called out my mother's name. "Katie love? You alright?"

"Yes. I'm just looking around," she said as she walked back in the room, composed. "I love the furnishings, Jake. Much more comfortable and inviting." She smiled sweetly at me.

"It's all Aly. I was just telling Notting here that Aly didn't go with me on this last trip." My mother's eyes flashed wide, mildly shocked. "She stayed here getting acclimated and getting the apartment ready."

"I see," she said, glancing around the room, and sat next to Notting. He rubbed her back affectionately, looking at me with a tight-lipped grin I couldn't place. Something in his eyes made me feel weird inside; my mother, too, was acting strangely. She looked at Notting. "When is Dump expecting us?"

"At noon. Sienna says he sleeps until about 11."

"Aly will be back about 10:30 or so," I informed.

My mother nodded, and Notting moved to get up. "Welp my love. I'm going to take a walk and make some calls. I will meet you at Dump and Sienna's at noon."

Wait, what? Notting looked at me for a long moment with his mouth open like he wanted to say something to me, but nothing ever came out. He turned back to my mother and kissed her on the lips. *Wow.* He'd never done that before in front of me.

"Where are you going, and why is she staying here?" I looked back and forth between them. "Sorry Mom, but you know what I mean."

She smiled softly. Restless, she sighed. "You and I need to talk."

"I'll see you soon, son." Notting squeezed my shoulder firmly and walked out the door.

"What's up?" My insides began to ball up. The last thing I wanted was to get a solo lecture from her, *Jesus Christ.*

"Are you sure Aly won't be home soon? Maybe we should go walk in the park." She was fidgeting with her purse handle, and I could see that each breath she took was deeper and deeper.

"Mom, look, if you're wondering what's going on with Aly and me…I asked her to marry me and I'm not sure what our…"

Her mouth hinged open. She closed her eyes and held up her hand. "Stop. I don't want to talk about Aly. What ever you decide with Aly, I'll support you. I'm actually surprised you two haven't eloped yet."

My heart started to race as my thoughts darted back to London and her surprise visit there six months ago. "Are you sick?"

She smiled, and her eyes closed shut again. She shook her head no. *No, yes, I don't want it to be true?* Or *No, no, I'm fine?*

"Spit it out then. What's wrong?" A burning urgency ran over me. "Don't be dramatic. Just say what you have to say."

She gulped, sucking in a deep breath. "Notting and I…well I wanted to do this during your visit home, but you avoided us." She sighed, shifting nervously in her seat. "And Notting reminded me that you still needed to finish your media tour, so we held off."

"Are you guys getting married? What?" The unknown pressed down on my shoulders.

"Jake this isn't easy for me, just be quiet, please." She sat up straighter, looking down at her lap, smoothing out her sky blue skirt. When she looked back at me, her eyes pooled with tears. My heart raced. "First let me say that I had no idea all this time, up until Christmas, when I decided to find out for sure. There are so many things that have happened between Notting and I, so many years have passed…that led me to believe, that led up to this…" She dug in her purse, taking out a tissue. She dabbed her eyes. "You've…"

"Mom! Cut the shit…say it!" I barked, insistent. I watched her chest rise and fall. *Was it fear I saw on her face?* "Just say what you have to say." I begged, under my breath and sat at the edge of my seat.

"Your father, Michael…" My mom looked like she was gonna pass out. *My father*…she must have found out about his cheating after all this time.

"Mom…look…"

"Notting…" Her voice rose over mine, interrupting me, "is your father, not Michael."

I stopped breathing.

Chapter 17

JAKE

"You're kidding, right?" Dump's gravely voice echoed in my ears. I sat staring at him, unfocused. Aly stood behind me silently, rubbing my shoulders. "What the fuck is going on… and she said she *just* found this out?"

"That's what she said," I confirmed.

"And Notting *just* found all this out, too?"

"Yep."

"Fuck." Dump's once meaty hand rubbed his bald head. "What did he say to you?"

"I haven't seen him yet. I left my pad at some point. I don't even remember what I said to my mom when I left. Next thing I knew, I was walking the park, and then Aly met me sitting on a some bench."

Sienna rubbed tenderly at Dump's arm. "Aly called and asked me to let them know when Notting and Kate left. But they called and said they'd be coming over later. Kate said she'd let us know," she explained somberly.

I glanced back and forth between everyone. "Dude, I totally blacked out," I admitted and that scared me. "Like, I seriously don't recall what I did between the time Kate's crazy confession and Aly meeting me on that park bench."

"Man, I'm sorry. This is some fucked up shit goin' on. Me dyin' of cancer…"

"You're not dying," I countered firmly.

"Uh, yes I am, my friend. I'm sick as fuck. This shit is eating me from the inside out and it doesn't look good."

Anger simmered inside me. "Fuck!" I tried to hold back my frustration and fury. I grabbed the back of my head, bending over my lap and taking in deep breaths, but I couldn't hold it in. I stood, rushing past Aly and Sienna.

Aly came after me and stood at a distance, watching my meltdown. I paced back and forth in front of the window, looking down onto the city streets below. Tears streamed down my face.

Dad…Dump…Why?

Sorrow was etched on Aly's face. Her fingers pressed to her lips as she stood there, quietly watching me. She wiped her own tears from her cheeks. "I think we should go, Jake. We can come back tomorrow."

"I need to stay here with Dump. I haven't spent any time with him since we've been back."

"It's only been two days. He just got home from the hospital. We can come back tomorrow."

"No!" I shouted. "I'm staying here. I need more time with him, today, not tomorrow. There might not be a tomorrow." As soon as I said that, I turned around and Sienna was standing there.

Fuck.

"What do you mean, there might not be a tomorrow?" she shrieked. "There's gonna be a tomorrow! And a next day and a next day." She began to bawl and rushed past Aly, then threw her arms around me, sobbing.

———

A week later, Bobby and I sat in some random Mid-Town pizza joint, waiting for Devon. Nadine had finally come to visit, and I was glad she was keeping Aly busy. Her visit couldn't have come at a better or worse time, but it allowed me the space to sort out my immediate life. I felt as if I was floating in a dream. I was completely disconnected from the space around me.

I knew I was with Bobby and chewing on a pepperoni pizza slice, but it didn't seem real. It tasted like plastic. I wasn't sleeping and to top it off every time I went to my guitar and held it, nothing came to me, nothing at all.

In a matter of a few short months, my perfect life, the one I'd been wishing, hoping, and planning for with Aly, imploded. Dump was fighting for his life, my father wasn't really my father, and Aly was having a change of heart about going to school at NYU. She admitted to not being sure in the first place and complained about the volleyball team not being up to par. I wondered if she was making it all up. How bad of a team could it really be? I reminded her of what she'd told me – *"My goal is to get my degree. I can play volleyball anywhere. As long as we're together, it'll all be good."* She'd looked at me with regret in her eyes, and it made me sick.

"So why is Aly changing her mind now about where she wants to go to school?" Bobby asked through a mouthful.

"I knew it." I shook my head at my recollection.

He cocked his head and stopped chewing. "What do you mean you knew it?"

"I just knew it," I said, throwing my pizza crust onto my paper plate. "She always kinda wavered, and now apparently this team really sucks, *and* her dad mentioned it once."

"What are you gonna do?"

"What can I do?" I raised my voice. "I can't force her to stay."

"Are you gonna break up?"

My stomach soured at his question. He stopped chewing as he waited for my answer.

"You know, I don't know." Anger roused inside me and for the first time, I wanted to tell *her* to fuck off. I felt like she'd led me on. "If she leaves, I'm not gonna have a long-distance relationship. Fuck that."

Bobby's eyes grew wide. "It's not that bad."

"I'm glad it works out for you," I said flatly.

My phone rang out. It was my mother *again*. I'd yet to talk to her since she'd told me about Notting being my real father. Notting hadn't reached out to me at all, and I was harboring resentment about that too. Why hadn't he reached out to me? I was his son, after all.

I was drowning in my thoughts when Devon finally joined us, forcing me to be in the moment. We spent the rest of the afternoon mapping out our next three months. It was the first time, Notting wasn't a part of it. I refused to reach out to him. He was the parent. He and my mother were the ones who created everything about me. He was the one that needed to reach out first, in my mind. We were leaving with Eva in October, with or without Notting's experienced advice.

Top priority – I needed to find another guitarist, because Devon was now our drummer.

———

The August heat was steaming, the air thick with moisture as we strode out of NYU. Aly stopped as she pushed the bright yellow crosswalk button. She dropped her grey backpack at her feet. I picked it up and slung it over my shoulder. She pulled her long hair up, piling it on the top of her head, tying it up with an elastic band, and turned to face me with regret. I'd surprised her at volleyball practice. I'd looked around for Nadine, thinking she might be hanging around too, but she wasn't anywhere to be seen.

From my private view, hidden behind the gym stands, it seemed obvious Aly was better than the girls she was training with. In each drill they ran through, she was faster and the most consistent with her hitting. Sure she wasn't a middle blocker, but her vertical jump was off the charts for her height, and her defensive skills and ball control were spot-on. She never let a ball hit the ground, and her passing was impeccable. I watched as Aly made impossible recoveries, getting the ball up, and the disappointment time and time again when a teammate would let it drop.

I knew the difference between a Division 1 and a Division 3 school – these girls looked like a bunch of high schoolers compared to Aly. Aly needed to be with a Division 1 or 2 school. My heart sank deeper into my chest at the realization that I couldn't hold her back from her passion.

She threw me a quirky grin. "You're a stinker." She pointed her finger at me.

I laughed. "Am I?" I sniffed my underarms, and she shoved me.

"Stop it!" she guffawed, looking over her shoulder. No one minded us. "What are you doing here anyway?"

"Just left the guys…" I chuckled at her embarrassment of me. The light turned green and I grabbed her elbow, prompting her into the street. "And thought I'd try and catch you." I flung my arm over her shoulder, and she grabbed my hand with the both of hers, kissing my wrist. "Where's Nadine?"

"She hooked up with Sienna. She tagged along here and then took off to meet her."

"Huh," I nodded, thinking. That was a good thing. Sienna needed someone to lean on other than me. I wished she'd stop texting me. I didn't blame her, but I had too much other shit to worry about. "Let's grab a cab," I suggested. I was eager just to be home, alone with Aly. It'd been strained the past week since the nuclear detonation of my family life, and since Nadine's arrival, we'd barely touched each other. "I say we grab some Chinese and hole up alone for as long as we can."

She sighed, smiling. "I'd like that."

"Only like?" I teased.

She gave me a playful leer. "I've missed you."

"I've missed you more." I nuzzled her ear and kissed her neck. "Mmm. Salty."

"Eww, gross." She removed my arm from her shoulder and laughed. "I'm sure I'm the stinker."

"You never stink." I winked and stepped into the street to hail a cab.

I'd decided to order Chinese for delivery. When we arrived home, I quickly uncorked a bottle of Pinot Noir and poured a glass – I noted that I was starting to like the wine thing a little too much. I watched myself pour it to the rim, but what the fuck, there was no harm in a couple of glasses. Aly got into the shower, and I tried to relax on the sofa. We were alone for the time being, and I was feeling more normal than I had in days.

I grabbed the down-filled pillow that sat next to me, reclining back into it, thinking about Notting and *Michael*. I tried to picture my dad's face, remembering him. He had dark hair and a strong build. I recalled how his dark eyes danced when I caught my first line drive in Little League, and he told the story to all his friends, including Notting. *My dad*, Michael, was proud of me.

I sighed, missing him. Did my mother cheat on him with Notting? Notting always made it sound like he was in love with her from afar. My brain couldn't handle the thought. They were *both* cheaters, my mom *and* dad…what the fuck. Now it all made sense, especially why I looked nothing like my dad at all. Michael would never know that he wasn't my father. Or maybe he did know now, if you believed in Heaven and all that shit.

I detected Aly's fresh citrus scent before she even stepped into the room; she went from strawberry to grapefruit. I loved them both. She sat next to me, then pulled the towel from her head, and her damp hair fell over her bare shoulders. She was wearing a strapless cotton blue tie-dyed sundress. I loved when she wore strapless *anything*. She had amazing shoulders. I leaned over, kissing and sucking the smooth skin on her shoulder. She moaned, pleased with the feeling.

"You like that?"

"Mmm," she purred and her hand cupped the side of my cheek. I scooted closer to her, tenderly tracing little kisses all the way to her neck, and she embraced me. "You make me crazy. I miss you." She reached under my shirt and her hands ran softly over my skin, sending an instant jolt through me.

I shifted my position, running my hand along her thigh up to her waist, guiding her to rest back. The hem of her dress pooled at the bend of her hip. She wasn't wearing any underwear again, and was as hairless and smooth. The sight of it made my junk pulse. Every time, it made me want to eat her up. I loved making her cum. I ran my hand over her smooth leg as she wrapped it around me.

"I'm sorry I've been so out of it," I whispered, taking her mouth to mine. I'd missed the sweetness of her. "I shoulda made..."

"Shh." Her breath tickled my lips, and she kissed me deeply, shutting up my excuses. "Stop talking. Nadine'll be back soon." She pulled my shirt over my head, and I slipped my hand between her legs, feeling the warm wetness of her. She sighed passionately. The buzz of the doorbell rang out and clubbed at my eardrums. And just like that, the moment was over.

"Nadine?" I whispered as I pulled Aly's dress down over her thighs.

"This isn't happening," she whimpered and pulled me back down on top of her. "No, it's not Nadine. She said she'd text on her way back."

"Huh. Miguel woulda called, letting me know it's the food." I gave her a quick peck and hopped up, grabbing my shirt and slid it over my head. "Hold up!" I shouted when more buzzing rang out. I peaked through the peephole, and my heart froze in an instant. It was Notting, Miguel, and the

Chinese food delivery guy. "You gotta be kidding me. It's everyone but my mother."

Aly sat up. "Who?" I ignored her and just opened the door so she could see for herself. My heart thundered in my chest as I locked eyes with Notting, my real father.

I felt woozy.

"Hey." I gave Notting a weak smile and looked past him to Miguel, and then to the delivery guy.

"I tried to stop him, Mr. Masters, but he rushed past me, and I didn't want to call the authorities because I know he's your family." He moved imposingly closer to Notting, like he would take him down if I ordered it.

My family. You mean my father.

I looked back at Notting. "No, Miguel. It's fine. Thanks." I stepped into the hallway and grabbed the bags of Chinese food, thanking and tipping the slight Asian delivery boy. When I turned around, Notting was already inside the apartment. I stepped back in and kicked the door shut.

Aly stood up and ran her hands over her dress, nervously staring between the two of us, and quickly moved past Notting without a word. She took the brown sacks from my hands and kissed my jaw, disappearing into the kitchen. My mouth went dry and tightness crept up neck.

"Hey," My voice cracked. I had no idea what to say to him.

"Hey." Notting moved to sit on the sofa, and I studied him. "You got another glass?" He pointed to the open wine bottle sitting on the table.

"Sure." I walked into the dining area and retrieved a glass from the cabinet. Handing it to him, my question slipped out. "Did you ever wonder?"

149

Notting shook his head. "It never dawned on me." He looked at me somberly. "If I had one inkling, Jake, I would have questioned Kate in an instant. I don't know what to say of all this."

"Me neither." I was beyond confused. I still missed my dad. Michael was my dad. No matter what he did, what my mom did, or how Notting fit in. Cheating on my mom aside, Michael was my dad.

"What happened? How did this happen?" I laughed cynically, grabbing at the hair on my head. "I mean I know how *this* happened." I gestured between us. "Was Mom married? You were my dad's best friend, Notting. What the fuck?"

He sighed heavily, shaking his head. "I'm ashamed, Jake. I've always been ashamed of my love for your mother. You know this," he reminded me. I already knew all this, but it was different now, now that I knew he was my real father. I couldn't wrap my head around it. This man who'd been a part of my life, *my entire life*. "Kate and Michael weren't married yet. She was confused. She chose Michael."

Chapter 18

ALYSSA

I stood as close to the kitchen door as possible, leaning my cheek against the cool wood and trying to eavesdrop, but I couldn't decipher anything. I'd left my phone in the bedroom, and now I didn't know when Nadine would be back. I looked at the clock; an hour had gone by. She'd said at least an hour. I slumped, turning back to the brown paper sacks that stared at me. My stomach rumbled. I was hungry, even though emotions were tearing up my insides. I wished I could hear what Jake and Notting were saying.

I decided to eat without Jake. With all the insanity, who knew how long they'd be talking anyway? I tore open the bag, taking out the white cartons by their thin metal handles. My stomach churned and my mouth watered. I glanced at the clock again, and then decided just to go down to the lobby and wait for Nadine. I identified the chicken chow mien and grabbed a fork. Me and the 'mien would sit and wait for Nadine downstairs. I exited through the service door in the kitchen.

I threw Miguel a nod and a smile, and watched him talk to one of our older building residents. I sat down on one of the many lounges that peppered the granite lobby. The woman he spoke to lived on our floor. I opened the box of chow mien, and the steam rose upward, filling my nose. I was happy it was still heated. I stuck my fork into it and took a mouthful. The old lady was complaining about the mail delivery and pointing her skeletal finger at poor Miguel's chest. As if he had any control over the inefficiency of the United States Postal Service. Every time she lifted her arm, her unfortunate little Pomaranian's head jerked upward with the leash, and it yipped and whined. I wanted to grab the leash from her bony hand and poke her in the chest.

I couldn't take the lady talking down to Miguel anymore, and got up, walking outside into the warm evening air. Cars and cabs swooshed by, and I kept feeding myself while I took in the movement around me. I eased back against the warm stone wall of our building, just outside the doors, and watched the locals stroll along to wherever it was they were going. I was devouring the noodles, and realized I should probably stop, or Jake wouldn't have anything to eat.

"Hey Aly." A male voice startled me, and I jumped, looking up from my food. It was Marty.

"Hi." I said, chewing faster and swallowing my mouthful. "Sorry." I shrugged impishly and wiped my mouth with the back of my hand, and then my hand on the side my cotton dress. "I don't mean to be so gross." I laughed off my boorish conduct. "Sorry, I wasn't expecting you."

He smiled looking down at his feet. "You're not gross." He laughed. "I'm sorry for coming unannounced. I've just been trying to get ahold of Jake since SNL, and haven't heard back."

I nodded, sadly. "There's some family drama going on."

His eyes went wide. "I'm sorry to hear that. I hope everything is okay?"

I sighed. "It will be. It's a big deal thing." I nodded again. "I'm sure Jake will fill you in."

Marty shuffled his feet closer to me and handed me an envelope. "I was gonna leave this for you, actually."

"Me?"

"Yeah. I know Jake is really busy as it is, without the family drama, and I just didn't want to bother him anymore. So I left my contact information for you, and inquired if all was good." He backed away from me, and seemed to have trouble looking me in the eye.

"Marty. I'm not going to bite you."

He laughed nervously. "I know. I feel bad for catching you off guard, and I know Jake wouldn't like me speaking to you alone, like this." He backed away farther, like I had a disease. "Jake sent me a text to block several weeks off in October for that Eva tour, and I just need to talk to him more about it."

The smile fell from my face, even though I didn't mean for it to, and Marty caught it. "I'm sorry. Did I say something wrong?"

I composed myself. *Fucking Eva.* "No, no." I focused on the first part of his statement. "Why would Jake mind you talking to me? Like this?"

He cleared his throat. "Um, he just said that you're off-limits, and I want to respect that."

My eyes tightened. "Really." It wasn't a question.

Marty smiled, and his eyebrows rose up his forehead. "I *am* a paparazzi after all."

He instantly lightened my mood. "You're a friend now, Marty. I don't think Jake would have you around if he didn't trust you."

Marty gave me a tight grin. "Okay, well, in that case, you have my information, and, well…just let Jake know that I need to talk to him."

Just as Marty strolled away, Nadine pulled up in a cab, waving animatedly at me. She whipped open the door and trotted up to me. "What. Is. Up?" she practically shouted in my face. "Dude, do I have something to tell you!"

"Are you drunk?" I wondered, and didn't doubt it.

"No! But I wish I was. Let's get drunk." Her eyes bolted wider. "You're gonna shit when you hear this. I'm kinda sick about it." She grabbed my wrist and dragged me towards the door. Just as we stepped inside and our heels hit the granite, we ran into Jake and Notting.

Jake gave me a gloom-laced half-smile, and he placed his hands on my shoulders, piercing me with his impossible blue eyes. They were darker than normal, and matched his mood. The warmth of his hands against my skin gave me the chills. I wanted to kiss him, love him, take away all the pain and confusion he must have been feeling. "We're gonna go for a walk, and I'm not sure when I'll be back." He noticed the food carton in my hand. "I'm glad you ate."

"Hey Notting. How's it going?" Nadine chirped happily. I wanted to slap her.

"Hello, Nadine." He tipped his head. "How are you liking New York?"

"I want to move here," she gushed, curling her arms to her chest. "I just have to talk Aly and Jake into me living with them." She laughed mildly, looking between all of us. I knew she meant it.

"I'll catch up with you guys later," Jake announced, and walked away, dragging his feet.

"Good to see you, Nadine. Aly." Notting saluted us and followed Jake out the doors.

———

Nadine sat with a bowl of rice and the rest of my chow mien in her hand, shoveling bites into her mouth. "I'm freaking starving."

"What the hell did you do all day with Sienna?"

Nadine shook her head as she bit off a noodle. She chewed and held up her hand, pointing at me to wait. She took a deep breath. "I think she's losing her mind."

Breath escaped me. "I would, too, if I knew Jake was probably gonna die."

She shook her head fervidly. "No. I get that. But she thinks Jake is going to take care of her."

"Okay," I droned, looking confused.

"She was talking crazy, like she was gonna move in with him…or you guys. She just kept talking, like – *"God forbid Dump doesn't get better…Jake said he'd take care of me. Dump said Jake would take care of me."*

My stomach sank, and my thoughts bounced around. Of course he would make sure she was okay and settled. What a nightmare. "Yeah. Of course Jake wouldn't just abandon her."

"No, Aly, this was different." Her eyes sprung wide, looking at me like I was stupid, then she shrugged. "But then again, I don't know what I would do either, if I might lose the love of my life." She sighed soberly. "Shit, man, I've never been in love."

"It's a pain in the ass."

155

"I want someone to be a pain in my ass." She grinned and stuffed another forkful in her mouth.

"But seriously. How is he? How's Dump? Did you see him?"

She shook her head no, chewing.

"What did you guys do?"

"We went to some place called the Meatball Shop." Her eyes went big. "Dude, you totally have to go there. They have all kinds of meatballs, gourmet shit, and they have homemade ice cream sandwiches."

"What are you, a foodie now?

"You fucking better believe it!" She placed her empty bowl on the coffee table. "I've dreamt about coming here, and eating and drinking and walking and breathing Gotham my entire life. Who knows when I'll be able to afford coming back?"

I smiled, uneasy. My mind was still on Sienna. "Did you *not* wanna see Dump?"

She looked solemn. "Is that bad?" Her green eyes danced around my face.

I shook my head. "No. I mean, yes and no. It's depressing. It's awful, and I'd feel the same way if I came to visit you for a fun time and got thrown into miserable circumstances." I sighed heavily, thinking of my own sad situation.

Nadine shook my knee. "What's up?

"Well, you know about Notting and Jake."

She threw her head back. "Crazy times. I mean, what the hell is going on?"

"I'm going crazy. *I am.*" I pointed to myself.

"Why?"

"What's that saying, sometimes love isn't enough?"

156

Nadine pushed herself forward. "What are you saying?"

"I'm saying that I can't stay here."

"What. The. Fuck." Her hand covered her mouth, then dropped into her lap. "Does Jake know?"

"I think so, but we haven't talked about anything because of what his mother just sprung on him." I slumped downward, deeper into the sofa. "The whole idea of this life is amazing, and if I wanted to just be a wife and tag along in Jake's life, then it would be cool. But I want to do my own thing right now, and I thought I could do it here, at NYU. But I don't think I can. I'd be an idiot to not take these next four years and just do the right thing by me and my parents."

"Dude, you can't live your life for your parents," Nadine said to the ceiling, picking food out of her teeth.

I sneered at her. "I'm not an idiot. You know what I mean."

Nadine looked around the room. "You guys have it all, Aly."

"Not yet, we don't." I thought about Jake's upcoming tour and Eva.

An hour passed by as I filled her in on the entire SNL night, and how Jake sprung the Eva tour on me. All Nadine could do was shake her head in disbelief. She couldn't fathom saying no to someone like Jake. I lined up all the sorry reasons why things were so messed up, and she kept lining up why things were so right for us. She thumped me on the forehead more than once, trying to convince me to marry him. Finally, I got up and moved to a chair on the other side of the coffee table. Just as I was about to continue with my four-year-plan, Jake came through the door with Marty.

Marty smiled sheepishly and waved. Nadine stood up, smiling with a curious glint in her eye. I looked at Jake and Marty, and back at Nadine. Marty leaned over and asked Jake something I couldn't make out; then Jake pointed toward the hallway. Marty had to use the bathroom.

"Who's that?" Nadine whispered to me and smiled at Jake. "How's it?"

"Been better." He placed his keys on the foyer table.

"What's goin' on?" Jake's tired eyes hopped back and forth between Nadine and I.

"We're talking about your future," Nadine offered.

I huffed and my mouth hit the ground. "Nadine, shut up."

"What?" She threw her arms out. "Not gonna lie. This whole thing here…" She made a circling gesture with her hand. "Is some jacked-up shit. You people need to figure it out and live the happy life you've been planning for. Sorry, Jake, about all the family stuff, but you guys need to take care of you guys." With her poorly strung-together and lamely timed words, she plopped back down on the sofa.

Jake just shook his head, and Marty came waltzing back out, looking hip and nerdy all at the same time, with his mussed hair and pressed button-up tucked in beneath his slim-fitting khakis. He wore tan boat shoes. What an adorable nerd he was. I smiled, watching him shift nervously, and then Nadine's loud voice broke the silence.

"So who are you?" Nadine smiled coyly, batting her eyes.

Oh my God. Jake threw me a horrified look, and I tried not to laugh.

"Uh, I'm Marty."

"I'm Nadine. Aly's best friend in the whole entire world, and the rock in Jake's shoe," she announced, matter-of-fact and pleased.

This made Marty laugh. "Great to meet you."

"So what do you do?" Nadine tilted her head, tucking her blonde hair behind her ears as if she was sincerely curious.

Jake moved over to me as Nadine talked up Marty. "What's wrong with your friend?" he murmured in my ear, and smiled in spite of himself. He folded his arms around my waist.

"I'm the band's videographer," Marty answered proudly.

Nadine studied him more closely. "That's right. You're the guy who did the interview with them when they announced Dump had cancer."

I wanted to stuff my fist in her mouth. Why did she have to sound so brash?

"Yes. That'd be me."

She nodded. "Nice to meet you, Marty."

"Likewise."

"So what are you doing right now?" she asked him directly.

He gulped. I don't think he was used to talking to girls in social settings, especially girls like Nadine. "I'm just headed home."

"You gotta work early?"

"I kinda work my own hours."

"Great!" she sang out. "You wanna grab a drink? My treat!"

Marty didn't know what to do with himself and looked over at us. He pushed his specs higher onto his nose, stood up taller, and gulped again. "Sure."

"Right on, Marty. I promise Nadine won't eat you alive." Jake looked over to Nadine, laughing. "Right? You promise?"

159

Nadine smirked playfully. "Oh no. I may only be motivated to have a taste."

"Oh my God. I can't take this," I said, laughing, and untied myself from Jake's arms. "Marty. I'm sorry about these two. Nadine's harmless."

"I'm just fucking with you, Marty," Nadine smiled, shoving his shoulder. "Please come out with me. I know these two don't wanna go anywhere, and it's still early."

"I would love to escort you out for the evening." He tipped his head.

"Sweet!" Nadine jumped up.

In a whirl, they vanished. I was still standing in the same spot, wondering how Marty's timid nature would make out against Nadine's boldness. Marty would probably have the time of his life.

"Wow. What just happened there?" Jake asked as he moved to the sofa.

He appeared to be upbeat, and I was dying to know how his talk went with Notting, and to feel his skin against mine. I walked over to him. "Don't get comfortable." I nudged his knees as I stood in front of him. His eyes hung low, and I could see desire flickered as he sat up, grabbing my calves. His hands ran up under my dress and over my thighs and butt, resting on my hips. He nuzzled my belly, and the heat from his breath made my knees go weak and my fingertips tingle.

"You're still not wearing any underwear," he muttered against my body.

"I wasn't planning on going anywhere."

He massaged my hipbones with his thumbs, rubbing gently down over my groin. I wanted him to keep going. I wanted his mouth and his velvety tongue prodding me. As if he read my thoughts, he lifted my dress, and the heat of his moist mouth took me. I gasped in ecstasy, and thought I would collapse.

"That fast?" he said, his voice deep with desire. "I'm getting' pretty good."

I panted. "Almost, but not quite." I took his lips to mine. "I'm gonna fall down if you don't lay me down somewhere."

He scooped me up in his arms and hauled me off to bed.

Chapter 19

ALYSSA

It was annoyingly bright, and I squinted my eyes trying to get a glace at the clock. It read 7:15 AM. I turned to look at Jake. He was still sleeping, looking yummy and rumpled. His full lips puckered out as his face squeezed into the pillow. I wanted to kiss them, but I didn't. I didn't want to wake him. I knew he'd tossed and turned the whole night. Every time I rolled over, he was up, the light from his phone cast over his face, reading or texting, doing who knows what.

I slipped out of bed to make coffee, and I peeked in on Nadine. She wasn't there. *Oh my God. No, she didn't!* I thought, smiling. "She fucking did. I just know it," I said out loud, and laughed quietly, padding in to the kitchen. I looked for my phone on every surface. I sighed, realizing I'd left it in my purse in the bedroom. I got the coffee brewing and snuck back into the bedroom to retrieve my phone when Jake's horse voice startled me.

"Alycat, what you doin' creepin' around?" He rolled over to get a better look at me.

I giggled. "Isn't that what cats are supposed to do?"

"Creep on over here." He patted the space next to him.

163

I dug in my bag and looked at my phone. Good girl, Nadine. She did text after all, letting me know she was with Marty and watching a movie over at his place. That was at 3 AM. "Nadine stayed with Marty last night," I snickered.

Jake looked at me like he was hearing things. His face bent and his eyebrows furrowed. "No way."

"Yes way." I showed him the text message.

"Slut." He smiled.

I huffed and grabbed my phone from him. "It's probably the best time Marty's ever had in his life."

Jake laughed out loud. "I wish I was there to watch how *that* all went down. He probably pissed himself." He laughed harder. "Speaking of." He got out of bed, holding an obvious pee boner, and I watched his bare buns disappear into the bathroom.

Anxiety flushed through me. I didn't want to leave New York. I didn't want to this to end, not even for a minute. I wanted to have it all. Why couldn't he just move back to California? My stomach turned. I sucked in a deep breath and forced the issue from my mind. I wouldn't leave until he left on tour with Eva, *if* that's what I decided to do. Fucking Eva. I punched the pillow like it was her face as I got out of bed to get coffee.

Jake met me in the kitchen with his drawstring pj's hanging low. "Nice view." I fingered his cute butt crack.

"You like that?" He threw me a crooked grin and scratched the back of his neck. I sipped my hot coffee with all its creamy goodness, enjoying the moment, admiring his tattoo of me and my musical hair. Maybe I would just say yes and get married. Fuck it. Go to school here. Have babies and just be his for the rest of my life. I smiled at the thought, the simplicity of the choice.

"I hear wheels turning."

Ugh, he knew me so well. "I want it to be like this forever."

"It can be." He tapped the spoon on the side of his cup and then stuck it in mouth, looking over at me, melting me with his mussed hotness. "If you stay."

Crash.

I took a big gulp, as if I needed to wake up more. Maybe the caffeine rush would stop my already out-of-control heart, and I could just die happy right there. I couldn't believe he was finally calling me out on it. Just when I was thinking about it, maybe we did have a connection like no one else. He read me like I was an open book.

"Look Aly. I've been wanting to talk to you about it." He took a sip of his coffee, and I watched the steam caress his face. "With all this shit going on with my mom and Notting… and Dump. I just don't know. I know you're not happy."

"I am happy, Jake." I stepped over to him. "What makes you think I'm not happy?"

"I watched you the other day, at NYU, for a long time. You're not gonna be happy there. I know it." His face wore an expression that made my stomach sink: wretchedness on his face again. He looked as if we were breaking up. Just like he did all those years ago. "I just don't know what to do about it all."

We stood side-by-side, leaning against the counter, drinking our coffee, in silence. We were at a crossroads, two semi-trucks headed in different directions. Tension and guilt spread over me.

"Move back to LA. Just 'til I finish school."

He scratched the back of his neck. "Aly, I'm not gonna be home anyway."

He didn't say anything else. My heart froze and my limbs turned to ice. "What are you saying?"

He placed his coffee cup on the counter and turned to face me. We were so close I could feel his aura wrap around me like a warm blanket. "Aly, you're the blood that courses through my veins. I'd rather slit my wrists and bleed out than not have you in my life. You're my anchor. You're the reason for any of this."

I could feel it all slipping away. That woeful saying popped in my head – *when love isn't enough*. I wanted to be sick. The heaviness of truth constrained me. I didn't want the truth. I didn't want *this* reality. I wanted the reality that we'd planned for.

"I'm not going anywhere yet. I'm not gonna give up on this."

He reached out and pulled me over to him. I wrapped my arms around his warm bare torso and pressed my cheek to his chest. "I can't have you stay here knowing it's not what you want or need."

Now I really felt I was going to be sick. "Are you breaking up with me?" I said, shocked by his words.

"No. No I'm not. I don't want to be without you."

"Then what are you saying?" I tried to pull away, but he held me tightly.

"I'm saying that you..." he paused, treading, thinking. "We need to do what's best for both of us."

"And?"

"And maybe you should go to school where it's best for you, not for me."

"So basically you're kicking me out?"

"Aly, stop it."

My mind reeled. *Breathe.* I *did* need to stop, because he was right, but I didn't want him making the choice for me. "Look," I said, forcing myself from his grip. "I'll make that choice, unless you're using this as some excuse to get rid of me. I mean where is this coming from, anyway? I don't believe you can make a call like that based on one afternoon of watching me play. There's more to school than playing volleyball." Now I was lying to myself, but it was the truth, sort of. I had to get an education somewhere, volleyball or not.

He shook his head. "I'm going to leave this up to you, but I know." He placed the palm of his hand on his chest. "I feel it, Aly. You're not happy. Yeah, sure, you're happy with us. I want *us* as much as you do. But I can't have you here, with everything else going on, knowing that you could be some-where excelling and living the way you want to."

So now I was a burden? "I can take care of myself, Jake. I know what I have to do. I love it here. It might not be the most ideal place to play volleyball…" I stopped, catching the words I was saying. They sounded ridiculous, even to me. Volleyball was what saved me from my Jake misery in the first place. It was a part of me like the skin on my body, but so was Jake. "You know what, never mind. You're right." I stood taller, rigid. "I'll figure it out."

Jake smiled softly, but it didn't reach his eyes. They were a pool of murky blue sadness.

"What else? You look like you have more to say." I prod-ded, and my nerves tightened around my veins. He stepped away, leaning against the other counter, facing me.

He sighed and folded his toned arms to his chest. "All this shit that's happened, that's happening right now with Dump and my mom, just has me thinking about life, Aly. My whole world has been turned upside down," he paused, searching my face. "And then I have you here." He rubbed his face with the palms of his hands. I stood paralyzed, waiting for him to continue. What was he trying to say? *Me here — me here what?* Worry coursed through me.

He grabbed my hand and suggested we move into the living room, *our* living room, the room I'd decorated for us to begin our lives together. I let my hand settle loosely into his, not wanting to hold on too tightly. I didn't want him to think I was desperate, even though I felt it like a looming storm brewing inside me. He might not tell me what he was really thinking if he thought I would break down.

I sat down lightly onto the sofa and tucked my legs up underneath me. "What's on your mind?" I inquired, trying to sound upbeat.

"I just want you to be happy, Aly."

"Okay. I am happy." I smiled as sincerely as I could, but he wasn't looking at me. He just stared at his hands that sat in his lap.

"I was so focused on you coming here and being with me and going to school, just those two things. I mean, I knew we discussed the whole school thing, and it all seemed like it would work and it still might." He finally looked at me. "It still might work the way we planned it. The way we spoke about it, I should say." He stopped there and just looked at me, his blue eyes intently taking me in. "You knew you had reservations, Aly." He shook his head. "And you never told me. I had to hear about it from your dad."

My stomach went sour. I tried to ignore that fact. I still wanted to ignore it. "Jake, I just want to make the right choice, and as far as I'm concerned, you're the right choice."

His shoulders slumped and he moved closer to me. Then he leaned over, kissing my shoulder. "I wanna always be your first choice." He continued with the little tender kisses, his lips warm and soft against my skin, and my insides turned to mush. "I just want you to make the right choice for your future." He sat up. "Like I did when I left California."

I felt slight panic arise. I knew he was right, but I still didn't know what I wanted to do. I really felt like I wanted to try and make this going to school in New York thing work. "I need time to think about it. That's why I put off school to the spring in the first place."

"So you knew you might change your mind?"

I was embarrassed. I felt stupid for not being honest with him in the first place. "I didn't know what I wanted to do about school. All I know is I want to be with you."

I felt so juvenile, so inadequate at that moment. I sounded so young and dumb, playing back the words that had just fallen out of my mouth, but they were the truth. Just like Jake's words – all he thought about was having me with him. We were both young and dumb. We sat for a long while in silence. Jake turned on the TV and we just sat, staring at it. I didn't even know what we were watching. He finally took my hand in his, and this time I held it and brought it to my chest.

I was holding on to it like if I let it go it would all slip away for good.

—

Nadine finally breezed through the door at 10:15 AM. Jake and I attacked her with questions. She held up her hands for us to halt with our torrent of words, as she laughed wide-eyed in disbelief that we could be so concerned about her whereabouts.

"You know this is all *so* flattering that you both care about what I've been doing." She crumbled into the chair next to us, looking worse for the wear. "Oh, Jake, if you weren't sitting there half-dressed with your sexy half showing, I would almost believe you really cared."

I held in my laugh and shot a glance at Jake, and he was actually blushing. Then I guffawed. "Oh, look, Nadine! You embarrassed him."

"No she didn't," he stated firmly and slowly, grabbing the pillow next to him and covered his chest. "Nadine, stop staring at my tits."

We all laughed heartily. Nadine was the first to quiet down, and looked contemplative. "You know. I think I could be in love with Marty."

My mouth fell open, and I quickly shut it and glanced at Jake. He looked horrified. "Um, what?" I asked, as if I missed what she said. Maybe I was hearing things.

"You gotta be kidding me!" Jake snickered. "Nadine. Do. Not. Fuck with Marty. He's a nice kid, and…"

"Kid?" Nadine cut in. "He's only a few years younger than you, Jake. He's the same age as me."

"Nadine, you can't be serious. You *just* met him, and…"

"And he's not your type!" Jake barked loudly and stood up. "Are you fucking kidding us? Did you fuck around with him?" Jake hovered over her like an anxious mother hen.

"Oh my God!" I nearly spit, holding in my laughter. Jake looked as if he was seriously concerned. He couldn't be. Could he? "Jake!"

"What?" He looked over at me, and then laid his eyes back on Nadine. "Did you?"

Nadine looked at me, alarmed. "He isn't seriously serious, is he?" Her forehead crinkled with concern.

"Jake, stop it!" I laughed anxiously.

"Okay, calm down!" She sat up straight, holding her hands up. "No, I didn't fuck him." She looked at me thoughtfully. "But if he tried, I probably woulda."

Jake slapped his forehead, collapsing down on the sofa. He fell over onto me, burying his head in my lap. "What is going on with our life, and the people in it?" His muffled warm breath seeped over my thighs. I lifted my leg, forcing him to sit up.

"What's the big deal if she did, anyway?" I wondered out loud.

"Yeah!" Nadine chimed.

"First of all, the guy works for me, and second of all…" Jake began to stammer. "I just…I don't need you getting him all jacked up in the head. The guy probably never had a girlfriend, and…and now you come strolling into his life." He got up, looking at the both of us like we'd lost our minds, and disappeared into the other room.

"Oh my God," Nadine said under her breath, covering her mouth. "Is he really upset?"

I nodded. "I think so." I was still smiling, trying not to laugh. "I can't believe how upset he his."

"I can hear you!" he shouted and came from out from the hallway, pulling a shirt over his head.

"What is going on with you?" I demanded. "Why are you freaking out?"

He shook his head, a forlorn look stamped on his face. "Nadine, I just don't need any more bullshit happening around me. I don't know Marty all that well, but what I do know is he's a good guy, and you're leaving back to California. When are you leaving anyway?"

Nadine pouted. "In a few days, on Monday."

"Okay, and when are you seeing him again?"

Nadine looked sheepish.

"Are. You. Seeing. Him. Again?" Jake asked, agitated.

I had to do something. Jake was acting like a crazy person. "Hey." I placed myself in front of him. "You stop this. She's not a child, and neither is he." I stood on my tiptoes and gave him a quick peck on the lips.

"I just don't want him getting all fucked up in the head because of her." He threw his arm out at Nadine. "No offense, Nadine. I just can't deal with stepping on one more piece of shit."

"I get it," Nadine said, remorsefully. "I'm sorry."

"Don't be sorry!" I cried.

She smiled slyly. "I'm not sorry." She shook her head, and threw Jake a surly glance. "Don't be a dick, Jake. He's got balls, and asked me to hang out again. He's gonna be here in an hour. We're gonna go to the Museum of Natural History. You two should come with us." She spun on her heels and walked towards the guestroom. "I think he's…what's a good word for him?" Nadine said, turning back to face us. She looked at the ceiling and crossed her arms to her chest, tapping her lips with an index finger. "He's groovy, smart, and unlike anyone I've met. So why not?"

Chapter 20
ALYSSA

I never did like tourist crowds, and being in a sea of people when feeling the weight of uncertainty pressing down on me was nearly unbearable. I wanted to talk more. All of a sudden, I felt the urge to hash out our differences, and get to the bottom of what would be the best for the both of us as a couple and as individuals.

All I could hear in my head were the echoing of his words – *"I'm gonna be gone anyway."* What the hell was that supposed to mean? That it didn't matter where I was at, because he would be gone? Basically, it was the sad truth, and I had to deal with it, and dealing with it back in Los Angeles was the best thing for me. He was right. Why would I want to stay in New York, when he'd be gone anyway? It would be one thing if I loved the volleyball team at NYU. I could see myself staying here and being happy with my school life, but without volleyball and him, New York didn't make any sense. Not any more.

We finally made our way through the throngs of school children and tourists at the entrance. I had yet to visit this museum, and I kept thinking about the movie *Night at the Museum* with Ben Stiller and Owen Wilson. Immediately, I wanted to go find *"Dum Dum"* the Easter Island talking Tiki. I took out my map, and I felt Jake's arm surround my shoulders.

"I've never been here before," he admitted.

"Really?" I questioned. I wasn't really surprised that he hadn't. It made me feel pleased to know we were experiencing something for the first time together.

"Never really wanted to." He shrugged.

"I did. I'm glad Nadine had the idea."

"It was my idea," Marty piped, looking back over his shoulder. I didn't realize he could hear us, let alone would be paying attention to what we were saying. "This place is awesome. Sometimes I come here to read."

My first thought was, *what a nerd*, and then I glanced at Nadine. She was smiling up at him as if she really thought he was cool. I scolded myself for being snarky. I loved to read too, but in my house or when I was waiting somewhere. It never crossed my mind to venture out to a public place purely for the enjoyment of reading.

The clicking of heels on the beige travertine floors and the sound of hundreds of voices swirled together, flooding the halls. We made our way to *Dum Dum*. We stood in front of the gigantic Tiki, staring and waiting as if it'd say something to us at any second.

Jake moved towards it so quickly, he made me jump. He wrapped his arms around it. "I loved you in *A Night at the Museum*."

"There's a sign that says not to touch him." I pointed.

"Oooo!" Nadine's voice rang out, trumping my concern. "Take a picture!" She grabbed Marty's hand, dragging him over to the massive piece of stone. "Okay! Be funny!" Nadine ordered.

I held up my phone and snapped away as the three of them posed on one leg, made corny faces and embraced each other humorously. "Okay. I think I got some good ones," I announced and a bit of jealousy ran through me that I wasn't in any of them.

I considering each image as the three of them had moved ahead of me. I watched as Nadine hung on Marty's arm as Jake lumbered a step behind, his hands crammed deep into his pockets – a sign he was uneasy. Finally he noticed I wasn't beside him, and he turned, looking for me. When he spotted me, he held his arms out to the side and waved at me to hurry it up.

Suddenly a sinking feeling overcame me, and the people around him seemed to blend into the exhibits. This was it. This part of our lives together was ending. I felt it like turbulence on a plane, and it made me sick. I forced a smile, pretending, trying to suppress the words of fear and anxiety that were about to gurgle out of my mouth. Jake reached out, wrapping his warm hand around my neck, pulling me into him as we walked in silence.

"Are you okay?" I knew I wasn't. I wanted to talk. I wanted to try and work the tension out. "I know you feel it."

"I do." He squeezed me tighter to him.

"What's gonna happen?"

"I love you." I barely heard him say it, and by this time, we'd stopped in front of some bird exhibit. "I feel lost." Jake's voice was barely a whisper, and he didn't look at me. I took in his profile in the dim lighting as he stared up at the fake trees and foliage. I reached out and played with his earlobe, and he finally looked at me. "I don't want to lose you, Aly." He shook his head. "I feel on the verge of empty."

175

"You'll never lose me." He wouldn't. I would always be his.

"You say that now, but the reality of it is…" he paused, shaking his head. "Neither of us will want to be alone for too long." He turned, walking over to a nearby bench, sitting down. "Come here."

He held out his arm to me. I felt like I my tongue was attached to the roof of my mouth. I took his hand and sat down next to him, feeling the stone's coolness instantly seep through the thin fabric of my dress. What? He wouldn't be able to keep his dick in his pants for too long if I wasn't around? Was that what he was trying to say? I searched his face, and his eyes were pained, squelching my harmful thoughts. I gulped down my doubts, but really, why would he say such things? My breathing became shallow, searching for what to say. Then he spoke again.

"My life is in the shitter. I mean, yeah, whatever I know people have it worse, like Dump. He's all I think about, and I feel guilty for thinking what I'm gonna do about not having him on the road with me. I think about him and how sick he is whenever I start to feel sorry for myself about my dad not being my dad. My mom not *knowing*…" his voice trailed off and he shook his head in disbelief. "How could she not know, not have one little inkling, not one! And then Notting? Fuck!"

His voice rose in frustration and I felt like a jerk for thinking of only myself and *my* feelings. "He's been dragged through the mud. Notting's my fucking dad, Aly. He's been my dad the whole time. He's the one who raised me as his own and now I'm really his. It's the craziest, most fucked up thing in the world."

Hearing his words made me feel insignificant. Jake's world was being rocked, and with my inevitable departure I hoped that wouldn't capsize it. I leaned close to him, wrapping my arms around his neck, nuzzling the side of his face, whispering in his ear. "I'm sorry." I softly kissed the side of his jaw. "I can't imagine…"

Jake suddenly laid a kiss on my lips, shutting me up. "Marry me, Aly," he whispered into my mouth. "Let me take care of you. None of what I said matters. Only you. You're the only constant. The only thing, the only person in my life that's been real."

My mind spun, and I felt a pang of guilt and desperation, because I wanted to say yes so badly. "Jake," I breathed in and held it.

The corners of his mouth turned upward ever so slightly, but misery was radiating from his eyes. "You're still not saying yes."

"You know I want to."

"Actually, I don't."

"I do."

"Then why not?" He stared at me intently. His blue eyes shimmered like a pool lit up in the night.

I thought about what he'd said to me right before we sat down. "For one, what you said just a minute ago, about neither one of us wanting to be alone for too long. Why'd you say that?"

"Because it's the truth."

"Okay, we get married, and I go to school back in LA, and then what?"

"That's different."

I huffed. He wasn't making any sense. "Why is it different?" My stomach began to turn. "Because we won't be together, and what? You'll end up in someone else's arms because you'll be lonely?"

"Because we'll be married." Jake held my hand and brought it to his mouth, kissing each fingertip. "Do you know that your parents are the only ones that I know of, out of all my friends, who seem to have done the marriage thing right?" He nodded. "I believe in that."

I could have melted, hearing his words and seeing the way he looked at me, with the most sincere expression of promise and love. But all I could think about was his mom, Kate, and Notting. I gulped. "Jake we don't need a piece of paper. Kate and Notting never had a piece of paper, but have had each other's hearts from beginning." I squeezed his hand, shifting to face him directly. "Your dad…"

"He's not my dad," Jake cut in bitterly, shaking his head. "You know I've been giving this a lot of thought. He didn't want to be with my mother; he could have asked her for a divorce instead of cheating on her, and she and Notting could have been together a long time ago."

Jake took the words right out of my mouth. "Exactly. That's what I was going to say. They had the piece of paper and it didn't matter. It doesn't matter."

"But it matters to me," he said sternly, looking at me with forceful eyes. "But you know what? I'm done here." He leaned over with his elbows on his knees, shaking his head. His next words were only a murmur, and they tore at my heart. "I've asked you to marry me I don't know how many times. I'm not asking anymore. When you're ready to marry me, just say when, and I'll be there." Jake stood and tucked his hands in his pant pockets and just stared down at me. "I think I've said that before too, but I mean it this time."

I had to pick my chin up from the ground. My nerves were shot, and I felt my eye twitching. A bit of anger bubbled.

"Four years is a long time, Jake. Are you trying to tell me that while I'm in school, we're free game?"

He slumped. "I don't wanna fight with you, Aly. I want you to be happy, but I'm not delusional in the fact that four months after you left London, you were hanging out with Sporto again."

"And you were still sleeping with Sophia," I spat out resentfully and crossed my arms to my chest. "How dare you."

Jake stepped toward me. I wasn't having it, and turned, swiftly walking away before I said more words I'd regret. He never admitted to sleeping with her after London, but I knew it my heart he had. How did it get like this? We were so happy just a couple of months ago. All because I wasn't ready to be married and I wanted to go to school and follow *my* dreams?

Jake sprinted in front of me, stopping me in my tracks, and wrapped his arms around me. He kissed my forehead and breathed me in. A huge lump formed in my throat. We just stood there, not moving, like mythical Greek statues: entwined forever, cast in our tragic star-crossed love affair.

"What's gonna happen?" The heat of my breath against Jake's chest warmed my face. He held me tighter.

"You tell me, Aly. It's all in your court. What are you thinking?"

I wanted to fall at his feet. The weight of our future sat upon my shoulders like a ton of bricks. "I was thinking I'd leave when you left on tour with Eva." I felt Jake's hold on me recede, and he took in a deep breathe. I pulled my arms from their tucked position between us and wrapped them around him. "You were right."

"I knew you wouldn't be happy at NYU as soon as I saw you that day at practice."

"I'm sorry." I began to cry. "I wanted it to be, I wanted it to work out so badly, Jake."

"Hey, stop." He lifted my chin and kissed away my tears. "Aly we made it this far. Nothing's gonna keep us apart. We'll always find a way."

"I'm sorry about the apartment. All the money you've spent," I sniveled. The guilt overwhelmed me.

"That apartment is ours. It'll always be there for you and me. You come whenever you want, even when I'm not there." He kissed me softly on the lips, and the warmth of them made me weak. I ran my hands up under his shirt. Feeling his skin beneath my hands made me want all of him bare against me. The all-too-familiar yearning and desperation filled me.

We were once again on borrowed time.

Chapter 21

JAKE

The metal door handle was greasy beneath my hand. I released it as soon as my palm slid around. *Disgusting*, I thought. What was wrong with people? *We're in a financial institution for fuck's sake!* I looked around, wondering if the scumbag was inside, and I spotted a barrel-bellied man, tucked neatly into his black well-tailored suit, gnawing on a hotdog with sauerkraut dripping from the bun. You can buy nice things, but you can't buy class. What a tool. It had to be him. Stupid fuck.

I made my way to the bathroom of the American Express office to wash my hands. I was there to pick up a credit card that I'd decided to get Aly. She was leaving in a week. I wanted her to have the freedom to come and go from New York whenever she wanted. I wanted her to leave all her things in the apartment. She could buy whatever she needed when she got back to California; I wanted New York to be her second home.

She was right. We didn't need a piece of paper to be committed to each other, I told myself. I wasn't looking forward to Aly's departure, but as much as it was torturously at the forefront of my mind, I was in survival mode with my band shit. Dump was stable, and his bone marrow was testing clean: zero cancer. I was now hopeful that he'd survive, but it would still be a long haul until he'd be back on the road or in the studio with us. Devon had stepped in seamlessly and I was relieved, that was one less worry.

I scratched my name down, *Masters*, and my representative's name, *Cheryl*, and waited my turn. I watched Cheryl from a distance. She was tall, very attractive, yet an imposing woman in her mid-fifties with black shoulder-length hair and big, dark eyes. She always wore the same thing: a cream-colored blouse with a slim-fitting black knee-length skirt. She never deviated, and I wondered what she was like outside of work, she barely smiled at anyone, always business. I wondered if she smiled more at home. I watched as she said her goodbyes to an older couple and walked over to the reception desk, inquiring with the young studious girl who sat there. Cheryl looked up and waved me over, no smile.

She extended her hand to me. "Hello Mr. Masters," she nodded as she gripped my hand firmly. This woman seriously needed to get laid; she was too uptight. And then a personal question popped out of my mouth.

"Cheryl, are you attached?" Her yes popped out with surprise, but she quickly settled back to her cool demeanor. "I'm sorry, I know it's a very personal question. But I've been your client for years, and I was watching you now, and I'm just wondering."

"Why, do you want to ask me out on a date?" Her head tipped back. I could see her suppressing a smile as she pressed her lips tightly together. *Ah ha! I got you!* I thought, laughing internally. "I don't date younger men, Mr. Masters." She turned to face me directly as we reached her desk, and she gestured for me to sit. Her lips lifted upward (barely), and I couldn't counter her assumption. Whether she was serious or not, I let it ride.

"Fair enough," I smiled, winking at her.

Her mouth hinged open, then clamped shut, and an even bigger (for her) smile appeared on her face. She breathed in deeply, looking down at her hands as they pressed flatly into her desk. Without looking back at me, she turned to face her computer and began typing away.

"Ah, I see. You're here to pick up a credit card for an Alyssa Montgomery, correct?"

"Yes, that's correct."

Cheryl took a set of keys into her hand and unlocked her desk drawer, pulling out an envelope and handed it to me. "Ms. Montgomery has been added as a joint account holder." She paused, taking me in, and then she barely smiled at me, again. "You are aware that you will be responsible for any charges made to this account."

"Yes. I'm aware," I nodded, smiling.

Cheryl nodded back. "This type of account has no limit."

"Yes, I know that too."

She stared at me a bit longer, as if I'd lost my mind. I could tell she wanted to ask more questions, but her professionalism wouldn't allow her to. "Very well."

I leaned in and decided to offer up some information. "I trust her."

She pursed her lips. "I certainly hope so, Mr. Masters. I'd hate to see someone take advantage of your generous, trusting nature."

I shook my head. "I'm only trusting with her. I've known her my entire life, since we were in grade school. She's actually the only person in the whole world that I can say that about."

Cheryl's face softened. "She's a very lucky woman."

I contemplated her words. "No, I'm the lucky one."

———

After my visit with Cheryl, I stood outside, pulling at my shirt as it began to stick to me in the humidity. I watched the bustling street as the people and cars rushed by, and I thought about just walking to Dump's for a quick visit. It was slightly cooler than it had been in days, and the thick rain clouds of a summer storm loomed, it would be nice to get rained on, I thought. I looked at my phone, and the time read 1:18 PM. Aly was still working out. I admired that in her; she was focused. I began to stroll toward 57th Street and watched the men and women as they approached me, none of them looking me in face. I was just another human, making my way to my destination. That's what I loved about New York; blending in was easy to do. The city swallowed you up, churning you around in its mouth, not caring who or what you were. It would spit you out, dead or alive.

I thought about making the move back to Los Angeles and pushed it out of my mind again. The truth of the matter was, I didn't really want to. I held on to the dream that once Aly graduated college she would want to come back to New York. I was setting it all up to have her bicoastal. She would see soon enough that she could have the best of both worlds.

It took me forty minutes to walk two miles to Dump and Sienna's pad. I didn't tell them I was coming, and hoped he was awake. When he answered the door, he was wearing a white surgical mask and looked as thin as I ever saw him, but the ashen look of near death was gone, and he was in good spirits.

"How's it?" I threw Dump a lopsided grin as I dropped down into a red leather chair. "You're lookin' good, brother." I smiled, relieved that he was looking better.

He just nodded and pressed his lips together in a tight smile. "Yeah, it feels good to feel good. I was so used to feelin' like shit, I forgot how it was to feel normal." He coughed, making a gurgling sound.

"You feelin' normal? That cough doesn't sound good."

"Nah, far from it. This cough?" He pointed at this throat. "Smoker's cough. I'm just happy the nausea is gone." Dump shook his head. "Man, I really thought I was gonna die."

"I told you it wasn't gonna happen, man!" I said excitedly. "That's not in the plan. So what's next for you?"

He pursed his lips and sighed. "Not really sure. Just tryin' to get healthy and get rid of this cough. Supposed to go back in a month for my three-month testing."

"What's up? Why you lookin' like that?"

"I'm worried about Sienna," he admitted and rubbed his hand over his face. He removed the mask, throwing it on table next to him. "I know I've been sick, but she's afraid to come near me, like I have AIDS or somethin'."

"Dude, you gotta give her time, including yourself."

"And then she tells me she wants to have kids, but then she won't fuckin' touch me."

My stomach sank. "You guys have been through the wringer, man. Give her some time," I repeated.

"Maybe Aly can talk to her." Hearing Aly's name made my heart lurch. I hadn't told him Aly was leaving.

"Um…" I was at a loss for words, but Dump didn't notice and kept talking.

"I'm pretty sure I can't give kids, man." He leaned forward, agitated, covering his bald head with his huge hands.

"What's goin' on?"

"Dude, this fucking chemo shit ruins you. It destroys the ability to reproduce, like it fries your sperms'n shit. Chicks too; it dries you up, leaves you barren."

It dawned on me that I'd heard that before, but then, *miracles* happen. "You can't be sure."

"I'm pretty sure." He looked at me with sad eyes, and his gravely voice pitched higher. "I shoulda jerked off at a sperm bank to save my guys, man. I read about it after Sienna started getting all weird."

I could barely take what I was hearing. I had my own worries about Aly, and I felt like a dick for not wanting to get involved, but I had to do it for him. "I'll talk to her."

I didn't think I'd end up talking to her so soon, but as I walked out the door of their building, I heard her call my name. Sienna waived at me from the distance, smiling. She came trotting up to me, looking happy enough, and I wondered if Dump was just being paranoid.

"Hey! It's been a while." She smiled, her teeth glowing bright white at me as she reached out and rubbed my bicep. "How are you?"

"Great. I'm great." I smiled back. I tried to sound convincing even though my stomach knotted tighter with each breath I took. "Just wanted to say hi."

"Where's Aly?"

My mouth clamped shut as I thought about how much I would divulge, and as soon as it did, Sienna knew something major was up. "You're not breaking up, are you?"

I shook my head no, and a lump grew in my throat – *Motherfucker!* I sniffed, gulping it down. "She's leaving next week to go back to school in LA."

Her face fell, the smile wiped away by concern. "Are you okay?"

"As good I can be, I guess." I shrugged. "Look, we're gonna be fine. The band is leaving anyway for three months or more, and it's probably for the best right now." What else was I gonna say? I wanted to believe it.

Her hazel eyes flickered. "You wanna grab a drink?"

Huh? "What's your vice? Sprite?" I smirked, knowing she didn't hit the hard stuff.

"Vodka soda these days."

I almost choked, coughing it out. "How does Dump feel about that?"

"I don't drink at home," she said, looking away from me.

I stepped back to get a better look at her. She looked put together, wearing a cream sleeveless blouse, neatly tucked into a pair of cut-off denim shorts. Her long legs met a pair of flat metallic-colored sandals. I felt for Dump. If the cancer didn't kill him, losing Sienna certainly would. "Are you okay?"

She licked her lightly glossed lips and ran her hand through her long brown hair, looking up at the sky, then laughed nervously. I knew that kind of laugh. I made that kind of laugh. "I'm not turning into an alcoholic, if that's what you're alluding to."

"I didn't say that."

"Jake, this whole fucking thing with Dump has taken its toll. Don't you fucking judge me for having a few drinks. I'm not the one who's had problems." She glared at me, adjusting her white leather fringed bag on her shoulder.

I held my hands up. "You're right. I'm sorry. I'm just surprised. You were always the one telling us how stupid we were for drinking."

"That's when we were in high school, and I didn't know what real life stresses were." She looked disgusted with me. *What the hell?*

"Hey, calm down."

"Sorry I asked." She turned away sharply and walked toward her building's front doors. "I'll talk to you later. Dump's expecting me back anyway," she muttered. It was obvious to me she wanted to talk; Dump didn't have to worry about that after all. All I had in me, though, was to wave at her. She turned back one last time before she walked through the door.

"We'll have a drink next week after Aly leaves," I shouted, making sure she would hear me. She looked at me expressionlessly and disappeared when the doors swung shut. I stood there dumbly, staring at the doors, waiting for her to come back out. She never did.

I don't know how long I stood there staring before it started raining on me. I didn't care that I was getting soaked. It felt good. The air was warm as I walked on, thinking about everything and nothing at all. As soon as it stopped raining and the clouds parted, the sun hit the pavement, sending visible waves of moisture up all around, making the humidity triple. I didn't know how long it took me to walk all the way home, either, but my shirt was somewhat dry and the sun hung low over Central Park.

Aly was sitting on the sofa with a bowl of grapes in her lap when I came through the door. She stopped chewing as soon as she saw my condition and sat up on the edge of her seat.

"What happened? Are you okay?" she asked urgently, tearing the towel from her head.

"I'm fine, just walked home and got rained on." I laughed it off.

She stood, sashaying over to me, and her perky boobs danced underneath her nearly see-through slip dress. She looked closely at my face and I stopped myself from grabbing them. Instead, I wrapped my hands up underneath her arms. She softly rubbed my forehead and ran her hands through my semi-damp air.

She sighed before she spoke. "One week."

I tensed up. "Don't remind me." She began unbuttoning my shirt, and I grabbed her wrists. I wanted to beg her not to leave, and kissed her instead when her fresh scent penetrated my senses. Chills ran up my arms as we held each other tightly. "I can't live the kinda life I wanna live without you, Alycat."

She held my face with her hands and kissed me. Her tongue swept the inside of mouth. "Ditto." She kissed me harder and whispered, "We're gonna make this work, right?"

"I'm gonna do my best," I reassured her. I picked her up, cradling her, and walked into our bathroom. Aly sucked at my neck as I gently dropped her down. Her hand wrapped around my arousal, making me moan. "Fuck, I want you," Aly whimpered and stomped her foot.

"What, baby?" I rasped, and kissed her hard and deep, guiding her toward the shower. "Let's get wet."

"I can't. I just started," she whined, and it took me a second to realize what she'd meant by it.

"So what, we'll be in the shower." I lifted her slip up and over her head, exposing her perfect contours, dropping it to the floor. I ran my hands over her ass, grasping it firmly, pressing myself against her pelvic bone.

She sighed into my ear. "Why do you do this to me?" she griped, looking me in the eyes. "It totally sucks being turned on when you're on the rag, just so you know, but I'm really *not* in a good way today." She wagged her finger at me. "The first day is always the worst."

"I don't care," I asserted and kissed her tenderly, trying to coax her into it. We'd never done it when she was on the rag, but I didn't care one bit. I used to think I'd care, claiming that I'd never fuck anyone like that, but with Aly it was different. I wanted her all the time, no matter. "It'll be fine."

"I'll tell you what," she smiled seductively and reached into the shower, turning it on. "You don't have to worry about me."

"Oh but I wanna worry about you," I countered. She stepped into the shower, pulling me in with her.

"You can make it up to me in a few days."

"A few days?" I shook my head, pained. "That's too long. I'm not gonna see you for a couple months, unless you promise to come to see me. Promise to meet me somewhere."

Warm water cascaded over our bodies, pooling between our chests. Aly rested her cheek against my shoulder. "I'll try. I promise."

I was never one to get blown standing up (if I had a choice), and we ended up dripping wet in our bed. With my obsession of having her in the shower, this had become a thing with us. I was an easy John when it came to Aly's mouth being wrapped around me, and watching her have me in the mirror was like watching our own porn movie. I was gratified within minutes, but I wanted more, and I wanted to please her.

Aly darted off into the bathroom as soon as I was finished. "You need to get back here. I'm not done with you," I shouted. "Hurry your sexy ass up!"

She crept back out holding a towel, wiping her face. "I told you." She smiled demurely, standing next the bed looking down at me. "This was my gift to you."

I smirked. "Get over here." I grabbed her wrist, yanking her down next to me, and she squealed, giggling. I loved her laugh. "I got a little present for you too."

———

The scent of her was overpowering. I tasted her, the sweet bitterness of the dark chocolate she always ate before bed. I felt her, the silkiness of her skin, and my favorite spot on her entire body, her hipbone. Sweet citrus penetrated my senses, as if she just crawled in bed with me after her usual long bath, but she wasn't there. It wasn't real. I rolled over, opening my eyes. The bed was still tucked in neatly where she used to lay, I'd barely moved all night. The pill did its job. Ambien. Thank God for the miracles of modern medicine. I'd not slept in five days. Sienna swore by it, and I was desperate, so I took it, making myself feel better with the knowledge it was non-narcotic.

I'd be needing more of those Ambien pills, I was sure of it.

Since Aly left, I'd been in high gear, prepping to leave for our tour with Eva James. My nights were spent in an obsessive vacuum of what ifs. The guilt of not taking my mother's calls (we'd still yet to talk about Notting) and the pressure of the next record was driving me crazy. Our four-song EP was blowing minds and selling well, but I felt clipped, unable to spread my wings.

There hadn't been a melody in my head in a while, and no words that would string together either. It made me anxious. I'd never had a block like this, ever. I didn't know which way to go. All I knew was that I couldn't get Aly off my mind, wondering what she was doing at every free second I had. I didn't want to come off as needy, refraining from constantly texting her. She seemed to be fine with her decision to go back to California.

The hollowness I felt inside made me growl as I threw the covers off of me. Heavy-footed, I went searching for my phone, finding it attached to its charger in the kitchen. When I saw a string of notifications on my phone, my heart leapt, hoping to see Aly's name. Nothing. There was one from Sienna, and my heart seized when I read the message.

- *DUMP IS IN THE HOSPITAL. PLEASE CALL ME ASAP.*

I didn't call. I went straight to the hospital.

Chapter 22

ALYSSA

The fog was as thick as a rain cloud. I couldn't see the water. You wouldn't think the Pacific Ocean was even there if you didn't hear the waves crashing at the shore. I could barely see the volleyball courts nearest my position above on The Strand. The weather mirrored my mood: grey and weighty. My hair was accumulating moisture as I stood there. I pulled the hood of my sweatshirt over it, blowing into my hands and then stuffing them into its pouch pocket while I waited for my new trainer, Craig, to show up. Craig Hamner was a sand volleyball gold medal Olympian.

I also had a new partner. Her name was Emerson Willet. I'd known Emerson from my early club volleyball days. She was 6'2 and quick as a whip, considering her height and build. I was looking forward to playing with her.

I looked over each shoulder searching for them, glancing at the dog walkers and joggers getting their day started at 8 AM. Jake popped in my head for the ten-millionth time, and my heart grew heavier. I'd received a text from him just an hour prior. I never answered it because I was rushing to leave for the beach.

Dump was in the hospital. He had pneumonia. Not a good sign. They were running tests. I was confused by this news, because Jake had just told me that Dump was doing better and his tests had come back clean, cancer free. How could this be? My first thought when the words sunk into my head was to get on the next plane back to New York, to be there for Jake. Thinking of the credit card he'd given me, it would be so easy. I took out my phone and replied.

- *AT THE BEACH TRAINING. I'M SO SORRY TO KNOW ABOUT DUMP. I'LL BE PRAYING. I'LL CALL SOON. I LUV U.*

All I knew was when cancer returned, it wasn't good news, it was basically a death sentence. I prayed that this wasn't the case. My stomach tightened just thinking about poor Sienna. Holy shit, what she must be going through. I shook my head, forcing myself to stay in the present, wondering where the hell Craig and Emerson could be. Looking at the time on my phone, it was now 8:15 AM. I went to step down the stairs to go wait on the sand when I heard my name being called out.

My heart rose up my throat hearing Nathan's familiar voice. I whipped my head around, and Nathan was smiling at me, bundled in sweat pants. He had his hood over his head, like I did. His green eyes sparkled as he searched my face, and my breath caught. I was surprised at my reaction to seeing him in the flesh.

What were the odds that I'd see him, right there at that moment, right when I was to text Jake?

"What are you doing here?" He was just as shocked to see me. I'd never mentioned to anyone, other than my family (not even to Nadine. She'd certainly have choice words for me), that I was coming home. I was embarrassed that New York didn't work out, like I'd failed; like Jake and I failed, *again*. I didn't want the pessimists or my haters to have their fist-pumping moment. I wanted to focus on me: training and college – but now Nathan stood before me. I didn't know what to feel, because my heart was hammering in my chest so thoroughly it brought on tunnel vision.

I smiled, taking a few tentative steps towards him, not knowing whether to hug him or what. He made the choice for me and closed the divide between us, wrapping his rock-hard arms around me. His familiar scent of freshly-washed laundry swathed my senses. I hugged him back and pulled away quickly, giving him a wry smile. "Surprise!"

He laughed. "That's it?"

I sighed. "Change of plans," I said, throwing him a meek grin.

"Did you guys break up?"

My hands went numb. *Way to dive right in, Nathan*, I thought. "No. I just decided that Pepperdine was the best choice after realizing that NYU wasn't gonna do it for me."

He nodded. His penetrating gaze sent a prickly vibe down my spine, making me look away. "I'm supposed to meet my new partner right now, but I don't know where they are." I looked past him, as if that was what really mattered. What mattered was that I *not* pass out – I was struggling for air.

Nathan backed away from me, severing the tension that made my mouth go dry. "Okay, well. Um…" Now he was the one looking around. "I guess I'll be seein' you."

"Okay." I gave him a tight smile, feeling totally awkward because my tongue was wedged to the roof of my mouth.

"Maybe we can catch up sometime." He tipped his head shyly, endearing me to him. *I DON'T WANT TO BE ENDEARED! STOP IT!* I screamed in my head.

"Sure." I swallowed hard, desperate for moisture. I agreed without wanting to (or did I?). I watched him as he jogged away, disappearing into the fog.

What. The. Fuck.

Now I was totally pre-occupied with the urgency to talk to Nadine. *Oh man, is she gonna kill me.* I had to get to her before Nathan did. Taking out my phone I saw that Jake replied, but I didn't read it. I sent Nadine a text first.

- *I'M HOME. LONG STORY. CALL ME FIRST BEFORE YOU TALK TO OR ANSWER NATHAN.*

Just when I was about to read Jake's text, I heard Craig's voice calling out my name. He and Emerson were on the sand. How long had I been there, with Nathan? It could only have been a few minutes, but I felt like we'd stopped time. Damnit. I rushed down the stairs and scurried across the sand to meet them.

The hour and a half of practice was just what I needed to smooth down my frayed emotions, keeping my mind focused. Jake, Nathan and Nadine were at bay, but as soon as I was alone, I was consumed by all of them, shouting at me for attention, seeing their faces as clear as day in my mind. There were ten missed calls from Nadine and as many texts messages to match. I opened to read Jake's first.

-   *ALYCAT, WHAT I WOULDN'T GIVE TO HAVE*
    YOU NEXT TO ME RIGHT NOW. PRAY FOR
    DUMP.

My hand covered my mouth and I pressed hard on my lips as I held back tears. I wanted to go to Jake so badly. I looked up at the beachfront homes that lined the oceanfront and wondered how many of the owners were going through something similar, having a loved one knocking on death's door. Tears ran down my face as I questioned my choice of leaving New York. I missed Jake, and I wanted to feel his touch so badly.

-   *I'LL PRAY. PLS GIVE SIENNA A BIG HUG*
    FOR ME.

Jake replied right away:

-   *PLS LOOK AT THE TOUR SCHED & LET ME*
    KNOW WHEN YOU CAN VISIT & BUY YOUR
    TICKET. I WANT SOMETHING TO LOOK
    FORWARD TO.

I recounted the days in my head. The band was leaving on tour tomorrow.

"What the hell is going on? What. Is. Going. On?!" Nadine demanded to know, brushing the hair from her face. She was flushed. She'd ditched work and rushed over to meet me at The Kettle. She sat wide-eyed, waiting for me to answer as I chewed the French fries I kept shoving in my mouth. She grabbed my hand before I could stuff any more in.

I nodded, chewing faster, gulping them down. "I'm sorry. I just wanted to come home. It was all an upsetting blur. I didn't want to burden you with my continuing Jake saga."

Nadine let go of my hand, and I wiped my fingers on a napkin. She sighed. "Did you break up?" She looked away, not noticing as I began to shake my head no. She shook her head, too. "I can't believe Marty didn't tell me."

"I don't think he knew," I said, taking a sip of my iced-tea.

She looked back at me. "What drama? Did you break up?" she asked again.

"No." I slumped, "I'm just here, and he's just…somewhere."

Nadine cringed. "That doesn't sound good."

"I know and it makes me sick. There's this big void inside." I clutched my stomach. "He told me to pick a date on the tour to come see him. I'll do that when I get home."

Nadine's forehead creased, and she frowned at me. "Wow, is all I gotta say."

"What? No Nadine wisdom? No 'suck it up Alyssa, you guys are gonna be okay'? You're not giving me any hope with that look on your face."

"What do you want me to say?" Nadine grabbed a French fry and ate it while I watched and waited. "Well, school's already started, what are you doing?"

"I'm starting in the spring. I'm training now, and I'll see about getting a job. You know, settle back in." Just as I said those words, I felt a gust of cool wind blowing at my back from some jerk off holding the door open too long. When

I turned to throw an evil eye at whomever it was, I saw it was Nathan (of all freaking people), holding the door open for three of his buddies. I quickly turned around, hoping he wouldn't notice me.

"Shit." Nadine said under her breath.

"Did he see us?" I said in a low voice. Nadine smiled and waved. *Yep, he must be staring at us*, I thought. I took a French fry and pretended to be into it.

"Hey Nathan." She smiled politely.

"Hey girls." His deep, gentle voice tickled my ears, and I swiveled my head and watched him walk by.

"Hey," I said in return, smiling. My heart raced, and I wondered why he was having this affect on me. I knew I had missed him too, but this reaction?

"You're pink." Nadine's eyes narrowed in on me.

"What?"

She shook her head. "What's going on with you?"

"I don't know, Nadine. I ran into him this morning on The Strand," I huffed. "Aren't you guys supposed to be in school or something?"

"I was at work, Betch," her eyebrows cocked upward. "And besides, college isn't like high school, Aly. You can pick and choose your schedule." She glanced in Nathan's direction.

I pinched her knee, and she looked back at me, scowling. "Owww," she protested under her breath. "What the fuck?"

"Don't look over there. I don't want to give him the wrong idea."

"Oh, Alyssa." She was dismayed. For the first time, I didn't think Nadine knew what to do with me.

I sat in the middle of my bed, in my childhood home, as I always had, like nothing had changed, as if my time with Jake had been nothing but a intense hallucination. His words echoed in my head – *"Everything with you has always been a dream."* It really did feel like that. Vivid enough to leave an impression, but nothing tangible ever remained, with the exception of longing and heartbreak. The only proof I had that New York really happened were the pictures in my phone and the black American Express Card I held in my hand. I'd just finished studying Jake's tour schedule and strung together some dates that spanned across Florida, Alabama and Tennessee. I purchased my plane fare, one-way, into Miami. I would be joining Jake on tour in just a few weeks. As much as I looked forward to being with him, I wasn't sure how I'd feel being stuffed inside a tour bus with six grown men and who knows whom else.

Maybe I wasn't cracked up to be a rock star's girlfriend, let alone…*wife*. My breath hitched at the thought. *I could be his wife right this very second…always to be cast off to the side, peering over the crowd of clamoring fans, or alone, like now. Alone, alone, alone.* This thought made me stare at the ring he'd given me, snugly wrapped around my finger, the promises embedded with every shimmering stone. *Maybe it wouldn't really be that way.* I shrugged to myself. Sienna was a rock star's wife and she loved it. Sienna came and went. She had her own life, too, working as a model and traveling the world.

I pictured Jake's bright blue eyes. They held another world, along with his strong hands…and his thighs…and arms…and lips…and tongue. *Kill me.* Lust left me tingly and wanting him. I really did want to be his wife – his *everything*, as he wrote so many times – but after, *after* I finished school. I sank deeper into my pillows, feeling so utterly *alone*.

I'm not sure why school was so important to me, but it was, regardless of wanting to make my parents happy. I wanted something of my own. I didn't care if I didn't have to work, that Jake would and could provide for me. I wanted to do something worthwhile; I just wasn't sure exactly what that was, yet. I envied that in Jake; he always knew. Sure, I had volleyball, but that was just the start to an ending somewhere else. I was looking forward to the journey.

I was tired and feeling lonely, wishing Nadine was around. I even tried to text my long-lost friend Marshall, only to find out we crossed each other mid-air. He was on his way to Boston to meet up with Bobby and the band. My stomach burned with jealousy, even though I didn't want to be there. At least I would have a fly on the wall to keep an eye on Eva James. I loathed her, knowing she would try to make a move on Jake every chance she got.

It was late, and I wanted to evaporate into a dream state. I craved the feeling of Jake's hands running across my skin, his lips and tongue caressing every inch of me. The thought of it made me touch myself, and I had to hear his voice. I grabbed my phone and dialed his number.

Chapter 23

JAKE

As my band made their way to Pennsylvania from Boston for our next gig, I hopped on a plane.

Beep. Beep. Beep – the sound of the machines monitoring patients filled the air.

Life turns on a dime, I thought, shaking my head. Where did that saying come from, anyway? I was curious to know, and thought about googling it as I stepped away from Dump's hospital room. I leaned against the wall glancing around at the nurses, doctors, and other hospital staff in their muted pastel-colored scrubs. The doctors, with their white coats and mussed hair, all looked frazzled. Everyone seemed to be staring at a clipboard or a computer screen. The low hum of voices and machines tangled together with the smell of antiseptic and sickness.

I wondered if it was that smell or the thought of losing Dump making me feel queasy; maybe it was both. My breath caught as I locked in on Dump. I forced myself to swallow the lump forming in my throat, wishing Aly were by my side. I pined for the warmth of her.

I could see Sienna and Dump through the room's glass window. It framed them like a still picture from a sad movie. She sat at his bedside, holding his hand. Her head was down, resting on his ink-stained forearm, long brown hair splayed out over the white blanket that covered him. Dump had a ventilator stuffed down his throat. *Holy shit – definitely not good.* My knees buckled as I went to step away from the wall, toward them.

"Whoa," a gentle voice hummed, and a warm hand grabbed my elbow, steadying me. "Are you okay?" My gaze met a set of concerned brown eyes belonging to a short stout woman in bluish-grey scrubs.

"Yeah. I think so," I croaked out, quickly glancing toward Dump's room, not wanting to call any attention to myself. When I turned to face the nurse, still holding my arm, she was staring in the same direction.

"Do you know how he is?" I stammered, feeling like I was gonna lose it.

Gloom filled her eyes. "Are you family?"

I'm his brother. "No. He's my best friend."

Her somber expression made my heart cinch painfully. "You'll need to talk with his wife." She patted my arm and rubbed it. "I'll be over in a minute."

She left me standing there, barely. I felt as if all my bones would crumble. Of all the time that had gone by, knowing Dump was really sick, I never felt like I'd lose him. This time was different. All I felt now was grief, like he'd already passed. Without haste, I quickened my pace into his room and placed my hand on Sienna's back.

She sucked in a sudden breath, startled, brushing the hair away from her face. Her eyes were bloodshot and puffy, without a hint of makeup. Upon her realization that it was me, tears began to pool in her eyes. I instantly bent to embrace her before one word could come out of her mouth. There were no words necessary. I believed in miracles, and I prayed for maybe the second time in my life as I rocked Sienna against my chest, tears streaming down my own cheeks.

Someone cleared their throat. It was the same lady from a few moments ago; she was now wearing a white coat. She was a doctor, Dump's doctor. I released my hold on Sienna and stood, reluctant to speak for fear of hearing the answer. We silently watched as the woman checked Dump's vitals and the machines surrounding him. Finally, I couldn't handle *not* knowing exactly what was going to happen.

"What's his diagnosis?" *Diagnosis?* Who was I? I wanted to throw up. I placed my hand on Sienna's shoulder, more for myself than for her at that moment.

"Precarious…dire." She shook her head, extending her hand to me. "I'm Dr. Levy."

"Jake," I answered sharply. "What's going on with him exactly?"

"We have him in a medically induced coma. He has developed sepsis from the severe pneumonia, Pneumocystis jiroveci pneumonia. This type of pneumonia is seen in cancer patients." She paused, caring, but disheartened. "Victor hasn't improved." Dr. Levy's eyes drifted to Sienna, who was staring at Dump with wet eyes. I wasn't even sure she was listening to the doctor. "Mrs. De Luis needs to prepare herself, look into potential arrangements."

The ringing in my ears didn't stop until well after Dr. Levy left the room. I don't even remember saying or asking anything else after hearing – *make arrangements*. Sienna sat in a wet-faced daze, not realizing she had snot bubbling from her nose. I grabbed some tissues from a nearby box and gently wiped her face. She didn't move. She was in shock. I wiped her nose, and she finally grabbed the tissues from my hand, finishing the job.

Sienna's lips were pale. All the color had drained from her skin, as if she'd decided to die with him. Hopelessness scraped at my heart, tearing it apart. She kept sucking in small breaths, about to say something, shaking her head. She covered her trembling lips with her fingers, her words barely a whisper. "I can't do it."

I nodded. "I know." I whispered in return, not even sure if she'd heard me. Still standing next to her, I pulled her close and she rested her head against my waist. I held her shoulder snugly.

"Don't worry about anything. I'll take care of whatever it is we need to do," I assured her, not knowing myself how I'd pull through.

———

There were no theatrics when Dr. Levy removed Dump's ventilator, until I felt my throat begin to close. Sienna was silent. She was somewhere else, her body present and mind forlorn as we listened to Dump's labored breathing, a gurgling sound. I watched her, instead of looking at Dump. I didn't want to remember him this way; weak and deflated…a bag of bones. All she could do was stare vacantly at the shell of her beloved husband and best friend. I couldn't take it anymore.

"Sienna. I'm gonna let you be alone with him…"

"No!" she pleaded. "Please don't leave me alone." Her eyes looked wild, desperate as she looked upon Dump. She began to crumble, sobbing uncontrollably, and squeezed her eyes shut. I thought I would pass out, and I began to back away from her, suddenly I darted from the room. Before I realized it, I was running. I ran down the hall, not knowing where I was going, cutting corners and dodging people, finally spotting a sign for the stairs. I pushed open the door to the stairwell like there was fire licking at my heels, pushing at me to run for my life.

Click.

The door shut, and there was silence. A crushing grip took ahold of my lungs. I stumbled over to the landing wall, feeling like I had lead in my shoes, collapsing, gasping for air. I felt like I would suffocate. I ripped at the collar of my shirt.

"*Aly*," I whispered. I needed to talk to her, to tell her what was happening. I frantically patted my pants and shirt to locate my phone, digging in my right pant pocket to call her. Fumbling, I dropped it between my legs. As I reached down for it, it rang. It was my mother. Tears began to roll from my eyes. I was blinded by grief and my dead father's face filled my vision, him lying in his coffin. I shook my head, burying my face in the palms of my hands, rubbing my eyes to erase the morbid memory.

Thoughts thrashed through my mind: Notting, then Dump and Aly. Aly left me and now Dump was leaving me, forever, just like my dad. My mother – I stared at her glowing name on my screen – *KATE*. I hadn't spoken to her since Notting and I were last together, the day my life officially changed. Guilt that I'd cut her off completely overwhelmed me, like I was the one who'd been lied to and cheated on, not my father or Notting or her. But none of it was really a lie, just a weird, fucked-up scenario that people write about, and it was *my* life.

I answered the call. "Hello?"

"Jake?"

"Yeah?" I could hear her breathing heavily, but she didn't speak. "Mom. Dump isn't going to make it." As I heard the words spill out of my mouth, I really began to cry, and I wished she were by my side. "He's got fucking pneumonia and sepsis, and that shit took over. He's not gonna make it."

Thump. Thump. Thump. Thump.

The only sound I could hear was the calm, steady beat of my heart thumping in my ears. I was so still I could feel the rush of it coursing through my veins. I remained slack, leaning against the wall in the stairwell. I'd sat there, catatonic, for about forty minutes before my thoughts began to have purpose. She already knew. That's why she'd called. Bobby called her when he arrived at Dump's room right after I took off.

All that remained from my episode were the dried trails of my salty tears. I knew I needed to keep my shit together, for Sienna, and for Dump most of all. He'd kick the shit out of me for being such a fucking pussy. I could see him standing over me, saying, *"Get the fuck up man! My old lady needs you! There's no time for your baby bullshit!"*

That thought and the comforting words of my mother that were reverberating in my mind were all it took. I found myself embraced in Bobby's arms, holding him while he cried and he held Sienna's hand. We were all an extension of each other in that moment. Her head rested on Dump's chest. Marshall waited outside of the room. I wasn't sure how long it took us to leave Dump, but we finally did after Sienna asked for a glass of water, she could barely walk.

Everything looked fuzzy and unclear, as if I were looking through a soft lens or smudged glasses. My eyes felt like I had sand in them. I felt like was floating through my motions, an extension of myself as if I were watching from above. I couldn't feel the keys in my hands as I went to unlock my apartment door. Bobby and Marshall stood behind me, holding Sienna up, all of us barely breathing, cried out and in shock from Dump's passing.

I pushed open the door, and all the aromas that reminded me of Aly hit me, practically knocking the wind out of me. My mouth went dry. I needed her, yet I told her not to come. She begged me, and I told her I was okay, but I wasn't. I told her that we'd be sending Dump back to California, to his mother, who had no idea her son had died. Would his mother even care? I looked back at my three friends and motioned for Bobby and Marshall to take Sienna to the guestroom. Bobby picked Sienna up, cradling her in his arms as Marshall steadied her dangling head against Bobby's shoulder. Marshall sucked in a cry, covering his mouth as Bobby disappeared into the hallway.

"I had no idea he was so sick, sick enough to…" Bobby shook his head fiercely, looking down at his feet. He ran his hand nervously through his now short blonde hair, not wanting to say the word.

"I know. It came out of nowhere," I concluded.

"Oh my God. Sienna. What do we need to do? What needs to happen next? Did you call his mom? Is she coming?" Marshall's thoughts spilled out in a torrent.

"Marshall, just stop." My voice was hoarse and scratchy. I held up my hand and tried to steady the urge to scream at him to shut the fuck up. "I need to just fucking think, okay?"

Bobby padded somberly back into the living room. "How is she?" Marshall asked, going to Bobby, placing his arm around his shoulders and glanced down the hallway toward the bedroom. "Is she sleeping?"

"Dude what did she take?" Bobby looked at me. "She's out of it."

"I don't know." I looked around for her purse. "Where's her bag, Marshall?"

He pointed his black-painted fingertip at the coffee table. Her black tote bag leaned up against it. I grabbed it and riffled through it, finding one unmarked prescription bottle. I opened it, pouring them into my hand to get a closer look. I didn't recognize the several different types of pills.

"Do you know what these are?" I held up my pill-filled palm to Bobby and Marshall. Bobby grabbed one.

"Nope." He shook his head. "Never seen those before. You never seen 'em before?" Bobby asked me, as if I should know.

I scoffed, "What? Just because I popped pills doesn't mean I know what every narcotic is. I know it's not Vicodin."

Marshall cleared his throat. "Okay, calm down."

"No!" I barked. "You fuckin' calm down!" I pointed angrily.

Bobby stepped in front of Marshall to protect him. "Whoa, whoa." He held up both arms, motioning at me with open palms. "We're not the enemy here, man."

I sat down heavily into the sofa, leaning back. I covered my face, feeling the burn in my eyes. "I'm sorry, man."

———

The next several days were filled with preparation for Dump's funeral and transfer back to California. To my surprise and relief, Sienna pulled herself together enough to make decisions on her own. She'd left my apartment late in the day, the day after Dump's passing. She didn't tell me where she was headed and walked silently past me while I sat in the living room on the phone. She came back later that night with shopping bags.

I was sitting in the same place as when she'd left several hours earlier, only now I had a towel wrapped around me. I didn't expect her return, and was surprised to see her, especially because she'd ignored my texts. She'd plopped down heavily into the chair just adjacent to me. She stared vacantly out the window, looking hollow. I certainly knew how she felt, missing Aly. I felt strange sitting there in my towel, with nothing else on. I got up to go put some clothes on. When I came back, she hadn't moved.

I cleared my throat, not knowing what I would say exactly, and noticed she was wearing different clothes from when she'd left. It was mid-October, and fall was begging to make itself known; the cold began to creep in. She wore black leggings with leather patches on the knees and a billowy cream lightweight sweater that fell off her right shoulder. She looked exquisite in her grief. *What the fuck? She's my best friend's wife and he just died.*

Upon closer inspection, I noticed her hair was tangled in knots, even though it was pulled up in a bun, and she looked unkempt. "Did you go home?"

She ignored my question, not looking at me, and continued to stare vacantly out the window. I looked at the shopping bags and assumed she'd gone shopping for clothes to change into. "Did you go by your apartment?"

She sucked in a breath, and her mouth parted. "I'm never going back."

I was speechless, and knew that it had to be just the way she felt right at that moment. I probably wouldn't want to go back either. We just sat there, and I watched the TV quietly. Sienna didn't stir at all. Her hand still gripped the handles of the brown Barney's shopping bags.

I felt my phone vibrate; it was set to silent, sitting next to me. I glanced at the screen, only now seeing the many texts and calls that came through: Bobby, Marshall, Marty, Notting, Kate and Aly…I saw Aly's name flashing, but I couldn't bring myself to answer. I didn't want Sienna to feel any pangs of longing or jealousy if she heard me talking and confessing my love to Aly.

Sienna would never hear Dump's deep, raspy voice or loving words from him ever again, and the thought of it made my throat close up. *No*, I thought and watched Aly's name disappear from my screen. I wanted to respect the peacefulness and just sit there with Sienna, as I tried to grasp the meaning of our new lives without him.

Chapter 24

JAKE

I knew I wouldn't be able to keep my latest apartment under wraps for too long. The power of social media and the rumor mill always amazed me. I stared out the window that faced Central Park. The trees were bright orange, red, yellow, and brown, on fire with beauty. Just below the trees, on the old cobblestone-lined sidewalk, fans of our band stood, some of them holding candles. It was dusk.

RIP Dump!

You're the baddest ass angel in heaven, Dump! RIP!

A huge poster or canvas of Dump with angel wings and a halo, sitting behind his drum kit – seeing that one made my nose burn and eyes sting with tears. I wondered if there were fans in front of Dump's real apartment. It'd been three days, and Sienna still stood firm on never going back. I couldn't find it in me to go check on the place either. She'd been shopping every day since, replenishing her wardrobe. I didn't have the heart to ask her if she was going to look for a new place to live; she apparently thought she'd just move in with me. I'd let her stay, of course. I wanted to keep my word – I would take care of her until she got on her feet. I wouldn't be home anyway.

I turned and looked around my apartment, seeing Aly everywhere, wishing she was there. Even though Sienna and I were about to get on a plane back to California, I just wanted her comforting presence next to me. I couldn't get to her side fast enough.

My eyes shot over to the urn sitting on the foyer table. It was hard for me to believe that Dump was in that thing. I almost thought the top would fly off at any moment like a Jack-in-the-Box, and his hand would pop out, giving me the middle finger. I could hear him saying, *"Later, you motherfucker! See ya on the flip side!"* This thought made me smile. I knew Dump certainly wouldn't want us to mourn with tears. He'd want us to celebrate and party until we didn't know what day it was.

It was very quiet, and I wondered if Sienna was ready. Miguel had buzzed us that our car was there to take us to the airport, and our security had arrived.

"Hey, Sienna! You ready?" I hollered.

"Almost." I could barely hear her.

Finally, about fifteen minutes later, as I watched the fan crowd stand strong outside, she wheeled her two pieces of Louie Vuitton luggage out. She had shiny, flowing hair, big eyes that were no longer red or puffy, and fine features. It was hard to remember her the way she used to look when I'd first met her, all Gothed out: chin-length black hair, black eye-liner, and red lipstick. Though other than that, I supposed she hadn't changed in personality that much; she was still sorta shy.

"Sorry, I can't seem to move along. I could give two shits what I look like, and I had to pack for another trip. I'm supposed to work a job in Miami in two days. I'll fly straight from Cali."

I had no idea she had to work. She never mentioned it. Maybe she'd just decided. "You sure you're ready for that?" I worried.

"No."

"Maybe you should cancel."

She shook her head. "Dump wouldn't want me to."

"Yeah. You're right." I nodded sadly. We stood searching each other's eyes, until I couldn't take it anymore. "Lemme call Miguel to come get our bags." She turned away from me, picking up the black and silver urn, cradling it.

Then she picked up a manila envelope that held the papers for Dump's airplane ride. She turned and handed them to me without a word. I accepted them and opened it, looking inside. There was a Ziplock bag and instructions. I informed her that we had to place the urn inside the plastic bag and place the premade sticker on it. She nodded in understanding and went about taking care of it. It didn't matter anyway, because we were now flying privately, but it gave her something to do.

Everything was surreal.

I was the one who'd made the arrangements for Dump, with Bobby's help, after Sienna notified everyone to speak to me. She also didn't want to be the one to call Dump's mom. Sienna hated her, and Dump did too, but it was his mother and she needed to know her son had died. Maybe this news would be the news she needed to pull her head out of her ass to get sober, but for whom would she do it? I didn't know. Dump was her only child.

I kept replaying the sad and unbelievable conversation with Rita, Dump's estranged mother and the inspiration for our band's name – a woman who had always given zero fucks about anyone but herself.

"Rita?"

"Who is this?" She'd asked harshly. I feared she'd hang up on me.

"It's about Victor."

"Who is this?"

"It's Jake. Rita, I have terrible news. Are you alone? You might wanna sit down"

The line was silent, and I'd thought she'd hung up. "Hello?"

"Is he dead?" she snapped.

I instantly wanted to throw up. My stomach lurched and I couldn't say the word.

"Hello? Is he dead?" Her voice was angry. I could practically feel her hands at my throat.

"Rita, I'm sorry." I thought I heard heavy breathing, like she might be crying. "He had cancer, and he passed away the other night from complications of pneumonia."

"Sure." A muffled sound came through the line. "I bet it was drugs, and you all are covering it up. I know how you famous kids do that. Your people cover that shit up."

"No, Rita. You woulda been proud of him. He'd been clean for years." I waited for her to say something, and looked at the screen of my phone to make sure we were still connected. So I continued. "Um, we'll be coming back to LA tonight and are having a service on Sunday, and just wanted you to know..."

Then the beep, beep, beep of the disconnection sounded in my ear.

She'd hung up on me.

I told Sienna about it when she'd finally come through the door late that night; all she said was, *"Fuck her."* And then disappeared into my guestroom with more shopping bags.

My recollection stalled when Miguel rolled in the cart to take our bags down. Sienna stood clutching the urn to her chest as we rode down the elevator. She sighed heavily and moved her black thick-rimmed sunglasses from the top of her head down onto her face.

"Did you look outside?"

"Not today."

"Did you see all the fans?"

She licked her lips, biting the bottom one. "There were several across the street when I came in last night. I didn't want to look at them."

"Did anyone notice you?"

"Yes. But I ran into the building from the cab." Her replies were monotone and matter-of-fact, devoid of any emotion at all. "They were screaming and crying, telling me they loved me. I thought no one knew where you lived."

"You're kidding, right?" What she'd said annoyed me. She knew better. "You know that shit doesn't stay off the radar for long."

She didn't say anything after that. The door to the elevator finally slid open, and Miguel and our two security guys waited as we approached. The click of Sienna's black knee-high boots echoed off the marble lobby reminded me of Aly; her stride echoed the same way. The three imposing men in their black suits paced back and forth, their hands clasped behind them, glancing at us solemnly. They looked like FBI agents. Miguel spoke first.

"There are two SUV's. One has your four friends, and the other is yours." He looked at us seriously. "The crowd has grown," he said softly, looking around as other tenants walked in. "Some of your neighbors aren't very happy."

This made my temper ignite. I stood tall, grinding my teeth together. "My best friend just died, Miguel. Sorry someone like me lives in this building. They can all go fuck themselves."

I glanced, around making eye contact with a couple about my parents' age, waiting for the elevator. The petite woman in a sleeveless baby blue dress, with short blonde hair and shining blue eyes, looked familiar to me, but I couldn't place her. I'd seen her somewhere else before, other than my lobby. She gave me a sad smile before she vanished behind the elevator door. She probably wasn't the one who complained. I'd meant to ask Miguel who she was, but Alex, our Samoan bodyguard, stepped in front of him.

"Sir. We need to get going or your flight may be delayed. It's the tail end of rush hour."

"Sure," I said grudgingly.

Alex nodded and walked ahead of us, leading the way. "Brace yourself," he warned, and looked at David, our other linebacker-sized bodyguard. As soon as we walked outside, the screaming pierced my ears, and I couldn't hear anything else but my name. I was shocked at the number of cameras. It was almost like someone called and told them what was going on. Sienna gripped my arm and buried her sunglasses-covered face into my shoulder blade as camera flashes blinded us. Alex and Kyle did their best to shield us, but there were too many of them.

"How are you doing, Sienna?" – *What? How do you think she's doing?*

"Our condolences."

"When did Dump pass away?"

"Sienna! Are you going to be living with Jake now?" a female voice shouted. *Really? Who asks that?* I whipped my head around trying to see who it could be, but there were too many arms and lenses; too many unshaven, dark-faced men in the sea of fucked-up tabloid mayhem.

"Jake! Where is Alyssa?"

"Jake! How is the rest of the band dealing with this tragedy?"

Then a lens hit me in the nose as we stepped into the street to our waiting transportation, and I lost it. I grabbed the camera, butting a man straight in the nose with it at least two times. I stopped when I spotted blood in his mouth and nose. I heard Sienna's cries to stop and I climbed into the back seat, slamming the door shut.

I stared at Sienna and took her trembling body into my arms. "Get the fuck outta here already!" I ordered the driver. He eased his way through the bulk of camera-clad people standing in front of our SUV, still having the nerve to keep shooting pictures. Their hopes of getting an image they could sell to the tabloids. "Fucking vultures." I kissed the top of her head. I couldn't see Sienna's eyes behind her dark shades, but her tears spilled down her cheeks.

It was one of the worst days of my life. Everything that had transpired up to that moment was so fucked up beyond belief that I couldn't grasp hold of clarity. I held Sienna in my arms, the wife of my dead drummer, and prayed for the fourth time in my life.

I was thankful and grateful for the friends more successful and ballsier than me. I was offered to hitch a flight back to
Los Angeles at the last minute when word got out as to what
our plans were for Dump. David Todd, CEO and Founder
of one of the largest media conglomerates in the world, Red
Layne Media Ltd., owned the penthouse in the building where
I lived. He had that old school suave thing goin' on, with a
full head of brown, graying hair – reminding me of *The Most
Interesting Man In The World*. If Tom Brady and Marlon Brando
had a baby – David Todd was it.

Mr. Todd was as generous as he was shady, and by shady,
I mean there was some shit that I'd overheard once that made
my blood run cold, kinda like a mafia vibe if I had to describe
it. The one and only time I'd been up to his apartment, I was
standing at his door. Before I could knock, it cracked open,
and I heard voices.

"Clive, if that delivery doesn't make it, someone won't
be going home to their family. I won't be out twice," a heated
voice warned.

"Yes. Mr. Todd. I understand." And the door flung open
and my eyes met Mr. Todd's. He didn't even flinch, staring
at me with stony eyes. That's when my blood went instantly
cold. I knew he was testing me, to see if I'd react; I didn't. His
minion, Clive, took off without a word. I didn't dare turn to
see what he looked like. Mr. Todd placed his arm around my
shoulders when I walked in, pulling me to him, whispering in
my ear. "Mr. Masters, business is business, and sometimes it
takes you down some unfortunate roads." And he laughed,
patting me hard on the back.

"Mr. Todd, I give zero fucks about what you've got goin'
on."

As I recalled the surreal encounter, I graciously declined his free flight offer and explained that the entire band would be traveling back to LA and we would be going together – "The plane is yours," he insisted, bowing to me as he exited the elevator. "Whenever you need it." He whipped off his black tie from around his neck as he turned to face me. "You just make sure to let me know when your next European tour starts. Sloan, my assistant, she's a big fan. I'd like her to join you for a bit. You know as a gift to her, for all she does for me."

Fuckin' A – whatever you want, Mr. Todd, I'd thought, stoked about his insistence under the circumstances. I wanted one less thing to worry about.

It was a relief that Sienna and I didn't have to hassle with crowds or security while carrying Dump's remains onto a plane. As I dipped my head, we walked into the sleekest piece of equipment I'd ever seen. It was a Dassault Falcon – running in the rage of about thirty-five million dollars. I'd done a little research on what it would take to own one. I wasn't quite there yet and wasn't sure I'd ever be. In spite of everything, the jet was exciting, and the other guys felt the same. None of them had ever been on a private jet before. Sienna on the other hand, had many times. She was as unaffected by it as she was devastated, cradling Dump's urn in her arms as she sunk into the tan leather seat at the back of the plane.

I zoned out as soon as our flight attendant, Gloria, introduced herself and offered us drinks, not really hearing the captain or paying any mind to the emergency exit info they were attempting to explain to everyone. Let's face it; we would all more likely die if we fell out of the sky. As we taxied down the runway, I peered over my shoulder and watched as Sienna popped a pill in her mouth, knocking it back with who knows what kind of drink. I was still amazed that after all these years, Sienna decided to start drinking. In high school, all she did was give us shit about it. That familiar yearning gripped at my stomach. What was she taking? I told myself it was one of those Ambien's. I needed one of those too; wait, no I didn't. I didn't need anything.

Holy fuck. HOLY FUCK! My insides coiled, realizing nothing in my life would ever be the same – Dump was gone forever. Aly wouldn't entirely be mine until she finished college, and my relationship with my mother and Notting was glaringly on a new level.

I hadn't slept in days, and whatever Sienna popped in her mouth – I took one too.

Chapter 25

ALYSSA

Since the news of Dump's death, traffic on our street had grown heavy, congested at times. It was the first time since Jake's rise to fame that our homes were on the news. *'Local celebrity's passing stirs mourning from music lovers near and far.'* Dump's death took everyone by surprise. The NBC affiliate in Los Angeles wanted to interview me, but I said no.

Jake's yard became a small shrine to Dump overnight – causing Kate to hire security. Cops began to patrol every hour or so. She'd asked me not to alarm Jake about it. She didn't want to add any more stress to his life. *"This will pass, and things will be a new normal, Alyssa. Please don't say anything, he'll know soon enough."* I felt like a prisoner of sorts. I had his fans shouting *my* name as I'd dash from my car into the house. They were sweet of course, perched in the spot across the street where I used to hang out in high school, waiting to catch a glimpse of anyone tied to the band.

What a mess.

I had no idea what I'd say to Sienna when I saw her. Should I smile? Should I hug her? Of course I should hug her – *duh*.

In my restless state, I unconsciously ran my hands over my legs, back and forth, finally feeling the stubble growing on my calf. I looked closely at the dark hairs sprouting up. I was perplexed at how the hair on my thigh was practically nonexistent, smooth as silk, the opposite just a few inches away. I chalked it up to shaving. I should have never shaved my calves back in the sixth grade, I thought, crossing my legs in front of me and directing my thoughts back to Jake.

The time read 5:36 PM, and Jake should be sending a text at any moment. The butterflies swarmed up my spine at the idea of being with him again. My obsessive, lurking craziness took over as I waited for Jake's flight to land. I busied myself with something I shouldn't have been doing while I waited, searching hashtags - *#JakeMasters, #RitasRevolt #RR #EvaJames* – anything that would bring up anything at all about Jake.

What was I doing? I shouldn't be trying to find out anything, but guess what? There it was. As soon as I scrolled through Eva's hashtag, there were several pictures of Jake and her, smiling like a happy couple. I knew better than to trust anything on social media. It was all bullshit. Or was it? I just couldn't help myself. I kept lurking and lurking as my stomach boiled over with psychotic anger, completely forgetting that one of Jake's best friends had just died. Not actually forgetting, but not caring. All I cared about were the images of Eva and him in each other's arms, blissfully smiling at the camera. One of them was of Eva kissing Jake on the neck and his eyes were closed like he was enjoying it.

A moment captured. How many other moments like that were there?

I blinked several times, as if what I was seeing would change. But of course it didn't, she was still there, kissing his neck. I wanted to scratch out my eyes *and* hers. I took a screen shot of the image – because of course I wanted to continue torturing myself at a later date, and God forbid it vanish from the Internet.

I sucked in a deep breath and sighed out heavily, punching away at my keyboard. I whispered out loud to myself that it was nothing, that she was nothing. *Shit happens on tour.* I kept reminding myself I could be his at any moment I wanted, and twirled the ring on my finger. But doubt consumed me, because now all I could see was the image of Eva and him. Then I found myself going to Facebook and stalking Nathan. I typed in his name and clicked.

There he was – a gorgeous, smiling, perfect picture of Nathan stared back at me. I could almost feel his gentle, kind, sweet nature oozing out of my computer screen. I buried my face in my hands.

"What is going on?" I shouted into my palms, rubbing my hands up my face and through my hair. I picked up my phone, looking at the screen, hoping I'd missed hearing a call or text – nothing.

I punched in a text to Nadine.

- *I FOUND A PIC OF JAKE AND EVA. KILL ME.*

Immediately my phone rang. It was Nadine.

"Stop it!" she yelled. "This is his job, and you know this. He's just living his life."

Her words burned. "I know, but I can't stand it."

"Then why do you go looking for it?"

I could hear the wind. She must have been driving. "Where are you?"

"Driving home." I could hear the sound of the wind begin to fade and the music cease. "Aly, you need to check yourself. This is something he's gonna be doing for the rest of his life."

"I know. I don't know if I'm tough enough." A ping chimed in my ear. It was Jake, and my heart sprung into high gear, thumping erratically. "Jake just landed."

"When is the funeral or whatever they're having?"

"It's tomorrow, I think."

"I'll call you when I get home."

I didn't even say goodbye and tapped quickly at my phone to read his message:

- *ALYCAT. KATE & NOTTING ARE COMING TO GET US. WE'RE STAYING AT A HOTEL. HEARD IT'S A MADHOUSE THERE. MEET ME AT SHADE IN A HALF HOUR.*

Happiness surged through me, and I smiled despite the reason why he was back.

Why shouldn't I be happy? I was excited to be with Jake, and I could still be supportive with condolences for Sienna and the band's loss. I felt sad, but couldn't mourn something that I didn't feel a loss for.

I stuffed a change of clothes in a bag and headed for the door. I stopped short of pulling it open when I heard my mother shout out my name.

"Alyssa!"

I rolled my eyes. "Yeah!"

"Where are you going?" I heard her voice move closer. "There are cops parked outside, informing people that Jake isn't at this residence." She pulled her glasses from her face and looked at me somberly. "The news says the memorial is tomorrow."

She shook her head sadly, and I nodded. "It is."

"Kate called."

"And?"

"Are you going to see Jake?"

"Yes."

Her eyes roamed my face, hesitant to say more. Staring. Blinking. "Be careful."

Something in me stirred. "I'll let you know what's up, once I know." I said, facing the door.

"Nathan came by earlier." She announced just as I stepped out.

I paused for only a blip, wanting to ask her why she didn't tell me three hours ago. "Thanks." I pulled hard on the handle to shut the front door, barely feeling my hand on the knob. Why didn't Nathan just call or text?

All of a sudden, I felt the weight of circumstances truly hit me. I had no business getting upset about Jake and Eva when I still cared about Nathan. All of us had a past. I needed to get over Eva. I walked slowly toward my courtyard gate and could hear the commotion of car engines and voices. I froze. There was absolutely no way for me to leave my property without some sort of confrontation. My breath was labored and angst needled at my brain.

Just walk out there and get in your car - I ordered myself. Normally I'd walk to downtown Manhattan Beach, a short stroll up and down one hill but as I opened the gate and stepped out my name was shouted.

"Alyssa! Oh my God, oh my God!" I kept my head down, as if I didn't hear anything. I didn't make eye contact with anyone.

"Aly! Is Jake okay? What's the band gonna do?"

Everything after that mixed together with my adrenaline-induced tunnel vision, and I couldn't understand the words anyone was saying. The cops parked outside of my house kept the passerby at bay. As I looked up when I pulled my car door open, a bearded, burly cameraman and newswoman came quickly towards me. I slammed my door shut, letting them know I wasn't interested. The brunette with big green eyes and slender figure waved at me through the passenger side window, and I saw a cop stroll up to her. I knew her from the TV.

She was on FOX news, always reporting on strange stories. I supposed this was up her ally. She smiled gloomily at me, trying to show me she had some compassion in her, even though she wanted to drill me about things. I started my car and shifted it into reverse, finally looking at her and shaking my head *no* and mouthing *sorry*.

I was relieved to turn the corner out of my block, away from the frenzy of grieving fans. A few short minutes later, I pulled into the Shade Hotel's valet parking area. They too, knew who I was. My car door was opened by someone I recognized but I didn't know by name. He was the younger brother of a girl I went to high school with; she'd been on my freshman volleyball team. "Ms. Montgomery, Mr. Masters is waiting for you at the bar."

"Thanks." I returned his smile and opened the door to my back seat, taking out my bag. "I knew your sister. Tell her I said hello."

His eyes lit up. "I will."

Shade was a small, if not tiny, boutique hotel, and the lobby was also the bar. Jake sat staring at the front door, and his eyes penetrated me as soon as I walked in. Like a shock of electricity, my heart lurched and I couldn't touch him fast enough. He got up and paced quickly to my side, taking me into his arms, breathing me in. I held him as tight as I could.

"I'm so sorry," I croaked out. All the feelings of sorrow and empathy that were nonexistent earlier reared their heads, and I gushed with grief. I held on to Jake snugly, feeling that if I let him go he might expire, just like Dump.

"Hey hey." He held my face and kissed my tears. "Shhh. Stop. Come on. Let's go to the room."

"I'm sorry," I blubbered. "I don't know what's come over me. I didn't feel sad at all earlier." I finally looked up at him, getting a closer inspection, and noticed the dark circles framing his dimmed blue eyes. "Oh Jake." I touched his face, and couldn't come up with anything else worth saying. After all, what else was there to say?

We walked slowly to the room, anchored together, with me tucked safely underneath his arm. Finally being wrapped in his scent and feeling the warmth of him was a reprieve from my angst-filled days without him. I shoved away Eva and the what-if thoughts that wracked my brain, and looked forward to my next visit with him in Miami, just a few short weeks away. What hit me next when we walked through his hotel room door was something I wasn't expecting.

Sienna was in the king-sized bed, asleep, beneath the covers. Her lips were pale, and a pain-etched crease was prominent between her eyes; for a moment I thought she might open her eyes, but she didn't. Clothes were strewn about as if thrown in anger. An urn lay next to her head, placed caringly on the other pillow. My emotions erupted, spilling from from my eyes, and I clasped my hand over my mouth stifling a sob. I turned and left as quickly as I entered.

My shock and reaction sent Jake into a whispering stammer as he followed me out the door. "I…I…She didn't want to be alone. She was awake when I left to meet you. I…I'll get another room. Shit." His eyes pooled with moisture and he pulled me into his chest. "I'm sorry."

"Don't be sorry. Oh my God! Is that Dump in that thing?" I gasped for air. "I feel like *such* an asshole. All I cared about was seeing you and being with you, and I shouldn't be here. I should leave you guys alone to process all of this. I'm the one who's sorry."

"Please don't leave me. I need you."

———

At 11:30 AM the next morning, I sat in my car, around the corner from my house, watching cars I didn't recognize creep by. No doubt they were going to drive by Dump's makeshift memorial. The tribute blossomed into a sea of flowers and burning candles. Why did it have to be in front of Jake's house? In turn, mine. I sighed in frustration and adjusted the rearview mirror to look at myself. Pulling off my shades, I wiped what little mascara residue remained from under my eyes and retied my hair on top of my head, thinking about my night with Jake.

We left Sienna in Jake's original hotel room. I didn't see her at all while I was there. Jake went to check on her a couple of hours later, and she was still sleeping. He said she'd taken an Ambien. As soon as we settled in, he asked if I minded if he took one too. He explained how he'd not been sleeping well since the ordeal. What was I gonna say? I just shook my head to go ahead. What I didn't realize is how quickly it would work. I'm not sure if Jake realized that either. We ordered room service, comfortably cuddled, and began making out.

To my dismay, Jake stopped kissing me and practically threw me off of him. He sat up, rubbing his face, and shook his head, taking a drink of water. *"Damn, this stuff works fast,"* he'd mumbled, then laid his head back down on the pillow and pulled me back to him. As I was kissing his neck he fell asleep.

He was out cold by 9 PM. I ended up eating dinner alone, watching him sleep fitfully. He'd tossed and turned, mumbling like he was arguing with someone. Just like Sienna, he wore a pained expression, and he twitched for most of the night. While I worried about Jake, I felt mostly guilt for lacking one hundred percent compassion. I did feel terrible for everyone, but something in me cried out – *What about me!* I'd fought my feelings of selfishness. What was wrong with me? These people's lives had been turned upside down and all I cared about was where I fit in.

I sighed heavily, shoving my sunglasses back onto my face and wondered how Marshall felt about it all. I wished he still lived down the street from me so I could show up on his doorstep, like old times. I sent a text to Marshall, hoping he could meet me. Bobby didn't stay at the Shade like the rest of band. He stayed with Marshall, who had moved to West Hollywood.

I looked at the time on my dashboard. It was now 12:15 PM, and the memorial was at 5 PM. The service was to be at sunset, at the Manhattan Beach Pier. It was near the end of October a week before Halloween and weather had been mild, mainly on the warm side for fall in Los Angeles. Our cloudless sky and gentle tides would make for a beautiful backdrop to celebrate Dump's life. My face twisted with sudden wretchedness, tears mixed with grief and guilt. I was full of confusion; hungry and hollow, feeling like Jake was a million miles away.

My heart stopped when a figure approached my passenger side door. Through the blur of tears, it took me a moment to realize it was Notting looking at me. I reached back and grabbed a sweatshirt from my backseat, then dried the tears from my eyes and face, unlocking the door.

"Alyssa, darling. Are you okay?"

A tiny smile cracked my lips, and I shrugged. "I've been better," I remarked ironically. "Thanks for asking. I'm just on my way home to get ready for the service, and didn't really want to face any crowds or nosey media people, so I pulled over."

He slid into my passenger seat and shut the door. "Do you mind?"

I shook my head no, but I wanted to say yes – *I was just crying over your son.*

He continued with an easy smile cinched on his face. "I just passed you and turned around once I made it by the house. There are no paparazzi around, just a few fans. They must be down at the beach already. I saw NBC4 news truck just parking at the pier a bit ago."

I sighed, relieved. "Good." I could feel Notting staring at me as I looked out my windshield, feeling even more awkward. "How are you?"

"I'm great. Katie's great."

I glanced at him, meeting his gentle eyes and my heart sprung into my throat. Why did he have to make it a point to be here, now? "Why are you here?"

I didn't expect those words to roll out of my mouth, but now I waited for his honest reply.

He bowed his head thoughtfully. "I slowed to wave hello and saw you were crying. I…"

"Is loving someone really this tough?" With that question, the tears just rolled from my eyes.

"Oh love." Notting reached over, grabbing my neck, giving it a little fatherly pat. "You're so young, younger than Kate was." He shook his head. "I hope this isn't about another love triangle. Lord knows we don't need those in our lives."

I sniffled. "Not that I know of."

"No, I'm about certain Jake's made up his mind about you," Notting said it with reverence. I curled my hand in my lap, hiding the ring as I wondered if Jake ever said anything about his marriage proposal to me. "He's a special one, different. He's never been like most boys, about the females, but then you know that." He looked at me, taking his hand away. "I suppose he's a lot like his old pop."

"It's weird hearing you say that."

"I need to keep saying it." He nodded slowly, looking straight out the window. He brushed his air away from his forehead, pinching the bridge of his nose. "I still don't quite believe it myself. But I won't lie, I rejoice."

There was a long silence between us as we sat and listened to the radio advertisements. The awkwardness had eased, and I wanted to know more. "So you and Kate are officially together? I know that you've tried to keep what ever it was under wraps ever since I've known you."

"I suppose we are, but things are still a little precarious, you see." He sighed regretfully. "Katie has a tough time dealing with matters, and I'm not sure she'll ever really be able to let go of Michael. Sometimes guilt binds us to the past. He died thinking Jake was his son. I'm not sure Kate can ever come to terms with that."

"But he was having an affair." I blurted it out without wanting to. *Oh shit!* I felt dizzy and I wanted to sink into the earth.

"Where did you hear that?" Notting immediately asked, looking gravely at me.

I rested my head on the steering wheel. "Notting, I don't know what I'm saying."

"Well then, what would make you say such a thing?"

"Kids talk. One of my friends saw Michael one time, with a lady. I guess they were kissing or something. It's all rumors from years ago."

When I twisted my head to look at him and our eyes locked, there was something that told me he knew it too. A quiet understanding passed between us that no more would be said about it, or maybe just not right then.

This was some serious baggage floating between Notting and I. I had my own relationship issues, but part of the issue stemmed in him, the man sitting next to me. I loosely knew their story, and it was sordid. Infidelity was flying around like crows at a corpse. I changed the subject back to Kate. "How do you feel about Kate not letting go? I mean, are you just gonna wait forever? Is that what love is? You just wait for the love of your life to come around, while you suffer? Or just settle for something next best?"

I wanted to know the answer so badly for myself. Notting's jaw clenched tight. Shit, I shouldn't have been so daring in my questioning. My palms began to moisten.

"I have guilt, but I also love Katie. I've loved her ever since I set eyes on her. She had a choice, and she chose Michael, unknowingly pregnant by me," he stated plainly.

I couldn't argue with that, but how could he put himself through it all? All those years of watching them together, raising Jake, now that he knew Jake was his? And possibly knowing that Jake's father was indeed having an affair. I wondered if Kate knew too. My brain hurt.

Chapter 26
ALYSSA

An official announcement had been made. Friends and family would be gathering at the north side of the Manhattan Beach Pier to remember Victor "Dump" De Luis. Kate had arranged for the pier to be closed to the public from 5 PM - 6 PM – they would close the gates, and only the band, the families, and close friends would be allowed on. There was anticipation that there would be quite a local crowd surrounding the base of the pier. Jake had contacted KROQ after he realized the unexpected fan bumrush at his house. Five fans would be selected to attend and speak at the memorial service – *"What would you say to the world about Rita's Revolt drummer, Dump Del Luis?"*

It was 4 PM, and Jake finally rang me. I'd been anxiously waiting, pacing my bedroom, not wanting to disturb him on this dreadful day. He wanted to go down to the beach before the service. I'd tried to forget my conversation with Notting, but it stirred my insides, and a pang of fear prickled up my spine. I really hoped Notting would just forget what I'd divulged.

Wading through my troubling thoughts, I didn't realize we were driving away from downtown. I watched and wondered where Jake was driving; it couldn't be far. We parked on Highland Avenue, several blocks away, and walked undetected down the 16th Street ally toward the beach. We stood on The Strand. A crack team news truck was set up at the pier entrance.

"Can you fuckin' believe it?" Jake rasped. I could tell by the sound of his voice he was still exhausted. As I glanced up at him, I noticed the bags under his eyes had grown more pronounced. Maybe I just didn't notice how bad they were to begin with; he was very pale. His beautiful blue eyes wore a gray haze, and fine red lines pulsed around the whites of his eyes.

"Nothing surprises me anymore," I replied, and squeezed his hand, leaning into his shoulder. "You're on a whole other level."

He didn't respond, and tugged me down the 16th Street stairs. As we trekked across the sea of sand to the water, it sorta felt like old times. Jake kept glancing over at me. I wanted to ask him – *What?* But I didn't. I admired him, too, and prayed for some solitude with him before he left.

"Hey. I'm really sorry about last night," he said, almost bashful. He held my hand and swung our arms to and fro. He ran his free hand anxiously through his hair, but I had no words of comfort. We arrived at the ocean, and I watched the tide run over my feet, sinking them into the sand. I waited for him to say more. I tugged at his pinky finger as if it would get him going, and it did. "I'm a little embarrassed that I passed out. That's not what I had planned for you." As he said those words, he twirled me into his chest, embracing me and kissed me deeply. My nipples went instantly hard, sending chills up and down my legs.

"I miss you so much," I whispered into his mouth, and desire surged through me.

"I miss you more, Alycat." His warm tongue gently caressed mine, and his firm, soft lips teased me, making me want more. "I promise, when this is over, you and I will disappear."

"Mmm," I purred into his ear. "I can't wait."

He smiled down at me, kissing my forehead. He kept his lips lightly pressed to my skin, brushing them back and forth. I breathed him in, not wanting the moment to end, knowing that the foreseeable hours would be a shit show.

He exhaled restlessly. "The crowd is growing. We should get up there."

We walked tucked together until someone called out Jake's name. It was a male voice. When I looked around to see who it was, Marty was strolling somberly over to us. Jake patted Marty's shoulder. "What are you doin', man? Is everyone here?"

"Hello Alyssa." Marty threw me a pleasant grin, then turned to Jake. "Um, yeah." He pointed. "They're all up at the end of the pier."

"What are you doing?" I asked this time, curious as to why he wasn't with everyone else.

"I've never been to California. I've never touched the Pacific Ocean. You on your way up?"

"Yeah." Jake nodded and tugged me along.

The moment we got to the bike path at about 12th Street, the murmurs started. I heard Jake's name more times than I could count, and he waved kindly at everyone we passed. I felt the eyes prod us with each step we took. I glanced up from moment to moment, noticing some people had no idea what was going on, and others were snapping pictures like their life depended on it. But for whatever it was worth, they kept their distance, respecting the gravity of what was going down. I was just thankful that it wasn't a clamoring mob, like it was that one time in New York at his SNL performance. My heart thundered in my chest, and as soon as we made it through the sea foam green gates of the pier I began to relax.

What I hadn't noticed in my disoriented state was the number of people that were actually gathered to pay their last respects to Dump. There were hundreds of people all at the base of their pier. It was as if they appeared in an instant. I could hear the faint sound of Jake's music streaming off in the distance. I was in awe. Jake's cheek brushed mine as he said something to me, letting my hand go. I nodded at whatever it was that he said but didn't hear him. I was fixated on all the people gathered below me. Some held hand made flags with Rita's Revolt insignia, some held signs of band devotion, and more than I could count read *RIP Dump ~ We Love You*. That's when I choked up and my eyes searched for Sienna.

I didn't realize that Jake had actually vanished. I was alone in the drifting crowd of people that I didn't recognize, at the middle of the pier. A larger crowd was formed near the end, next to the red-roofed octagonal building that housed an aquarium. I kept searching for Sienna. Where was she? Who I didn't want to see was the person I locked eyes with, Eva fucking James. *Of course she had to be here.* If I could swallow her whole, I would. I looked past her without even a nod, as if I didn't see her at all, and to my reprieve, Nadine pushed past her with a bouquet of tropical flowers in her arms.

"Oh my God, Aly!" Nadine bellowed. "This is fucking nuts."

I nodded in agreement and looked around, as if taking it all in one more time would snap me back to reality. I felt like none of it was real.

"Can you believe these? Marty gave these to me!" Nadine enthused. She was beaming and smitten. I don't think any boy had ever given her flowers, let alone anything else other than heartache.

Her happiness coaxed a smile to my face. "They're beautiful."

"He's so cute, Aly." She sighed happily, her green eyes sparkled, and she stepped closer to me. "I know he's not my type at all, but maybe I didn't know what type was the right type."

I hugged her tight. I was happy for her, and not quite sure what I was feeling. I watched from a distance as everyone I knew, and didn't know, mingled about – accepting and giving condolences to Sienna. She looked beautifully broken, if that was even possible. She wore her dark black-rimmed shades, and her brown hair blew loosely in the wind. She appeared to wipe an occasional tear from her pinkish cheek. Her lips were as red as a rose, but her hair didn't stick to them. They were naturally lit up, unlike the pale skin tone of last night.

I wanted to go to her, but I'm not sure why I was afraid to approach her. Maybe I was just totally immature and something inside me was stirring up things I didn't want to address. I was completely uncomfortable being there. Jake stuck right by her side, basically holding her up. I'm not sure if it was jealousy I was feeling, but I wasn't sure it wasn't mixed in there. I just didn't have a place in the grieving moment. My place was on the sidelines, as was the place of my current (possibly imagined) nemesis.

Eva had her eye on me, with her short boy-cut hair and inappropriate (for the occasion, or any occasion for that matter) bright pink lipstick. She looked like a cartoon character; pretty, but a caricature nonetheless. She kept looking around, over her shoulder, quickly locking eyes with me and then looking away.

Of course I kept staring at her too, but I was looking in that direction. She looked like a bobble-head. Sure, I was being silently catty, but what the fuck was her problem? I laughed to myself. I was her problem. She wanted Jake. *Oh fucking well.* She could keep trying, because it was up to him to either ignore her or have her.

In a daze, I strolled back to the middle of the pier, reading all the plaques embedded into its cement surface along the way. Plaques that read the names of all the winners of the *Manhattan Open* – which was volleyball's most prestigious tournament, like the *US Open* was to tennis. I wanted my name forever cemented into the pier. That was *my* dream.

I looked over the massive crowd below me, and I could hear Jake's voice over a PA system. He was speaking about Dump. Tears welled up in my eyes. I could see him standing a head higher than the other people on the pier, Sienna stood next to him, holding the urn with Dump inside. Jake had his arm around her shoulders – *"…he was one of my best friends. If it wasn't for him, I don't think I'd be standing here."* Jake choked up, and I became a blubbering fool, standing there alone. *"Dump was a solid guy, a survivor of abuse, a living testament to recovery. He was my rock. He was a loving husband…and the best fucking drummer a band could ever have…."* Cheers erupted from the crowd, and I began crying so hard I couldn't hear anymore of his words. I took off to the entrance of the pier.

I felt like I needed to leave. I couldn't breathe. All I kept thinking was, *there is no place for me here,* and it was like my brain was stuck on repeat. I wiped the tears away from my eyes and face. I could see dozens and dozens of people gathered at the gate, watching. They were now watching me, the lone person walking away from what everyone else was trying to get close to. I heard my name in whispers. I thought about turning around, not wanting to cause commotion, but I just wanted to get out of there.

I nodded to the grey-haired cop wearing aviator shades and a totally disinterested expression. Without a word, he rolled it open, letting me out. I walked quickly past bodies large and tall, small and wide; children asking the same question – *"Mommy, what's going on?"* and then one comment, *"That's Jake's girlfriend, Alyssa."* Hearing that made me rush faster through the herd up the hill, and suddenly a large, firm grip held my elbow.

I gasped, jumping away from whoever it was, and I was even more startled when I realized it was Nathan. I snatched my arm away from him like the plague, clasping at my chest. I shook my head *No* at him and dashed faster away. What the hell was he doing here anyway! My mind screamed. I heard Nathan call out my name, and then he was pacing me.

"Hey! Are you okay?"

I ran across the street into the Green Belt, a wide mulch-filled path, densely filled with vegetation, shrubbery and trees. I headed towards my house, and he kept following me. "Nathan, leave me alone! I obviously want to be alone if I'm leaving Jake and everyone else down there!" I shouted angrily.

He jogged up to my side. "That doesn't make any sense."

"Why not!" I stopped in my tracks. "Why do you care? Why are you here? Why!"

Nathan stared at me, his penetrating green eyes hooded with perplexity. "Alyssa," he huffed, throwing his arms out to the side. "Jesus Christ! I just wanna know what the fuck, okay?" He calmed and stepped toward me, and I stepped backward. He sighed, shaking his head. "Are you okay?"

I could hear the faint drone of the PA system floating on the wind, but I couldn't interpret what was being said. What I did hear was Nadine's words loud and clear – "*...but maybe I didn't know what type was the right type.*" I felt like I collapsed on the inside.

"Nathan, just go. I'll be fine." I waved him off and turned walking away.

"Can I walk you home?"

I turned, astounded at his persistence, and stomped my foot like a five-year-old. "What are you doing here? Why were you there?"

I saw him swallow hard, and his lips parted. "I don't really know." Embarrassment splashed across his handsome, chiseled face, and my stomach sunk – *Oh my God, I don't want to feel this way!* My heart surged, because I knew he was there for me. Then he confirmed it. "I wanted to see you. I just wanted to see you, with him...and you're not with him. Why?"

Chapter 27

JAKE

Searing heat ran through my veins as I watched Aly and Nathan talk outside of her house. Nathan with his unzipped hoodie covering his head and his fucking sporto chest showing – what was he trying to prove? *What a dick.* Gone were the gawkers and mourners; it was finally quiet on our street. It was just the two of them, standing just yards away from Dump's flickering candle lit tribute on *my* front lawn. Their faces were somber, serious, and I wondered what they were talking about: *me*, more than likely. The thought of it pissed me off more. It'd been an hour since we'd left the beach, and she'd not answered any of my texts or calls; now I knew why.

I got out of my car that'd I'd parked on the street, two houses away from Aly's. She didn't even turn her head when I slammed the car door shut. I stood there for a moment, waiting for either of them to notice me as I walked up, but they remained engrossed with whatever they were discussing.

Why did she leave? When did she leave? What the fuck!

"What's going on?" I said loudly as I walked up the driveway. Aly startled and her chest heaved. Nathan's jaw clenched and he didn't say a word. He only looked back at Aly as if waiting for her to explain, I waited too, eyeballing the both of them.

"I'm sorry I left." Her voice cracked. She was about to cry. Nathan's manner changed immediately, growing concerned as he watched Aly struggle to account for her behavior.

That motherfucker was still in love with her.

Nathan cleared his throat and pushed the hood off of his head. "I'm gonna go, Okay?" He reached out, touching Aly's shoulder, dipping his head to look into her eyes. She shook her head in acknowledgement.

I wanted to shout at at him – *"Don't you fucking touch her!"* I didn't, and it took everything in me to keep my fists stuffed in my pants. Nathan quietly left without a glance at me, and I waited for Aly to explain herself.

Aly's eyes were pink from crying, matching mine. A deluge of feelings ran through me. I felt mad, sad, devastated, ruined, broken, and just over it. For the first time since laying eyes on her as high school freshman – I felt as if I didn't want to fight for our love anymore, and the thought of that made me sink deeper into despair, because I loved her so much.

"Why didn't you stay?"

"Because I didn't have a place there…"

"Your place is right here!" I patted my chest, right over my heart, heavily frustrated at her selfishness. "And then Nathan? Here? What the fuck?"

"Stop it, Jake," she whispered.

"Are you that self-absorbed that you can't just be next to me without me paying attention to you? Just be there for me? Be there for Sienna? Dump is dead, Aly! Sienna is a widow! She'd been with Dump since she was thirteen years old! She's a part of my family, you're a part of me…"

246

I could have lectured and soapboxed for hours, but watching the stream of tears roll from Aly's eyes down her cheeks took the air from my lungs. None of it mattered. She was somewhere else, and not with me. I wasn't even mad about Nathan anymore. I knew it wasn't about him either.

"I'm sorry. I just didn't know what to do. I was so overwhelmed, Jake." She sobbed into her hands. "I don't mean to be this way. I don't want to feel this way. I want to be there for you. I just don't know how. I guess I'm just not made for this."

I bit my lip and swallowed the words of encouragement. I didn't want to try and convince her that she was my perfect fit, because at that moment, that day, she hadn't been. If she didn't feel it, then it wasn't in her. You can't make people feel and do things they don't want to.

"Come here." I embraced her shuddering body, and cried too. "Shh, come on Alycat." I petted her hair that hung down her back. "This has been the most adverse time in my life, Aly. Trying to stay clean while dealing with my mom and Notting. I just want to toss a fist full of pills down my throat and wash them down with a twelve-pack. Dealing with Dump and Sienna and trying to keep the music going…I don't know what to say to you, other than I love you and I want you to be happy."

"I love you too." She squeezed me tighter and burrowed her face into my chest. I rested my cheek on her head. "I'm sorry. I'm sorry I let you down. I want to be here for you, to be strong for you."

"Me too," I murmured. I was sorry, because I knew at that moment things between us were different. I knew it was coming since before she moved to New York. I knew she always had doubts, and we both forced it, hoping it would work. "Sometimes love isn't enough."

Her head lifted, and her woeful eyes met mine. "You're so out of my league." She shook her head, and her teary eyes shimmered in the dimly lit porch light.

"No I'm not. I'm the same person you've always known…"

"No. You're so far ahead of me, Jake. I can't keep up. It's too much." She unwound herself from my arms. "I let you down today. I don't want to feel this way inside. Seeing Eva there made me feel things I hate feeling. I don't want to feel insecure, mad, sad, irate – I don't want to feel desperate. I want to feel happy, accomplished, like I'm headed in a positive direction, and all I can think about is you and what you're doing and who you're with."

"So what are you saying?"

"And none of this, none of what I'm feeling is your fault. You're just living your life. You're just trying to make everyone happy. I see it, I tell myself this, and it doesn't change what I'm feeling inside." She backed farther away from me. Puzzlement draped her face. "I can't even explain it. I'm fucked up."

"Aly, Let's go back to the hotel, please." I stepped towards her. "Please. I'm leaving in the morning. We're on tour still. We resume tomorrow. Eva already left."

"What's gonna happen?"

Aly's voice was barely a whisper, tickling at my jaw. I took her face into my hands, caressing her soft cheeks with my thumbs. "I'm gonna make love to you, and we're just gonna live, and I'm gonna love you every chance I get."

———

For that slice of time, we were consumed in an impassioned ring of desire. All of our problems waned with every stroke, kiss, lick, suckle and breath. Disappearing from our reality, Aly filled me with a vigor that only she could stir. My hands, mouth and cock couldn't get enough of her. Every moan and every whimper of pleasure from her made me harder, almost losing it. I had to pull out. I wanted to her to come before me. Fingering her, rubbing her smooth wetness, I kissed her all the way down to her navel, teasing her, until I took her into my mouth. She shook to her core, arching her back, crying out my name. She came into my mouth. Feeling her hot wetness spread across my lips and the pulsing of her on my tongue sent me over the edge. If I'd pressed my dick hard enough into the mattress, I would have come right then too. I flipped her over and slid inside her, gripping her hipbones. It only took a few pounding thrusts to see stars.

"Holy shit," I moaned. "Fuck, I fucking love you."

Aly straightened up as much as she could with me inside of her and twisted to kiss me. I wrapped my fingers through her hair, kissing her deeply, still feeling the remnants of pleasure. She detached herself from me, pushed me down onto the bed, and climbed back on top of me. Sticky and wet, I lay caressing Aly's taut body and wrapped my arms around her pulling her as close as I could. I didn't want to leave.

As if she read my mind, she sighed. "I wish things were different."

I kissed her ear. "So do I." Matching her sentiment, I rolled her off of me, turning to my side. "When am I gonna see you again?"

Her lips pressed together, and her eyes bounced around my face. "I bought a ticket like you said to do, for Miami, for a few days."

Hopefulness and relief rushed through me, but only for a moment. "And after that?"

She scooted away from me, laying flat on her back. "I don't know. Jake, I have so much that I need to focus on." She covered her face with her hands.

I gently lifted one of her hands off her eye. "The holidays are coming. I'll be home for a couple of weeks."

She perked up, lifting her head. "Here? LA?"

"No." Disappointment weighed on her. "Aly don't look like that. Come to New York. It's amazing at Christmas time."

"Didn't you hear what I said?" She reached up, rubbing my cheek tenderly. "I don't think I can. I'll have training. I'll be starting school right after the holidays."

What she was saying sounded like excuses. I wasn't the insecure type normally, but as soon as I realized unless I figured out how to carve a few days off in between booked studio time with a new producer, whom was specifically flying from Europe in order to work with me during his only free time during the holidays, I probably wouldn't see her. What the hell was going on with her?

Nathan popped in my head. That motherfucker. The tendons in my neck tightened and I roll onto my back. I was angry and hurt. I didn't believe she couldn't find a few fucking days to come and see me. What else was going on?

"So you're telling me that your coach and your teammate are gonna be wanting to train during fucking Christmas time?" My tone turned dark and bitter. I was hurt, because I felt she was playing hardball and I didn't understand why.

She huffed and burst off the bed. "I have dreams too, Jake!" Her voice elevated. "It's not just all about Jake fucking Masters!"

Whoa.

"Wait a second, that's not fair!" I retorted. "I never made anything about me! I've always put you first, Aly, as much as my career allowed. You're the one that *knew* you didn't want to move to New York, and you weren't honest with me." Her eyes sparked for a split second. She knew I was right. "I've been open to making this work between us, no matter what, and now you're trying to throw some made up bullshit in my face?" My chest felt like I had a thousand-pound elephant sitting on it. I struggled for air as I searched for my sweat pants, putting them on. Aly stood unmoving and stared at me with a look in her eye that I'd never seen.

"I love you so much, Jake." All of a sudden, she wilted, and her voice wisped like a feather. She bent down, picking up her bag, and dug out a black dress, slipping it over her head.

I was sick to my stomach and paced the hotel room. "What do you want, Aly?"

Her eyes narrowed, and she sighed heavily. "I'm not sure. You've had a problem being one hundred percent truthful with me. To save my feelings, or whatever it is you think you're doing when you try that shit. It always comes out, and I know I haven't been truthful with you either about stuff for the same reasons."

"Okay…"

"And I just need to stay here," she said loudly, cutting me off.

"Why the aggression? You're acting like *I* did something wrong?" I motioned. "You're the one I catch with what's-his-fuck! Is that what this is about?"

"No!" she shouted.

"Then what is it?"

"I'm not made for you." She looked forlorn and collapsed on the bed. "I mean, not in the way that makes up everything someone needs."

"Yes you are. You're the only one who knows me, Alyssa. Don't you see that? Don't you feel that?" I went to her, kneeling down to her, taking her hands in mine.

"Jake, you said it." She looked deep into my eyes. "Sometimes love isn't enough. I've said it, too." Her voice faltered.

Emotions trampled through me. I didn't know what to feel. "But someone like Nathan is?" I looked up at her. I wanted her to tell me the truth.

"This isn't about Nathan, Jake." She took my face into her hands and kissed me. "This is about me. I'm not Sienna. I'm not Eva. I'm not made like the type of girls for someone like you."

"I'm gonna ask you again. What are you trying to say?" I reached up, holding her wrists, and pushed her hands away from my face.

"I don't know. I just know that I hate the way I feel when I'm standing there watching your life unfold in front of me like a movie, and knowing that I want to do things that are so far off and different than what you're doing."

"Are you trying to say you don't wanna see me anymore?"

"No. That's not it at all. If you were here, I'd want to be with you ever day. I'd want to come home to you every day."

Eventually, we faded into each other's arms. Not really making a choice either way on where our relationship was headed. All we knew was it wasn't what either of us wanted. I wanted her with me, and she wanted me with her, and that wasn't going to happen.

Chapter 28
JAKE

As time passes, dipping back behind the horizon, the debilitating pain of loss fades into a dull ache. Hope is raised from the ashes, from once-in-a-while text messages, sprouting like a weed. Like the Northern Lights, it cascades, feathering, teasing with its illumination, hinting at warmth, but it's too far away to feel. You fill yourself with whatever helps you survive; good, bad and everything in the middle. Sometimes we stay delusional for far too long, feeding our demons, just to stay alive.

It'd had only been two weeks since I left Aly in California, and within those two weeks, we went from texting and talking several times a day to barely communicating at all. She was busy pursuing her dreams, and I was busy living mine – *right*. All I could imagine was her fucking around with Nathan during any free time she had. I knew old habits died hard. Thinking about Aly putting off having a life with me for the foreseeable future made me resent her. Regardless of her aspirations, I truly felt like she was stringing me along.

Eva sat curled up in a black flannel bathrobe, a white heart-covered scarf wrapped around her skull as she watched me strum my guitar. That's all I was capable of doing these days, was playing old melodies. I had zero inspiration. My separation from Aly was different this time. It didn't ignite the love-loss creativity as it had before. It was as if a big boulder blocked the exit of anything worth expressing. My guitar sat cradled in unmotivated hands as I watched Eva move about, unbeknownst to my scrutiny.

It was a relief to have Eva there. It was an easygoing friendship now. All the sexual tension from the past was gone. She would smoke her weed, and I would take swigs off of my flask filled with whiskey. The auburn liquid made me feel warm and quickly took the edge off. An edge I'd been teetering on for far too long became a distant memory. I jumped back into feeding my demons real good, and I could have cared less. Eva and I dissected the past and made our predictions about the future.

Maybe I'd stay numb until Aly came around.

"Sorry that I fucked with her." Eva exhaled a cloud of smoke and coughed lightly. "I'm jealous, but not in an *I want you* kinda jealous."

"There's nothing to be jealous about," I said flatly. "But control yourself, willya? Don't be a bitch. You acting that way kinda fucked things up for me."

"How so?" Her tone challenged my remark.

"I take that back. It just solidified some of the things she'd been grappling with."

"Like what?" she scoffed. "How perfect her little fucking life is? Give me a break." Eva's voice trailed off bitterly.

"There's nothing to be jealous about, just put it that way," I reiterated, changing my mind about divulging any of our issues with her.

Broken Notes

"Sure there is. You have the kind of love everyone is searching for," she remarked, not knowing she had no idea what was talking about.

"It's not what you think." I laid back against the hard bus cushion, bringing the flask to my lips. I watched Eva stare off, ruminating on her jealousy, and I wondered. "Are you seeing anyone?"

"Nope." She shook her head slowly, but didn't look at me.

"Are you fucking anyone?"

Her eyes darted to me, and she smirked. "Nope."

I nodded my head. "I don't wanna fuck you, if that's what you're thinking."

"Good. Because I don't wanna fuck you either." She smiled, and we both chuckled, but our laughs weren't the happy, easy kind. They were laced with woe.

"Hey, so…" I strummed the old tune. The only tune I'd been stirred to play. The one tune no one had heard before. "Listen to this."

I cleared the phlegm from my throat and sang the long ago song that I'd written for Aly – _I Swear_. Eva's eyes went dreamy and sad. They held a sense of longing as she watched me play, and I closed my eyes finishing the song.

"It's a duet."

"It's beautiful," she said softly and threw her arms out at me. "See, the kind of love that bitches all over the globe wished they'd find, including myself."

"You wanna sing it with me?"

Her eyes flashed wide, and a wave of nausea swept over me as soon as the words parted my lips, but I ignored it.

Eva happily agreed to sing the song with me, and we spent the rest of the night harmonizing, until she decided it was time for her to be nosey.

"What's up with you? All sad n'shit. Just tell Aly to get on a plane already." She crossed her legs under her and leaned forward, waiting for me to reply. I took a huge mouthful from my flask, finishing it off. She extended her arm, palm up. "Give that to me."

"You want some? Too late, it's all gone." I tipped the silver flask upside down.

"Nope. I don't think you need that thing anymore." A sudden surge of anger ignited in me, and I almost told her off, I didn't need a babysitter. She must have seen it in my eyes, and uncurled her legs, standing slowly. "I'm gonna go."

"Yeah," I said, clamping my mouth shut. I didn't say anything more. If I did, all the anger I'd been pushing down would explode right in her face.

Eva stopped as she got to the door of my bus and stared at me long and hard, stepping down and opening the door. We were at a rest stop, and the music and voices drifted in; whose, I didn't know. "Don't do this." I heard her say. "Don't be a fuckup, Jake." I heard her sigh, "…oh, and that song is amazingly raw and beautiful, thanks for sharing it with me." I sat there with my head leaning back against the hard laminated wall of the bus, my eyes closed, until I was sure she was gone and I heard door slam shut. I didn't take another drink, but I popped a pill. One I shouldn't have taken.

I didn't know what time it was when I crawled into my bunk or where the guys were, but when I woke to take a piss, they were back and asleep. I laid there, listening to them breathing deeply, thankful that none of them snored too loudly. I curled up, thinking way too much about Aly and how she told me she wouldn't be able to come to Miami for the days she'd planned. She'd been invited to some training facility with her new partner, in Brazil of all places. It was hard for me to be happy for her, even though I wanted to be.

———

In a blink of an eye, Halloween, Thanksgiving and our last tour were an afterthought, and I was back in New York. Holiday music blared and Christmas decorations were displayed wherever I turned. I was schlepping through three feet of snow to meet with Duncan Martin, a British producer, whom worked with nearly every award-winning, history-making band and artist known to date. He was a Midas and probably one of the very few producers who actually played more instruments than I did – now *that* inspired me. I made a mental note to begin listening to everything he'd produced.

Pushing through a garland-laced doorway of a Midtown-West recording studio, my heart clamored. I couldn't recall the last time I was nervous about meeting someone – maybe it was because I was unprepared. I hadn't written anything new in over three months. Two months had passed since Aly and I last saw each other, and it was like a cork plugged my flow and it was sealed with wax – nothin' was getting' out; it was weighing on my me hard. I had nothing to give, *and* to top it off I'd just signed on to something else new. I was hoping this meeting would spur something creative in me.

Aly was still in Brazil, unsure if she'd be back for Christmas, which was only ten days away. She'd planned on staying in Brazil right up until her classes began at Pepperdine University in February. She'd begged me to fly to her, but ironically, I was headed back to LA. We'd been commissioned to write a song for David Fincher, of *Girl With the Dragon*

Tattoo fame, amongst other music video and movie accolades. David's work spanned decades. He was producing and directing a new movie, set to release the following winter. As it happened, I'd be in Los Angeles for New Year's Eve until mid- January. Aly said she'd try and make arrangements to come home.

Distracted by the frustration and uncertainty of my musical conundrum, knowing my band's reputation hinged on it, I shook my head and pulled off my wool beanie and prayed – for the fifth time. I glanced around the unfamiliar room. The black painted walls of the entry area sported more gold and platinum records and discs than I could count. There were black and white pictures of old time, long-ago musicians taken back in their heyday. A timeline ticked by as I glanced to my right, the history of the establishment played out all the way to modern day. Familiar faces smiled back at me. Maybe I'd be on this wall soon.

So typical, I thought, of waiting around in places like these, for someone to come out. I could hear the distant sound of a guitar, and wondered who it could be. A cold bluster of wind rushed through the door, running up the back of my neck, prompting me to turn around. A slender man wearing a black wool overcoat, scarf, and fedora stopped in front of me, smiling. It was Duncan Martin, and he looked as ancient as Mick Jagger.

He held out his hand. "Jake Masters. Duncan Martin." I took his hand, shaking it firmly. "You're more handsome in person, though looks like you need some sleep," he commented abruptly, smiling and nodding matter-of-factly.

Nice backhanded compliment. I was taken aback at his directness. Even though I knew I looked like shit, it was strange hearing it from a man so openly. He whisked away without another word, going through a closed door, leaving it open. Was I to follow him? I stepped toward the door and ran into him as he called out my name, right in my face.

"Jake, geez man! Keep up!" he ordered enthusiastically. "I've only an hour today, and that started five minutes ago. Come." He waved me along.

"I'm sorry. I didn't…"

"Don't be sorry. Just pay attention. This is important business. I'm extremely thrilled to be working with you. I've read everything about you and listened to everything you've recorded, and I have to say you're supremely talented." He flung his coat onto a nearby chair as he spun to sit on the black leather sofa, crossing his legs.

I sighed, feeling my airways tighten. "Thank you, sir."

"Don't thank me. It's fact." He watched me closely as he rubbed the greying stubble on his chin. I could almost feel pressure on my face as his eyes scanned over me. "Are you sober?"

A jolt of fear and shock numbed my hands. I closed my mouth when I realized it was hanging open. I half-laughed, and he held his hand up to shut out the words, the excuses, I was about to feed him. I wasn't going to lie to him.

"Uh, uh." He shook his head, and displeasure marked his face.

"Mr. Martin. It's not what you think." A reluctant sigh parted my lips. "I have trouble sleeping, and at times I do take medication to help me sleep. As you've noticed, I haven't had very much shut eye lately."

He drew in a breath, and drummed the tips of his fingers on the arm of the sofa, contemplating. My heart thudded hard in my chest, and I reproached myself for contacting my old pill supplier in the first place. My first illegal shipment of pills, Ambien and Vicodin, arrived just the day before. The pills were burning a hole in my jacket pocket.

"Jake. I'm not here to reprimand you. I just want to know what I'm dealing with." He clasped his hands under his chin, inspecting me further. "I've seen it all. All the greats wade with the Devil, at war with the angels." He reflected on the past as he stared at the wall of pictures behind me. "I've created the greatest works with people who have no memory of how they became so great. Thankfully, many of them lived long enough to kick the Devil's ransom and realize their great fortune."

His honest words made a burn inch up my throat, and I swallowed it down. He'd probably never been in my shoes, but I didn't want to ask. I pulled myself together and told him a half-truth. "I remember every sorry step I've ever made, Mr. Martin." *Truth.* "I'm not on anything but Jim Beam and Ambien from time to time." *Lie.*

I admitted to Duncan I was stagnant in my vision these days, and he understood why as he repeated what he'd heard in the media and from my management – "Your whole world imploded. Losing a loved one is tough business." He smiled, almost wickedly. "What a vast canvas."

My hair stood up.

I didn't share the thing that dogged me the most. He had no idea that my dad wasn't really my dad and that my whole existence was based on deceit and disloyalty – past and present. "I've decided to share some music with you that no one has heard. Maybe resurrect something that was once very special to me."

"Once?" His eyebrows rose.

My stomach cinched. "It still is."

I took out my phone and mounted it to the speaker system, playing him some tunes that I'd written while in Europe, and then I played him *I Swear*. His head tilted with interest. His eyes darted to meet mine when he heard Aly's lithe voice fly out of the speakers. He wasn't expecting a duet.

"It's very raw. I can hear the emotion in both of your voices."

I felt a sting in my eyes and sniffed, looking away from him. "Yeah. That's the first duet I'd ever done, other than the one, *Talk About It*, that was a hit."

"I like it." He smiled. "Tremendously."

When I left Duncan, I wasn't sure what I felt, but it wasn't happy. I knew Aly would die a thousand deaths if she knew I'd played that song for anyone. But if I had to be honest, I was at a point where I no longer gave a shit what Aly thought. She clearly didn't care about me at the moment. I wrote the song, and it was mine to share.

I arrived home through a sleet storm and looked forward to being back in California, regardless of Aly being there or not. Part of me wanted her to stay in Brazil. I would be forced to focus solely on my music and the band.

I began to feel desperate for the first time about my future in making music. Self-doubt coursed through me with each step toward the elevator bank in my building. I waived at Simon, my other imposing doorman, and wondered where Miguel had been. I hadn't seen him in days.

As I stepped through my front door, I was shocked to see Sienna sitting on the sofa with three huge boxes stacked to the side of her. She had a pile of papers and envelopes sitting in her lap and at her feet. She'd been crying, and her brown hair was a tangled mess.

"What are you doing here?" I rushed to her side, caressing her mussed hair. She was in disarray. I inspected the boxes. They were filled with mail: fan mail, bills, bills and more bills. "What is all this? I thought you took care of all this." I waved a disconnection notice in the air. "Aren't you supposed to be in Milan?" I was beyond confused to why she didn't call me.

She sniveled. "I got a call from Mark, you know, our attorney. And he said that I was being evicted. and that…" she sobbed, dropping the papers she held and covered her face with her hands. "I didn't want to bother you anymore."

Sienna kept to her word and had never gone back to the apartment, staying with me periodically between her modeling gigs. I had no idea that she'd done nothing at all, as in *nothing*. She'd not paid one bill, nor had she told her building manager that she'd be moving.

"They're selling everything in the apartment to recoup the rent."

I stood from my crouched position. "Sienna." I leaned down grasping her shoulders, forcing her to look me in the eyes. "You can't let that happen. Don't you want to keep some of Dump's things? Your wedding pictures? Some of his shit?" I was flabbergasted. "What's Mark's number?" I grabbed the cream colored paper she'd let drop to the floor. It was the legal document notifying her of the sale – it was in two days. I ripped my coat and sweater off, throwing them across the room. I was sweating, even though I'd just come in from zero degree weather. I sat down next to her in a heap.

She threw herself backwards, sinking into the sofa pillows, and the air filled with the scent of Aly. My hands began to sweat. *I don't need this right now*, I thought. I looked at the time, and it was after 7 PM. I could call *Mark*, her attorney, to see if there was anything we could do, but it'd have to wait until morning. I let Sienna cry it out as I reached around her, taking a handful of letters from the box that sat next to her.

"Please don't." She croaked, touching my arm with her cold, pale fingers. "It's mostly fan mail."

"Don't you want to read them?"

"No. I've read enough." She wept. "I want to burn them."

On some level, I identified with the way she felt as I looked around my apartment – everything in it was Aly. "I know. I feel the same way sometimes."

Her breathing ceased. I glanced at her, and she was staring off around the room like I had been. Then her eyes met mine. "I'm sorry, Jake." Tears dripped from her eyes. "I know you've been going through a lot too. I don't mean to be so selfish. I swear, I don't. I just can't help it. I want it to all go away."

I reached for her and pulled her to me. "I know. Trust me. I know."

Chapter 29

Jake

Sienna pulled herself together, collecting all the scattered documents and fan mail littered around her feet. It was as if she went from envelope to envelope, searching for something that would change her life. There must have been over one hundred ripped open letters piled and scattered about. She apologized over and over again through fits of tears.

I stuffed a plastic trash bag with all the paper and bent to pick up one of the boxes to move it to the trash. Sienna stopped me, staring blankly into the stone fireplace that had yet to be used.

"Let's burn them."

I hesitated, staring at the grey stone hearth. Who was I to talk her out of it? If it would help her move on and heal, why not? I set the file box down, dropping the trash bag. I walked over to the fireplace and inspected it, as if I knew what I was doing.

"Okay. Let's go get some wood."

We didn't have to go far. As soon as our heels hit the stone floor of the lobby, Simon insisted on helping and arranged for wood to be delivered. Sienna and I, bundled up in our coats and hats, walked arm in arm around the corner to the market for some wine. We talked in circles, trying to convince ourselves that the life ahead of us would be better.

When we arrived a short time later back at the apartment, Simon was standing over a man who was tending to the fireplace. "Don't want'ya to burn the buildin' down." He pointed to the man who was halfway inside the chimney.

"Thanks man," I said, and took the wine into the kitchen to search for an opener. I grappled with what the next day would hold as I pulled each drawer open looking for the wine opener. I set down the bottle after I opened it and took my phone from my pocket. I set the alarm to wake me at 7 AM and sent Marty a text to be at my door an hour later. I would show up to Dump and Sienna's apartment to try and salvage anything I could.

I stood in front of a roaring fire, holding two glasses of wine, and wished it was Aly, who'd walked out from the hallway. As the seconds passed, I was surprised at how at home I felt with Sienna there. She'd put on loose-fitting sea blue pajamas and pulled her hair back into a ponytail.

"Thank you," she squeaked, covering her mouth in an attempt to stop the emotion from tumbling out. She was hurriedly at my side, taking a wine glass out of my hand. She sniveled the tears back. One lone drop spilled from her left eye. "Cheers to new beginnings."

I smiled sadly, reaching over and wiping the tear away. She tipped her head at me, taking a gulp from her glass. "To the future." I bowed. "Hold this." I handed Sienna my glass. "Move." I gestured and bent down sliding the coffee table out of the way and moved the sofa to directly face the fireplace. I then moved the boxes and bag filled with paper to arms' length.

Sienna sat down and finished off her glass as fast as it took me to blink. I did the same and walked to grab the wine from the kitchen. When I returned, she'd started to burn the letters. I was numb. I was hollow. I was as vacant as I'd ever felt as I watched my best friend's widow burn him away. She stared expressionless with each envelope she'd toss into the flames. Each time, a burst of red heat would rush upward and outward and the ash would replace its spouting rage. I watched her closely. She looked like a different person. I could barely remember her as she used to be even just a few months before. Her once full, youthful cheeks were slightly hollowed in that model way that made the lens love you.

She'd matured in a beautiful, ravaged way, and I wondered how long she'd been drinking and using whatever else she may have been using. Now it was clear to me that it'd been kept from Dump for longer than she'd let on. I could tell by how easily she drank her problems down her throat, and thought back to the Ambien and other unidentifiable pills we'd found in her bag.

My head spun in a light, content way – finally. I slumped back and watched silently as she balled up the white empty trash bag and tossed it behind where we were sitting. Before I realized it, we'd gone through two bottles of wine. I lazily watched Sienna as she dug into the first box, and she stood tossing the largest handful of paper into the fire. It snarled out at her angrily, making her stumble back onto the sofa.

"Whoa!" she laughed. "I guess the fans are pissed I didn't read their fucking letters." She laughed almost diabolically, and then her face twisted and her eyes welled up. "I'm sorry." She looked up at the ceiling, rocking back and forth. "I'm sorry I can't handle this. I'm sorry I don't care. You left me, and I know you didn't want to, but you're gone and I can't deal with it."

My stomach lurched. She was talking to Dump.

She wept, and the burn in my nose knotted my throat. I swallowed it down and squeezed her shoulder in an effort to comfort her and myself. She tipped back into me, and I held her close and she sobbed harder into my chest. I brushed the hair away from her face and kissed the top of her head. She was warm and soft, and it felt good to have her in my arms. It felt too good. I knew I shouldn't keep holding her with that thought drumming in my head, but I did, and I wanted to. I needed her there as much as she needed me.

"Nothing lasts forever." Her warm breath penetrated my t-shirt, and I agreed, kind of.

"Sometimes, and sometimes it's different, but the same."

She shifted to look at me, but remained in my grasp. "What do you mean?"

"Just like sometimes love isn't enough. Love doesn't keep two people together. There's all the other life shit that gets in the way. Two people with different dreams, different timelines, different ideals."

A weak smile crossed her lips, and she nodded in under-standing. Our faces lingered close, too close, and she whis-pered, "Thank you for being here for me." Her breath, sweet with wine, washed over my face. "I'm sorry for taking over your home."

Our eyes held each other's, and she inched closer to me. I held her tighter and I went to say not to worry about it, and something foreign inside me swelled. I wanted to tell her to stay for as long as she'd like, that I wouldn't be home any-way. But instead I kissed her. She immediately pulled away, touching her lips. Shock flickered as her pupils dilated. I went to apologize, but she moved in so swiftly, kissing me back, holding my face, and I let her soft lips brush over mine.

She whispered into my mouth, "Thank you."

I gently pushed her away and closed my eyes, but I didn't fully release her. My mind raced and my heart raced but I pulled her back to me and we lay there, saying nothing at all. Her thoughts were probably the same as mine – *What the fuck was happening? What am I doing?* But we kissed again, and this time our tongues softly blended together and my hands began to roam. Our unacquainted bodies pressed together, inviting and needy. Neither of us spoke; we just breathed each other in, knowing if our voices sounded it would halt whatever was happening.

When I awoke at 7 AM when my alarm sounded, I was curled up, uncomfortably and alone, on the sofa. Sienna wasn't by my side. Why would she be, anyway? I reflected on the night, and breathed a sigh of relief that we'd had enough sense to not go any farther than making out, even though my body wanted more. *I'm fucking going to hell*, I thought as I rolled over, stiff from sleeping on the sofa. I had a throbbing headache from drinking an entire bottle of wine with no dinner.

I rubbed my temples, sitting up, and the painful pounding kept forcing my eyes shut. Squinting at the light filtering through the grey haze of the early morning, I noticed Sienna's bag was at my feet, and some of the contents had fallen out. An orange prescription bottle caught my eye, and an instant pang surged to the very core of me. The kind of pang that makes your entire body numb, a craving so profound that it overtakes every sense. With shaky hands, I reached for the bottle – *Hydrocodone*.

Perfect, I thought as I removed the cap, and a flash of guilt coursed. I knew I should put the bottle back, but instead I tapped out a couple chalky white pills. I didn't think twice, tossing them into my mouth, swallowing them dry. What was the difference? It was a pain med, just like the Vicodin I had in my bedroom. I needed the physical and psychological pain to melt away, just like my dreams of having Aly with me. *Fuck it*, I thought, as I lay back and waited for them to take affect. The relief was a rush, unlike the Vicodin. I felt them take ahold of me within twenty minutes. I stood and it was as if I floated.

I felt zero pain. I felt energized.

Marty arrived promptly at 8 AM. I'd arranged through *Mark*, Sienna's attorney, to pay the outstanding rent owed. I wanted to get my hands on Dump's drums and written music. No one really knew that Dump wrote music, and I knew Sienna would one day be happy to have something that was his.

I went to say goodbye to Sienna and lightly knocked on the guest bedroom door. "Sienna?"

I heard faint music and tapped on the door again. This time I turned the knob and cracked it open, peering in. She was sitting in the middle of the queen-size bed with her legs crossed in front of her. She was reading a book – in a lacy black bra and panties. When our eyes locked, my fingers tingled. *What the fuck?* I cautioned myself, and looked away.

"Um, I'm sorry. I didn't mean to walk in on you." She didn't reply, and I turned to leave. "I'll be back later." I shut the door and exited the hallway so fast I wouldn't have heard her respond. I needed to get the fuck outta there.

I grabbed Marty by the elbow and towed him out. "Let's go."

Marty adjusted his glasses. "What's going on? Everything okay?"

I sighed. *I almost fucked Sienna last night.* "Sienna never went back to her place, and never paid any bills or rent since he died. We need to salvage what we can over there and make arrangements for some sort of estate sale."

"Wow." Marty slapped his head and pulled on his gloves as we exited the elevator.

Ten hours later, I was standing back at my front door with a satchel full of papers; Dump's music, poems, sketches and pictures he held dear – pictures of Sienna, who looked so different now. I couldn't even take a moment to look at them without wanting to lash out at someone. At one point while sifting through their things, their love letters, I wanted to vomit for crossing the line, but something pulled at me. I felt like I needed her. My hand shook as I reached out to open the door. I retracted balling it into a fist. I began to sweat. I reached into my pocket, took the cap off the bottle, and popped the oval horse pill in my mouth. All I wanted was to curl up in bed and fall asleep. I wanted to dream of better times, easier times, simpler times. I wanted to vanish into oblivion.

I wasn't sure what to expect when I came through the door, but it was dark, save the lights from the street shining through the windows. It smelled like fire and ash. I looked toward the hallway and could see a dim light from the guest-room, Sienna's room, illuminating the rug in an oblong rectangle – her door was open. My heartbeat speed up as I thought about how I left her in the morning, and how she'd been practically naked. I thought about how good she felt in my arms, and I wanted more.

When I approached her doorway, it was as if she was waiting for me. She must have heard me come through the door. She was staring at the entrance as I appeared through it. She lay under the covers with a book resting on her chest. The only light in the room was coming from a little reading light she'd attached to the headboard. A look of relief glinted in her eyes, and I could see the rise and fall of her breathing beneath the white down comforter. I believed her flared reaction to be anticipation. She knew, like I did, that last night wouldn't be the end.

She watched me as I removed my coat and my clothing, leaving it in a pile on the floor, Without a single word spoken, I crawled in next to her, taking her warm body in my arms. Her heated breath flooded over my chest as she burrowed her face into me, and her cool fingers ran over my skin.

This night, I only held her as her tears wet my chest. Only our breath would be heard.

Chapter 30

JAKE

For the next eight days, Sienna and I lived together as if we were a couple. We went about our daily business, meeting for lunch, shopping, and going for long walks in a winter wasteland that was Central Park – not to mention popping pills together like they were vitamins. Each time our eyes met, it was as if we both wanted to talk about what was going on, but neither of us had the courage to. We were in total denial of our reality. There was nothing unusual about our relationship on the surface. The band and Marty knew Sienna had continued to stay with me during her transition, but below the exterior behind the closed door of the guest bedroom, we pushed the envelope a little farther – never acknowledging what we were doing was wrong – or was it?

Dump was gone, and Aly and I had essentially broken up. Aly and I agreed to remain tethered, but that was it. If I had to choose, it would be Aly, but she wasn't an option. I wasn't going to fight what was happening between Sienna and I.

Life rolls on.

It was Christmas Eve, and I was leaving for Los Angeles first thing in the morning. Sienna too was spending Christmas back home in LA with her family, though she was leaving later than I. I lingered over my silver suitcase sitting on the bed I once shared with Aly. Staring at the stack of t-shirts I'd just placed in it, I was stoked I'd be in warmer weather and thought about staying longer than just a few weeks. I wanted something new. The rhythm had returned since Sienna and I had begun our adventure, if that's what you wanted to call it – new musical hope flickered, but with it were dark secrets – all fueled by booze, pills and lust. The thought of what went down just the night before made me prickle with desire. After eight days of kissing, caressing and fondling, we finally made each other come – and the sound of her ecstasy still echoed in my brain, making my blood rush. I kept telling myself it was innocent enough because I didn't stick my dick inside her, even though I wanted to.

I cursed myself – *I can't go there again.*

Tap, tap, tap.

It was as if Sienna read my mind and appeared there to test me. "What time do you leave?" Her soft voice pitched higher than normal.

My nerves prickled up my spine. "Before dawn." I didn't want to face her, she was something I knew I couldn't keep playing with.

"Okay. Um, if you don't have any plans tomorrow night, you're more than welcome to join me. My LA agency is having a holiday party."

I felt her presence disappear as I pretended to organize my things. Confusion and regret increased inside me. I had to clear the air with Sienna. I had to finally address what we'd been doing and set boundaries or something. I had to define what was happening between us. I turned and hurried to find her, running into her in the hallway, and words rushed out of her mouth before I could form any of my own.

"I'm sorry, Jake." Her voice trembled. "I know we shouldn't be doing what we're doing. I'm sick to death when I think about it. I'm so sorry for putting you in this position. I just…"

"Hey, stop it." I brought her close, resting my cheek on her head. My nerves were eased by her remorseful commentary. "I don't know what happened either, but you can't blame yourself. It's me too. I'm sorry."

"You don't think anybody knows? What if someone finds out? Oh my God, the media will have a field day." Fear hitched in her voice as she moved away from me, shaking her head violently. "All those lunches and walking in the park arm-in-arm. I just know those motherfucking paps had to have taken pictures."

"Stop worrying, Sienna. No one's gonna suspect anything. It's not like we were making out in public."

"No one can know."

"Shhh. No one's gonna know anything." I gripped her by the shoulders, looking deep into her big, hazel green eyes. She pulled away, rubbing her hand over her forehead.

"I need a drink."

I followed her into the kitchen and she grabbed two glasses from the shelf. "You want one?" She asked as she reached for the whiskey.

"Yes."

We clanked our glasses together. The amber liquid burned going down, and I sighed loudly. "Don't worry."

"Okay," she whispered, and her face crinkled. "Uhh! God! Why?" She slammed her glass on the counter, and I swigged the last of the liquid in mine down my throat.

I grabbed her by the neck and pulled her to me, kissing her on the temple. Her arms wrapped securely around me. I shifted to look at her and cupped her gorgeous, pale face in my hands.

"Everyone has a secret," I said, and lowered my head to kiss her. Her lips met mine, pressing into me eager for more. "And this is ours."

We stood entangled, feeling things we shouldn't have been feeling. With a soft touch to my cheek, she left me standing there with a hard on. I felt like she wanted me to follow her, but I couldn't. I wanted to, but the desire wasn't enough to coax me into doing something more regretful than I already had.

That night, we slept separately.

I awoke at dark-thirty, squinting at the clock on Aly's side of the bed. It read 5:30 AM. I ignored the sinking feeling I had at seeing Aly's beautiful, smiling face in the picture of us lit up by the clock's light. I was glad I had enough sense not to continue with Sienna – what the fuck were we thinking anyway? I hopped in the shower, and was ready by the 6 AM pick-up time I had scheduled. I wheeled my luggage past Sienna's door and stopped for a moment, almost going back to say goodbye.

I shook my head, deciding against it.

Cloudy and cold, the wind pushed at my back as I jogged to my hotel, ending my early morning attempt at running. I mostly walked. I was determined to detox. I had the shakes and hot flashes from weaning myself off the pills. It was like having the flu, an extended version. At least this time it was bearable. The last time was forced rehab, cold turkey, and I literally thought I'd die from the pain. This time, I thought I'd do it myself under the radar of prying eyes, with the guidance of Amy, my long-time sponsor. I'd shown up on her doorstep unannounced straight from the airport.

I knocked on Amy's olive green door. At least I'd hoped it was still Amy's door. I looked over my shoulder. My eyes leered over every car window and every bush. I was a professional at spotting cameras and their owners – *motherfuckers*. I appeared to be in the clear. If anyone woulda spotted me, they'd think I was in Hawthorne to buy drugs; instead, I was there to get off them. *How the hell did I get here…again?* I clutched at my stomach. I was feeling nauseated, and it took every bit of strength not to pop the pills in my mouth.

"What the fuck?" I heard her voice through the door as she unlocked it.

"Merry fucking Christmas." I smiled wildly, holding my arms open wide when she opened it. "I'm back."

She pursed her lips and leaned against the door jam, trying not to smile. Her hair was wild, like she'd just had sex. "You know you coulda called."

"What? You getting busy in there?" I winked at her.

She cracked a smile. "Come here, you, give Sissy a hug."

I embraced her warmly, feeling her bony back beneath my hands. She smelled my neck and released me. It wasn't uncommon for her to act strangely, so I didn't think anything of it, but she looked at me with narrow eyes as I moved past her into her living room. I glanced around. Nothing had changed, except for her wimpy attempt at holiday décor.

I sat down, and she hovered over me, running her hands through my hair, and then smelled them. "You're using again. It's coming out of your pores."

Heat flashed over me. I nodded in admission; what else could I do? She was like a drug-sniffing dog.

"If it matters, that's why I'm here, and I haven't taken anything since yesterday and I'm sick. I don't wanna go back to rehab." I took out the unmarked prescription bottles and tossed them onto her cluttered coffee table.

She snatched them away as quickly as I tossed them down and walked into her adjacent bathroom. I could hear her flushing them down the toilet. What she didn't know was I had more in my luggage still sitting in the trunk of the rental car.

"What happened?" She came out with her skeletal arms hitched on her hips.

I gulped for moisture. "I need water." I was totally perspiring. The withdrawal was really beginning to take effect. She held up one bottle and shook it, pills rattled inside it. "What? Why...?" I wondered out loud why she didn't flush them all down.

"You'll be taking some of these," she said over me as she walked to her kitchen, filling up a glass of water from the sink. "It'll help you come down, and not completely crash. If you can handle it, that is."

She walked over, handing me the glass, and I gulped half of it down in an instant, lying back. "How many of these were you taking a day?"

I didn't want to admit it. "Eight, ten, I really don't know."

She winced and nodded. "I guess that's not too bad, some people take twenty or more." She uncapped the bottle and handed me two. "Take these. Tonight you'll take two more." She scratched her head. "You should really just check yourself in..."

"No. I don't want anyone to know."

I fell asleep on Amy's couch. When I woke, I was covered in a soft, mustard colored quilt, and ambient music faintly filled my ears. It was dark and the room was lit by candle-light. I sat up, still feeling shaky. *How fucking long would this really last?* I patted my pockets for my phone and dug around in the cushions. Looking up, I scanned the kitchen counter surface and spotted it sitting there with my wallet. I didn't remember taking them out, but then again. I was pretty out of it when I arrived.

There were a so many text messages and voice mail notifi-cations I didn't even count them. I just scrolled through look-ing for *Alycat* – and there it glared, her name and the number 5 next to it. I eagerly tapped over and over at the screen, willing it to react as fast as my mind was spinning:

- *MERRY CHRISTMAS. I MISS YOU SO MUCH. I COULDN'T GET A FLIGHT OUT THAT WOULDN'T COST AN ARM AND A LEG, BUT I ARRANGED TO COME BACK ON NEW YEARS EVE. KISSES. HUGS.*

- *<3 <3 <3 WHERE ARE YOU?*

- *NOW I'M WORRIED. PLEASE CALL ME OR TEXT ASAP TO LET ME KNOW YOU'RE OKAY.*

- *JAKE? WHAT'S GOING ON? I JUST CALLED YOUR MOM I WAS SO WORRIED AND SHE SAID YOU LANDED EIGHT HOURS AGO. I HOPE EVERYTHING IS OKAY.*

- *I TRIED CALLING. I'LL BE LEAVING YOU ALONE UNTIL I HEAR SOMETHING. I LOVE YOU. I HOPE YOU'RE OKAY.*

A part of me felt happy she was worried. Those texts were the most I'd heard from her in weeks. My hands shook, and I wondered if it was from the adrenaline or from withdrawals.

"Amy?" I called out and focused back on my phone. My mother, Notting, Marty, Bobby and Eva had tried to contact me – wishing me Merry Christmas. I felt a tinge of disappointment when I didn't see Sienna's name – but it was a good thing. She needed to leave me alone, and I needed to leave her alone.

Amy came out from her bedroom, and she didn't look like herself at all. She wore a black, form-fitting long sleeve, v-neck dress. Her hair was curled, and she wore knee-high boots. A red scarf was wrapped around her neck.

"Wow, you look great." I marveled at her transformation. "Where's my hippy chick?"

A quirky grin sprung to her face. That little tick she had made an appearance, a slight head tip and pursing of her lips, then a glance over her shoulder. "My boyfriend prefers me to dress more elegantly."

My eyebrows shot to the top of my head. "Reeeeallllyyyy?" I sang out. "Who is the unfortunate bastard?" I laughed, and she moved past me with a slap to the back of my head.

"The luckiest man in the world is actually a retired doctor. His name Michael Cohen. He's a psychiatrist."

Hearing he'd been a head doctor made me laugh out loud. I wondered how old he was; he had to be eighty or somethin'. "How convenient." I hunched over, really finding it funny. I could hear her giggling. "No, but really, I'm happy for you."

She grabbed her keys from the counter. "Make yourself at home. You can stay here tonight and tomorrow, but you'll have to get the hell outta here because my sister and her family are coming."

"Merry Christmas," I said to no one when the door clicked shut. I fell back onto the sofa and kicked my feet up onto the coffee table, contemplating what I would do while I traced the green and red Christmas lights with my eyes. They were strung around the entire room like crown molding. There wasn't tree, nor presents, only the lights indicating that it was the most joyous time of the year – *yeah, whatever*. "Woo fucking hoo." I twirled my index finger.

I'd sent my mom and Notting a text telling them I'd just woken up and Merry Christmas. They replied basically ordering me to meet them for breakfast in the morning. An uneasy, gnawing feeling ate at my stomach, and I wondered if I was getting ulcers again. I held out my hand. It shook a little. I supposed it was time to take another two pills. Tossing those back dry, my mind went to Aly again. I'm not sure why I wouldn't call her, and I sat there staring at my phone. I didn't feel like texting her, either. She knew she could have charged airfare to my credit card, if she really wanted to be there with me, but she didn't. That was the truth of the matter.

I socked the cushion. *Fuck her.*

I took in a deep breath and continued to check out what went on with everyone on Christmas Day, which I'd slept away. Going to my social media accounts, liking pictures of friends and people I'd found interesting. Everyone appeared to be having the time of their lives, while I sat alone like the pathetic, drug addicted loser I was. I proceeded to tap on the *Following* tab and thumb-scrolled through what everyone else thought was worthy of a like – in an instant the rush of alarm numbed every inch of me. Nadine – *NotNad* – liked a picture of *Whoisnate*. Nathan was standing with his arm draped around Aly's shoulders. I clicked on the picture, and they were standing in front of a brightly-lit Christmas tree.

The motherfucker was with her in Brazil. How long had he been there with her?

I scrolled through the rest of his pictures. He didn't post very many; posts were weeks and weeks apart. The picture caption read: *Merry Christmas Southbay! From Brazil, with Love.*

"Fuck you!" I roared. My head pounded so hard it felt like a jackhammer let loose against my skull.

My heart sank into the pit of my stomach. If I didn't have an ulcer before, I most certainly did now. My hands really shook, and I couldn't peel my eyes from the picture, Nathan's sappy smiling face taunted me. I wanted to punch his eyes out of the back of his head. I tapped at my *Favorites* programmed into my phone, and hit Aly's name at the top. The phone began to ring. What would I say to her? I had no idea. I wanted to cuss her out, call her a fucking lying whore.

Five rings and she finally picked up. "Jake?" Her sweet voice sounded, and my eyes stung with tears in an instant. I hung up the phone.

I thought about all the shit that had gone down over the last several weeks, and I felt as if I was spiraling downward. I felt dizzy, and all of a sudden I was gonna puke. I ran to the bathroom and hurled, spitting and heaving, expelling what felt like all my vital organs. *I wish*, I thought, as I dropped to a heap on the floor.

Death would be too easy. I'm not that lucky.

Chapter 31

ALYSSA

My heart pounded violently in my chest, bringing on ringing in my ears and the tunnel vision so fierce that my sight went black for split second.

Jake's text:

- *I KNOW NATHAN IS IN BRAZIL WITH YOU.*

"What's wrong?" Nathan grasped my shoulder, steadying my weakened body. Then he hugged me to him. "You okay?"

I shoved him away and stumbled back. "I need to sit down." I glanced around, practically staggering over to a wooden bench just outside the restaurant we'd just left. It was 11:30 PM on Christmas Day.

Why was I there with Nathan? Why?

I should have gone home. I didn't have to stay in Brazil, even though my partner had. *Oh my God. We just had the most amazing time together,* I thought, and glanced at Nathan, who looked handsomely disarming with the ocean breeze rustling his hair. The most puzzling and exacting truth was, I wanted to be there with him. I chose him over Jake, thinking Jake was too busy for me with his music *and,* a la Jake – what he didn't know wouldn't hurt him, because in my mind I wasn't doing anything wrong. Nathan and I hadn't even kissed, I rationalized with myself. I hid my unsteady hands under my thighs, trying to get a grip. I didn't want to tell Nathan anything, but it came out anyway.

"Jake knows I'm here with you." I shook my head, and there was a long silence, with only the subtle sound of waves crashing at the shoreline.

I felt the vibe in the air shift and Nathan's eyes on me. "So what?" He practically spat at me.

Confusion increased inside me. "Nathan, why do you keep coming back? When you know I'm fucked up."

"I could ask you the same thing." He laughed resentfully and paced. "You keep coming back to me, too, Alyssa. It's like we're all fucking ping pong balls or something, except I don't have another girl waiting in the wings." He paused, huffing, his own realization shedding light in the darkest corner. "That oughta be the decision maker right there."

"Stop it."

"It's the truth and you know it."

"No it's not! You're just being an asshole." His words burned me to the core, because it was true. I knew Nathan was always ready to pick me up when I was down.

"Than you're really more delusional than I thought," he continued.

What?

I jumped up. My thoughts were tangled. "Wait, what are you trying to say?"

Nathan's green eyes grew stormy. "Alyssa I didn't force you to be here with me, and you know Jake's always off with some other girl, some *"It has to do with the band"* thing." He mocked quotations, referring to Eva, and stepped farther away from me.

I thought he was implying that he or Jake was always the other guy in waiting for me.

I folded back onto the bench and a chill ran over me. I sighed heavily, thinking about Jake's text and how I would reply. I'd just tell him the truth. Nathan was there with his family, and I had no idea when I'd committed to staying that he was even *in* Brazil. I couldn't help that his mother was Brazilian and that he happened to be there the same time as me. What I *did* have control over was spending time with him. Jake was probably having a meltdown.

"I should probably just get back to my place," I said, distraught.

"Sure," Nathan mumbled.

As I walked ahead of him, a bit of agitation sparked. "You know, it's not like you didn't know what you were dealing with. I haven't led you on," I reminded him.

Nathan joined my side, with his hands buried in his pockets. I kept glancing at him as we walked along the boardwalk at Copacabana Beach. He looked despondent, making me feel that much more like a total failure as a human being.

"It's the same old story."

"I don't want it to be though."

"Actions, Alyssa, actions." I nodded in agreement, but I didn't think he noticed. It would probably be the last time I would see him on any personal level, and I panicked inside. There was so much about Nathan that I loved. I didn't want to *not* have him on some level; selfish, but the truth.

As we came to the front door of my building, he stopped. He wasn't going to walk me in. I held the heavy glass door open, wedging my foot in front of it, and turned to say one last thing. "Nathan, whatever's vibing between us, it's real. I've always cared so deeply, but…"

"But there's Jake," he interrupted, standing taller and more rigid. "Look Alyssa…"

"No. Just don't say anymore." I held my hand up for him to stop. "I'm sorry if you're the casualty of my uncertainty."

"We're stuck in a vacuum." He turned to leave, and I wanted to go to him so badly, to feel his strong arms around me and breathe in his fresh laundered scent. In all practicality, he was the perfect fit for my current life, but I just couldn't choose. I was jammed in the middle of something I didn't know how to get out of, having feelings for two guys.

I bet this was exactly how Jake's mom felt when she had to choose between Notting and Michael. The thought of it made my heart ache for Jake. He didn't deserve to have so much distress and sorrow thrown at him. He was born into a shit situation and didn't need one taunting him. Especially after Dump's passing. *Ugh, I'm such a sorry excuse for a human.* Jake, nor Nathan for that matter, didn't deserved my lack of esteem.

"Thanks for an amazing time, Nathan," I called out, as if that would make it better.

He waved at me unhappily. "It's always an amazing time with you, Aly. I'll talk to you soon."

I watched him walk away until he faded into the night. My thoughts suffocated me.

Jake wouldn't pick up the phone that night, or any other of the three days after that. We'd only exchanged texts, and he was basically over fighting for me with Nathan and I didn't feel like arguing my point of his double standard – he was allowed "friendships" with old flames and I was not? *Whatever,*

I thought sourly. I was both grief-stricken and angry. Even though I knew I was wading through all sorts of swampy feelings, it was clear to me that I'd made a choice after all. I chose Jake that last night with Nathan; otherwise I wouldn't have let Nathan walk away.

It was December twenty-ninth, and summer in Rio De Janeiro was in full swing just as winter in America was taking grip. I'd been told, begged, and almost kidnapped by my Brazilian friends in an effort to keep me from missing New Year's Eve – the biggest party of the year, other than Rio Carnival in February. Two million partygoers would be lining the famous beachfront on December thirty-first to see the live music performances and the firework display at the stroke of midnight. I'd miss the ritual of wearing an outfit of white, red, yellow or green, which are believed to bring luck, romance, prosperity and health for the coming year. *I should probably stay. Lord knows I needed help with all that.*

I'd spent the last few days trying to enjoy the waning hours of my time, hanging out with the friends I'd made *and* stopping myself from calling or texting Nathan to say goodbye. I didn't want to give him any wrong ideas. I'd spent my last day alone, walking the Ipanema Beach and swimming in the impossibly warm turquoise water. Spent from my day in the sun, I was anxious for the day to end as I packed the last of my things. I would miss it there, but I knew I'd be back. Brazil was a hotbed for volleyball, and I looked forward to returning in the future. All I wanted at the moment was to plant my ass in an airplane seat and to see Jake. I'd stopped bothering him, but he knew I'd be returning for New Year's Eve. I zipped my suitcase and heaved it off the bed. My room was naked and white.

Gone were the colorful sarongs I'd hung from the ceiling like a canopy, and I'd given the tea lights and plants to our housekeeper. It was 11 PM and I refrained from texting Jake, even though my angst was eating a hole in me from the inside out. I crawled into bed, and thoughts of Jake and more romantic times filled my mind. I wanted to put all this nonsense behind us.

The continuous ping of my cell phone woke me, and I reached over, grabbing it. It was barely getting light outside, and the time on my phone read 5:53 AM. There were missed calls and messages from both Bobby and Marshall. As I scrolled, there was also one from Kate, Jake's mom. My heart sprung into my throat.

Jake – something happened.

I listened to all the messages. No one had heard from him in nearly a week, the same amount of time as when he fell off the grid with me. Worry coursed through me, forcing me out of bed and pacing my stark room. I dialed Marshall's number.

"Aly?" Marshall's sleepy voice cracked.

"Yeah. What's happened?"

I heard rustling and Bobby's voice came on the line. "Hey Aly."

"Hey. Tell me what's going on." My voice rose higher in a near panic.

"He's okay. Sorry to have worried you. I guess he's been lying low with Sienna." A pause. "And he's a mess again, from what I understand."

"What does that mean, Bobby?"

"I think he's using again. Hey aren't you coming home?"

"Yeah, today, I'll be home around 2 PM." I couldn't wrap my head around Jake using drugs again; he'd been so against it and determined. "What do you mean he's using? Are you sure? I mean, the last time I talked to him he was with Amy, his sponsor. He can't be."

"Well, we saw him after he found out that you were with Nathan, and he was pretty fucked up."

So they knew, too. "Maybe he was just drunk." I sighed, totally freaked out. "Let me talk to Marshall."

"Hey." Marshall's quiet voice filled my ear.

"Marshall what the fuck?"

"Girlfriend you tell me." I felt as if insinuation laced his voice.

"Oh my God, I'm not gonna be blamed for Jake's relapse. He's a big boy. I wasn't doing anything wrong, Marshall. You know me better than that."

A beat passed, almost as if he didn't believe me. "I know, but you know how he gets."

Yeah – The pot calling the kettle black.

I worried, though, and a sick feeling crawled up my throat. "I think I'm gonna throw up." I lay back down on my bed, closing my eyes. "Marshall, Nathan is just a friend to me. He was here with his family; nothing more happened."

"It just looks bad, Aly." He paused, looking pained. "We ran into Jake the day after Christmas, and he was definitely high. He was all erratic and super sketchy."

I nodded, grabbing my forehead. "How did you find out he was with Sienna?"

"Jake's mom was looking for him, and we called Sienna, you know, because she's here too for the holidays, just to see if she'd heard from him. Then to our surprise, she said he'd been staying with her."

"Hmm. Okay. Well maybe she'll slap him around. She's always been against drug use." My feelings swirled. "Marshall, will you pick me up from the airport?"

Chapter 32
ALYSSA

Standing in the long customs line at the airport was grueling. I itched to get out of there. Like a crack head, I was paranoid everyone was staring at me – it seemed as if, every time I looked up and around, I made eye contact with someone checking me out. I fidgeted with my bags, my hair, my cuticles, my phone – which had no reception. That was the worst part. I had no idea what had transpired while I was flying. I was beyond anxious to get to Marshall to see if anything had developed with Jake. To top it off, I just had to pick the line with a family with three little kids and the parents who'd never traveled in their entire lives, until now. They spoke with a heavy accent I couldn't place, and searched for one passport they should've had ready to present to the Custom's Agent.

Kill me.

Finally, I was rolling my luggage up the winding ramp into the main arrivals terminal, and immediately began searching for Marshall. Hearing his voice call out my name sent a rush of relief through me. I searched the faces in the crowd spotting his, and not surprisingly his hair was different. It was a light violet, and had grown a bit longer in the front. He looked as happy to see me as I was him.

"Sweetie, you look worse for the ware." He hugged me tightly and patted my back, stepping away from me just as fast, his sideways stare roamed over me.

Gee, thanks.

"Oh my God! Stop it!" I ordered, half laughing at his motherly-ness.

As we walked to his car parked in the garage across the road from the International Terminal, I shivered as the cold wind whipped my hair around my face. I wasn't used to the cold, let alone drizzle and dreariness. The thin sweater I was wearing wasn't cutting the fifty-five-degree temperature, cold for Southern California. As my teeth chattered together, I explained exactly what had gone on since I'd left for Brazil. I still wasn't sure how Jake found out that Nathan was with me.

"I have no idea, Aly." He shook his head, perplexed as I. "Jake doesn't seem the type to lurk around." Marshall shot me an ironic glance. "I did see the picture of you and Nathan posted on Instagram, but Jake doesn't follow Nathan, does he?"

I shook my head. "No. I don't think so." I laughed it off. Maybe he did. "But I still wasn't doing anything wrong."

Marshall shrugged off my comment and opened the trunk of his little black Volt, a newish electric car. "You know the band is playing at the Roxy tomorrow night."

Tomorrow was New Year's Eve I thought as we drove out of the airport parking garage. We took the beach route home. My insides tightened. "Jake never mentioned them playing anywhere in LA."

"It was a last-minute thing, I guess."

I'd heard what Marshall said, but was still stuck on Jake. "Bobby didn't mention anything about Jake at all?" My tone was desperate, but I didn't care. I leaned my head against the window and watched the stormy Pacific Ocean speed by me. There wasn't a soul on the beach. Even though the weather sucked, I was relieved to be home.

"No. We've just been spending quality time together."

A sentimental seventies love song played on the radio, making me feel more sorry for myself. I reached up and tapped the radio tuner to another station. Most of them were running commercials. "You should really get satellite radio."

"I know. Just add that to the list of things to do." It was his turn to poke at the radio buttons. "Bobby's been kind of depressed since Dump died. It's really been strange for me too, watching everything change so permanently."

Permanently. "Death and taxes, right?"

"Sadly."

As we turned down my neighborhood street, my hands began to get damp. What if Jake was at his mom's? *I mean he'd have to go there to visit at some point, right? What if it was today?* Would I go over there? But as we got closer, my strange worry extinguished when I saw there were no cars in their driveway. *Of course I would have gone over there*, I thought.

I groaned as I opened the car door. "Thank you for coming out of your way to pick me up."

"Anytime. I love you, Aly. Anything for you." He looked at me fondly.

"I'm so proud of you, Marshall. You've kept your shit together with relatively no drama and I couldn't be more envious, in a good way." I smiled sincerely at him.

Marshall put the car in park and got out, helping me with my bags. "Why don't you come up to WeHo before the show tomorrow, like around seven? You know you've never been to my place." He tsk'd and wagged his finger at me. "We can walk to The Roxy from there."

My stomach grew nervous, and a sinking feeling gripped me. "Jake knew I was coming home today and I haven't heard from him." Marshall didn't know what to say. He looked as woeful and I felt. He too knew it wasn't like Jake. I wheeled my luggage up my driveway, thanking Marshall again. "I'll let you know about tomorrow after I talk to Nadine. If I don't hear from him, I'm not going. He *knew* I was going to be home. After everything we've been through and all the bullshit he's put *me* through, you'd think he'd see the bigger picture here."

Marshall's face turned downward. His mouth hung open like he was gonna say something, Instead, he smiled at me and waved, ducking into his car.

I drew in a huge breath as I stepped through my front door and called out, "Is anyone home?"

Silence. I was totally alone.

Nadine twirled a piece of her blonde hair around her finger as she smacked her gum, scrutinizing a fashion magazine. She kept scoffing as she turned the pages. "You can't possibly compete with these images. No wonder girls have eating disorders, seriously."

I just shook my head. It was the same comment that she'd made a million other times. I wasn't gonna bite. I would usually follow up by saying, *"Don't hate on the skinny girls."* And she'd say, *"These girls are photo-shopped. It's a proven fact. Nobody looks like this."* And I'd say, *"Nadine. Not everyone get's inches taken off."* And she'd tell me not to brag and I'd pump her up. And say, *"being tall and gangly isn't always a selling feature."* Because Nadine harshed on herself way too much, and I never understood why. Guys flocked to her and her voluptuous figure. She had a flat stomach, shapely legs, and boobs I'd probably pay for someday.

"Shut up over there. You're not fat. Those girls are like six feet tall. Stop comparing yourself and eat some popcorn." I walked back into my living room and placed a bowl of lightly salted organic air-popped popcorn in front of her.

"Is this how you've managed to stay super skinny?" She threw a piece at me. "I hate you." She tossed a couple pieces in her mouth. "I say that with love."

I leaned forward and yanked the magazine away from her and flung it over my shoulder behind the sofa. Her green eyes cast a wounded look at me. "There, and no. You try working out three hours every day. I could eat a cow's ass, speaking of, let's go to In N Out. I need my burger fix."

Nadine was staring into her bowl of popcorn and sighed. "Marty's here and he hasn't asked me out yet. It's fucking New Year's Eve for Christ's sake."

A zing of shock stabbed through me. Marty's name went right along with Jake. "Well, if it makes you feel any better, Jake still hasn't reached out."

"Have you?"

"No. Why should I? We had plans to spend New Year's Eve together, *tonight*. He's being a baby and a double-standard wielding jackass." I spat intensely, my curiosity provoking me along. "When's the last time you heard from Marty?"

"Before he left." She pulled her knees to her chest and balanced the bowl on her knees. "He did say he thought it was sad how Sienna was leaning on Jake so hard for support. You know she's moved in to that apartment you guys shared, and now she's here and they're together. Maybe…" She looked at bug-eyed.

A weird feeling engulfed me. She was insinuating something that I didn't even want to think about. I shook my head violently. "No. Don't even go there. That's just gross and… and there's just no way."

Her forehead creased. "I don't now. Crazy shit goes down when life changes so dramatically." She moved and put her empty bowl on the table. "Aly, I'm just sayin'."

"Well don't *just be sayin'*, it's just wrong. Sienna and Jake are like brother and sister." I looked warmly at Nadine. "Sometimes friends are closer and more important than your family."

Nadine's face got a little pink and her lips curled up all goofy. "Awe shucks." She bounced out of her seat. "We're going to the show. Get ready."

"You think we should?" I moaned and sank back into the sofa, unenthusiastic. "I'm so not in the mood to see Eva prancing all over the stage." I shot straight up. "Now that's the person I'm worry about." My eyes narrowed at the thought.

"Screw her." Nadine grabbed her purse and pointed at the clock. "It's seven PM; we'll leave by eight and go grab some din."

I thought of Marshall. We shoulda been to his house already.

Sunset Boulevard was packed with club-goers and party people shuffling up and down the famed street, all gussied

296

up to ring in the New Year. Some people in skimpy, nearly nothing outfits with their buttcheeks and boobs hanging out, despite the cold weather; some wearing jeans and t-shirts and the standard leather biker jacket. It was 10 PM. Red taillights from the bumper-to-bumper traffic glittered brightly, making it seem more Christmasy. (If that thought wasn't looking at the positive side of my current situation, nothing was). I still hadn't heard from Jake, and Marshall said that Bobby was concerned about the situation. Apparently they'd not practiced at all for the show. Jake had only sent a text informing them of the opportunity – *'Eva asked us to play at The Roxy NYE. Be there. Load in at 5:30.'* Jake never returned their calls or texts inquiring about more info.

We'd swung by Marshall's to pick him up – late. He was miffed we didn't take the time to come in and see his place, but he shook it off with a flip of his lavender hair in his typical understanding way, saying, "Well, seeing you're *both* empty handed." He'd looked cock-eyed at me and shot a glance at Nadine. "Etiquette, girls! You never show up to someone's new place without a little house-warming gift. We'll just have to plan something next week." He tsked, and folded femininely into the back seat, smiling in good humor.

We pulled into a parking garage just a block east of The Roxy; $25 dollars to park. Total parking rape, but it was New Year's Eve. We all split the fee. I wore a standard little black dress with black thigh-high boots. I attempted to look the part, even though I felt as if doom and gloom oozed from my pours for all to see. My mind swirled with concern over showing up *without* having talked to Jake.

What if he didn't want me there?

I shivered from the cold as I trailed behind Nadine and Marshall, fiddling with the black velvet hat I wore. I tucked my hair inside of it in an attempt to go unrecognized and stared at the venue sign in the distance, a red neon 'R' flashed back and forth, dancing for all to see. Only *Eva James'* name appeared on the Marquee underneath it. Earlier in the day, Nadine said she'd heard on the radio that KROQ was giving away tickets for a *Rita's Revolt* Secret Show. This was it. My heart thundered in my chest. We crossed the driveway where band load-ins took place, and where they and roadies congregated, smoking and whatnot. I was too afraid to look in that direction, worried I'd lock eyes with Jake.

Why was I even there? Of course he didn't want me there. He would have called me.

"This is a bad idea," I said out loud to no one. Marshall heard me.

"Stop it. It'll be fine. You two just need to work things out. He loves you, and you love him. That's all that matters." Marshall pulled me to him. His arm felt strong around my shoulders as I clung to it for comfort. "He needs you, Aly. He's a mess without you."

My attempt at being incognito was working. I walked past the throngs of fans and people milling about out in front, taking the curb like a balance beam all the way to The Rainbow Room driveway, a bar just adjacent to us. My heart raced as Nadine and I waited for Marshall to return with our passes.

Nadine waved her hand wildly. "Marty wants to meet me. Come on, they're just about to go on!" She held her glowing cell phone in my face, smiling happily, and my windpipe narrowed.

Marshall took my hand in his. "Come on. It'll be fine."

I sucked in a deep breath. "You guys go. I'm coming. I just need a minute." I took in another deep breath and exhaled heavily, watching my warm breath filter out into the cold night air. My body was numb.

Nadine didn't hesitate to take off. "Hurry!" she'd shouted as she vanished into the building, all eyes on her perfectly round rump. Each time the door opened, I heard Jake's voice. My heart felt like it was chipping apart. He really didn't care if I was there or not. It was as if he'd forgot about me, about us, about everything. I ran my thumb against the ring he'd given me. What happened? All because I wanted to pursue my dreams? And wanted to remain friends with Nathan?

This couldn't be the end.

Chapter 33

ALYSSA

The dank smell of beer, booze and old dirty floors filled my nose as my eyes adjusted to the darkness of The Roxy's interior. Dim lights barely penetrated the darkest corners of the venue's black painted entry. Screaming and shouting from fans blended with the strumming of a guitar. Then Jake's voice filled my head, and my knees buckled.

I entered the main room. It was packed, and there he stood, lit up like a rock god, with his hair messy and falling in his face. He held a microphone and took a long swig from a beer bottle. He held it out over the crowd, and their piercing screams rattled my eardrums. They went wild.

"Cheers, Los Angeles!" he shouted out, and the screaming sent my ears ringing. "It's good to be back." Jake hung his head and placed the beer bottle down on the stage, pinching the bridge of his nose for a long moment. The crowd grew quieter. The white lights from the stage lit up the entire room. He combed his hand through his hair, tossing his head back, giving me a clear view of his face. The hair on my arms stood up, and a surge of longing penetrated me to the bone.

His head suddenly balanced straight and he looked out over the crowd as if searching, almost like he'd felt what I'd felt. I feared he'd see me at the back of the room. His eyes scanned the crowd, waving and nodding at people he knew. He looked at every face and in my direction. My heart raced faster as his eyes passed right over me. *Phew.* I could tell by the look in them, he was lit up on something, and my heart sunk even deeper into my gut. I walked closer to the stairs that led down to the stage, but it was entirely too packed to go any further.

I glanced over at the VIP area, and I could see many familiar faces, including Nadine and Marty. Marshall stared out at the stage with his hands pressed flat together under his chin, praying. His eyes were sparkling as he stared at Bobby, totally in love. Bobby strummed a light tune. Then I spotted Sienna, and a shock jolted me. My eyes shot to the stage. Devon sat behind the drum kit. I hadn't notice. I gulped, and my eyes sought out Sienna again. She had a soft smile on her face as she waited patiently for Jake to continue.

A smile? Even though the band was like family, I wouldn't want to be there to witness what had been and what would never be again.

"This is weird." Jake's voice drew my attention back to the stage. He licked his lips, pointing behind him, and his mouth pressed tightly together. I could tell he was holding back tearful emotions. "This is our first show without Dump. RIP, man!" He looked up toward the heavens, and the crowd went crazy and quieted just as quickly. "Who can hear Dump sayin' – *'Get to fuckin' playin', man?'*" Another volcanic eruption came from the crowd. Bobby began playing a familiar, soft tune I couldn't place.

"I've got something new. Well it's not really new, it's actually really old and different. Dump was actually the only one to really dig it back when I played the idea for him several years ago." Jake nodded and he looked over his right shoulder to the side stage. I spotted Eva. "It's a duet," he announced, and the crowd went hysterical.

As soon as I heard those three words, something in my head popped. The rhythmic, simple guitar melody vibed through my body, and my stomach churned with unease. I wanted to run from the room but I was paralyzed, watching Jake as he smiled at Eva. She joined him on stage.

I wanted to be wrong. I told myself that it had to be a spin off, but I wasn't wrong. Jake reached down, taking something from a fan. It was a shot glass. "Thanks, man! Cheers!" He knocked back the dark liquid. His face grimaced as he swallowed. "Don't drink and drive." He nodded, half smiling, and the crowd cheered and laughed.

"This song is dedicated to all the fucking lovebirds out there! I hope it lasts for you."

What the fuck was happening?

The words that were meant just for me, for us, burst out into the room filled with five hundred people, and I couldn't breathe. Half of them held recording devices, and soon the entire world would hear it. The song Jake wrote for us, for me, when we were still in high school, before his super fame, when our dreams of a life together were so fresh and new, now taunted me. It was no longer ours; it was now officially theirs. The deep velvety rasp of his voice wrapped around my heart, crushing it. *How could he?*

And then the worst happened, and I knew it would unfold as I watched Eva's smiling face standing next to him, her sweet falsetto sang out the words that were once mine. Tears began to roll from my eyes. When their voices embraced at the chorus, it was too much for me and it was as if Jake knew it. His eyes landed right on mine. He stopped singing, and I heard my name, but I was blind.

Just as I turned to push through the crowd of people behind me, Jake jumped from the stage. I didn't want him. I didn't care that he was coming after me. I wanted out, and I shoved people out of the way as I ran through the doors to the street. I ran toward where we parked our car, but didn't have the keys. I sobbed and screamed words of hate, searching the street for a cab, holding my arm out as if I was in New York City. I heard my name. Jake was running toward me, stumbling and pushing people out of the way. "Aly! Wait, please!"

I shook my head, and finally a cab stopped. I rushed to open the door. "Please go!" I cried.

"You don't want him?" The man pointed. Jake was just feet away. "No! Go!"

The cabbie tore away from the curb, nearly running Jake over. I heard him shout *"Motherfucker!"* but didn't look out the window.

"Miss, are you okay?" the balding driver asked. *No stupid ass, I'm not okay!* "Yes. I'll be fine. We just broke up," I said, wiping my face with my coat, but the tears wouldn't stop from coming.

It was 11:30 PM and I would be ringing in the New Year alone, in the back of a cab. My phone was blowing up with Nadine and Marshall's texts and calls. I didn't want to talk to anyone. I didn't care to read the texts. I just wanted to go home and forget about Jake forever. He wasn't worth it anymore, and now I wasn't sure he ever was, with what just happened. He'd just proved he didn't care at all about what we had or about any future we'd talked about.

I barely had any cash on me to pay for the ride home. I had the cab driver pull into the bank around the corner from my house for an ATM visit. It was 12:13 AM. As we pulled up in front of my house, I had to blink twice. A shock ran over my skin when I saw Nathan leaning against his car, parked in front of my house, talking on his phone. I quickly rubbed up under my eyes and smoothed my hair. I didn't want him to see me like this – embarrassed and broken. Why the hell was he here? It didn't make any sense. As I fumbled to pay the cabbie, Nathan opened the car door.

I swung my legs out and hung my head. "Why are you here?" I tried to rush past him, but he grabbed my elbow and pulled me to him. I lost it. I sobbed, collapsing against him. "Why?"

"Shhh." He squeezed me. The comfort I felt in his arms made me cry harder. I didn't deserve his soothing affection. "Nadine called me."

"You're supposed to be in Brazil, with your family. Why…" I stepped away from him.

"I lied. I wanted to spend New Year's with you there, if you were gonna stay. We all came back the day after Christmas, as planned."

"Nathan, *why* are you here? I'm crying over another guy breaking my heart!" I yelled at him, as if he was the one who'd broke it.

A confused look creased his forehead. "Because I'm your friend, and Nadine asked me to check on you. She's on her way here."

I wiped my face with my hand and my running nose with my coat and tried to hold back the tears of guilt, sadness, and anger. "You shouldn't be here." I shook my head. I wanted to tell him he was the reason Jake broke my heart, but that wasn't fair. Jake would have done it anyway. He had it in him to be the most terrible person on the face of the planet.

"I need to be alone."

"I don't think you do."

"Nathan, I'm confused, okay? I'm totally heartbroken. Jake did the most fucked up thing he could have ever probably done to hurt me. And at the same time, I'm relieved you're here." I swung around with my arms out. "I'm going crazy. *This* is making me crazy. I need to be alone," I cried out to the sky, desperate for answers.

Headlights swung wildly around the corner, then another set came quickly behind. It must be Nadine and Marshal, but who else? I faced Nathan again. "Can we just talk later, please?"

Tires screeched, scaring me numb, and I hopped back, ready to run. The black truck hopped the curb, stopping just short of the tree in my front yard, and the door swung open.

"Aly!" I was blown back by Jake's voice. Nathan swung around to face him. Jake stumbled from the car. The look on Jake's face when he locked eyes with Nathan was pure anger and hurt. His eyes darted to me, and he shook his head. "Can we talk? Please."

"No. We can't. Go away!" I screamed.

"I think you should leave." Nathan stepped in front of me, standing taller.

"Fuck you, Sporto," Jake spat and took a few drunken steps towards us.

"Look at you." Nathan pointed in disgust. "You're a real fucking winner, aren't you?"

"Fuck you," Jake growled. "Why don't you go on home? You don't live here."

Another car whipped around the corner, stopping in front of my house. This time it *was* Marshall and Nadine. They got out of the car quietly, alarm etched all over their faces.

"Oh my God." Marshall's voice rang out into the night, and I worried the neighbors would come out, including Jake's mom. I wondered if she was home. Maybe she would pull him away.

"Get the fuck outta here!" My eyes shot to Nadine, and she pointed and walked toward a couple of men. One held a camera. He was filming all of us.

"Jake what's the problem?" The camera guy asked loudly. Jake's eyes wouldn't leave Nathan's.

"What's the problem?" Jake repeated the man's question, pointing at Nathan. "He's the problem. He's apparently stuck on someone else's fiancé."

Nathan's eyes shot to mine, and I almost passed out. "Is this true?"

My mouth hung open, and nothing would come out. I didn't know if it was or wasn't. "Jake, stop it!" I begged.

"Yeah, Jake, stop it," Nathan laughed cruelly. I'd never seen this side of him. He was almost wicked. "Maybe you made a mistake, because don't you think your fiancé would have spent Christmas with you and not me?"

A rush of heat engulfed me at hearing Nathan's words. Jake flew into a fit of rage, charging Nathan, and they both tumbled to the ground. Shouts from everyone around pierced the night air, and we all tried to pull Nathan and Jake apart.

Jake's fists hit Nathan in the face and neck. Nathan was bigger than Jake and sober. My heart raced and fear pumped through me. I didn't want Nathan to hurt Jake.

"Stop it, Nathan! Leave him alone." I rushed toward them just as Nathan socked Jake right in the jaw, sending him flying backward onto the pavement. Blood rushed from Jake's mouth.

"Oh my God! Jake!" I scrambled over to him.

"Motherfucker!" Jake leaned up on one arm, attempting to get up and I pushed him back by the shoulders. He spat the blood that pooled in his mouth.

"Jake. Please. Stop."

Jake's eyes were bloodshot and sorrowful. "Aly. I'm sorry."

"You're not fucking sorry for anything you do!" Nathan shouted at Jake. "You're just a selfish narcissist who thinks he can do whatever he wants to whomever he wants because he's famous. Aly, you can't want this for the rest of your life!"

I was out of breath, and my mind reeled from what was happening, trying to find words that wouldn't come. My mouth hung open. I looked from Nathan to Jake, bleeding in my arms. Revulsion draped over Nathan's face as he stared down at us.

"I can't compete with this, can I, Aly?" He backed away, touching his split cheek, and his green eyes narrowed as he winced. He was hurt too, but I held Jake and not him. "No, I can't," he said in realization.

Sirens came from the distance, and two cop cars were in front of my house in an instant. I looked around, and a few neighbors stood around. I thought of my parents, who were probably on their way home too, because I'm sure one these neighbors probably called them to inform them that their daughter and her rock star boyfriend were causing problems again.

Before my parents arrived home, Jake was hauled away on DUI, Assault and Battery, and Possession charges. Nathan got to leave once he proved he was sober, and witnesses attested that Jake attacked him first and he was only defending himself. I begged to differ on the defending part. Nathan didn't have to knock Jake's teeth out, literally.

Just like when I was a freshman and Jake was a senior and he had his first run-in with the law, my parents stood at the foot of my bed, hovering over me for answers.

My mother stood with her arms crossed at her chest. "Thank God you're okay and didn't ride in the car with him, Alyssa. He was very intoxicated. You could have died. Not to mention the drugs?" Her hand covered her mouth. "Kate's going to have a fit when she finds out he's not sober, good Lord."

"Oh geez."

"Don't you *Oh Geez* me, Alyssa." She frowned at me.

"I'm not helping him this time, Alyssa," my father cut in. As a criminal defense attorney, he'd helped Jake in the past with his legal troubles. "He's a grown man. He's had one too many chances."

I wondered why I still felt a connection to Jake. Even after reminding myself over and over again of the impossibly hurtful, most selfish thing he'd ever deliberately done to hurt me. Drugs or not, he had to know what he did with that song was wrong.

He wasn't any good for me, not at all, not anymore, I told myself. But I still wanted him.

I love him.

Higher Octave

A HEAVY INFLUENCE NOVELLA

Book 2.5

An Excerpt

Ann Marie Frohoff

Chapter 1

A golden pink haze hovered over the Malibu hills as the sun began its decent from the sky, as if it were about to take a dip in the ocean. A light, foggy, ocean mist began to roll towards the compound I'd been staying at for the last three months – the Promises rehab facility. It was the beginning of April, and the spring season fluttered and bloomed around me as I sat waiting for Bobby to visit. Other than calls and texts, it'd been over a year since I'd seen him last.

It was the third spring season to come since my complete fall from grace. The music went completely silent.

I was a free man. Free from answering to a manger, a label, a band or a girlfriend. My entire life was a sad *E! True Hollywood Story* and *Behind The Music* – literally. I'd watched those episodes more times than I could count. I even recorded them so I could watch whenever I wanted and it was a lot. *I'm a free man*, I thought, but I wasn't really free. I still thought about Aly every day and what I'd done. *All* the things I'd done and continued to do while I was in and out of the four other rehab facilities around the country.

Aly was in her last year at Pepperdine University. The pull of her was real and more intense as the days went by at Promises. I'd stayed away from Promises on purpose, knowing it was too close a proximity to her, to keep me from wanting to see her. Now there I was and there she was, just over the hill, and I felt the grip on my heart. I could have left Promises whenever I wanted, but I didn't have anywhere else to be. I wasn't sure about where I was headed or if I even wanted to make music. Though my notebooks were filled with lyrics and my head was filled with melodies, I'd yet to touch a guitar to string anything together. I wondered if Aly thought about me at all anymore. I had to come to terms that she'd ended up with Nathan. I had to give it to the guy; he never gave up. He loved her and treated her better than I ever did. She'd spat in my face when she found out that Sienna and I had been sleeping together.

The thought of Sienna sent a wave of nausea through me.
I'm sorry, Dump.

Sienna and I used each other in so many ways. We both went to the first two-rehab facilities together, in and out, fucking around until it wasn't fun anymore. Until Sienna began losing jobs and the band got dropped from our label. The media went to town with speculation about our supposed sordid relationship. Even though Aly and I weren't involved romantically, we maintained close contact, and the news sent her bursting through the doors of a Phoenix rehab facility. Sienna and I never admitted to anything. We'd kept our intimate moments to ourselves and let the media run amok, but when Aly confronted me, I told her the truth. That was the real end of our relationship and the last time I'd talked to Aly.

A flutter to the right of my ear startled me, and I swatted the air, noticing two hummingbirds at the red bird feeder right above my head. I marveled at their hovering tiny bodies and nearly invisible wings.

"Thank you," I heard Bobby say, and I turned to see Lydia, one of the many staff counselors, pointing in my direction. A smile sprung to my face. Bobby looked great. I stood and was surprised that my knees were a bit weak from excitement.

"Hey man!" I met him halfway, in the middle of the grey flagstone patio. We were the only ones outside. "Thank you, Lydia." I waved to her, and she vanished inside with a smile. "Welcome to my humble abode." I bowed.

Bobby grinned, looking around. "Can I smoke out here?"

"Yep."

"Do you mind?"

"Nope." I shook my head and I led him back to the table I'd sat at. "I'll just sit on this side so the breeze will carry that shit in the other direction." I'd always hated smoke, and blamed cigarettes for killing Dump. "I'm gonna keep sayin' it. Stop smokin'. I don't want to have to bury you for some cancer bullshit."

Bobby frowned and lit up anyway. "My dad smokes, my granddad smokes, and my great granddad smoked until he was eighty-nine. I'm goin' with good odds."

"Fair enough."

"Why *are* you still here?" He looked at me, perplexed, as he bit his cig between his teeth and lit it.

That's the million-dollar question. "Don't really have any-where to be."

Bobby sucked on his cig, inhaling deeply, and blew out a stream of smoke. He nodded and smiled at me like he had a story to tell. He leaned towards me with his elbows on the table. "I came here to tell you I'm getting married."

A shock tingled at my fingertips. Wow. "Damn. Congratulations." I sat back into my wooden chair. "Holy shit, man. So you and Marshall?" I knew it was Marshall, but I wanted to make sure.

"Yeah." His eyes beamed with confirmation. "He popped the question two days ago. He's been a great fuckin' partner, Jake. I love him. He wants kids, and I kinda do, too, ya know."

I was truly happy for them. "I'm stoked for you. Seriously."

"You're the first person I've told."

Thinking about Marshall made me think about Aly. I was sure she knew they were getting married.

"When's the wedding?"

"June fourteenth." That was just around the corner, and as if Bobby read my mind he explained, "I know it's fast, but I'm leaving on tour and Marsh is going to Paris for an interview at *some* high profile fashion house." He waved his hand with raised eyebrows. "I should pay more attention."

"You guys going traditional? Like a real wedding?"

He nodded with a corny grin. "Marshall wants a wedding. I'm gonna let him do whatever he wants."

Having Bobby sitting right in front of me had me all jacked up with happiness. I hadn't felt uplifted in a long time. I almost forgot what it felt like. "Man, it's good to see you." I leaned in slapping my palms on the Beachwood table. Guilt crept up my spine, and I leaned back, shaking my head. "I'm sorry I haven't been communicating and you felt you had to drive over here."

He blinked twice, looking a bit serious. "I wanted to. I miss you, man. How are you?"

"I'm actually really good. Been writing a shit ton, but not sure what I wanna do with it all."

Bobby sighed and snuffed out his cigarette in a little silver cup. His eyes searched mine, an indication he had more to say. "What? What else you got?"

"If Marshall really goes for a traditional wedding, I want you to be my best man."

"Sure. I'm down, man." I said enthusiastically. "*And* I'm gonna be the best godfather your kid will ever have. That is, if you'll allow me the honor."

Bobby chuckled. "Of course." He nodded, taking me in for a beat. "And you know if it's traditional, Aly will probably be Marshall's best chick."

This time, my hands and arms went numb and heat flashed over me. "Okay. Is what it is." I shrugged, sucking in a deep breath. I gestured with a serpentine wave of my arm. "Life rolls on."

Bobby's smile was tight. "And there's more."

My heart was already pounding like a jackhammer, and now it felt like it would pop out from my ear. "What?"

"Nathan asked Aly to marry him, and he may be at the wedding too."

I could barely spit any words out, and felt like I was choking. I sprung up and walked to the mini fridge next to the barbeque. Anger, jealousy and loss ignited in my stomach. Taking a can of Coke in my fist, I wanted to throw it through the window and watch the glass shatter like my heart. Instead, I sighed deeply, controlling my emotions, and took a big gulp as if it were a shot of whisky.

"Sorry man. I didn't know how else to say it." He shrugged, gesturing apologetically.

I belched unexpectedly and patted my chest. "Damn. I never drink this shit," I said, staring at the can and then back at Bobby. "You know she's right over the hill?" I pointed with the can in my hand. "That's why I haven't left here."

"I'm sorry." He said looking as pained as I felt. Fuckin' Nathan. I didn't want to ask if she'd said yes. I assumed she did, otherwise Bobby wouldn't have said anything. My memory flashed with Aly's hurt, tearful, and angry face as she threw the ring I'd given her at my face when I'd confirmed my despicable relationship with Sienna.

I sniffed, took another drink, and cracked my neck. "Thanks for telling me." I held my can of Coke out to him. "Cheers to everyone's happy endings. I guess it's really time for me to move on."

But for some reason I couldn't, and I didn't understand why. I stayed at Promises for another two weeks, talking to Lydia about it. She told me to keep journaling and to play music again.

No shit.

———

I hadn't felt as clear headed as I felt at that moment in years, looking out at the massive red Golden Gate Bridge. It was a warm summer day and the bay breeze cooled my sun-heated skin. I was being a full on tourist standing there taking a picture of it with my camera phone. Then I decided to take a selfie. *What the fuck, why not?* I held the camera out at arms' length and smiled with the bridge behind me. *My first selfie, all by myelf. A new beginning. A new life*, I thought. I'd not posted anything on social media in over three years, and decided this

318

was as good of a time as any. I was working on a new solo record, and decided right then it was time to announce it.

"Marty," I called and strolled toward him, as I downloaded all the deleted social media apps back on my phone. "I'm going to announce my solo endeavor."

His eyes batted with surprise, and he pushed his glasses up on his nose. "Wow. Okay. Are you sure you're ready?"

"Yep. This day. This time. I finally feel a real sense of freedom and…" I breathed in happily. "Hope. I'm feelin' hopeful." I nodded and refocused on my task at hand.

Boom. I tapped *post,* and there it was, my mug on Instagram – the caption: *I'm back! Get ready Killas. New solo tracks are comin'.* That post fed the rest of my accounts, and my phone began to explode with reply push notifications. It was music to my ears, and fire burst inside me. An excitement I'd thought I'd never feel again.

Marty stood next to me, smiling, taking his own pictures. He'd never been to San Francisco. I'd rehired Marty to drive me around and to be my wingman. With a conscious decision to move on from the past, to make amends with those I'd hurt so deeply, included my mother and Notting, I was more determined than ever to bury the past behind me. I'd done so much damage, it was hard to choose where to begin, but I started with Marty.

I'd not driven a car since my third DUI. Two happened within a sixth month period, and I'd spent almost six months in jail with heavy fines and a massive settlement. Not that I couldn't drive; I just didn't want to. I'd almost killed a teenaged girl running a red light, t-boning her car a year and a half prior, and I had not touched a steering wheel since. I'd be on probation for another three years, thus the desire to be alone behind the wheel was a million miles away.

I swam in my eager thoughts of a new life, as I prepared to run face first into my old life at Bobby and Marshall's engagement dinner. They'd moved to the little bay side town of Tiburon, just south of San Francisco. Marshall worked in San Francisco as a fashion design assistant, and Bobby still toured as a hired hand with various bands from time to time. The success from our band, *Rita's Revolt*, allowed Bobby a very comfortable life. Money from all of our music publishing would always be coming in, and it made me feel good that I'd made the choice to include him and Dump in the publishing rights, even though I'd been the one to write all of our songs. I thought of Sienna and sincerely hoped she was doing well. I didn't think she'd be at this dinner, but a bit of fear ran through me. I didn't want my past to cause any drama for Bobby and Marshall.

"Hey, Marty."

"Yeah?"

"Have you heard anything from or about Sienna?"

I strolled over to Marty, dodging a sea of Japanese tourists, young and old, exiting a tour bus. I smiled at the ones who'd stared at me, wondering if any of them would recognize me. Japan was one of our biggest fan bases, but if anyone did, no one said anything. I'd literally fallen off the face of the planet musically after Dump's death, and especially after that stunt at The Roxy with the song I'd made with Aly. Other than bad tabloid press – I'd vanished.

"No, I haven't." He shook his head with concern.

"Yeah. Me neither." Sienna told me to leave her alone. She'd apologized to me as if it were all her fault we'd done the unthinkable. She'd said she wanted to start a new life with none of us in it.

Marty looked at his watch. "We better get going."

My heart speed up. "It's now or never."

I had no idea what Aly looked like anymore.

———

The cool bay breeze rustled my hair, and my date's heels clicked on the cement sidewalk, echoing off the surrounding cottages. We snaked up and around a short hill to Marshall and Bobby's home, just a few blocks away from my small hotel. All I could think about was how it would all unfold. I just wanted to get it over with.

A horizontal dark wood fence surrounded a small well-maintained yard of a one-story contemporary home with Balinese accents. Little white lights were strung up the slender tree trunks of what looked like prehistoric bonsai trees, and cracked-glass lanterns the size of grapefruits hung throughout their branches.

When I stepped into the house I wondered whom I'd see first. I turned into the vast living room. Oversized contemporary sofas and white upholstered chairs sat on sealed cement floors. Dark wood coffee tables and end tables sat upon groovy patterned-blue hued area rugs. The ceiling was vaulted, and beams and silver ducts were exposed. Modern silver lighting fixtures hung down here and there, and cactus and succulent plants accented the sparse setting. It was an open floor plan, and the kitchen was at the far end.

I scanned the crowd, looking for Aly. She was somewhere near. I could feel it. I heard Marshall's voice and turned and the first set of eyes I met were Aly's. She smiled and waved. I did the same, and looked back at my companion, whose long blond hair flowed down her back over her black body hugging dress. She was beautiful, no doubt. I wondered what Aly thought of seeing us together and I looked around for Nathan, instead I spotted Nadine.

"Alyssa!" Marshall's voice sung out and I tried not to follow his movement. His hair was still lavender, and he wore a white button up and cuffed white pants. His feet were bare, and his toenails were pink. "Look at you, you're so ravishing in that red dress! Holy moly! *And* when did you cut your hair! I love it!" Marshall cooed at Alyssa, it was hard for anyone not to stare at them.

Marshall was pinging off the walls, and Bobby went over to greet them with arms wide open, embracing Aly tightly. "You look great. Wow." He complimented Aly and put his arm around Marshall's shoulders.

"Oh my God! Let me get a picture of you two! I'm so excited for you guys." Aly said and she dug in her little black clutch, taking out a phone, and turned to place her bag on the arm of the sofa nearest her. She glanced up over the room, in my direction. I was staring at her, right over the shoulder of my date and our eyes locked. She looked away quickly and turned back to Marshall and Bobby.

"Okay, get ready." She held the phone up clumsily. I could tell she was nervous and it made me want to go to her. Bobby gave her a gentle smile and mouthed *breathe*.

"Nadine, will you please take our picture?" She sang out and jumped in the middle of Marshall and Bobby.

I couldn't take it anymore and had to go say hello. I grabbed the hand of my date and strolled over to them.

"Long time no see." I said smiling, letting go of Lillianna's hand. I couldn't help but give Aly an adoring sweep with my eyes and extended my arms for a hug. I had to feel her. She didn't move. "Shorter hair suits you. Polished elegance. The lady in red *is* ravishing." I complimented, but she wasn't having it.

I tilted my head and then stepped to hug her. Aly loosely wrapped her arms around me and I breathed her in. "You're beautiful, but you know that," I said softly in her ear as I backed away. She looked flustered and her cheeks were bright pink – *Yes! I got to her.*

Nadine introduced herself to my date and they chatted politely enough, but I cringed, like a permanent tick, at Nadine's intrusive questions. Lilliana answered with light-hearted grace:

"We're just friends."
"My name is Lilliana."
"I'm from Scandinavia."
"I'm a model."

I couldn't stop smiling at Aly and the forced enjoyment that was stamped on her face. I knew her so well. I could have laughed out loud. If it were like old days, she would have turned to me mock gagging. It was killing her as much as it was killing me. The tension seemed to subside as we continued to break the ice, with the exception of me continuously glancing at Aly's hand, the one with the ring on it. I wondered if she noticed. It was as if she kept trying to hide it with her other hand – maybe she was.

Bobby announced that dinner was now ready and being served. He slid open doors that I thought were a wall, exposing another vast room that held two fourteen-person tables. They were elegantly decorated with three vases filled with banana leaves and Birds of Paradise. Masculine granite-colored table settings were expertly placed.

"Open seating, my friends!" Marshall clapped his hands.

Aly didn't hesitate to sit down, and Nadine sat across from her. I couldn't help myself and sat right next to Aly and my date sat across from me, next to Nadine.

"Well then. Seeing this is gonna get interesting." Nadine clucked her tongue and shot me a brief stare, one that Lilliana missed. "I'm gonna grab a bottle."

I gave a hearty laugh, and Lilliana laughed with me, even though she was totally clueless. Aly huffed. "Are you fucking with me? Leave me alone," she leaned over, whispering to me.

Aly glanced at Lilliana, whom had zero idea what was happening. Lilliana struck up a conversation with a person behind her. It looked like someone Marshall worked with, a well put-together stylish male. I'd seen them chatting earlier.

"I'm just happy to see you. Just trying to catch up." I said quietly, smirking. I wanted to waggle my eyebrows at her, but she would have probably knocked me out.

"Mmhmm." Aly took a big gulp of wine, trying to ignore me.

Nadine returned with the bottle she'd promised, clunking it down on the table.

As we sat being served our salads, Nadine shared what she'd been up to, and so did I. We ate our dinner of Chilean sea bass and Asian-inspired stir-fry with saffron rice. I asked Aly every question I could think of about her school, her travels playing volleyball, her parents, and brother and sister, Kyle and Allison. I explained to Lilliana that Aly and I grew up next door to each other, and that was it. I didn't ask once about Nathan or the ring she wore. It was as if they didn't exist. Lilliana shared her latest travel adventure to Morocco and how she fell off a Camel and broke three ribs.

"I'm just starting to work out again. I gained so much weight," she'd said as she sipped her champagne.

Aly sighed, rolling her eyes at me and excused herself with the empty bottle of wine. I got up a moment later and followed her. I walked into the kitchen and didn't see her right away. I searched the perimeter and noticed a nook off to the right of the kitchen. A wine chiller sat under the small counter and Aly stood next to it. I looked around as I made my way toward her, making sure no one was watching me.

"Hey." I said, trying not to scare her. She glanced over her shoulder as I slid the door halfway shut. I could no longer see the kitchen. That meant no one could see us.

"Jake, what are you doing?" She turned back, focusing on opening the bottle. "Aren't you worried your date might come looking for you?"

"No." I kept my voice low.

"What do you want?" She practically whispered.

I stepped up next to her and leaned against the counter, watching her spin the opener into the cork. "I just wanted to say I'm sorry. One last, *sober*, time." I swallowed hard, trying to control myself.

She closed her eyes. "Okay."

"Let me help you."

I stepped behind her and wrapped my arms around her. Feeling her warmth shocked to life what I thought was dead. I knew she felt it too because her breath hitched. I ran my hands over her smooth arms and held her hands in mine. She let go of the wine bottle and opener and laid her hands flat on the counter. I placed my palms on top of hers hands, coaxing our fingers to curl together. Then wrapped our arms together, around her.

Chapter 2

Alyssa Montgomery. Aly. My Alycat, I thought as I held her. The ring Nathan gave her mocked me beneath my grip – *'I won. She's mine.'*

Nah, not yet, motherfucker. Not until she says I Do.

I would ignore it. I wouldn't say one word about it. She wasn't married yet; that's all that mattered to me. Her little red dress accentuated her tiny waist just right. It beaconed me to take it in my hands, to spin her around to face me, but I remained still. She was killing me without even knowing; or maybe she did.

I'd mentally one hundred percent prepared to see her. I'd convinced myself that she'd moved on after Bobby informed me of her engagement. It was just the kick in the pants I needed. I'd resigned myself to thanking her for fueling my musical fire; I had to give her that. Everything I'd written was a derivative of my experiences and longing for her. I knew this and looked forward to finding other inspiration. I'd never wanted that before. I had a new future in music, and I was devoted to healing and staying clean and healthy. I'd reinvented myself. This was what I'd believed, until I laid eyes on her again. The connection was instant. The invisible unrelenting bond gripped and smothered me. I was pulled to her as if I had no control. I didn't have any control. When she had stepped into the room, she radiated a force so extreme it rushed to me and swallowed me whole.

And now here I was…no control, holding her, hoping it wouldn't be the last time.

Having her in my arms again and filling my senses had me losing my mind. Standing behind her I wanted to press my growing desire into her backside, but I abstained. She was fighting me, and then she wasn't. I knew she still wanted me, too; otherwise she would have turned, said something nasty and left. She allowed me to touch her, to kiss her and feel her skin without bolting from the small room. I knew she was as tortured as I.

When her voice quivered with the words – *"I don't dream about you anymore."* It stung, but I knew she was lying. Maybe she didn't dream of me as often, but I knew she did. Especially when I felt the longing release from her when her breath caught for a brief second.

I still had a chance.

I kissed her other shoulder and backed away, clearing my throat. "I'm sorry. I can't help myself."

She remained still for a long silent moment, finally facing me. Her eyes were glassy, and she was flushed. "I can't be here with you."

Yes you can, you can do whatever you want. "Have dinner with me when we get back to LA."

"You're not hearing me, Jake. I can't do this with you any-more. I had years to think about this." She twirled away from me. Bewilderment cloaked her face. "I wanted this moment, right now, to happen. I prayed for it. Like all the other times." Her hands moved under her chin in prayer and she stared at me long and hard, but instead of saying more she moved to exit and slid the milky glass door all the way open. People in the kitchen looked in our direction, but went back to their business. "I don't want to spend the rest of my life on a roller-coaster, worrying if you're gonna freak again. Worrying if you're gonna…" She threw her arms out, vexed and shook her head. "I'm happy you're sober. I love you, Jake. I always will."

She spun out the door, but I grabbed her hand and pulled her back in, embracing her. "For now," I whispered and kissed her forehead, letting her go. "It's not over until it's over." I almost pointed to the ring on her hand.

We didn't speak for the rest of the night, but I kept meeting her gaze.

Until next time.

The next morning, Marty packed his bags into the car as I sipped on my coffee overlooking the bay. "Aly's probably asleep in one of these little hotels."

"Mhmm. Where's Lilliana?" He changed the subject. I supposed he was over my obsession with Aly. I'm sure everyone was.

"She's staying. Visiting friends or some shit." I could care less about Lilliana. I'd only invited her because I thought Nathan would be there, guarding his treasure. I took him not being there as another sign of hope.

Marty grunted arranging the bags. He stomped his foot. "Are you gonna just stand there? Hand me your bags."

"Did you just stomp your foot?" I scoffed.

He rolled his eyes at me. "I'm tired. Hand me your bags."

"Why, Martin." I wagged my finger at him and bent to grab my bag. "Did you drink too much last night and fuck around with Nadine?" Marty ignored me, snatching my bag away from me, and it made me snigger. I tsk'd at him. "You don't wanna disappoint your parents by your continued hanky-panky with the likes of a non-Jewish girl, do you?"

He stood rigid, not amused by my teasing. He adjusted his glasses. "It's none of your business."

"Oh come on. I'm just fuckin' with you." I slapped him on the back kindly and shoved him out of the way. "Get in the car. I got this."

I could tell Marty wasn't feeling well. He was the most disheveled I'd ever seen him. He wasn't wearing his signature, neatly pressed button-up dress shirt. He wore a black zip hoodie over a t-shirt. That never happened. I wanted to offer to drive, but a real fear loomed over me about it. Maybe I'd try to drive around once I figured out where I'd be staying.

"Marty, man, sorry that I can't drive. I thought about it, and I need to…like, do it around a familiar hood."

He ran his hand over his head. "It's okay." He sighed. "We didn't sleep at all. I need at least seven hours' sleep. I'm never drinking that much again. She certainly loves that champagne."

I chuckled. "You can sleep on the plane."

"Yeah."

Marty was flying back to New York from San Francisco. He'd moved into the guestroom of the apartment Aly and I used to share after he'd helped Sienna clear all her shit out of there. I told him he just had to pay the utilities and make sure it was always ready for me to come home. I'd not set foot in the place since I hit rock bottom. I'd yet to sell it because of Aly. I almost put it on the market the day after Bobby told me about Aly and Nathan. Now I was glad I hadn't. I'd give it one last shot with Aly. No matter how long it took, until she married me, or someone else. If she married someone else, I'd sell it with everything in it, including the black and white portraits of her that'd traveled with me all over the world.

Would I really do that? I don't know. Maybe I wouldn't, probably not.

At the airport, I encountered a few fans and took a few pictures. The meaningful well wishes were uplifting, and they'd all mentioned the post I'd made of myself in front of the Golden Gate Bridge. They were all excited and looking forward to my new music. It'd been a long time since I casually interacted with fans.

I floated through the airport with a stupid smile on my face and actually said hello to a few people. I would have never done that in the past, ever. There was something to say about being twenty-five and living the kind of life I've led. I was a survivor. I had stories to share. I'd be sharing them soon enough. I rewound the conversation Marty and I'd had on the way to the airport:

"You need to come back in about a month."

"Jake. I can't be driving you around."

"Nah. I got that figured out. I'm gonna start this new solo project, and I want you to document it all. I want to share the good, the ugly and the resurrection."

I finally got a smile from him.

I called my mom as soon as the plane touched down in Los Angeles, and she was beyond delighted to oblige. I'd avoided her and Notting for basically the last several years. Ever since I'd found out that Notting was my real, biological father. I'd wanted to protect my mother from the knowledge of my cheating "father", Michael, a man whom I truly loved and had fond childhood memories of. Now Michael, my dad, died not knowing that I wasn't really his, and what did it matter anyway? My mother had her own skeletons, major. It was just all so fucked up. I never really talked to her about the entire ordeal. The only person I really felt sorry for was Notting, and I wasn't sure I felt sorry anymore. He got his son and the love of his life, even though he'd waited thirty years.

Holy shit. Was that bound to be me?

Notting and my mother Kate reminded me so much of what I didn't want to address; everyone's infidelity, everyone's lies and secrets, including my own. Maybe if I took the time to actually invite my mom into my life…

Fuck. I want a real chance with Aly…or anyone, for that matter.

I almost said my thoughts out loud as I stood curbside waiting for my mom, looking around as if people would be reading my mind. It was hot, and the mixture of heat and the smell of jet fuel and car exhaust nauseated me. I hadn't stood curbside since I don't remember when…probably high school, usually because it would have been too crazy with fans. Today I took it all in stride and stood for pictures and signed autographs. I'd never asked anyone's name before, but as I stared up from the black ink that stained the blue piece of paper I held in my hand, I decided what the hell. Happy brown eyes sparkled at me over a grin so big, it tugged at my heart. A teenaged girl with wavy black hair bounced on her toes. I winked at her as she took the paper from my hand.

"How old are you?" I knew I probably shouldn't have asked that, and before I could apologize, her words rushed out so fast I couldn't help but smile.

"Fourteen." She bounced. "I'm gonna be fifteen next month. Thank you so much. I had to do a double take standing at the baggage carousal. I was like is that! Wait, is that?" She cocked her head with grand gesture. "Oh my God that's… and it's you! Thank you! Can I take a picture with you?"

I chuckled. "Sure."

Our faces appeared on the screen of her phone, and she snapped three.

"Okay thanks so much! Your music changed my life. I'm so happy you're okay. I prayed so hard for you, because you're so amazing you don't even know!" She hugged me so quickly and took off. I barely had a chance to wave before another person came up to me. There was a small crowd for about twenty minutes before I realized my mom had pulled up, and she was watching the whole scene. It was the first time since I was a senior in high school that I'd interacted with every single fan that wanted a moment with me.

I was stoked to be home, my real home. It was also a bittersweet moment, because Aly's house seemed to mock me when I got out of the car and stared at it. It looked the same as it ever did, but she wasn't inside it. She lived in Malibu with roommates, apparently. When she'd shared that bit of info with everyone at the dinner table the night before, I wanted to ask if she had her own room. She probably did, and I surged with jealousy at the thought of Nathan in her bed.

"Where's Notting?" I wondered when I didn't see his truck in the driveway when we pulled in. "He's at work."

"What?" I was shocked. He didn't have to work anymore. "Where's he workin'?"

"He's been consulting at an agency in Beverly Hills. He's bored."

—

I lay on my mother's bed and sunk into her pillows. The smell wasn't the same. I used to come into my mom's room when I was younger. It would make me feel safe, like everything would be okay. It wasn't just hers any more; it was Notting's, too, yet it gave me the same safe, homey feeling as it did all those years ago.

My mother startled when she noticed me. "Oh geez, Jake!" she gasped, holding her chest. "I didn't expect you to be there. What are you doing? Are you feeling okay?"

Her motherly hand came over and covered my forehead and moved to my cheeks.

"*Am* I okay?" I gave her a worried look.

A wry grin popped to her lips. "Your temperature is okay." She pulled the hair from her shoulders into a ponytail, wrapping it up into a bun, all the while giving me a long, loving once over. "I'm happy you're here. I pray every day you'll have another day on this Earth."

My nose burned instantly, and I swallowed the little lump in my throat. Instead of my usual negative outburst or condescending remark, I accepted her love. "I know."

I nodded and bent to sit up. *Ouch.* My balls were getting squished. I pulled at the waist of the black board shorts I wore, tearing open the Velcro fly closure, loosening the snug fit. I'd gained a few healthy pounds, more muscle from working out. I probably should stop trying to fit into my high school clothes. I hadn't worn a pair of board shorts in more years than I could count, and I hadn't stepped in sand in probably just as long.

"I love you, Mom."

She gave me a soft, crinkly-eyed smile. My beautiful mother was getting older, finally. She'd looked younger than her years for more years than I could count, but finally, the years were knocking. I couldn't help but feel deep guilt for being a pain in the ass. No doubt her worry over me helped carve the lines on her face.

"I love you, too," she said and crawled underneath the covers next to me.

"I'm sorry for everything. I know I've said sorry so many times it doesn't mean anything anymore." The words made me think of all the times I told Aly I was sorry, too.

She patted my arm. "I know you're sorry. Let's not dwell. It's taken me a long time to let go of the past, and I just want to keep looking forward."

Me too. "Does Notting always come home late?"

"Not usually, no."

I tucked my arms behind head. "Mom."

"Yes."

"Did Notting ever tell you that we've talked?"

"Of course, you know that." She rolled over onto her side to face me. "But he never shared, in depth, what was said. Just that you two bonded. It was actually a contention between us for a long time, him keeping your confidence."

I inhaled deeply. My heart began to thump rapidly, and I cleared my throat. "Mom. Did you ever hear that Dad cheated on you?"

Hearing her exhale heavily, I turned my head to see her wounded eyes staring back at me. She bit down on her bottom lip with a furrowed brow and said, "I'll assume *you* did, or you wouldn't be asking."

"Did you believe it? Or did you know?"

She tipped back onto her back and bent her knees up. "I knew."

"And you just let him get away with it? How long did you know?"

She pushed herself up and gathered the pillows against the padded cream-colored headboard, thinking.

"I'm sorry. You don't have to answer that. It was a long time ago, and you've moved on, finally." I reached over, rubbing her arm. "I'm happy for you and Notting, no matter what the story is."

Her eyes pooled with tears, and she wiped them away with a swipe of her hands. Her words came out slowly as she pulled her knees to her chest. "I think because of what you're going through with Alyssa, you understand the complexity of what some people go through when being in love. Not everyone has a hard time. They meet someone and it's just that one person. There's no fight from another, no third party, or love triangle. I loved Michael very much, we had a great life together, but in the end I'm not really sure why I chose him. I hate to say it was a mistake."

But it was a mistake. I was Notting's son, not Michael's - I wanted to say.

I was riveted by her words. It was the most open she'd been about her life before me, and I wanted to know more. I wanted to know her side.

To my surprised she remained open, and spoke more, "Are these the things Notting shared with you? Did he tell you about Michael?" she asked cautiously.

"No. Did he know?" I asked pointedly, thinking maybe he did know and that's why he stuck around, waiting for her to find out on her own. But then my dad was killed in a car accident and I thought she'd never find out. I'd kept that agonizing secret, that ate away at me, for nothing.

"We never discussed it." She shrugged and her chest heaved with a sigh. "Jake. I have so much culpability in how our relationship came to pass." She reached over taking my hand and rested it on her stomach. "You're my greatest accomplishment, and Michael loved you very much. He said the same thing about you." She released my hand and cupped the sides of her cheeks as she attempted to hold back tears. "I didn't know. I really didn't know that you could have been Notting's son. I look into your eyes and see mine. I…but now that you're a grown man…" She closed her eyes and shook her head. "The older you got, I'd see you standing next to Notting…it was so obvious. You're built just like him. You have his hands. I didn't want to think about it, I…I pushed it so far down until I couldn't take it anymore. I just had to know, so I took a paternity test."

Tears dripped from her eyes. "Michael always felt like he'd won. He was proud and arrogant. Notting saw me first. He was so sweet, nothing like Michael, in the Cavern in Liverpool. I was so young. Michael and him were best friends, and… well everything happened the way it happened." She sank, exhausted from the memories. "Michael took care of me. He dominated me."

"Mom…" I squeezed her hand. "As much as I wanna know. If it's too difficult to talk about…"

"No. You have to know. It wasn't until I had you that I found my voice, and Notting was always there to listen. He was my biggest advocate, and after a while, Michael just faded into his own world. Notting gave me the courage to stand up to Michael." She hugged my hand to her chest and kissed my knuckles. "You don't need to know all the pessimistic details. Here we are. As it should have been."

Chapter 3

It'd been several months since I last saw Aly. The last time I'd seen her was at Bobby and Marshall's wedding in June, and she'd attended with Nathan. There's not much to say about it, other than she looked gorgeous in a cerulean blue strapless dress. It killed me to spy Nathan fawning over her. I left as soon as I made the rounds at the reception. I didn't even bother saying hello to her. I'd tried to pretend they didn't exist.

I'd been keeping track of Aly, once again through her brother Kyle, just like I did during our three-year separation while Aly was still in high school. My big plans to inject myself back into her life backfired when I found out she would be away playing beach volleyball in some foreign country all summer. Then my new aspirations at a solo career took me back to Britain until right before Christmas.

Six months flew by in a blink of an eye.

During that time, Kyle went and got married in Vegas. Nothing eventful. No one was there, and he'd settled in Hermosa Beach, the next town over. He had a baby on the way. I couldn't image myself with a kid. I was only twenty-five, after all. Who does that anymore? I guessed Kyle did.

His wife was the epitome of the sexy librarian. Lacey was her name and he'd met her at his tech job. She was of average size and decent figure, though she hid beneath knee-length skirts and oversized blouses, but I saw through all of that. When I first met her, I'd recognized something bubbling beneath the surface. Her pouty pink lips and almond-shaped green eyes caught my attention. I was stoked for Kyle.

I wondered if my generation was getting married younger than my parents' generation; first Marshall and Bobby, and now Kyle and Lacey, not to mention Dump and Sienna right out of high school. It just seemed so young to choose whom you'd spend the rest of your life with. Yet there I was, ready to marry Aly if she walked through the door and said yes. I had zero interest in a relationship with anyone else. Sure, I wanted to get laid and have a good time, but nothing else. I pondered the difference between all of us being ready to settle down, vs. Aly being against it. My stomach curled with resentment that she was now engaged. Ready to marry Nathan. But what did I expect? I put so much bad energy out there I wouldn't have wanted to marry me either.

There I was back at home, like a teenager, depending on other people to give me rides. Notting was even back into pseudo-managing me.

Full circle.

I kicked my feet up onto the padded leather ottoman in front of me and watched Notting's tattoos dance on his arms as he wrestled with some of my mother's painting canvases. Seeing his tattoos made me touch my own, unfinished, tribute to Aly. Looking at it, I wanted it finished. The strands of black hair needed a blue outline, the same blue that filled the music notes.

"Not, you know this is the first time in my life that I don't feel any pressure. Like zero." I strummed the chords, plucking a tune I'd been mixing with some lyrics. "I think I'm gonna finally finish this tattoo, too," I announced, with one last strum, and then slapped my left bicep.

He swiveled his seat to face me and moved the blank canvas he had between his legs, leaning it against the sofa arm. He'd been screwing in metal wall mounts into the wood of the canvas' frame. My mother was on a new kick. She'd begun painting.

"Life is good, eh?" He smiled, and his handsome face folded together like an accordion. His new reading glasses balanced on the tip of his nose. I saw myself in him. I had his teeth.

I bobbed my head. "So so, but better than before. There's no struggle." Except for Aly.

He stood and adjusted his black wide-legged sweat pants. "I've been talking to your old booking agent."

I perked up. "And?"

"They're ready when you are."

I held my breath. "Okay." I was nervous, and I found it odd, almost like it would be my first time on stage. I'd played to sold-out stadiums and for millions of people watching award shows, but this was something new. I wasn't sure when I'd be ready. I'd never been on stage without my friends.

Notting looked at me fondly over his rimless glasses with a smile, as if he'd read my mind. "We'll hire a drummer and a bass player and go from there. Simple."

———

Gabe Sherman was serious about his job. He was precise. He was stoic. He was articulate, and most of all, accommodating. He had to be, I supposed; he was my driver. A handsome Clint Eastwood lookalike, he'd worked for the same limo service for over twenty years, which catered to studio executives and A-list celebrity clientele. Gabe was directly recommended to me by one of the new producers I was working with on my solo project. He was also the driver for several rock and music legends when they came into town. Gabe and I developed a similar relationship as I had with Marty, part friendship and part business.

It was nearly show time.

The famed Hotel Café in Hollywood with its dramatic red curtains as the stage backdrop. That's where Notting had arranged for me to play my debut solo gig. I had to admit I was excited, and a bittersweet sensation crawled over me as I thought about Dump. I was thankful Bobby was back home from his last tour, and he was more than stoked when I asked if he'd play with me. We'd practiced and then hired a guy Bobby recommended, Trev Stoneham, aka Stoney, as a drummer. It was nearly like old times – in my garage at first; then we moved to a rehearsal space. Six weeks later, the day came.

Load in at Hotel Café was at 5:30 PM, and it was about 4 PM on a Thursday in mid-March. Cool and breezy, the trees rustled with each bluster of wind, and dark clouds began to roll in. I hoped it wouldn't rain too hard or too long. I didn't want the fans to get soaked. I'd heard there was a line at the venue trailing down the street. It'd begun forming at around noon. I was elated and relieved. There was a bit of fear in me that no one would come, since I'd fallen off the face of the planet in complete scandal.

I'd arranged for Gabe to drive me for the evening, and he'd pulled up right in front of my driveway. I stood in my garage packing my very first acoustic guitar in her case and rubbed her smooth glossy surface. Every time I picked her up, she sang to me in an authentic, fine voice, so different than any of my other guitars. It would be the first time I'd be performing on stage with her, she was my most prized possession, and I thanked God I'd left her in her case that one time, thinking back to when I'd busted my other acoustic guitar in a doped-up mad rage over something stupid – *well, I didn't think it was stupid at all, but still.* She was the one that wrote all those hit songs with me, and now the world was going to finally meet her.

As I was loading my guitar and backpack into the backseat of Gabe's black Escalade, time stopped. A car I didn't recognize pulled into Aly's driveway. My mouth went instantly dry. I didn't notice the driver, only her in the passenger seat.

Was she with Nathan?

I leaned into the back seat and unzipped my backpack, pretending to look for something, peering out the back window. Then relief flooded through me when I saw Allison, Aly's older sister, step from the driver's side.

I backed out the truck and looked over at them and Allison was waving wildly at me, smiling cheerfully. I couldn't really place Aly's expression, but it sat between shock and joy. I waved back and shut the door and slowly trudged back toward my garage. I wanted so badly to go say hello to them, but I didn't want to be intrusive.

"What?" Allison's voice sparked, and I turned, smiling. She threw her arms out. "You're not gonna come and say hello? I haven't seen you in like…years!"

My heart raced so fast that I couldn't feel my feet as I walked toward her. She was bursting with elation in her prim office attire. It warmed my heart that she was so happy to see me. Allison met me halfway on the sidewalk and hugged me tightly when she got ahold of me. I closed my eyes. When I opened them, I couldn't help by look in Aly's direction. She'd moved to the trunk of the car, throwing me a gingerly smile. I wanted to kill myself. She'd gotten more gorgeous, if that was even possible. She was in workout gear, as usual, showing every bit of her natural beauty.

"How the hell are you?" Allison slapped my shoulder, grabbing my attention.

I chucked, focusing back on her. "I'm great."

"You look great." She motioned at me with her hands. "So what's up? Are you living back here?"

I looked back at my house. "Just temporary." My eyes drifted to Aly to see if she was watching us, she was. I drew in a deep breath. "How are you, what've you been up to?"

"Just surviving at my sucky job." She laughed, rolling her eyes. "Not really. It's okay. I just wish I'd hit the lotto."

"Right?"

"Just picked this kiddo up from the dealership. Her car needed some TLC."

My insides fluttered, staring over at Aly.

Allison's eyes roamed over me with a smirk on her face, and she looked back at Aly. "Alyssa, get over here." She waved her arm and looked back at me. "Just because you two aren't together anymore doesn't mean you can't be civil and grown up about it."

Fuck.

Aly reluctantly strolled over to us. "Hey."

I tipped my head with a playful gleam. I couldn't help myself. "Get over here."

I reached for her hand, and her cool figures wrapped around mine, sending a deep charge through me. I'd noticed immediately she wasn't wearing the ring Nathan gave her. I told myself that didn't mean anything as I pulled her to my chest, hugging her. She'd probably taken the ring off to work out. That's what most people did.

"What are you doing?" She pointed to Gabe's truck. "Is that yours?"

I shook my head no. "It's my driver."

Aly and Allison both nodded, more than likely remembering how I'd almost killed someone the last time I was behind the wheel.

"Where you off to?" Allison gave me a strange look, almost like she knew. Maybe she did, but I wasn't going to say anything.

"I'm just taking care of some music stuff, you know."

Allison gave me a tight grin. She knew, she nodded, and Aly looked between us, confused. "What's up?"

"I've got to get going." Allison said, changing the subject. "Gotta say hi to Mom before I leave, too, or I won't hear the end of it."

Allison disappeared behind their tall courtyard gates. "Uh, okay, well." Aly sighed, closing her mouth, and a bit of dejection overcame her. She crossed her arms, rubbing her bare shoulder. "It's freezing. It was great seeing you."

"Yeah, you too." I lingered on that last word, wanting to say more, but she turned and trotted back to the trunk of Allison's car, taking out her own black backpack and a brown Trader Joe's shopping bag. We'd waved our goodbyes and I shuffled back to Gabe, who was leaning against the side of his truck, watching the whole thing. I'd yet to share with him any real information about my life. He didn't seem like the type to buy tabloid mags, seeing as he had the type of clientele who usually appeared on the covers.

"Awkward, yeah?" He scratched his head, feeling it.

Maybe he did know what was going on.

"Yep."

Chapter 4

The line outside The Hotel Café was thick, and the excitement charged through me, erasing any anxious feelings I had about the show, or Aly for that matter. As soon as I opened the car door, fans began to scream, waiving excitedly. I waved in return bowing my head with hands in prayer, thanking them as I was whisked into the side door. Bobby arrived alone, still looking like the Bobby from years past, tucking his pack of cigs in his back pocket. He wore a worn out t-shirt and black Levi's, and dirty-worn out Van's tennis shoes. Marshall's fashion sense had certainly not affected his husband in the least.

We did our sound check, and Bobby, Stoney and I discussed what would go down during the show. I explained to them how Marty would be filming our performance. Gabe stood off near the loading area door, waiting for his wife and a friend. He'd asked if he could invite them to meet me – *"My wife loves your music…"*

What could I say? I was humbled to know this. Bobby asked what the plans were for my music, and I explained to him and Stoney that I didn't have anything firm, that the show was just feel it out, film it and release the footage – throwing the cards up and to see where they lay.

I'd removed myself from an intense political conversation Bobby began to have with Stoney, whom you wouldn't think would know anything of politics by the way he looked, all long-haired heroin chic – though he was sober. I was dead set on having only recovering and/or non-users or drinkers in my camp. As soon as I'd heard Congressman blah blah blah and The White House this that and the other roll off Stoney's tongue, I dashed to grab something to drink.

Marty finally arrived, clumsily making his way through the side door with his camera bags and tripods. A camera dangled from his neck; he must have been outside snapping shots. I watched with amusement as he began setting up his cameras to record the new lease on my musical life. Everybody in attendance had a chance to be captured on camera and to appear in the video. The video would be used to announce my solo career to the masses and the music industry. This was just between a hand full of people. Though the rumor mill was churning, I had everyone hanging with anticipation.

As I stood at the bar, I watched Gabe usher two dark-haired women out from the back of the stage area. I wondered which one was his wife, when my eyes were drawn to the taller one in particular. She was one of the most gorgeous women I'd ever laid eyes on, a statuesque raven-haired fair-skinned beauty. I could see her ocean-blue eyes from where I stood and her lips were full and pink, yet they didn't look false at all. Her eyes shimmered in the light as she looked around in a bit of awe. I stood taller and smoothed my shirt when I saw Gabe point in my direction. The other woman with short, shoulder length-brown hair, led the way. I assumed she was Gabe's wife. She beamed up at me with her fairy-like features when Gabe introduced her. She was a whole head shorter than her friend.

"Jake, this is my wife Margo and her friend Grace."

Grace, indeed.

I smiled at the both of them and extended my hand to Margo. "It's nice to meet you. Thank you for coming."

Margo grasped my hand, shaking it vigorously. "I love your music. I always have, since your early days. I told Gabe here when we first saw you play, when you were just a teen… watch out for that kid." She wagged her finger at me. "We saw you play at Gibson Theater, which is something else now…" she looked up thoughtfully, trying to recall the new name. "Well anyway, you know, at one of those awards shows. Gabe was driven someone famous."

Margo giggled and looked at her friend, finally releasing my hand, and I extended it to Grace. She placed her delicate hand in mine, and I felt as if it would snap if I squeezed too hard. "Grace." I bowed my head and I wasn't sure why, feeling compelled like she was royalty. She smiled faintly at me. "Thank you for coming," I said and out of nowhere I felt an urge and brought her hand to my mouth, kissing the top of it. She tilted her head toward me and I dropped her hand gently.

"You're too kind, Jake." This time the smile reached her eyes, and she blushed. This warmed me, and not in a sexual way. There was something about *Grace*. I glanced at Gabe and Margo and they both wore satisfied expressions.

Margo clapped her hands. "Let's get a drink." Just as she spoke and moved to the bar, the venue opened their doors and people began to fill the room and I excused myself.

I lurked around the heavy red curtain, side stage, to watch Grace. She moved with finesse, and there was a despairing allure about her. I wondered how old she was; she looked quite a bit younger than Gabe and a slightly younger than Margo.

I noticed she wasn't wearing a wedding ring.

———

"Thank you all for coming," I spoke into the mic as hoots, whistles and clapping filled the small room.

The venue was a sit down kind of joint, where people sat at cocktail tables with candle centerpieces, to watch performances. Tiny metal lanterns hung from the ceiling, with cutout designs casting a dim light. Standing room was in the back or off to the side. I heard someone shout out Bobby's name, and cheers from a small group off to the left got Bobby waving and more clapping ensued.

I cleared my throat and looked at Bobby. "I gotta thank this guy. The last time he played with me, I think I may have mowed some of you people down in that audience, when I jumped off the stage and ran out the door…and never came back." Laughs filled the room. "Nah, but on a serious note. Thanks for being here. Things are different, and I'm stoked to have you all sharing this moment with me and to Bobby for playing with me." I gestured to Bobby, on the verge of getting emotional; then my eyes landed on the audience, specifically on Grace. She was staring at me thoughtfully, with such a reverence that it touched me to my core. I could barely take my eyes off of hers. The silence stirred me. "That's Stoney back there. I'm sure some of you know who he is; he's played with some great bands." He raised his sticks, and clapping and hollers permeated all around. "Thanks, man, for being here for the cause."

I sucked in a breath and continued, "On a business note, all of you that are here should have filled out a Photo Release Form. If you haven't, please raise your hand, and Marty over there will bring you one."

About twenty people raised their hands, and Marty and a few venue staff quickly got the documents signed and collected all of the forms from everyone in the room. "This is going to be a very special evening. Thank you for wanting to be apart of it…some of you will be getting your close up."

The Hotel Café erupted in applause.

I strummed my girl, and the vibration from her caressed my arm and inched its way through my entire body. The more intensely I stroked her strings, one by one, people began to disappear from the room, until the only two people that were left were Grace and I.

That moment made me fall in love with music all over again; there was no separation from my heart and my hands. The pure bliss of watching Grace enjoy my emotionally raw lyrics from song to song, playing out my love and my pain for Alyssa and Dump, for my mother and Notting, and my taboo time with Sienna. My melodies cascaded over Grace, bringing her to tears.

When I was finished, the crowd's intensity brought me back to the ground. "There's my soul. I just laid it out for all of you."

———

I slipped on a clean dry t-shirt, and all I could think about was Grace and how emotional she'd gotten. I needed to see her and thank her for making the night so special for me. I couldn't recall ever affecting a grown woman in such a way. I didn't get that chance to see Grace again. She and Margo left as soon as my set was over.

"Gabe, what's Grace's story?" I inquired as nonchalantly as I could as we drove home. "She got all emo, you know."

There was such a long silence that I thought he didn't hear me, but as soon as I opened my mouth to repeat myself, he spoke. "Grace's husband died almost two years ago."

My stomach sank. "Damn." I shook my head, disturbed by this knowledge.

"This was the first time she's been out of the house."

What? "Gabe, she's had to go out of the house."

"Other than taking her kid to school." He glanced at me, gripping the steering wheel. "She has a young son, about four years old now…" His voice trailed off.

"No wonder she lost it, hearing some of my songs." Love, loss and death filled them.

"Yeah," he said somberly.

For the next week, I stood over Marty, hovering like a drone, watching him edit the footage from the performance. I was ecstatic. The sound and picture quality were insanely good, and I'd become obsessed with watching Grace.

"Send me stills of her." I pointed at the massive Apple monitor we had set up in my mother's spare bedroom. I'd arranged for Marty to have what ever he needed, like he would have had back in New York. I wanted the work done in front of me. I was now a micro-manager.

He nodded. "She's stunning. I don't think I've ever seen anyone so perfect. She's perfect."

"She's pretty amazing."

"How old is she?" he asked.

"Thirty-nine."

"Geez." Marty scratched his head. "She looks younger than that. I would have guessed ten years younger."

I nodded and wondered if I'd ever see her again, seeing that she lived in my town, albeit as a recluse. I pondered Grace's existence and my own, and thought about Aly. Kyle informed me that she was finally graduating from college in May. I would be there to watch her walk, Nathan or not. I didn't plan on letting her go so easily. Not until she was married to him.

Maybe I would change her mind.

Feeling as if I'd conquered climbing Mount Everest, I collapsed onto the sofa in my mother's house. I finally felt like I could go back to New York. It was now mid-April and warming up in the city. The release of my video, *I Am Here*, exploded with more than 1 million views in a matter of hours. Within two weeks, it had over 100 million.

I was back.